Blade snatched up her hand. "Come, *chère*, don't take on virginal airs after setting me afire. You've let me go too far to turn back."

"I'll call for my cousins."

"And the upright Lord George will see us wed this very night." Blade pulled her to him so that his lips nearly touched hers, and whispered to her. "Then surely would I gain release from this pain in your bed instead of in this chair."

Twisting her body, Oriel ducked down and escaped the circle of his arms. He reached for her again, but she slapped his hands away.

He chuckled and called after her.

"You're a lovely, kissable coward, Oriel Richmond. Come back and let me teach you how to play my lute."

A door slammed in the library, and he heard her footsteps in the gallery fading rapidly.

Something was wrong with him. His only purpose in wooing Oriel was to gain entry to Richmond Hall, yet he risked being tossed out by pursuing her so relentlessly that he nearly had her on the floor of the withdrawing chamber. God rot her. She tempted him by her refusals and her defiance and her scorn.

He would show her that virtue was a pallid and tedious thing that evaporated when boiled in the cauldron of passion. . . .

LADY DEFIANT

Lady Defiant

Suzanne Robinson

Bantam Books
New York · Toronto · London · Sydney · Auckland

This edition contains the complete text
of the original hardcover edition.
NOT ONE WORD HAS BEEN OMITTED.

LADY DEFIANT
A Bantam Fanfare Book

PUBLISHING HISTORY
Doubleday edition published September 1992
Bantam edition / January 1993

FANFARE and the portrayal of a boxed "ff" are trademarks of
Bantam Books,
a division of Bantam Doubleday Dell Publishing Group, Inc.

Grateful acknowledgment is made for permission to reprint from
the following:

*Beowulf; The Oldest English Epic: Translated into Alliterative Verse with a
Critical Introduction* by Charles W. Kennedy. Copyright © 1940 by Oxford
University Press, Inc.; renewed 1968 by Charles W. Kennedy. Reprinted by
permission of Oxford University Press, Inc.
The Book of the Courtier by Baldesar Castiglione, translated by George Bull
(Penguin Classics, Revised edition, 1976), copyright © George Bull, 1967.
Reprinted by permission of Penguin Books Ltd.
The Art of Courtly Love by Andreas Capellanus, translated by John Jay Parry
(Columbia University Press, 1990). Reprinted by permission of the publisher.
Life in Medieval Times by Marjorie Rowling (G. P. Putnam's Sons, 1979).
Reprinted by permission of G. P. Putnam's Sons and Batsford Ltd.
A History of Private Life, Volume II: Revelations of the Medieval World, edited
by Georges Duby, Cambridge, MA: The Belknap Press of Harvard University
Press. Copyright © 1988 by the President and Fellows of Harvard College.
Reprinted by permission of the publisher.

ISBN 0-553-29574-8

Published simultaneously in the United States and Canada

Bantam Books are published by Bantam Books, a division of Bantam
Doubleday Dell Publishing Group, Inc. Its trademark, consisting of the words
"Bantam Books" and the portrayal of a rooster, is Registered in U.S. Patent and
Trademark Office and in other countries. Marca Registrada. Bantam Books, 666
Fifth Avenue, New York, New York 10103.

PRINTED IN THE UNITED STATES OF AMERICA
RAD   0 9 8 7 6 5 4 3 2 1

To my sister, Nancy Woods,
who possesses
both talent and imagination,
and who makes a gift of them to everyone,
especially me.

Chapter
1

Northern England
December 1564

Since young noblemen had always gazed through her as if she were a window, Oriel couldn't stomach them looking at her as they would a fat rabbit now that she was an heiress. She had spent the last eight of her twenty years as an orphan cast into the lair of two aunts and dependent upon their mercy. Aunts were one of God's plagues.

In order to avoid the plague, on this bright and icy morn on the last day of December, Oriel had taken refuge with Great-uncle Thomas in his closet where he kept his papers, books, myriad clocks, and other instruments. Oriel had burst in upon him, out of breath from running as usual, and caught him directing the hanging of his newest picture, a portrait of Queen Anne Boleyn.

She smiled at him when he glanced at her over his shoulder. He sighed, for he always knew when she was hiding.

"Little chick," he said, "how many times have I admonished you not to gallop about? Such unseemly haste little befits your dignity and degree."

"Aunt Livia searches for me," she said as she wandered over to examine a model of a printing press. She picked it up, feeling its weight in her hands. "Uncle, why do you suppose things fall down instead of up?"

Sir Thomas waved his serving man out of the room while he straightened the portrait. "Is this a new riddle?"

"No. I just bethought me of the question."

"You're always thinking of unanswerable questions. You won't find a worthy husband if you're too clever."

Oriel glanced at the likeness of Anne Boleyn. "She was clever—a great wit, so you say—and she married King Henry VIII."

"And got her head cut off."

Sir Thomas subsided into his chair, groaning as his body met the cushions. His great age was a marvel to Oriel, for he had seen more than sixty-one years. Walking-stick thin, his skin almost transparent, his hands shook, yet he could still set quill to paper and produce a fine Italian script. He had taught her Greek and Latin in her girlhood, and given her solace when Aunt Livia cuffed her for answering back or Aunt Faith had made fun of her wildly curling hair and its auburn hue.

"God's toes, Uncle, I won't get my head cut off."

From the ground floor came the sound of a bellow honed by years of shouting at hapless grooms on the hunting field.

Sir Thomas lifted his brow at her. "Get your ears boxed, more like."

"She wants to put me in a farthingale and stomacher." Oriel wrinkled her nose and looked down at the scandalously plain and comfortable wool gown she wore. "And she wants me to put on a damask gown, so I told Nell to give out that I'd gone riding. I think another suitor comes today, but I'm not certain. Uncle, I hate suitors."

From the floor beside his chair Thomas picked up his journal, a book bound in leather and decorated with gilded oak leaves. "You must be patient. Some girls come into their beauty late. The young men won't ignore you forever."

Oriel looked down at her hands. She was twisting her interlocked fingers. "Did you—" She gathered her courage. "Did you know that I'm twenty and no one has ever tried to kiss me? I think there's something wrong with me."

Uncle Thomas held out his hand, and she went to him. He took her hand and patted it. "It must be quite terrible to fear being unwanted."

Oriel nodded, but found she couldn't reply.

"I think you're pretty."

"You do?"

"Upon my soul I do."

"Even if I don't wear brocades and silks?"

"Even without the brocades and silks, but you could do with some new gowns," Thomas said. "Look at that one. It binds your chest, girl."

Oriel knew how to avoid chastisement. "Tell me about your new picture. You knew Queen Anne long ago, didn't you?"

"Yes." Thomas rested his head on the back of his chair and gazed at the portrait. "You can't tell from the portrait, but she was all wildness and courage, was Anne Boleyn. And our good Queen Bess takes after her. It was her wit and fey courage that captured old King Harry's heart."

Thomas sighed and glanced at Oriel. He seemed about to speak, but didn't. After a short silence, he continued.

"He never captured hers, though. It had been taken, and Henry Percy had it always, may God rest his soul."

"How so?" Oriel asked. This was a story she'd never heard.

"I forget. Have I told you about that Italian fellow, da Vinci?"

"Ohhh—ri—el!"

"God's toes, she's coming."

Oriel bounded for the door, threw a kiss to Uncle Thomas, and scurried through his chamber, the withdrawing chamber, and a short passage, then down a side stair. Hugging herself, she scampered along the frost-ridden lawn beside the east wing of Richmond Hall, through the gardens and back into the house.

She crept into the Old Hall and stood at the base of the main stairs looking up. Aunt Livia's stiff skirts disappeared above her, so she tiptoed after the woman, her own skirts lifted to her ankles. Stealing into her own chamber on the third floor, she snatched up her new cloak lined with squirrel fur and dashed back downstairs. As she went she could hear Livia's booming voice in her great-uncle's closet. Someday Livia would have a fit from her own choler.

Aunt Livia wanted her to don a farthingale and a gown as stiff as cold leather. Oriel couldn't remember why, at the moment, but Livia's reasons never made sense anyway. Proud of her stealth, Oriel hurried to the stables. She must go riding so that Nell wouldn't be caught in a lie.

She returned an hour later. Having galloped the last few leagues, she was flushed and damp with sweat when she entered Richmond Hall once more. Livia was waiting for her. Oriel paused upon seeing her aunt, then gripped the carved stone newel post. Livia descended upon her from the first landing. A tall woman, she had the bulk of one of her hunting horses, and a habit of flaring her nostrils like one of them, as well. Though Oriel matched her in height, she did not in weight.

Once she would have shrunk away from Livia in anticipation of a slap. No longer. Oriel lifted her chin and her shoulders and met Livia's gaze.

Livia came to rest on the last stair and swore at her. A fleshy hand twitched, and Oriel glanced at it, knowing how much damage that beringed fist could do. Then she stared at Livia. The woman swore again and put her hand behind her back.

"You strain all courtesy, girl. Would God I had the chastening of you still."

"No doubt."

"None of your clever retorts," Livia said. "Have you forgotten that Lord Fitzstephen comes this day with his son? A match with his heir is above you, but Lord Andrew knew your father and has asked to meet you for some passing strange reason of his own."

"Not so wondrous, Aunt. I'm an heiress now, or has your memory failed you? Grandfather saw to the matter."

"You're the one with the unfit memory. Why, your Aunt Faith and I took you in—"

"Who did you say was coming?"

Livia vented a storm of a sigh. "How haps it that you remember French, Italian, Latin, and Greek, but fail to remember the names of your suitors? Yesterday you even forgot to come down for supper."

"It's another suitor," Oriel said with a long-suffering sigh.

Each visit from an eligible man increased her suffering. Grandfather had been dead only a few months, but Aunt Livia and Aunt Faith couldn't wait to rid themselves of her. To their chagrin, Grandfather had left part of his fortune to Oriel—several caskets stuffed with jewels collected over the whole of his lifetime. Livia, as the wife of his eldest son, had expected to get most of them. Faith, the widow of the middle son, had wanted them all. Oriel, the only child of the youngest son, shouldn't have received a thing, and they begrudged her even the dust on top of the caskets.

She was a living reminder of riches lost, and they wanted her gone. Thus she had been forced to entertain the suit of every likely man in the county. For Oriel, the business was an ordeal. Never a great beauty, left with but a poor inheritance by her parents at their death, she'd spent most of her time at Richmond Hall studying with her great-uncle or riding.

Aunt Faith's daughters Agnes and Amy were too young to provide companionship, while their sisters Jane and Joan harbored a spiteful resentment toward Oriel. Why this was so remained unclear, except that Jane and Joan were as plain as their names and bore spite toward anyone even the slightest bit more presentable than themselves. Livia's sons were much older, except for Leslie, and even he was away much of the time.

"My lady!" The steward came bustling toward them, his chains of office clinking as he moved. "My lady, Lord Fitzstephen and his son are here."

"God's mercy." Livia shoved Oriel up several steps. "Get you gone until I send for you. And put on a suitable gown, you addled goose."

Oriel bolted upstairs, but stopped on the landing of the third floor and looked over the rail. The stair took right angles several times, and as she looked down to the bottom floor, she saw the swirling edge of a black cloak and heard the scrape of a sword sheath and ching of spurs.

She heard a voice. The voice of a man, a young man. Low, soft, and vibrant with tension, it caught her attention, trapped it, tugged at it. Hardly aware of her actions, she reversed her steps, following the voice as it floated up to the second floor and then faded toward the great chamber. Oriel darted after it, hovering on the landing, her upper body bent toward the sound.

What was it that drew her? She listened, and heard the voice respond to her aunt. There was something different about this voice, something beyond the lure of its deep, quiet tones. Ah. An accent.

This young man spoke with an accent. Slight though it was, it gave the voice a distinct character. The *r*'s blurred, and sometimes the vowels stretched out. A French accent. How did the son of a border lord come to have even the barest of French accents? Aunt Livia had spoken to her of the visitors, but she hadn't listened.

Oriel cocked her head to one side, but the voice was muffled now that its owner had entered the great chamber. She stole along the gallery, with its latticed windows and walls lined with paintings, until she neared the doors to the great chamber, where all noteworthy visitors were entertained.

Livia was speaking. "Are you certain you wouldn't like to retire for a while? I've sent for my niece, but your comfort is my greatest concern, my lord."

"Thank you—"

"But we must needs make our visit a short one," the accented voice said. "I take ship for France soon."

"A pity," Livia said. "Though I understand that you must attend to your holdings there. Your dear mother was French, and through her you hold a title?"

"Yes, my lady. I am called the Sieur de Racine. But at home I am called Blade."

Oriel peeped around the open door and saw her aunt standing beside the fireplace. The great chamber was the largest room in the house. Lofty of ceiling, paneled in carved and polished wood, it contained the largest fireplace outside the kitchens. Its chimneypiece had been carved of Italian marble, and its shining floors were covered with intricately woven Turkey carpets, a luxury of which Livia and cousin George were proud.

Upon one of these carpets, near Livia, stood an older man whose tall figure was thickened with age. He seemed to possess only one expression, a scowl, which he directed at a man standing with his back to the room, gazing out the windows. All Oriel could see was a tall figure made even taller by a soft cap, the sweep of a black cloak, a silver sword sheath, and a pair of mud-spattered boots.

The young man spoke again, and as he did, he turned to face his hostess. Oriel beheld a pair of grey eyes so bright that they seemed silver. Straight brows echoed the dark brown-black hair beneath the cap. Now that he faced her, his body framed in the light of the windows, she could see the line of his mouth, with its full lower lip and contained tension. His hand rested on the hilt of his sword, and a heavy gold signet ring surrounded the third finger.

He walked toward the two by the fireplace, and as he came near, one of his brows arched. She caught the impression of much-tried patience, of skepticism and barely concealed mockery, all smoothed over by a grace of manner that spoke of the French court, rather than the border castle in which he had been born.

All at once he threw his cloak back over one shoulder, and rested his boot at the base of the marble chimneypiece. Oriel cocked her head to the side, fascinated by his smooth movements. He moved as if he was dancing in a masque. She was staring at a long leg, tracing the knot of muscles in a thigh, when he suddenly looked past Aunt Livia and saw her. His eyes widened, and he faced her without speaking.

Drawn by that unwavering silver stare, Oriel came out of hiding. She barely heard her aunt's admonishments. She spared Lord Fitzstephen not a glance. Her whole attention fastened on this dark, graceful creature with the alluring voice and argent eyes. They stood opposite each other without speaking, and Oriel found herself trying to memorize the Sieur de Racine with her eyes. He met her gaze with a puzzled stare of his own, but soon, when she remained silently gawking at him, one corner of his mouth twitched.

"Mistress," he said.

The sound of his voice broke the spell and wove another just as compelling. This was a suitor from whom she wouldn't hide. When she didn't reply, he glanced at Livia in inquiry.

"Oriel!"

She jumped. Livia's brassy voice shattered her reverie, and she came to herself. What had she done? She had entered unannounced and stalked a young man like a huntress pursuing a deer. For once Oriel cursed her forgetfulness. She had to say something.

"I—I . . ." He looked at her again, and she noticed a smooth cheek, the sharply angled line of his jaw, those startling eyes. All her wits scattered. "What was your name?"

This time both brows arched, and that arresting mouth drew down. "Marry, lady, do you forget the names of all your guests?"

"Oriel." Livia hurried to them and gripped Oriel's arm. "I marvel greatly at your lack of courtesy. Look at you. Your gown is besmirched, and you're flushed. And your hair. Have you never been taught the use of pins or caps? Jesu Maria, come with me."

Livia nodded to both men. "We will see to the bringing of wine and bread, my lords. Pray rest yourselves here."

Shutting the great chamber doors, Livia rounded on Oriel. "Worthless girl, your head is stuffed with learning and no sense. I'm going to the kitchens. Be off to your chamber and prepare yourself."

Livia stomped downstairs, leaving Oriel to rush to her chamber and call Nell to aid her in changing her gown. Never had she imagined that her aunts could produce a suitor she would care to meet at all. But this one—the mere sound of his voice and sight of his body had dashed her prejudice asunder. This man she could imagine touching, an act she had so far avoided when confronted with the countless others her aunts had dragged to Richmond Hall.

As Nell laced and buttoned her into a gown and fussed with the small ruff at her neck, Oriel shuffled her feet with impatience. She was afraid the man would vanish, and she had forgotten his name in her obsession with his person.

What was it, that name he'd said? Blade, that was it. At last Nell was finished, except for her hair, and Oriel dashed back down to the great chamber. One of the doors was half open, and she couldn't stop herself from peeping around it to catch sight of the young lord again.

They had been served wine and bread. The father was sitting before a table laden with a flagon, wine cups, and a tray with a loaf on it. Lord Fitzstephen was still scowling, and his complexion bore a flush. He poured himself a drink and downed the wine, sighing as he finished the whole goblet. His son, however, prowled about the great chamber, his cloak still about his shoulders and swinging with his strides. He stopped abruptly by the fireplace and glanced back at his father. The older man tore a chunk of bread from the loaf and began eating.

"May God damn you to the eternal fires," Blade said.

Oriel had been about to push the door open, but paused as she heard the young man speak. The father said nothing. His mouth was full and he chewed calmly.

"This is the fourth girl you've dragged me to see, and the worst. She's also the last."

"Clean her up and she'll be worth looking over. Jesu Maria, did you see that wild hair? Almost black, but with so much red to it there must be a spirit of fire in her to match."

"I care not. Did you think to buy my return to your side with a virgin sacrifice?"

"It's your duty to stay by my side and produce heirs."

Blade crossed his arms over his chest and purred at

the other man. "It's my duty not to kill you. That's why you're alive, dear Father."

Lord Fitzstephen slammed his drinking cup on the table, and wine splashed out. He stood, rested his hands on the table, and glared at his son.

"I haven't raised a hand to you since you took up with that foul thief, Jack Midnight."

"No, Father, you're wrong. You haven't raised a hand to me since I was sixteen and big enough to hit back. I haven't forgotten those lashings, or how you left me bleeding and locked in a bare stone chamber when I was but fourteen."

A fist pounded the table so that the flagon and cups clattered. "My heir should bide in England, not France. You still fear me, or you wouldn't run away."

"You always did twist the truth to suit your illusions," Blade said. "As I told you, I'll come back when you're dead. There's nothing to keep me here now that you've driven Mother to her grave."

"Your mother was a weakling, and you're a coward, afraid to marry a feather of a girl like that Oriel."

"God's breath!" Blade took several steps toward his father, then halted and cursed again as he tried to strangle the hilt of his sword with one hand. "I won't do it. I won't marry her. She has eyes like dried peas and a pointy little face like a weasel, and she can't even remember my name."

"It's Blade." Oriel pushed the door back and stepped into the great chamber.

It had taken all her courage not to run away. His disdain had been so unexpected. He'd said those words so quickly she hadn't understood their meaning immediately, and then she realized that while she had been enraptured, he had been offended by her and her appearance. All the years of encountering youths and men who paid her slight notice came thundering back into her memory. The evenings spent watching while others danced, the hunts spent pursuing a deer or fowl while other girls were instead pursued themselves—these had driven her to seek comfort in learning and solitary pursuits.

Until today she'd scorned to seek the favor of men, for there lay the path to great hurt. She had forgotten herself and her fear this once, for the prize entranced her without warning, danced before her in the guise of a dark-haired lord with eyes like the silver edge of a cloud when lit by the sun behind it. She had forgotten, and now she paid the price.

When she'd spoken, both men had frozen. Neither had spoken as she entered, and now Blade approached her. Oriel held up a hand to stop him, and he hesitated.

"If it please you, my lord, let there be no pretense between us." Oriel stopped and swallowed, for her voice trembled. "I see that you like not my person and have no time or desire to make yourself familiar with my character. Likewise, I find myself unable to countenance a suitor with so ungentle a manner, be he ever so handsome and endowed with a goodly estate."

"Mistress, my hot and heady language was the result of being near my lord father."

"Whatever the cause, I have no wish to deal with you further. Good day to you, my lords."

Oriel turned her back on Blade and made herself walk slowly out of the great chamber, down the gallery to the staircase. She lifted her skirts and was about to dash upstairs in a race to beat the fall of her tears when she heard Blade's voice calling to her.

He was at her side before she could retreat. His cloak swirled around her skirts, and his dark form blocked out the light from the gallery windows. She could smell the leather of his riding clothes. He put a hand on her arm, and she sprang away, shaking it off.

"Mistress, stay you a moment."

"I have work, my lord." She must gain her chamber before she betrayed herself with tears.

"I swear to you, my words were hastily spoken and

ill-reasoned on account of my anger at my father. A meanness of spirit overcomes me when I'm in his company for long, and this time I struck out at him and hit you instead. I take an oath before God that none of my insults are true."

"Ofttimes we speak our truest feelings when our words are least guarded, my lord."

She brushed past him and mounted the stairs with as much dignity as she could summon. Halfway up he was still looking at her from below.

"Lady, I go to France soon, and would not leave this kingdom without your forgiveness."

Oriel looked down at Blade. Even from this height he appeared as tall as a crusader tower and as beautiful as a thunderstorm in July. In a brief span she had been enthralled and rejected, and if she didn't get away from him she would throw herself on the floor and weep for what she had lost almost before she knew she wanted it.

"Of course. As a good Christian I can hardly withhold my forgiveness, and you have it. It seems to be the only thing in Richmond Hall you want. Once again, good day to you, my lord."

Chapter 2

In love when I have been
With them that loved me
Such danger have I seen. . . .

—*Sir Thomas Wyatt*

France
January 1565

The Loire Valley was the heart of France. A spy who wished to prize secrets from courtiers made himself a familiar of those nobles whose chateaux graced the banks of this azure river. This was why Blade rode alongside the water toward the chateau of Claude de la Marche, mistress of princes, cardinals, and spies. Though he loved the Loire, this time he failed to notice the beauty of the frost-covered countryside. He burrowed his nose into the fur lining of his cloak hood and pondered the unlikely source of his vexation.

He had enough worries to beset him without thinking about that fey creature who couldn't remember his name, yet the image of her face wouldn't go away. He'd loosed his cursed tongue, scimitar fashion, and cut her instead of his father. He'd gained the habit from Christian de Rivers years ago, and found it useful when employed correctly.

The face of a weasel—what drivel. He could see her face now. Small, pointed of chin, and wide of forehead, it more resembled the face of a fairy, and her eyes reminded him of the trees of the Loire Valley in spring. She hadn't replied to his letter apologizing for his lack of courtesy.

There were matters of great weight straining for his attention. He shouldn't be thinking of Oriel Richmond. He shouldn't, at the moment, be thinking of anything English. For he was in France, and the smallest slip in manner or of tongue could mean his death. He muttered to himself in French and glanced back at his servant and bodyguard, René.

René had been with him since he was a boy. He had first been employed by Blade's mother, and had stayed when she died eight years ago, though many of her servants had gone back to her estate on the Loire. Lady Fitzstephen had asked René to protect her son, and no argument on Blade's part could dissuade him from his task. Though of middle age, he could still lift his charge over his head and match him at fencing.

"*René, venez ici.*"

"*Oui, mon seigneur.*"

"I'm worried, René. Our lady queen takes a great risk with her plan. Mary Stewart may be queen of Scotland, but her life's ambition is to wrest England from Elizabeth, and her cursed French uncles will help her. The queen has forgotten that Mary Stewart owes more of her character to her Guise relations than to her Stewart ones. Cunning and ruthlessness were reborn in the shapes of the Guise brothers."

"*Oui*, my lord, but one cannot follow every intrigue hatched by the Duc de Guise or the Cardinal of Lorraine."

"It is the cardinal who presents the greatest threat. If it would gain him control of France or England, he would draw and quarter his own firstborn. With as many mistresses as he has, he's sure to have a firstborn."

"So," René said, "that is why we travel in weather unfit for dogs. The lovely Claude de la Marche has succumbed at last."

"I received her invitation upon returning from England. I'm surprised you didn't read it. You read everything else."

"It was sealed, my lord."

"And you never read sealed letters?"

"Only those I have time to work upon, my lord."

"I shall remember." Blade lifted himself in the saddle as they emerged from a stand of bare trees. "Look. I never tire of the sight of the chateaux, though mine is by far the most beautiful to me."

Less than half a league distant, a chateau rose from the waters of the Loire. Its high white towers, crenellated and topped with conical roofs, swam before them, a diamond balancing between river and land. The weak January sun set the silver rooftops ablaze. Claude's chateau was much smaller than those of the king or great princes, yet it contained all the beauty of decoration in the Italian manner—foliated scrollwork, scalloped shells, pilasters, and fluted columns abounded.

Castle La Roche, his English home, seemed a monstrous cavern when compared to this enchanted place. Mayhap his view of it was distorted by the past. Although there were whole chunks of his childhood shrouded in the blackness of lost memory, what he remembered had been sufficient to send him to France as soon as he'd been able to go. He remembered incessant battles. He remembered always living in fear that some unsuspected offense by his mother or him would ignite his father's fury. He remembered taking refuge in study, only to find that gradually he himself had fallen prey to a demon rage.

At first he struck out in anger at his tutors when they criticized his work. Then he began to dream. He dreamed of killing someone, a faceless man who evoked such rage in him that he attacked the man with fists and feet, beating him until he lay dead. After such a dream he woke in a sweat, his chest heaving as though he'd ridden fifty leagues. Terrified, he would spend hours begging God to forgive him for his own nightmares. Even more of his time was devoted to controlling his temper. He swore a vow to God that he wouldn't strike out at others for his own shortcomings, as did his father.

As he grew older, the nightmares changed. The faceless man turned into one of his tutors. Then one day when he was sixteen, he was killing his tutor in the dream, his hands squeezing into the flesh of the man's neck, when he blinked, and the tutor transformed into his father. He woke screaming. That night he vowed to leave Castle La Roche.

Two years later he succeeded in convincing his father to send him to Oxford, only to be captured by the highwayman Jack Midnight along the way. He'd been struck on the head and had lost his memory. During this time, he joined Midnight and his band. When he regained his memory, his greatest concern had been to conceal from those who knew him his father's monstrous nature, and his own secret rage. His French inheritance had come as a blessing from heaven.

He gripped his reins tighter and shifted in the saddle. He'd allowed himself to drift into memory—a dangerous luxury when he would encounter Claude soon. Putting old unhappiness aside, he stared at the spires of the chateau and recited proverbs in French to keep his thoughts from straying.

It wasn't long before he rode beneath the chateau gate. Soon he was inside and shaking frost from his hair. A servant murmured that madame awaited him in her chamber, and he followed the man up the spiral staircase in the east tower. The stair was a graceful curve of white marble with a central support carved with foliage and panels that reached high above his head. As he mounted the steps, he could see the underside of the flight of stairs above, seemingly afloat in the air.

On the second floor he entered a withdrawing chamber. The servant paused before a door and knocked, then opened it and bowed. Blade ducked through the entryway, which was a bit low for his height, and found himself in a chamber hung with great tapestries depicting hunting scenes and scenes from Greek mythology. Claude awaited him, having contrived a pose beside a table laden with food and wine. A gilded and velvet-covered canopy bed rose behind her. The whole effect of woman and chateau was one of luxurious fecundity, warmth and sensuality layered over with an elegance of presentation that concealed a preoccupation with physical pleasure. Claude waited for him to take in the full measure of her beauty before calling him and coming to him with arms outstretched.

"Ah, *mon chèr* Nicholas, you have taken so long to come to me. I have been desolate."

White, plump arms surrounded him, and Blade kissed her. The scent of lilacs nearly smothered him, and he scraped his hand on a diamond button. Abruptly he was reminded of Oriel Richmond in her simple wool gown, her hair flying about as if mussed by pixies. Claude's beauty was as full-bodied and rich as her chateau, and her hair was her best feature. Pale gold, silken, and gently curling, it lay in cascades about her shoulders, for she had purposely left it undressed.

"You have ignored me for so long, *mon ami*, that I thought you had forgotten me."

Blade freed himself from her arms. It wouldn't serve to show eagerness, for Claude had at least twenty noble French fools capering about her feet.

"Indeed, madame, I had thought myself far too unimportant to cause you even a moment's unease. I have been in Italy visiting an old friend."

Claude waved her hand, then began pouring wine into crystal goblets. "When one is out of France, one is cast from heaven. Did you have company on your journey?"

"Claude, in faith, I think you pry to see if I've a mistress."

"La, I already know that."

Blade sipped his wine to cover his wariness. He ran his tongue over his upper lip to distract Claude, and once her gaze was fastened on his mouth, he answered.

"Know you my habits so well?"

"The whole court knows your habits. My friends make a great game of tracing the antics of ladies and their lovers. The Vicomte de Tallart wagered that you would fly from Louise St. Michel to Marie de Bourbon within three months. I have confounded him."

"Then I am a wager."

Claude set down her goblet and placed her hand on his cheek. "*Non*, my sweet, you are the prize."

She pulled him to the bed and sank down upon it, drawing him with her. He didn't leave it until late that night when the chamber was cast in darkness except for the unsteady light from the fireplace. He rose and wrapped himself in a silk cover from the bed. Then he padded across the carpet to crouch before the fire and stare into the yellow flames.

He'd used his body in the service of his queen and country many times before, but never had he experienced this weariness of spirit. Apart from the first year, when he'd been enamored of the pleasure and intrigue, he had grown to view this aspect of his missions as the most draining. Making love where there was no affection wasn't making love at all. More and more he felt as if his body was a thing apart from himself, an instrument.

He'd found it was an instrument much desired at the

French court by women, and ofttimes by men, as well. Yet each woman who succumbed transformed herself in his mind into a tool much like himself, though none were aware of his thoughts on the matter. So, as the new year progressed, he conceived of a desire for something more. What this might be, he couldn't guess. He knew a discontent that burned in his chest, a heavy molten chain surrounding his heart.

He looked at the bed, but Claude was still sleeping. Soon, perhaps in a few days, he would lead her into conversations she would consider gossip. The gossip would eventually light upon Charles de Guise, Cardinal of Lorraine, uncle to Mary, Queen of Scots. His friend Christian de Rivers, and Cecil, Queen Elizabeth's chief minister, discounted the cardinal's ability to make mischief in England. Blade knew better. The cardinal's spies infested every court in Europe, and in spite of being occupied with persecuting French Protestants and scheming to control the French boy king, he hadn't given up on putting his niece on the throne of England.

Neither Christian nor Cecil understood Charles de Guise. Blade had understood him ever since he'd watched the man laugh at the antics of a Protestant heretic dancing on the charred stump of a leg in the flames that burned him alive. The cardinal at once combined bigotry, blind faith, a love of great art, and unmatched desire for power. Elizabeth counted upon the cardinal's desire to wrest power from Catherine de Medici, the queen mother, and the religious wars of France to keep the de Guises from meddling in English affairs.

Blade knew that few temptations would be more irresistible to the cardinal than seeing one of his lineage rule both Scotland and England. And he had trained his niece to believe the crown of England to be rightfully hers as the niece of Henry VIII. Lately the cardinal had entertained many English visitors at a banquet given for Elizabeth's ambassador. Whenever the cardinal sought out English company, Blade grew wary.

The covers on the bed stirred, and Claude's blond head poked out from under them. "Nicholas?"

"I am coming."

He slipped beneath the sheets. Claude threw an arm across his chest and shoved him into the pillows. Her hands kneaded the muscles of his arms and pressed into the flesh of his buttocks. He resisted the urge to thrust her hands away and was relieved when she left off exploring his body, climbed on top of him, crossed her arms on his chest, and grinned at him.

"I am well content with my wager. I've taken you from Louise St. Michel and given myself more pleasure than I thought possible. The vicomte will be furious." Claude giggled.

Blade shoved her off his body and began to free himself of the tangle of covers. With a cry of protest, Claude grabbed him and pulled him back beneath her.

"What ails you?" she asked.

"I dislike being treated like an amusing trinket you hang from your girdle and display to your friends."

"Oh, poor sweet infant, I've touched your pride. Does it not flatter you that so many compete for your favors? The vicomte would give a purse of gold to be here."

Blade scowled at her. "I trust you haven't invited him."

"Of course not."

"Nor anyone else."

"*Non.* I've no desire to share, but you know the court. Even the cardinal made a jest about my penchant for you."

Blade went still. "And what does he know of it? We have never met."

"La, he and I had a great quarrel but a fortnight ago. He dared to leave my bed to write letters." Claude slapped Blade's chest. "To write letters! I told him he hadn't worked hard enough if he could still pick up a quill. He fell into a rage. His face turned crimson and he sputtered like an overheated pudding."

"I don't believe you. The cardinal? God's breath, Claude, you try to make yourself important by claiming a powerful man as your lover." Blade cast a sideways glance at the woman.

"I do not," Claude said. "He is my lover."

"*Sacré Dieu,* I think not."

Claude sat up and glared at him. "He is. You may ask the vicomte or St. André, or your stupid St. Michel."

"That I won't do," Blade said. "I do not ask people about the lovers of a cardinal."

"Very well. I can prove it another way. I saw the letter he was writing."

Stretching his arms wide and yawning, Blade shook his head. "You could make up any fantasy you wished and claim you saw it in a letter."

"*Non,* this letter was too odd. Its very strangeness will be my proof, for it spoke of times long past, and events of no importance to France."

"Let us send for something to eat." Blade sat up and scooted toward the edge of the bed.

Claude captured him in her arms from behind. "You'll have no food until you admit I am beautiful enough to snare the Cardinal of Lorraine."

"Let go," Blade said. He groaned when Claude boxed him lightly on the ear. "Very well, tell me of this wondrous letter. Mayhap I will believe you."

"Oh, it was most strange. The cardinal was writing to someone about the old English king, Henry VIII. He told someone to inquire about Henry's second queen. What was her name? Anne? He told someone to find out about Anne and an old lover, who was also named Henry. Imagine, the great Cardinal of Lorraine bothering to find out whether some dead queen had a lover."

Blade said nothing. He allowed Claude to pull him

back down on the mattress. She smacked kisses all over his face and chest.

"Are you listening to me?"

"What?"

"I asked if you believed me."

"Oh, I suppose I must. The story is too unimportant and passing odd. I'm sure you wouldn't make up so unlikely a tale."

Claude continued babbling about how she would preen herself before the vicomte and enjoy her victory.

Never had Blade been forced to play his part so carefully as in the hours and days that followed. To leave beforetimes would arouse Claude's ire. He didn't think her clever enough to suspect his reason for wishing to be gone, but he couldn't risk arousing the curiosity of the cardinal, who no doubt watched Claude's doings as he did nearly everyone else's.

Thus it was a fortnight before he could take his leave of the garrulous Claude and ride back to Paris at an unhurried pace. Once safely behind the high gates of his town house, he summoned René, who was unpacking.

Settling in a chair, Blade propped his booted feet on a table and winced at the ache of muscles strained from long days in the saddle. When René entered his chamber, Blade had his eyes closed against the glare from a window.

"*Mon seigneur.*"

Blade opened his eyes and beckoned, and René went to kneel beside his chair.

"We leave for Calais tonight," Blade murmured. "Ready my traveling clothes and food—nothing else. I want to be in London as soon as possible. Give out that I've decided to spend the winter in the country."

"But we've only just—"

Blade stared at René.

"*Oui,* I will attend to it. I know that look."

Less than a week later, Blade had slipped into a river boat at the London docks on his way to the queen's

palace of Whitehall. By the time he reached the palace
the sun was setting. Instead of going to the palace gates,
he went to a nearby tavern after dispatching René with a
message. He then climbed the stairs to a rented chamber
and fell into bed. He was asleep in less than a minute.

> *With lullaby be thou content,*
> *With lullaby thy lusts relent.*

At the first word Blade grasped the dagger he'd
placed beneath his pillow and sprang at the singer. The
invader was sitting beside him, and didn't move when
the tip of the dagger met the flesh at his throat.

"As bloodthirsty as of old, marchpane."

"Christian, you sodding whoreson."

Christian de Rivers laughed, snatched the dagger,
and threw it at the door. It hit the wood and quivered,
its tip embedded in the panel.

"Years at the French court and you still sound like a
doxy's brat."

"Only in your presence." Blade rubbed his eyes and
yawned. "René found you. What o'clock is it?"

"Past midnight, and the queen is furious that you
sent no word of your coming."

"There was no time. I gained some news that
couldn't be set to paper or trusted to a messenger."
Blade looked at the door. "René guards without?"

"Yes. Now, what has sent you flying out of that nest
of civilized murderers, my comfit?"

"Anne Boleyn."

"A dead queen?"

"The queen's mother."

Christian rose, picked up an iron poker, and stirred
the dying embers in the fireplace opposite the bed.
"What have France and Anne Boleyn in common?"

"The Cardinal of Lorraine."

Blade took satisfaction in having startled his mentor.

There had been few times he'd been able to accomplish such a feat.

"Out with it, marchpane. You've had your amusement."

"The cardinal has taken a sudden interest in the affair of Anne Boleyn and Lord Henry Percy, who was heir to the Earl of Northumberland."

Christian tossed the poker aside. "Why?"

"I can but guess."

"Do so."

"I believe the cardinal seeks to find proof that Anne Boleyn and Henry Percy were married." Blade swung his legs off the bed and worked his shoulders free of kinks.

"Cardinal Wolsey broke up the match," Christian said. "Vows of betrothal were exchanged, but no consummation took place. . . . Ah."

"Yes, what if there was a consummation?"

"Then the church would consider a marriage to have taken place, and any other marriage thereafter would have been null. And—"

"And thus Henry VIII's marriage to Anne would be invalid in the eyes of Protestant and Catholic alike, and our queen would be the illegitimate issue of a royal liaison."

Christian approached him and leaned on the bedpost. Blade sank back on the bed and covered his eyes with the back of his arm.

"The Catholics consider Mary Stewart the rightful queen," Blade said, "and if our Bess is proved a bastard, many will clamor for Mary in her place. If the de Guises are concerning themselves with the marriage of Anne Boleyn and old King Harry, there can be but one reason. It is part of a greater plan—one involving Mary Stewart and the northern English Catholics. But how they will find proof of this consummation I don't know."

"Let me think."

Christian rested his forehead against the bedpost. Blade had almost fallen asleep again when he felt Christian's weight on the bed. He looked at the older man, and was surprised to see him staring at the bare wall by the door in horror.

"We could have civil war."

"I know," Blade said. "For the past five years I've watched France travel that road. At Vassy the Duc de Guise and his men slaughtered Protestants for singing too loudly. They raped girls and then hung them from the roofs of buildings for target practice."

"God, Blade, we've just rid ourselves of that wretched Mary Tudor."

"So you see why I made haste to come to you."

"Yes, marchpane." Christian smiled at him. "I am well recompensed for my tutelage."

"Can you search the court records, and those of Cardinal Wolsey? There must be something written upon the matter. We have to find out what the de Guises are about."

"I'll begin tomorrow."

"And while you're at work, I shall visit your lovely wife and she will feed me. I haven't seen Nora in more than a year."

"Don't get too fat, marchpane, for I've a feeling you're going to be back on your horse soon, despite this foul new year's clime."

"Me?"

"Don't look at me with such offense. You brought this plague to my doorstep, and you'll damned well see to the curing of it."

Chapter 3

Jesu Crist and seinte Benedight,
Blesse this hous from every wikked wight.

—*Geoffrey Chaucer*

Northern England
January 1565

Oriel's attention had strayed to a passage from Aristotle's *Politics* that waited for her in Uncle Thomas's library. It spoke about all persons alike sharing in government, and if Aunt Faith or cousin George knew what it said, they would have burned all the Greek books. Aunt Faith and cousin George didn't like strange ideas.

With reluctance she transferred her thoughts to her trencher and the mutton and roast quail upon it. January waned, and soon it would be Lent, the time of fasting and fish. She hated fish, almost as much as she hated Hugh Wothorpe. She stole a glance at her latest suitor. They were in the great chamber, which had been set for the midday meal, and her aunts and seven cousins were gorging themselves. Hugh Wothorpe was draining his goblet of wine, and a drop of it had trickled from the corner of his mouth. He wiped it away with his napkin and cleared his throat.

"Mistress, have I mentioned that my ancestry hies from the line of Edward IV?" Hugh didn't wait for her reply. "Few in this realm can claim so mighty a lineage, and still fewer can call it Plantagenet."

She had eaten a good deal of quail, and the food had made her sleepy. She allowed Hugh to drone on about his ancestors, which were his only claim to eligibility as a suitor. She had tried to make allowance for his boorishness, for he'd been kept in the Tower since he was a child by Henry VIII, and only released when Elizabeth came to the throne. He knew little of the world. He worked hard to cover his ignorance—and failed.

"Mistress Oriel, don't you feel well?" Hugh asked.

"I fear I'm surfeited with meat."

"Lord George keeps a fine table," Hugh said as he looked about the chamber.

The yeoman ushers were marching in with a course of sweets. In Hugh's honor and at George's order, the French cook had constructed a subtlety of marchpane in the form of his coat of arms. George was Aunt Livia's firstborn. He had inherited the title of Lord Richmond and his mother's beefy frame. He was a great one for proper gestures such as the subtlety. Presiding over each meal with pomposity, George always insisted on the ceremony of the ushers bowing to each course. Each dish was escorted by gentlemen in waiting.

Oriel found the ritual tedious, as did George's youngest brother, Leslie. She heard him talking to George in that too-nice tone he used to shred his brother's peace. Their mother preferred Leslie, who used her partiality like an apothecary's lancet to jab at his brothers until they bled. She turned her attention away from the two, for she disliked seeing either of them hurt. She allowed herself to ponder a new thought that had come to her this day.

"Lord Hugh, have you ever wondered how trees know where to put out branches?"

"Branches?" Hugh looked down his long nose at her, as if she was speaking Persian instead of English.

"Yes. Why don't trees put out branches all over their trunks? How do they know which way to grow?"

"God has caused them to grow in the appropriate manner, as he causes all manner of creatures to thrive."

"But how?"

"Fie, mistress, this is a bootless question."

Aunt Faith, her skinny aunt, was frowning at her from the table opposite her own. Aunt Faith resented Oriel's new wealth when she had four daughters to marry off. Jane and Joan were of marriageable age, being fifteen and seventeen. It seemed that neither would leave Richmond Hall, however, before their sisters Agnes and Amy came out of the schoolroom. All of them had that unfortunate shade of brown hair that looked as if they stood on their heads in ashes. Not one of them had eyebrows, and only little Amy had a chin. When they wore ruffs, their short necks disappeared.

Livia boomed at her from beside Hugh. "Oriel, since you and Lord Hugh have so much about which to converse, show him our west courtyard."

Given no choice, Oriel conducted her suitor downstairs and out into the western court. Richmond Hall was built on a rectangular plan, and the hollow formed by the wings of the rectangle was split by a gallery, thus forming two separate courtyards. Three stories of latticed windows with lead frameworks looked down upon the courtyards from all sides. Aunt Faith had ordered the shrubbery cut in formal designs, so that the visitor was presented with bushes pruned in the shape of cones, balls, and rectangles.

In January the courtyard flora were covered with protective sheets, and these had been layered in white by yesterday's snow. Bundled into heavy, fur-lined cloaks, Oriel and Hugh walked up and down the snow-covered paths because they had been ordered to do so and Faith would spy on them to see that they obeyed. They had been walking some ten minutes when Hugh stopped abruptly.

"It's hopeless," he said to her.

"My lord?"

He looked away from her and wiped his nose with a large kerchief. "You may not have noticed, mistress, but I—I have not much facility with company, especially with women. Until Her Majesty released me, I only had my gaolers for companions. When I was young, I was a kind of pet with them."

"It must have been terrible to be kept in the Tower for so long."

"My room was a good one, and I was allowed exercise. But you're a clever girl. I can see it in your eyes." Hugh wetted his lips and went on. "You already know how poor I am."

"Yes." All the Tudors made a habit of killing or beggaring any dangerous rivals to the throne.

"I am ashamed. Everyone says I should be proud of my lineage, but how can I hold up my head when my hose need patching and my boots don't have soles? I've been living on the charity of noblemen for so long that they bar their doors when they hear me approach."

Oriel watched Hugh stomp his feet and realized the snow must have wet them almost as soon as he set foot outside. She took his hand and began pulling him toward a door in the western wing. Once inside, she led him to the windows.

"Stay here and walk up and down to keep warm. I'll return anon."

She scampered upstairs. On the way to her own chamber, she stopped to filch a pair of Uncle Thomas's shoes and a pair of boots. Uncle loved shoes. His collection required several tall cupboards and even more chests. He had shoes of velvet and brocade, slippers and boots—embroidered shoes, plain shoes, jeweled shoes, and even a pair sewn with feathers. When he traveled, he carried at least forty pairs with him.

This harmless vanity endeared him to Oriel. He would miss the two old pairs she'd taken. In her chamber she threw open a jewel casket, plucked a necklace from it, and a set of buttons. Thrusting them into a velvet bag, she returned to the gallery where Hugh still paced. She produced the shoes and boots from beneath her cloak after making certain that they were alone.

Hugh flushed, but took the footwear with hands shaking from the cold. He stuffed them under his cloak. "Won't there be an outcry when these are found missing?"

"No. I'll tell Uncle Thomas I gave them to a poor rat catcher and a beggar."

Hugh's flush deepened to crimson. "You are kind, Mistress Oriel. I—I would marry you if you wished."

"Shhh! Don't say that. Aunt Faith may be nearby."

She and Hugh looked up and down the gallery. It was still deserted. Oriel drew near Hugh and lowered her voice to a whisper.

"I've something for you, but you must promise never to tell where you got it."

She opened the velvet bag. Buttons spilled into her hand. Mounted in oval gold settings, each contained a square-cut ruby, and there were four of them. The necklace spilled out after them, a flat piece of lacy gold set with pearls and diamonds. Hugh gasped and then stared at Oriel. She thrust the jewelry into the bag and shoved it into Hugh's hands. He clutched it, still gaping at her.

Oriel lifted a finger. "I give these to you. They will keep you for a long time. But you must promise to go away and not ask for my hand."

"Fie, mistress. You but need to refuse me. You don't have to bribe me."

"I know, but I have boxes and caskets full of such baubles left to me by my grandfather. I've no need for these, and I would worry about you if you left in your present state. Take them. If not for yourself, for me, for I vow I'll sleep not a wink if you don't. Do you promise?"

Hugh's eyes filled with tears. "I promise. And if you should ever need aid of any sort, call upon me, dear Oriel."

"My thanks," she said. "Now you should go to your chamber and dry your feet. God give you a pleasant afternoon, my lord."

She fled the gallery, fearing Hugh might change his mind and refuse her gifts, and made her way to Uncle Thomas's library. In truth, the library belonged to the owner of the Hall—George—but Great-uncle Thomas had lived with the family so long and inhabited the room so much that it had become known as his. As she approached the chamber from the second floor gallery, she heard Uncle Thomas arguing with someone. Her pace slowed, for she recognized Leslie's voice.

She was surprised to hear him, for Leslie abhorred the country and preferred to spend most of his days in the south in London. He loved attending court and gambling and dicing and carousing, pursuits unavailable to him in the north country. His greatest desire was to obtain an appointment from Her Majesty as one of her gentlemen pensioners, for then he would be eligible for control of leases, wardships, and licenses, which would relieve his penurious state as a younger son.

To her astonishment, Leslie's voice was raised in ire. Leslie was the only male Richmond to possess a ready wit and charm to match, and rarely lost his temper. When she had first come to Richmond Hall he had taken pity on her and befriended her. She had been grateful, for Leslie had been a high and mighty youth of thirteen, and she only twelve. He had protected her from George's and Robert's teasing. It had taken Oriel little time to realize Leslie's favored position at Richmond Hall. Aunt Livia considered him the most engaging creature put upon the earth, and he could wind the sour Faith about the heel of his boot with no objection from the lady.

"I know not," Uncle Thomas was saying.

"A pox on your knowing and not knowing. You were there. I remember the story."

"Contentious whelp, begone with you. At once! Out of my sight."

Oriel had her hand on the half-open library door when it was swept aside and Leslie charged out of the chamber. He stumbled over Oriel and caught her up in his arms. Lifting her, he set her aside with a mumbled apology. She watched him storm down the gallery and take the stairs two at a time. A tall man, he shared with Oriel the same dark black-red hair and slender build. When that auburn head had vanished down the staircase, she went into the library.

"Uncle?"

Thomas looked up from behind a great pile of books spread over one of the tables. Piles as large as this one littered two other tables.

"Uncle, what's wrong with Leslie?"

"Naught. You know Leslie, always up to some foolish scheme to gain a fortune. Last spring he tried to convince me to pay for his experiments in alchemy. He wanted to make gold."

"Oh, no. I hope he isn't doing that again. Marry, he near blew himself to the New World messing with potions and such." Oriel went to the table, stopped opposite Thomas, and picked up a book. Its binding was cracked, and the clasp rusted. "Where did you find these?"

"I sent for them from my old house in London. I haven't been there in so long I was worried they might suffer from lack of attention, and I was right. By my faith, I shouldn't have neglected them."

"I'll help you," Oriel said. "You'll need a list of them and a notation of the contents and condition of each one. You'll tire yourself most thoroughly if you try it by yourself."

"You're a good girl." Thomas pinched the bridge of his nose. "I need fresh air. I've been at work since sunrise."

After calling to his manservant for a cloak and walking stick, Thomas invited Oriel to come with him.

"I'm going to the chapel, and the ground will be slippery with all this snow. Lend me your arm, child."

The chapel lay east of Richmond Hall on a wide lawn, and a path covered with flagstones connected the two buildings. It was an ancient structure of creamy stone, over three hundred years old. Built by a Richmond ancestor upon his return from France, it was a small replica of the French cathedrals of Saint-Denis and Chartres.

They slipped into the chapel nave. It was some time before evening prayers, and the altar was deserted, though lit with candles. Oriel never missed vespers, for the setting sun illuminated the western rose window over the main doors and transformed the chapel into a place of light and shadow. Beams of red, green, white, and Chartres blue made the ribbed stone vaulting and marble floor glimmer with color. At that moment of sunset, the chapel was transformed into a mystical place, a tribute to the spirit of man and God.

"Come," Uncle Thomas said. "I want to look at my new tomb inscription."

As no one lingered in the chapel, Oriel lit a torch from a candle stand and walked with him down the south aisle. They passed window after window of bright glass panes and pointed arches until they found the spiral staircase that led down to a short tunnel and the old family crypt. Shoving open the heavy, iron-studded door, Oriel held the torch high. She stepped aside so that her uncle could enter. The crypt was as deserted as the chapel, and demon black.

Thomas chuckled, and the sound echoed off the walls and tomb effigies. "You used to be afraid to come down here."

Oriel glanced around the crypt at the long lines of tombs, each with an effigy of its owner resting atop the lid. She held the torch close, and could just make out rounded arches, wide stone pillars, and, inset into the walls, more tombs.

"I'm a grown woman now. And besides, ghosts and shades don't walk in daylight."

"True."

Thomas went to a long marble box surrounded by a work cloth and sculptors' tools. In the face of the tomb was carved the newly finished inscription. Oriel held the torch aloft to reveal the Latin words: *"In Nomine Patris et Filii et Spiritus Sancti. . . ."*

"A fine piece of work, Uncle." Oriel studied the intricately carved head of Thomas's effigy.

"Yes," Thomas said and held up a finger. "And you should remember it. Have your effigy carved when you're young, and you'll look a fine spectacle to your descendants. I had my likeness done before I was thirty, and the sculptor used it as a model."

The old man touched the tip of the marble nose. Oriel smiled at him, but grew puzzled when he suddenly rubbed his chin and frowned at the effigy.

"Er, Oriel, my child. Someday, if I am gone, you may find my tomb inscription full of wisdom and aid in matters of great import. The world is a perilous place."

"I will remember, Uncle Thomas."

"By the rood, I know you will." Thomas turned away from the effigy and began walking. "I've never seen a maid with a memory like yours. I do believe you could memorize the entire Bible. In Latin and in English."

Oriel put her hand beneath Thomas's arm as they

mounted the stairs. "That reminds me," she said. "Did you know cousin Robert and cousin George have quarreled again? Last night Robert said all the problems of highwaymen and thievery hereabouts were no doubt due to heretics robbing decent Catholic folk. George nearly burst his doublet."

"Ridiculous. Robert has never recovered from the family's changing religion. He's such a stiff, bigoted young colt. I'm sure a good part of the reason he keeps his fat, disguised priest and his mass is to irk poor George. Robert is a lamentable soul."

Oriel sighed and nodded. "Yes, and if he doesn't stop his tongue, he'll attract Her Majesty's attention. She cares not for meddling with men's souls and doesn't inquire into a Catholic's mass as long as he worships quietly, but Robert has never been quiet, and now he refuses to attend the established church."

"If old King Harry were alive," Thomas said, "Robert would find his head on a pike atop London Bridge."

After returning to the warmth of Thomas's library, Oriel gathered quill and paper for her catalog of her uncle's books while he sorted them. Unfortunately, she grew distracted, reading each book she picked up. She was reading a collection of the poetry of Sir Thomas Wyatt when her uncle woke from a doze by the fire. He snorted and sat up, straightened the cap he wore to keep his balding head warm, and rose. He picked up the book he'd let fall in his sleep and brought it to the growing pile at Oriel's writing table.

"I've remembered me of a thing," he said. "Your aunts are constantly at George about your marriage. They say it's a disgrace to the family that you're twenty and unmarried, and you should have been a wife seven years ago. What say you to this Hugh fellow?"

Oriel snapped her book closed. "Uncle, he's a pitiful creature. Why, they hardly taught him his letters in the Tower, and he never learned of hawking or hunting or dancing or even fencing. He feels unmanned. Poor Hugh."

"No match for you, my girl. You need a man who won't get himself lost in the maze of your wit, and one who can protect you. Robert was right, you know. The roads are dangerous, crawling with vermin of all sorts. And what if there's rebellion? Our cloth-headed Catholic neighbors might take issue with the queen over religion. Too bad that young Blade, er, Nicholas Fitzstephen, offended you. I've heard his sword could slice a fairy's wing, and he's set all the queen's maids sighing on his visits to court."

"He's mean."

"Now, child, I thought you'd come to understand his discourtesy. If I had a father who beat me for laughing aloud or for falling off my pony when I was nine, I'd do more than give him barbs and threats. I remember hearing years ago that Andrew Fitzstephen near killed the boy with his whip. That was after he'd done the same for the mother and the boy tried to stop him."

"I know, I know, I know." Oriel pressed her palms to her ears. "Don't speak of it, I pray you. Such talk makes me long to steal into Fitzstephen's castle and put acid in his ale."

"Then you forgive the boy."

"Marry, Uncle, what choice have I? But I still remember what he said."

Oriel rose and stood in front of a window. She bent her knees and ducked until she caught her reflection in a pane.

"He was right. My face is so pointed I look like a weasel—no, a ferret." She stuck her tongue out at her reflection.

"A hedgehog, perchance?"

Oriel turned and grinned at her uncle. "Or a dolphin."

"A squirrel."

"A rich squirrel," Oriel said. She sat down in the

window seat and put her chin in her hand. "So I'm to be hounded into marriage."

"Hounded apace, may a pox take your aunts."

"Then you must come to my aid. Bethink yourself of all the men I could marry, and I will make a list as well. I will be the one to choose my husband, not them."

"The choice belongs to George as your guardian."

"But George I can bend to my way of thinking." Oriel rose and approached Thomas. She whispered in his ear. "And hark you, if he listens to Aunt Livia or Aunt Faith, I shall run away with the man I choose."

"Only if you're able to remember his name, child. Only if you remember his name."

Chapter
4

*One must therefore be a fox to recognize traps,
and a lion to frighten wolves.*

—*Niccolo Machiavelli*

Blade cursed and threw his goblet at the chimneypiece. The crystal shattered against the stone, and wine splashed, making a carved column appear to bleed.

"The queen's gone mad."

Christian de Rivers, who had been standing near the fire, gave his mantel a rueful glance, but otherwise maintained his somnolent pose. "Why say you so?"

"Don't pretend ignorance. No doubt this is your contriving, this idea to send Matthew Stewart to Scotland. What care you if he's married to old King Henry's niece, whose son is a Catholic and has a claim to the throne? Margaret Lennox has plotted her whole life to claim England, and Matthew is as dangerous."

Blade paused to glare at Christian. They had been

sharing a rare moment of repose, for soon Blade would leave London, and each time they parted, neither could be sure of seeing the other alive again. Tempestuous as their friendship was, Blade was grateful to Christian for rescuing him from the highwayman Jack Midnight.

Eight years ago the thief and his band had fallen upon Blade's traveling party on their way to deliver their young master to university. In the skirmish, Blade had suffered a wound to the head and awakened with no memory of who he was. Midnight, a dispossessed farmer turned outlaw, carried a deep-seated hatred of the nobility. He'd turned this hatred into a quest for vengeance against any hapless aristocrat who fell in his path. Thus he'd abducted Christian as a child and trained him in thievery, only to lose him. By an unhappy chance, he found a replacement in Blade, a better one, for with no memory, Blade had believed Midnight's claim that he belonged to the band of highwaymen.

Looking back, he'd decided that his previous misery had contributed to his loss of memory. Rough as Midnight had been, serving him had been preferable to succumbing to the lust to kill his own father. Besides, the life of a highwayman allowed him to drink deep of the wine of recklessness and freedom. Christian had felt the same.

From Midnight they had both learned the lawless arts. Christian had been rescued by his father, the Earl of Vasterne. A later encounter with Jack Midnight brought Christian face-to-face with Blade. In spite of Blade's fury at being plucked from the dubious comfort of Midnight's band, Christian forced him to take up residence at the earl's palace while he ferreted out Blade's true identity.

At the moment they had returned to the de Rivers mansion on the Strand, for Christian's inquiries into the matter of Anne Boleyn's betrothal to Henry Percy had come to an end. He had also consulted with Elizabeth's chief minister, William Cecil, who had reacted with alarm at Blade's news.

Having to wait idle for over a fortnight had given Blade the temper of a starving boar. His fear of encountering the French ambassador had kept him from court and from the company of his friends, except for those of low degree who would not frequent the court or mansions of ambassadors. His carefully tended reputation as a dissolute would protect him from suspicion of intrigue, but he would rather few knew of his presence in England for the moment.

As time passed, he grew more and more apprehensive, for he knew the Cardinal of Lorraine. His network of agents was extensive in London, and whatever Christian discovered, the French minister would as well. The specter of civil war loomed large in his mind. He'd seen the results in the horror of the auto-da-fé, where Lorraine and his allies had publicly burned scores of French Protestants, even children. The thought that the cardinal might acquire the power to perform the auto-da-fé in his beloved England tortured him. He knew Christian felt the same, which made this latest action by the queen seem so foolish. To allow so dangerous a rival as Matthew Stewart to prance off to Scotland to consort with that country's Catholic ruler seemed the trick of a witless fool.

Christian was no fool. Blade drew his brows together and studied his friend. "What foul scheme have you hatched with our glorious Queen Elizabeth?"

"I've hatched nothing. I'm not a chicken."

"No, you're a villainous, intriguing, deceitful serpent." Blade slumped back in his chair and stretched his legs out, crossing them at the ankles. "And having learned my trade at your side, I begin to think there's a plot afoot. Knowing Her Majesty, the true intent is buried well below the headstones I see popping up at my feet."

When Christian remained silent, Blade smiled nastily and continued. "So," he breathed. "Let me think. The son of Matthew Stewart and his Tudor wife is Henry, Lord Darnley, in whose veins flows the blood of both Tudors and Stewarts. But if I remember me well, our friend the Cardinal of Lorraine called Lord Darnley *'un gentil huteaudeau'*—an agreeable nincompoop."

Christian left the fireplace and came to stand before Blade with the table between them.

"I've tutored you well, comfit."

"Since the Queen of Scots is determined to wed, unlike our own virginal majesty, it would be far more agreeable to her for her cousin to marry an agreeable fool than a disagreeably clever man."

"And now that you've discovered me of my deepest secrets, mayhap you'll close your mouth so that I may give you news of the witness to Anne Boleyn's betrothal."

"A dangerous gamble, Darnley is."

"Made more perilous by the interference of the Cardinal of Lorraine at this most delicate time. Which is why you must go to this witness and prize from him the truth of the betrothal." Christian straightened and folded his arms over his chest. "You have an instinct for peril, marchpane. I thank God you recognized the significance of your news and came to me quickly."

"It's as I thought, then. The cardinal seeks to destroy Elizabeth's claim to the throne by finding proof of this prior betrothal and consummation."

"And the only witness left alive was a lifelong friend of Henry Percy—Sir Thomas Richmond."

Years at the French court had given Blade the facility to hide his reactions. He lowered his eyes and traced a scratch on the surface of the table with his fingers.

"Sir Thomas Richmond," he said. "There are no others?"

"No, they're all dead and have left no written word on the matter. If the cardinal wants proof of a consummation of vows, he'll have to get it from Sir Thomas, but you're going to get it first, preferably by stealth, so that no one will know what you've done."

"Christian."

Christian swept around the table and put his hand on Blade's shoulder. "A happy chance that it was you who discovered the danger, for I can send you to Richmond Hall. I've already bethought me of a plan. There is an heiress at the Hall, one the Richmonds are seeking to marry to a highborn suitor. You, my comfit, will be that suitor."

"Christian."

His friend pounded him on the shoulder and laughed. "Think you I haven't heard the talk about you at the French court? The queen mother employs her maids in waiting as seductive spies so successfully that they're called the Flying Squadron for their flying skirts. I shall employ you in like manner."

"God rot your twisty mind, Christian de Rivers." Blade threw off his friend's hand. "You delight in circuitous maneuvers, and this is a good one, except for a small impediment."

"What impediment?"

"Not long ago I insulted this heiress of Richmond Hall so grievously that she's bound to puke at the sight of me."

Blade thrust himself out of his chair and faced Christian. Once, the fury he beheld would have given him pause. Now he merely lifted one brow.

"Apologize," Christian snapped.

"I have. She liked me not one whit more for it."

"Then you must pursue one of the other girls of marriageable age."

"No one would believe my suit."

"Why not?"

"You don't know Mistress Jane or Mistress Joan. Cheese-witted little hedgehogs, both of them. I'm surprised their tutors were able to stuff enough learning in their heads to enable them to write letters."

"Dissemble. Pretend to be enamored of one of them."

"God's blood, Christian, even I cannot play a part so contrary to my nature. They're stupid, man. I hate stupid women. I hate stupid men, for that. And there's no use chastising me. You must trust my experience."

Christian took Blade's place in the chair. Blade clasped his hands behind his back and paced back and forth beside him. After long moments of consideration, he threw up his hands.

"We must find someone else to go to Richmond Hall."

"No, marchpane. This knowledge must go no further than we two. Curse you, Blade. Why did you pick this one girl to insult? You've plied your charms on many less likable."

"I was with my father, and I lost my temper."

"Ah, no wonder." Christian was silent for a moment. "I have always regretted sending you back to your father once we discovered who you were all those years ago. Why did you not tell me what he was like, instead of pretending everything was well?"

Blade turned his back to his friend. "Think you I'd speak of what he really was? Have you ever told your father the whole of your experiences with Jack Midnight?"

"God forbid."

"One learns to dissemble before the world, as one learns to be what one's oppressor wishes. You know that. It's what makes us useful as spies. We change colors, wear mask upon mask, hoping no one will ever think to look beneath and find only another mask." He faced Christian. "I don't wish to speak of this. As I said, I've insulted Oriel Richmond and she detests me. There's naught to be done about it."

Christian slapped the table with his palm. "There's

no help for it. You must return all remorseful and beg to be forgiven. You're enslaved by her charms. You've suffered every moment since you left."

"I didn't say Oriel Richmond was stupid; only her cousins."

Christian rose and poured himself a goblet of wine. "You will think of a way to convince her."

"She'll think I'm after her wealth, or that I'm a fool."

"If you're diligent, she'll be so smitten she won't have the wits to be suspicious."

"The thing's impossible," Blade said. "She'll toss me out like a false beggar."

Christian grinned at him. "Take heart, comfit, for 'the easy attainment of love makes it of little value; difficulty of attainment makes it prized.'"

"Christian de Rivers, you're a pig."

A fortnight later, on a day in mid-February, Blade rode through a quiet, snowbound forest on his way to Richmond Hall. René and four of his liveried retainers rode behind him. He was cold, cold and disgusted with himself, for he'd yet to conceive of a plan that would assure him the welcome of Oriel Richmond. He'd written to Lord George and received permission to renew his suit. George was anxious to rid himself of his cousin, it seemed. She tested his patience. No doubt the man shrank from the eternal skirmishing between his mother and Oriel he'd spoken of in his letter.

Strange how agitated he'd grown at the thought of encountering Oriel again. She had appeared in his dreams, a phantasm surrounded by the dark auburn fire of her own hair. It was a preoccupation he'd forborne from mentioning to Christian. To confess himself haunted by memories of a girl he'd insulted with thoughtless barbs would amuse Christian and inspire unending mockery. The thought of being at Christian's mercy was as lowering as the idea of facing Oriel.

If it weren't for the danger to kingdom and queen, he wouldn't have ventured north in winter. Blade huddled deeper into his cloak and rubbed his nose on the fox fur of its hood. Snow and freezing rain had turned the road into a mire. His stallion, a roan, danced with impatience under his restraining hand. He had to go slowly or risk riding into a hole.

The road to Richmond Hall had received a new coat of snow last night, and much of it lay concealed. It wound through a forested dale, skirting thick stands of trees covered in white. Their trunks marched like dark columns as far as he could see. One old relic blackened by a lightning strike had fallen across the road under the weight of the snow in its branches.

Blade held up his hand, and his men halted. He dismounted and trudged over to the tree to see if it was movable. He thrust his gloved hand through the layer of snow on the trunk, then turned to shout at René. As he turned, he heard a familiar buzzing sound and ducked. An arrow smacked into the tree trunk beside him.

Shouting at René, he vaulted over the trunk. He landed on his feet, threw back his cloak, and drew his sword as a dozen howling men darted out from behind snowbanks and trees. Shoving back the hood of his cloak, he raised his sword to meet the attack of a man who leaped over the tree trunk. The man raised his sword high and brought it down. Blade countered; their weapons clashed. Blade jabbed his foot into the man's stomach and shoved him backward. He hit the tree trunk, but bounced back, aiming at Blade's chest. Blade knocked the sword down with his own, then stomped on his attacker's foot.

A second man jumped on him from behind. Blade fell to his knees, jabbed the man with his elbow, and thrust the point of his sword up just in time to impale the first man as he raced in with his own weapon aimed at Blade's neck. Blade leaped to his feet. The second man scrambled out of his reach.

Past the fallen tree René and his men were fighting off as practiced a band of highwaymen as Blade had seen. Though clad in rough wool and scraps of richer clothing taken from past raids, they worked together, each man taking on an assigned victim. He saw one of his men fall, hit by an arrow from the bowman who had aimed at Blade from his perch in a nearby tree.

Blade ran for the tree trunk, placed his hands on it, and gathered his strength for another spring across it. He heard footsteps and turned. Something hit his shoulder. His whole body arched, and he felt a sting. He looked down at his left shoulder and saw blood. Shoving his back against the tree trunk, he faced his assailant, his left arm hanging limp and useless.

"Midnight."

His assailant lowered his sword. "God's arse, it's my lost treasure." He gave a bark of laughter. "You've grown into a man of a sudden. Well met, my love. Mayhap I won't kill you after all."

"You won't find it any easier now than before."

Blade lifted his sword, but Midnight did not. The highwayman put his hands on his hips and laughed in spite of the brawl taking place nearby. He whistled three times, and his men halted their attack. The two sides faced off, Blade's men surrounded by the thieves, but neither side moved to resume the fray. Midnight took a step toward Blade, who backed away until he hit the fallen tree.

The highwayman looked much the same as he had years ago when Blade served him. His black hair had turned more silver, and he bore a scar on his jaw from a sword cut, but those eyes still flashed bright black at the anticipation of a fight and the smell of blood.

"What do you here in the north, Midnight? Your realm is far south near London."

"Well, my novice, our good queen has made the hunt more difficult out London way. Blackheath's no longer a place of frolic and fun. It's safer in the north. And I had a good offer."

Blade kept his sword pointed at Midnight, but his head was growing lighter than the rest of his body. "Leave off, or I'll carve you like a capon, and you know I can do it."

"Yes, I've seen you best swordsmen of the first fencing house. But not with a hole in your shoulder." Midnight took another step.

"Stay away, you whoreson piss-prophet."

"Ah, there's my Blade, my apprentice. You were a wondrous good thief. Come, I only want to rob you. I promise not to kill you."

Midnight ventured another step, but Blade's sword made a silver arc and nearly sliced his stomach open.

"Your presence here is no accident, I trow. Again I ask why you're here."

Shrugging, Midnight looked from Blade's wound to his face. A slow smile formed on his lips, and he held out his hands, away from his body.

"Peace, my lodestar. I've no secrets from you. It's a patron I've found. One who appreciates my arts and needs a ready band of men. You see, I'm collecting funds for my old age."

Biting the inside of his cheek to keep his vision from blurring, Blade kept his sword aloft, though it grew heavier each time he breathed. "What patron?"

"Now, my treasure, you know I can't tell you that."

His sword wobbled, and Blade felt his arm tremble. "I said, what patron."

"Look at you, you're bleeding. Throw down your sword, my treasure." Midnight laughed at him. "God's arse, boy. Come now, surrender."

He blinked hard, and tried to lift his weapon as Jack Midnight swooped down on him. His knees buckled, but his fall was stopped when Midnight caught him. He heard René shout at him, but he was too weak to answer. He couldn't stop his eyes from closing, and when he opened them again, he was on the ground propped up against the fallen tree. Midnight leaned over him, stuffed a rag into his shirt, and held it against his wound.

Midnight shouted to his men. "Take the rest of them into the forest and lose them in it. Leave the stallion."

Blade felt the highwayman's hands at his belt. He was relieved of his pouch of coins. He fumbled for his dagger, but he was too slow. Midnight plucked it from its sheath.

"For shame, love. You were always such a blood-thirsty little wolf cub. Would you deny me my reward after such travail? I am sparing your life."

"My men . . ."

"They're alive, but only for the fondness I hold on your account." Midnight pulled Blade upright and began wrapping his cloak about his shoulders. "Don't fight me, you fool. You're bleeding, and I'm trying to get you back on your horse before you grow too weak to mount."

"I'll cut your tongue out for this."

Midnight laughed and turned Blade toward the stallion. "Not for a while, I'll wager." He put the reins in Blade's hands and placed his foot in a stirrup.

Blade found himself shoved into the saddle. The back of his horse had never seemed so high before, and he peered around at the tops of trees.

"God's arse." Midnight leaned over from his own horse and latched onto Blade's arm before he toppled from the saddle. "Where were you bound, love?"

"Rishmon . . ."

"Richmond Hall?"

"Mmm."

"Odd fortune, that. Ah, Blade, I vow I'll rue my foolish mercy."

The highwayman dismounted and climbed up in back of Blade.

"God's blood, what'er you about?"

Blade tried to shove Midnight off. He cursed as his wounded arm was jolted, and dizziness nearly overwhelmed him.

"Be still," Midnight said. "It's your own blood you should be worried about."

"You won't turn me into a thief again. I'm not—"

"You think me such a fool that I'd try to keep you? I'd as soon befriend a viper as try to make you into a proper thief all over again. Now be still. If I don't take you near the Hall, you'll fall off your horse and bleed to death."

Blade laughed helplessly. He felt as if he'd drunk a cask of wine. Midnight kicked the horse, and they began to move.

"You're losing your wits along with your blood," said the thief.

Attempting to hold his head steady, Blade tried to stop chuckling. "There's no help for it. You don't know what a favor you've done me. I couldn't have thought of a better plan if I'd spent a month—marry, the ground seems a league off."

"Hold!" Midnight hauled Blade up by the neck of his cloak. "You stay still or I'll knock you senseless."

"Just drop me in a heap at the gate," Blade murmured. He closed his eyes and smiled. "I'll cast myself on the mercy of a certain green-eyed fairy who dwells within."

Chapter
5

She would be scolded again for riding in the snow. Anticipation of Aunt Faith's whining had slowed Oriel's pace as she walked her mare toward the stables. She had lost track of time, and since the clouds were thick, she couldn't guess the hour from the sun. She was hungry, so it must be past time for dinner. She'd been pondering Uncle Thomas's strange behavior of late and thus forgotten how long she'd been gone.

The past few days he'd started when she came into his chamber or the library, and he'd taken odd fancies into his head. Only three nights ago he had insisted that she read all of old Sir Thomas Wyatt's poems. While the reading was enjoyable, she did think old Wyatt could have left off feeling sorry for himself. He seemed to have let the scorn of one woman ruin his enjoyment of life and then poured out his torment on paper.

She had finished the collection this morning and fled the house in search of nature and air free of the staleness of old tragedies. Wyatt must have loved Anne Boleyn above all else. What would it be like to have a man so in love with you? Oriel sighed and patted her mare's neck. She wasn't likely to inspire such passion. She knew that she irritated folk, especially noblemen.

Taking deep breaths of icy air, she gazed around her, letting her eyes feast upon the white world that had lifted her spirits. She glanced past the Hall to the gate near the horizon and pulled her horse up. Two men on a single horse rode up to the massive red brick pillars. A second horse followed them. As they approached, Leslie rode up to them, shouting.

He reached out and took the reins of the overburdened horse. One of the riders slipped off it, mounted the second horse and galloped away. Meanwhile, his companion slumped forward in the saddle. The moment his horse began to walk, he dropped unconscious to the ground.

Oriel kicked her own mare into a trot that brought her across the lawn to the gate.

"Oriel, come quickly."

She left her horse inside the gate and trudged through the snow to join her cousin. As she knelt beside him, Leslie pulled aside the hood of the fallen man's cloak to reveal the face of that young man who had called her a weasel. Her heart decided to stop beating for a moment, then she forgot about her own concerns.

"It's, it's . . ."

"Nicholas Fitzstephen."

"That half Frenchman," she said. "The Sieur de something. He's hurt."

"Of course he's hurt, you wigeon. You stay with him while I gather men to carry him inside."

"Hurry. He's cold and as pale as his shirt."

Oriel rose, went to the roan stallion, and searched its saddlebags. She drew out a blanket, then stumbled back through the snow to throw it over the young man. His head was resting in the snow, so she pulled him up and gathered as much of him as she could in her arms. He was heavy, and his head fell back over her arm. She drew him close, so that his head rested on her shoulder.

Putting her hand to his face, she found that his skin was almost as cold as the snow in which they rested. Fearful, she searched beneath his cloak and found a leather doublet soaked and icy with blood. He'd been stabbed. Oriel swore and looked at his face again. His hair was soft and dark, and reflected the shine of the snow surrounding them. But what worried her was his pallor. She remembered the dark rose of his lips, and their present blue color alarmed her.

He lay so still in her arms that her fear grew, and she looked up, intending to shout for Leslie. Relief flooded her when she saw her cousin trotting ahead of several men, yet she couldn't stop herself from yelling at them to hurry. Though anxious to get her charge inside, she relinquished him to the servants with a surprising reluctance.

Following them inside, she ignored Aunt Faith's hysterics and directed the men to put the wounded man upstairs in the guest chamber next to that of Uncle Thomas. While she was supervising his transfer to the bed, Livia charged in with George and Robert at her heels. She boomed questions at Oriel and Leslie while Faith, Jane, and Joan hovered in the doorway. When the two girls began giggling, Livia snarled at them, and all three scattered.

"If you'd hunted these rogues down when I demanded it, this wouldn't have happened," Livia said to George. "They've hounded travelers for two months now, and you've done nothing."

George scowled at his mother. "I've ridden the countryside until my backside ached."

"I've sent for the apothecary," Livia said as she left. "Come, Oriel. It's not meet that you should be here when they strip him."

Oriel allowed Leslie to herd her from the room, but she was back as soon as the patient was tucked beneath a pile of blankets.

Motioning to a serving man, she said, "Stoke the fire high. This room must be hotter than an August day. And bring hot water and cloths." She pointed to a stack of pillows. "Jonathan, when I lift him, stuff those beneath his head and shoulders. We must keep his shoulders above his legs. That's well done. Now, go heat bricks, lots of them, and put them between the blankets."

Livia's apothecary arrived, out of breath, his black cap askew. "Mistress, there is a wounded man?"

"Yes, it's the Sieur de—it's the son of Lord Fitzstephen."

"The Sieur de Racine?" The apothecary bent over the young man and clucked. "Hmmm. Hmmm. Hmmm."

"Will he live?"

"I think so, but he's bled a lot, mistress. Is he a choleric man?"

"I don't think so."

"Good. Do you know his birth date? I should consult the stars."

"Shouldn't you sew up his wound?"

"Yes, mistress, I'll do that. Press hard upon the wound while I ready myself."

She was proud of herself. Though she felt giddy at the sight of needle piercing flesh, she remained throughout the apothecary's ministrations. Soon the wound was cleaned, stitched, and bound, and the apothecary was gone. He left instructions that she wait for a few minutes before transferring the pillows from his head to his feet.

This done, Oriel dragged a chair to the bedside and

sat looking at the wounded man. Servants came with hot bricks, followed by Leslie, who stood beside her chair.

"Saints, dear coz, our drowsy home has been invaded. What a stir he'll cause awake if he can upturn the household in such a manner when asleep."

"Who was the man who abandoned him to you?" Oriel asked.

"I know not. I never saw him before. A strange fellow. He said I must take great care of his treasure—meaning Fitzstephen, I suppose."

"And then he ran away?"

"Yes," said Leslie. "A most curious occurrence."

"Oriel!"

Both Oriel and Leslie started at the trumpet call of Livia's voice as she invaded the chamber.

"Oriel, what do you here? The apothecary said you sent him away."

"I can watch the Sieur de—"

"Racine," Leslie said.

"I can watch the Sieur de Racine as well as he. There's naught to be done but watch and keep him warm."

"After you sent him from our house like a cheap peddler," Livia said, "I'm amazed that you now wring your hands over him."

"Christian charity, Aunt."

"Ridiculous," Livia said. "But mayhap if you attend him, I'll gain a betrothal from it."

"I think not," Oriel said.

Livia went away, contenting herself with a disgusted snort. Leslie left as well, and Oriel spent the rest of the day beside the unmoving patient. She sent for books, and spent much of the time rereading Wyatt's poetry.

Before nightfall Leslie reported that Fitzstephen's men had been found, including the one called René, who insisted upon viewing his master before receiving care himself. All the men were suffering from the cold and needed nursing. One had an arrow wound, but would live.

As evening wore on, she fell asleep. Uncle Thomas came sometime during the night and insisted she go to her chamber. She agreed only after he promised to set Nell in her place, and she was back again the following morning.

She hadn't slept well, for she kept thinking of the dangers even a shallow wound meant, and then chastised herself for dwelling upon the welfare of the man when she'd managed to put him from her thoughts, for the most part, since he'd left. Now she sat beside his bed once more. However, she'd promised herself she'd leave the moment he woke. She wouldn't want him to know she had lingered at his side like a puppy.

If she hadn't had her nose tucked in the Wyatt poems she would have had some warning. Instead, she glanced up to find him staring at her, his face flushed, those silver-grey eyes bright with the slight fever that had come upon him. He stared at her, and she at him. Oriel stopped breathing as he continued to hold her gaze as though he wanted to devour her alive. Then he closed his eyes, and to her chagrin, chuckled softly and murmured to himself.

"Vain imaginings."

He sighed and turned his face from her so that she saw only tousled dark hair and the angle of his cheek.

" 'Stay me with flagons,' " he whispered as he drifted into sleep again, " 'comfort me with apples: for I am sick of love.' "

Oriel stood, and her book dropped to the floor. He didn't stir, so she bent over him. "What mean you by that vile remark? My lord? A pox on you and your pretty face and your sleek body and—" She clamped her mouth shut.

She had returned to her chair and was scowling at her patient when Joan and Jane came in.

"Mother said we should help you," Joan said. She

was the older of the two, and the one with the most wits.

Jane bobbed her head. "Yes, we should help."

"We're to help you," Joan said by way of making herself clear.

Oriel lifted her gaze to the ceiling and groaned. "I need no help."

"Food is coming," said Joan. "We sent for food. Sick people need food."

She spoke slowly. "Joan, he can't eat if he isn't awake, and I would have sent for food if he could eat."

"Oh." Joan sat on the end of the bed.

"Don't do that! You'll jostle his wound."

"Oh."

Joan started to wriggle off the bed, thus jarring the sleeping man. He moaned, and Oriel pounced on Joan. Grabbing her cousin's hand, she yanked the girl off the bed. Jane whined a protest and Oriel rounded on her.

"Having you two for nurses will make him worse, not better."

Jane stared at her. "Mother said we were to help."

"We're as good at sitting as you," Joan said.

"And what if his fever worsens? You two will gawk at him like two cows in need of milking."

Oriel didn't finish, for her patient turned and sighed; his lashes fluttered. She swore, then shoved Jane into her chair.

"He wakes. Don't tell him I was here at all. Do you understand?"

Both girls nodded without curiosity, and Oriel glanced at the stirring figure on the bed. His eyes opened. He stared at the top of the bed frame, then lowered his lashes again. Oriel raced out of the room, giving him a last glance over her shoulder. He'd opened his eyes to study the top of the bed again, and she darted out of sight.

She avoided the sick man's chamber the rest of the day. It wasn't her fault that her daily habits kept her nearby in Uncle Thomas's library. Once she heard that fabulous voice raised in annoyance, but it faded, and she continued her cataloging of her uncle's books. After the evening meal, she and Uncle Thomas were back in the library, where they had taken refuge from the rest of the family. George and the rest of her cousins were playing cards, but Oriel found she couldn't pay attention to any game with that man upstairs. She kept imagining she heard his voice. All of a sudden, she did hear it, along with a crash.

"God's blood! Get you gone, evil wenches."

She raced for the sick chamber with Uncle Thomas behind. She ran into Jane and Joan, who were scrambling out of the room, hot towels in their hands. They raced past her like frightened cattle, and clambered down the stairs. Inside, Oriel beheld the wounded man and a chamber in near shambles. He sat up in bed, naked except for the bandage on his shoulder and the covers over his hips and legs. He was glowering at her, and breathing hard. Beside the bed lay an overturned basin of water and several towels still steaming from the heat of the water. Beside them lay a chair, overturned.

"What ails you, my lord?"

"Those two harpies tried to scald me." The young man winced and put a hand to his bandage. "A plague take them."

Uncle Thomas came in, surveyed the room, and righted the chair. Sitting in it, he gazed at the patient, who was staring at Oriel. She reddened and busied herself with picking up the basin and wiping the spilled water.

"Fear not, young Blade. I'll warn Jane and Joan away, though I doubt they'll have the courage to come near you again. I am Sir Thomas Richmond."

"I thank you, sir. I am Nicholas Fitzstephen, but I see you know who I am." Blade craned his neck so that he could see Oriel kneeling beside the bed. "I find my-

self cast upon your mercy. I'm in need of a gentle nurse
—one who won't try to boil me."

"Oriel will protect you," Thomas said. "She's at-
tended you without pause since you arrived, but Jane
and Joan replaced her when she grew weary."

"Uncle!"

Oriel popped to her feet and gave Thomas a look of
dismay. Thomas stared back in surprise.

"Ah-ha!" Blade said. "Then it wasn't a dream."

She hastened to explain. "I've an interest in learning,
and have knowledge gained from our apothecary, and
so I'm better suited than the others for nursing."

Blade sank into his pillows with a smile that turned
her face a deeper shade of pink. "Marry, lady, then God
has bestowed upon me a great blessing. Might I trouble
you for a change of dressing? This one chafes now that
your cousins have gotten it wet."

Thomas rose. "I'll send for the apothecary."

"Uncle, don't go."

"You but need to slit the bandage, child."

Thomas was gone. He'd left her with this man apur-
pose, she knew it. Swallowing, Oriel turned to face him,
wishing he would cover his chest so that she didn't have
to gaze upon all that smooth flesh.

She hesitated between the bed and the door, but finally came back. Taking a pair of scissors from a table
beside the bed, she began to cut the bandage. Her hands
were separated from his skin by a wet cloth, but she still
felt the heat of his flesh as she worked.

"My lord, part of the dressing has stuck to the
wound. I will try to be gentle."

"Arrrgh!"

"Fie. Such a great noise for such a small pain."

"Small?" Blade swore and tried to put his hand to
the wound. "Marry, woman, it felt as if you'd torn me
open afresh."

"If you carry on so, what a thunder you must make
when you're grievously wounded."

Blade lifted his nose and looked down the length of it at her. "The greater the wound, the more silent I become. You may ask my man René. See this mark?" Blade turned toward her and lifted his right arm to reveal a long scar that went from his back to his navel. "When I got this, I was as quiet as a pilgrim in a cathedral."

She looked at the scar and lifted a brow. "How brave, my lord."

"Hmmmph."

"Raise yourself, please."

Blade's good humor returned, and he smiled as she surrounded him with her arms and began unwinding the soiled wrappings from his shoulder. Each circuit brought her face close to his, and she could feel his warm breath on her cheek. She shivered and felt her body begin to tingle in strange places.

She came near again, and breathed in his scent, all wood and spice. Her lungs began to work hard, and she had to stop herself from fleeing as he murmured something unintelligible and lifted his body toward her. Luckily she finished unwrapping and straightened to gather the bandage. Her hands were shaking, and she prayed he didn't notice.

While she worked, he continued to stare at her in silence. She could still feel the heat of his body and was relieved when she could move away from him without the appearance of haste. Dropping the wrappings and bandage in the basin of towels, she wiped her hands on the front of her gown and fastened her gaze on it. He shifted his weight and cursed.

"The wound pains you?" she asked.

"No more than most."

"Let me see."

She came close and studied the reddened wound and its stitches. She touched the flesh near the threads, and quickly lifted her eyes to his. She found that he had been studying her. For long moments they stayed as they were, he half lying on the bed, she bending over him, growing warmer with his very nearness. He drew a deep breath, and his hand lifted to touch one of the long curls that had drifted onto his chest.

That simple movement woke Oriel. She lifted her hand from the wound, but Blade caught it.

"Please? Your hand on the wound is soothing. So warm."

"I should find the apothecary."

"I don't need him with you so near." His hand tugged on the curl.

She snatched the curl from his grasp and bounced away from him. Standing over him, she gave a most indelicate snort.

"God's breath, my lord, how can you find comfort in the presence of a weasel?"

He groaned and lay back on his pillows. The covers slipped lower on his hips, but he failed to notice.

"Saints and apostles, I thought you forgave me for my rancorous barbs." His hand darted out and caught her skirt. "I insist that you forgive me."

"I have. Now loose me."

Oriel dug in her heels, but he dragged her to him and captured another lock of hair.

"You haven't, you ill-tempered sprite. I'll content me with nothing less than true forgiveness, not courtesy."

"I'll not repeat myself." She slapped at his hand, but couldn't free her hair.

Blade began to rise from the bed. "Oh yes, you will, or I'll kiss you."

"No!"

"Thank you for being so obstinate," he said, grabbing her shoulders.

Thoroughly alarmed, Oriel twisted in his grasp, but even wounded, he was the stronger. He put a hand on the back of her head and forced it down to his own. She watched his lips draw close and fall open. Crying out, she thrust her hand between them and covered his mouth with her fingers.

"I forgive you!"

Beneath her fingers his lips moved, and she tingled again. His tongue tickled her skin, and she yanked her hand from his lips. He burst out in a chuckle and released her.

"Beshrew you, Oriel Richmond, for depriving me of the succor of your lips."

Oriel dashed out of his reach and scowled at her tormenter. Drawing herself up to her full height, she looked down on him.

"I shall fetch the apothecary, my lord." She turned sharply and marched to the door.

"I need no apothecary, and I'd much rather have your nursing to make my blood rush," Blade put a hand on the covers over his groin, "and my body stir."

"I shall fetch the apothecary," Oriel said again, for all her clever retorts fled when she saw his hand spread out in so blatant a gesture.

He smiled at her, and murmured in the same low voice that had enthralled her from the first. "Don't fly, chère. I won't hurt you."

Oriel paused. "I'm not fleeing you. I'm going to fetch the apothecary."

"As you wish. But I'll be on my feet by tomorrow, so you'd best accustom yourself to having me near. I've come to press my suit again, you know."

She knew her mouth fell open, but it couldn't be helped.

"Again?"

"Yes? Didn't Lord George tell you?"

She shook her head.

"Well, I have, with his blessing, so you must needs learn to accept me. Don't run away."

Oriel had raced into the gallery and looked back at him. He was still grinning at her and still hadn't covered himself. No doubt he sought to cozen her and beguile her with his body.

"I would never run away from the likes of you," she said.

"We'll see upon the morrow, *chère*."

Oriel lifted her chin. "We will not."

He wasn't listening to her. His gaze had fastened on her face and then dropped down the length of her body.

"*Mirabile visu, chère*, most wondrous to behold."

Oriel swore, picked up her skirts, and ran, heedless of those mocking eyes and his annoying laughter.

Chapter 6

I pray that love may never come to me
with murderous intent,
in rhythms measureless and wild.

—Euripides

Blade sat in the withdrawing chamber between Uncle Thomas's library and apartments and his own chamber and polished the hilt of his sword with a cloth. He was in a foul humor. He'd been caught off guard and attacked by that scurrilous bastard Midnight and there was naught to show for his suffering except a sore shoulder and, to his disgust, an uncontrollable desire for Oriel Richmond.

At first he'd blamed his rampant lust upon his wound. He'd awakened to find her close to him, her wild hair floating about her face, her wide green eyes fixed upon him. He remembered thinking he'd been caught sleeping in an elf's bower. Later she'd touched him, and with her touch transformed him into a vile satyr nearly mad with appetite. The violence of his craving for her had caught him unprepared, and he hadn't been able to stop himself from approaching her, which had frightened her.

Once frightened, she had avoided him, and no amount of feigned sickness had brought her back. After three days, he'd grown as randy as his own stallion. As the hours passed and Oriel stayed away, his indignation grew.

Who was she to ignore him? He had captured the hearts of French, Italian, and English women of high and low degree. He was being grievously insulted—no treated as if he were a leper. Each day that went by saw his frustration and his determination grow until he vowed to himself that no cloistered little spinster would scorn and defy him.

He'd been so disturbed by Oriel's rejection he'd almost lost sight of his real task, which was to search out any privy knowledge kept by Thomas Richmond about the vows taken by Anne Boleyn and Henry Percy. This evening he would join the family at table, and there he would begin his prying. He would make himself agreeable to the old man, mayhap by enlisting his aid in pressing suit with Oriel. Thomas had visited him several times, and he'd taken care to win the old man's regard by praising Oriel. Thomas seemed most fond of the girl, and perchance through her, he could court the uncle's friendship.

Meantime, since the evening meal was two hours away, he would spend the time setting lures for the elusive Oriel. Blade slipped his arm out of the black silk sling the apothecary had fashioned for him and rose. He crossed to a window seat and picked up an ivory lute.

The withdrawing chamber was a small room, the walls of which were faced in mahogany. The gleaming wood had been carved in rectangular panels two hand spans in length. These panels marched up and down the walls except where they were interrupted by a door set in a pointed arch, and by the fireplace, with its white marble chimneypiece. The size of the room, the paneling, and the fire combined to make the chamber warm and welcoming.

Carrying the lute, Blade returned to his chair near the fire and placed his right hand over the strings. Propping his sore arm on the chair, he plucked a chord, winced, and began tuning. He was twisting an ivory peg when someone pounded at the door. Before he could answer, the chamber was invaded by the three Richmond brothers, followed by Uncle Thomas.

"How do you this e'en, my lord?" asked Uncle Thomas. He shook his head when Blade offered his chair.

"Well, I thank you, Sir Thomas."

Lord George stalked over to the fire and thrust his hands out toward it.

"We've been hunting those thieves who attacked you," he said.

Leslie came to stand behind Blade's chair and leaned on the back of it. "Yes, but there's no sign of them since that fellow brought you to us. We'll have to start afresh tomorrow."

"I wouldn't," Blade said as he plucked a lute string.

"Why not, pray you?" asked Robert. He was the tallest of the three and had to duck as he lowered himself into the window seat.

"Your thief is Jack Midnight, a highwayman of surpassing talent and wit. By now he's fled the north country altogether."

Thomas leaned on his walking stick and surveyed Blade. "Know you this ruffian, my lord? How haps it that you're so familiar with thieves?"

"We've met before, near Blackheath, and he spared me for old times' sake."

"A most garrulous and merciful outlaw, this Jack Midnight," said Thomas, "that he would spare your life and those of your men when he hasn't spared others."

"As I said, we're old acquaintances."

"Curious company you keep," Robert said.

Leslie moved to stand beside Blade. "Ah, thievery. I've often thought rampaging about and stealing from rich fools like our George would suit me."

George scowled at his youngest brother, but it was Robert who responded. "You surprise me not, given your laziness and aversion to all honest labor. But I warrant even Mother would disapprove of your taking up such a vice."

"Even then," Leslie said softly, "she would love me better than you."

"Boys." Uncle Thomas's warning caused both men to close their mouths.

Thomas began to address another question to Blade, but Oriel's voice calling for George delayed him. She came in, clad as usual in a simple gown of russet wool and no cap. She directed her attention to George after a little curtsy to Uncle Thomas.

"Aunt Livia sends for you. She's furious about one of the serving men missing morning prayers."

"I've already fined the man," George said.

"It matters naught to Aunt Livia."

Robert spoke from the window seat. "Negligent servants and murderous highwaymen. This kingdom is under the devil's sway. The true religion kept such indecencies under abeyance. If the rightful queen were on the throne—"

"Robert!" George's face went strawberry red. "I'll have no treasonous talk under my roof."

"Peace," Leslie said. He left his perch on the back of Blade's chair and wandered over to prop himself beside Robert. "Good brother, why can't you keep your religious habits private? Her Majesty has said she likes not prying into the secrets of men's hearts if they give their obedience to her."

"To obey a heretic queen is a sin."

George swore. "More treason."

He stomped over to the window seat, but Uncle Thomas followed him and nimbly insinuated himself between his two great-nephews. George would have gone around him, but Thomas whacked his nephew on the shin with his walking stick. George yelped, hopped back out of reach, and bent over to rub his leg.

"Saints and apostles," said Thomas. "I'm tired of this unending quarrel. Robert, the family gave up the old religion when Queen Mary died. Queen Elizabeth has been gracious to us as a result, and even you have benefited from her generosity. Your flapping tongue will get us all tossed into the Tower."

Thomas came to Blade, who had kept silent so as not to call attention to himself. The old man put a hand on Blade's arm.

"My lord, Robert has an unruly and impetuous nature, but he's a loyal subject of Her Majesty. Mayhap you'll forget his hasty language."

"If Her Majesty seeks not to pry into men's souls, I can but follow her example."

Thomas smiled at him, then swept the young folk out of the chamber before him. Oriel took his arm without glancing at Blade.

"Come, child. We've time before supper to put some books in order."

They went out, leaving the door ajar so that he heard their footsteps in the short passage between the withdrawing chamber and Thomas's library. Blade crept to the door and listened. When they began a discussion about a translation of Plato, he tiptoed back to his chair and took up the lute again.

This family was like a boiling stew. Bubbles of contention burst into the open all about him. Robert was a fool, and his brothers and Thomas knew it. Only a fool and a fanatic would openly criticize the queen, especially in front of someone who wasn't a member of the family. Yet there were many such hotheaded young men among the Catholic nobility of the north. Robert had company of high estate, including earls and a duke. Most claimed to be loyal subjects, yet here was fertile ground for the designs of the Cardinal of Lorraine.

He needed to know more about Robert. Mayhap he could prize such knowledge from Oriel. To do so he would have to take her in thrall, smooth away her apprehensions with enticements irresistible. Blade struck a chord and smiled. The lute was tuned to perfection. He moved his chair nearer the door and began a song. He wasn't so foolish as to sing of love. Oriel wasn't a silly, adolescent miss. If he was to succeed, his wiles would have to be circuitous and indirect. So instead of a courtly love song, he chose to lure her with sound—the sound of Old French and of his voice, clear, strong, low, and beguiling. For this purpose he chose the classical *Song of Roland.* Even stories of war took on a sensual tone in French.

> *Sustenir voeill trestut mun parentet*
> *N'en recrerrai pur nul hume mortel;*
> *Mielz voeill murir qu'il me seit reprovet.*

> *I want to support all my kindred; no*
> *mortal man shall force me to deny them;*
> *I would sooner die than incur that reproach.*

As he finished a verse, he saw through the partly open door the russet fold of a gown. He continued to sing a while longer, then stopped. The edge of the gown disappeared, and Blade swore under his breath. Then a sly thought came to him. He began again, this time with an old poem he'd set to music himself.

> *A woman is a worthy wight,*
> *She serveth man both day and night,*
> *Thereto she putteth all her might,*
> *And yet she hath but care and woe.*

He smiled when a shadow appeared in the doorway. So pleased with himself was he that he failed to pay attention and shifted his wounded arm too abruptly. He cursed and his fingers tangled in the lute strings. The instrument twanged as he let it fall and clamped his hand over the injury. He was biting his lip when the shadow moved and fell on him. Looking up, he beheld his quarry hovering over him, and all plots and designs vanished from his head.

She gazed down at him, her eyes wide with alarm. He schooled himself to keep his own glance from wandering over her body in search of curves. Holding still, he waited, fearing she would leave if he even spoke.

"My lord, have you hurt yourself? I—I was in the library and heard you sing."

Blade had forgotten his shoulder. Now he made a great business of moving his left arm and spread his right hand over the sore place on his shoulder. He saw her gaze fasten on his hand, then dart back to his face. She was frowning, and he gave her a smile of slow, voluptuous warmth concealed by a veil of gratitude.

"I thank you, mistress. I but jarred the wound. I forgot it in the music."

Oriel turned away, and Blade searched for an excuse to keep her near. She surprised him by hesitating.

"I've never heard a voice so pure and strong as yours, my lord. A nightingale would envy you."

"My thanks again." Blade took up the lute. "Would you hear more?"

"But your wound."

"I've had many far worse, and idleness chafes me more than the cut itself. I will sing, if you wish."

She smiled at him, took a cushion from the window seat, and placed it by the fire. Perching on it, she rested her weight on one arm braced on the floor. She had taken a seat at least three arms' lengths from him. Undaunted, Blade pretended to shiver and dragged his chair to the fire.

When he resumed his seat, his knee touched her shoulder, but she couldn't move away or she would come too near the heat of the fire. God's blood, just the feel of her arm sent spikes of arousal shooting up his leg to his groin. He took a deep breath and scolded himself.

"Now, mistress, if I'm to play for you, you must give me a promise."

She gave him a wary look. "What promise?"

"You must promise not to run away if my singing displeases you."

"I can't envision ever finding your voice displeasing, my lord."

"Then I have your word."

"Yes."

The ruse succeeded, and he began to sing, this time quietly, as he would on a dark night in a bedchamber in a chateau. At first he sang of Tristan and Isolt and their tragic love, then of Arthur, Lancelot, and Guinevere. Night was falling, and darkness closed in around them, wrapping them in intimacy.

He felt her move away from his leg, so he shifted his weight so that his calf brushed her arm again. As he did so, he lowered his voice so that she leaned closer to catch his words. She was watching his fingers pluck the strings, and a strange glow lit her eyes as he strummed the instrument. Trapped in that glow, he forgot what he was doing, and his hands went still.

She looked up at him, her lips parted, and he saw the quick rise and fall of her breasts as she took shallow breaths. Neither of them spoke while the last chord he'd struck hummed in the air. His body hummed with it, and he let the lute slide to the side. He leaned down, moving slowly, slowly, until his lips met hers. He put his hand on her cheek to keep her close, and opened his mouth. Sunk in his own delirium, he followed her lips when they sought to retreat. They moved beneath his own, warm and lush and compelling. When she opened her mouth completely to him, he released his hold on the lute, allowing it to slide to the floor, and pulled her up into his arms. She braced herself against his body and tried to shove away from him. He disregarded the movements. Spreading his legs, he trapped her between them.

As he plunged his tongue into her mouth, he kept hold of her, and after a moment, she stopped wriggling and allowed him to run his tongue down her neck. Her hands snaked beneath his doublet to touch his skin and run up and down his chest. At the feel of her flesh against his, he captured her lips again and put a hand on her breast.

Oriel jumped and cried out. She pounded at his chest with a fist, coming too near his wound, and he yelped. She pulled free of his arms and fell backward to the floor. She landed on her bottom with her legs apart, and Blade laughed to cover the painful twitch her position caused at his groin.

"Cursed licentious villain," she said. She closed her legs and got to her knees.

Blade darted at her and snatched her hand. "No, mistress, you can't go. I've a mind to finish our game of pleasure."

"Release me!" She yanked at her hand, but couldn't free it.

"Come, *chère,* don't take on virginal airs after setting me afire. You've let me go too far to turn back."

"I'll call for my cousins."

"And the upright Lord George will see us wed this very night." Blade pulled her to him so that his lips nearly touched hers and whispered to her. "Then surely would I gain release from this pain in your bed instead of in this chair."

Twisting her body, Oriel ducked down and escaped the circle of his arms. He reached for her again, but she slapped his hands away.

"Keep your hands from me, you debauched lecher. You're deceitful and—"

Blade stared at her, fascinated by her trembling lips and watchful stance. "Marry, I do believe you're frightened."

Still on her knees, Oriel drew herself up and snapped, "I am not."

"Yes, mistress, you're quivering and pale, and you look like a milkmaid who's just been tossed behind a haystack by a miller's apprentice."

"I say again, I'm not afraid of you, Blade Fitzstephen."

"So you do know my name."

She stood up. "I have work."

"Is your word so worthless?"

"What mean you?"

"You promised not to run away." He picked up the lute again.

"I always keep my word, but you transgressed, and therefore my vow is made null."

"Then you're afraid of me, *chère*, and you might as well admit it. I'll wager you can't stay in this room for one more song."

He watched her face burn with ire, and inclined his head to her. "No doubt you fear to trust yourself in my presence now."

"Ha!" She stalked to the window and sat down. "One song, my lord."

He grinned at her again, then struck a chord.

> *The prettiest girl in our town*
> *Begged a boon of me:*
> *To graft for her a scion*
> *From my pear tree.*
>
> *When I'd done the grafting*
> *Entirely to her pleasure,*
> *With wine and ale she plied me*
> *In fullest measure.*

She was up and through the door before he could finish the song. He chuckled and called after her.

"You're a lovely, kissable coward, Oriel Richmond. Come back and let me teach you how to play my lute."

A door slammed in the library, and he heard her footsteps in the gallery fading rapidly. His smile faded as well when he realized how completely he'd lost all trace of design, all self-possession, at the feel of her body. Such lack of governance was unlike him.

With others he could bend his body to his will. He could make love to a dissolute French courtesan while plotting how to trap her into revealing her closest secrets. Yet when he kissed Oriel, his only thoughts were primitive, almost violent ones that drove him to seek release in her body with no heed to the price.

Something was wrong with him. His only purpose in wooing Oriel was to gain entry to Richmond Hall, yet he risked being tossed out by pursuing her so relentlessly that he nearly had her on the floor of the withdrawing chamber. God rot her. She tempted him by her refusals and her defiance and her scorn.

She knew nothing of courtesy in lovemaking. French women knew how to play the game of courtly love. They knew when to submit, for in succumbing, they gained much pleasure. Not her. Not Mistress Oriel Richmond. No doubt she thought herself too virtuous to succumb to him. He would show her different. He would show her that virtue was a pallid and tedious thing that evaporated when boiled in the cauldron of passion.

Chapter 7

Tell zeal it wants devotion;
Tell love it is but lust;
Tell time it is but motion;
Tell flesh it is but dust.

—*Sir Walter Raleigh*

In a town house in the city of Paris, on an icy night full of moaning wind, the Cardinal of Lorraine stood atop a marble staircase. Framed by a stone doorway carved to resemble Corinthian columns, he gazed down the winding stair at the body of the woman named Claude. In the light of a candle set in a tall stand at the bottom of the stair, her head rested at an unnatural angle.

The cardinal looked as if he were mildly annoyed as he gazed at the figure prostrate below him. A young priest in black that matched his shining hair emerged from the shadows at the foot of the stair and glanced from the woman to the cardinal. Charles de Guise sighed and came down the stairs slowly. He moved with a smooth glide, as if he trod on oil, and his red robes gleamed in the meager light. Their hue reflected the red tint in his golden hair and the healthy pink of his cheeks.

He reached the body, tucked his hands in his sleeves, and addressed the priest. "Most distasteful, Jean-Paul. I suppose she wished to avoid the *peine forte et dure*. Traitors should consider the possibility of torture before they act."

"*Oui, mon cardinal.*"

"The coach, Jean-Paul. There's nothing for us here."

They emerged from the town house and into the bitter night. Few lights shone in the city at this late hour, and the coach clattered away into blackness. Inside, huddling in the warmth of mink and miniver, the cardinal seemed lost in thought.

"You questioned the servants," he said, "and they gave you a list of her friends."

"*Oui, mon cardinal,* and I have traced them all, except for one."

"And who is this one?"

"That is what worries me. None of the servants seems to know. He only came to her at her chateau, and then only once for a few days, and gave no name. The servants said Claude was triumphant during his visit, and that she gloried in his presence. She called him— incomparable. They say he had dark hair, and grey eyes, and a manservant with long silver hair and the build of a man half his age. But the curious thing is that all of the servants remembered the young man's voice."

"His voice. This does not help me, Jean-Paul."

"Mayhap it will, Your Eminence, for there can't be many young and handsome noblemen with a voice that would charm an angel from heaven. That was the description I was given."

We must find this young man. Send men to all the ports, especially Calais and Le Havre. I don't like this mysterious visit to Claude. She never mentioned a beautiful young man with a siren voice. I despise not knowing things. I won't have it."

"*Oui*, Your Eminence."

The cardinal laced his fingers and made a steeple of them. "Claude was indiscreet. She spied on me and then chattered of her discoveries to others." He sighed and clicked his tongue against the roof of his mouth. "It's a pity that a man of God can trust no one, and most inconvenient that I have to burden myself with chasing after possible foreign intelligencers. I like it not."

"*Non, mon cardinal.*"

The cardinal lapsed into silence. He had found out through one of his agents that Claude was babbling about his privy affairs, and now his plans for his niece were threatened. He'd been careless, a mistake for which he was paying dearly. The handsome young man with the beautiful voice and no name, he was an ill omen. Could it be that the Bourbons were on to his plans, or perchance the Spanish? It might even be that the annoying English had divined his intentions. Elizabeth Tudor was proving a much more formidable opponent than he'd imagined she could be.

No matter. He would catch the spy, and soon. Then this small inconvenience could be turned into an advantage. After all, Claude wasn't the only one who could fall down a staircase and break her neck.

After Blade Fitzstephen had kissed her, Oriel had fled back to Uncle Thomas's library, closed the door to the connecting passage, and locked it. Thomas had fallen asleep to the sound of Blade's singing, but when she slammed the door, he woke with a snort.

She went to her table and began fumbling with the pile of books on it. She dropped one and started when it landed on the floor with a loud smack.

"What's wrong with you, child?"

"Naught, Uncle."

"He kissed you."

Oriel's head shot up and she gaped at Thomas. "He did not. I mean, he did, but—oh, why is he here? He doesn't need an heiress. He has that great fortress castle of his, and manors scattered from here to London, and in France as well. Why has he come back?"

"Scared you, did he?"

"He's vain, and arrogant, and, and—"

"And has set you aflame."

Oriel pointed at her uncle with a book. "Joan told me about him. He's slept in every noblewoman's bed at the French court."

"Not the Queen Mother's, surely."

"And he was an outlaw!"

"Now, child, you mustn't censure him for that. He lost his memory."

"But remembered how to kill people. Joan told me he's killed five men in duels. Over women."

"Rumor, prating gossip."

"Seneca says that gossip is the most knowing of persons."

"And Hesiod said that it was easy to raise and grievous to bear. Forget gossip. Only a while ago you told me no one had ever kissed you. Don't you like it? Be honest."

Oriel worried her bottom lip with her teeth. "In faith, I don't know. I hadn't thought upon it."

"Then do so." Thomas rose and came to her. He patted her hand and smiled at her. "Shall I tell you a secret?"

She nodded.

"You were right. The boy has no need of an heiress. Therefore, he has come back for some other reason."

"What reason is that?"

"Saints and apostles, girl, what reason think you? He's come back for you. I've been watching him, and hark you, that boy's undone. He writhes and chafes, for he's never suffered a mortal wound before. He runs mad with it."

"What mortal wound? He's healing well."

"The one you dealt him by your very existence, my oblivious little scholar. God's breath, Oriel, sometimes I see why your aunts despair of you."

"You're wrong. He must want my jewels and my lands."

"As you say."

This ready agreement caused her to cast a suspicious glance at him, but Thomas was leafing through the poems of Sir Thomas Wyatt.

"You will remember what I said about my tomb inscription, won't you?"

"What? Oh, assuredly, Uncle Thomas. If I've troubles or am beset with confusion, I should go to the chapel and read it."

"It will solve mysteries." Thomas rubbed the gilt lettering on the book of poems. "Wyatt had a great gift. I enjoy his poetry as much as I enjoy puzzles and the symbolism of flowers. Did I tell you I came upon one of my old books about the language of flowers? I put it on your table. Here it is." He opened the book in the middle and turned a few pages. "The bluebell symbolizes constancy, the gentian injustice, and the iris, the fleur-de-lis, symbolizes a message. Remember, Iris was the messenger of the Greek gods, and appeared to men in the form of a rainbow."

Thomas turned the book to show Oriel the illuminated drawing of the flower, then closed it.

"Now, why don't you go to your chamber and put on a nice gown? It's almost time to dine."

"What ails this gown?" Oriel looked down at her comfortable, soft skirt.

"Naught, but you should dress for your suitor."

"I didn't dress for the others, not even Hugh Wothorpe."

"None of the others followed your every move as if he lived by gazing at you."

"Have you an ague, Uncle?"

"Placate my fancy, then. Do it for me."

Oriel sighed, then relented. "Only for you."

"Of course, child. Why else?"

She went to her chamber and requested a gown of Nell. The maid gawked at her, which brought back her ill-temper. There followed an hour of torture. She was tied into a farthingale petticoat that, in her mind, made her look as if she was sticking out of the top of a cone. Nell had laced her into a patterned brocade gown of forest green, open in front in an inverted V to reveal a gold underskirt. A heavy gold girdle encircled her waist and fell in front to end in a pendant pomander.

The least offensive article was her mother's necklace, one of the few jewels she really valued. It was a gold chain from which was suspended a pendant. The pendant frame had been cast of beaded gold and held a green stone. The stone was polished and oval, and almost the same shade as her eyes. Yet the necklace hardly made up for the rest of her trials.

If the hooped cage of the farthingale weren't enough, Nell had attached a gold stomacher with whalebone stiffening to add further discomfort. Worst of all, her hair was pinned up and surmounted by a gold filigree chain braided through the coils. Now she didn't know which was the most uncomfortable—her legs, stomach, or head. If she hadn't promised Uncle Thomas, she would have cast aside gown and farthingale and pulled every last pin from her hair.

Instead, she turned her ire upon Blade, whose fault it was that Uncle Thomas thought she needed to change her habits of dress. She didn't want him in her home. He touched her when he shouldn't and made her feel most odd, and she didn't trust him. Mayhap he'd gotten himself into debt in France and needed a rich wife. No doubt that was the reason he wanted to court her, but he'd soon learn she wasn't the gullible fool he assumed she was. Thus armed with skepticism, she stalked downstairs to the great chamber where the family assembled for the evening meal.

To her relief, Blade wasn't there. Thus he wasn't a witness to the consternation of her family. Her cousins and aunts stared at her as if she was a shade come to haunt them. Joan made one of her astute comments.

"Mother, Oriel is wearing a gown."

"A green gown," Jane added in case someone had suddenly gone blind.

"Well," barked Livia. "At last you've seen fit to dress as your station demands."

Leslie came to her and bowed. "Coz, you're beautiful."

"You've a kind heart," Oriel said. Leslie had a habit of saying nice things to people, even his Aunt Livia. She glanced at her relatives. "Must they stand amazed? It's most loathsome to be stared at."

"I fear you must accustom yourself to being stared at—in envy by women, and with desire by men, coz."

"You needn't try to sweeten my temper with false compliments. I heard from Uncle Thomas that you've gambled your allowance for the next three months and want money."

Leslie held up his hands in protest. "Jesu Maria, coz, I wouldn't ask for money from a woman." He bent to whisper in her ear. "I'm much too clever to be in want for long. Everyone thinks of me as a charming but addlepated wastrel, but I'll show you all. I'm a man, for all I'm only twenty-one, and deserving of respect."

"Not another duel, Leslie."

"No, coz, but enough of this chatter. Here's our guest."

Oriel turned to see Blade come into the great chamber alone. He paused, and Oriel's ire returned when she beheld his dark beauty made even more alluring by being clad in black and gold. Black damask brought out the silver in his eyes, and he entered a room as if he was the French king gracing the *Salle des Etats*. He bowed over Aunt Livia's hand and kissed it in the French manner rather than kissing her cheek in the English fashion. Somehow, this small elegance annoyed Oriel even further.

He rose from kissing Livia's hand and took Aunt Faith's. As he bent over it, his gaze strayed to Oriel and stayed there. A taunting glint came to his eyes as he brushed his lips over the age-spotted hand of her aunt, and he straightened, holding her gaze with his own. He smiled at her, lynxlike, and whispered something to Jane, who giggled.

Before her face could turn red under his stare, Oriel sniffed and swept away to join George and Robert by the fireplace. Yet try as she might, she was aware of his least movement, the low, haunting cadence of his voice as he spoke. Indeed, he seemed to ensorcel each person he encountered, for he had Livia and Faith smiling benevolently at him in an instant.

He even charmed Leslie, who had his own full measure of male appeal. She realized, as unseasoned as she was, that a man who could charm men as well as women was one who bore watching. Such an ability gave him enough power to be menacing—yes, dangerous. In faith, the Sieur de Racine would find her much more alert the next time he tried to work his artifices upon her.

Oriel stopped in midsentence of her conversation with George and Robert, for Leslie was bringing Blade to join them.

"George, I was just speaking to Blade about Parliament."

"Parliament," George said. "What know you of Parliament, boy?"

Leslie clamped his hand over his dagger. "Beshrew you, brother. I'm not a boy, and I know more than you think." Leslie appeared to remember his manners, and

his hand dropped to his side. "We were speaking of the
succession. Most favor our queen naming Katherine
Grey as her successor, for old King Henry named the
children of Frances Brandon, his great-niece, as next
heirs. Hardly anyone wants the Queen of Scots."

"Not true," Robert cried. He pounded his fist
against his thigh. "Those of us of the true religion know
better. Mary Stewart is the only legitimate heir. By God,
she should be on the throne—"

"Robert!" George scowled at his brother. "I'll hear
no good words about that woman. She quartered the
arms of England with those of her own when Mary
Tudor died. What presumption."

Oriel had heard these arguments before. Neither
George nor Robert would budge in his opinion, and
they would fight all evening, thus ruining everyone's
meal.

"Cousins," she said. "I warrant our guest would
rather hear of some less contentious topic."

Leslie chuckled. "Yes, brothers. Let us ply Blade
with questions about French women. I hear he knows
most of them."

George opened his mouth to scold his youngest
brother, but the gentleman usher saved Leslie with his
call to dinner. To Oriel's chagrin, she was seated next to
Blade, a misfortune she could blame on Livia. Her suffering began immediately.

"I am most gratified, Mistress Oriel, that you
deemed my first appearance at table worthy of a change
of gown. Yet I fear no gown is needed to enhance your
beauty, and your necklace dulls under the green fire of
your eyes."

He thought she'd changed her habit of dress because
he'd kissed her. The arrogant villain.

"In truth, Lord—er—my lord, I do change my
gown upon occasion."

"Little wretch, you haven't forgotten my name."

"Faith, my lord, I have."

He stabbed a chunk of roast capon and examined it. "Shall I teach it to you? I've a thousand ways to make you say it. Most pleasurable, marvelous ways."

"A plague take you. I want to learn naught you can teach."

He dropped his napkin on the floor and bent to pick it up. As he raised his head, his hand slipped to her waist and brushed it lightly.

"You lie, *chère*, for I trow you enjoyed my lessons full well not two hours ago."

"Keep your hands on your food, my lord." Snatching up an empty goblet, Oriel slammed it down on the tablecloth and a serving man poured wine into it.

While the man poured, Blade glanced up and down the table. "Your venerable great-uncle hasn't joined us. Is he ill?"

"No, he often retires early, especially after a day of long work over his books and studies."

"He seems to have incurred the wrath of your Aunt Faith," Blade said. "She was complaining to Livia of his miserly treatment of her daughters and was most annoyed that he hadn't managed to die yet and thus leave Joan and Jane with the inheritance he promised them."

"You mustn't listen to Aunt Faith. She believes God put her on earth to be martyred. Uncle Thomas constantly points out to her how unlikely a saint she is, and she hates him for doing so."

The mention of Uncle Thomas reminded her of the old man's protests that this intrusive dissolute was enamored of her, and she sniffed. Uncle Thomas was too old. He knew nothing about love.

"Now what have I done to offend you, *chère?*"

"Don't give me that name. I'm not your dear one, and you presume too much."

" 'Alas, madam, for stealing of a kiss/ Have I so much your mind there offended?/ Have I then done so grievously amiss/ That by no means it may be amended?' "

She had been sipping wine. She swallowed, but her goblet remained suspended in her hand as she regarded this menacing creature. She'd thought of him as a vain, brazen hellhound, never as a lover of poetry.

"You have read Sir Thomas Wyatt?"

"Don't look at me as if I were a pig that suddenly began quoting scripture, *chère*. Shall I prove my civility?"

Blade cleared his throat and placed his hand upon his breast. " 'Count it the greatest of sin to prefer life to honor, and for the sake of living to lose what makes life worth having.' Or mayhap you prefer Homer to Juvenal. 'She spoke and loosened from her bosom the embroidered girdle of many colors into which all her allurements were fashioned. In it was love and in it desire and in it blandishing persuasion which steals the mind even of the wise.' "

She refused to look at him, for he was grinning at her and taunting her with his winter-sky eyes.

"I thought you a knave."

"But no longer."

"Now I see you're a learned knave."

"Peace, *chère*." He lowered his voice. "I'm not going away, so you'd best accustom yourself to me."

"I shall ignore you."

"Marry, you may attempt it." He grinned at her. "If you do, I may be forced to caper about under your window and sing songs to you of your beauty."

"No!" She regarded him as she would a cutpurse with the pox.

"Very well, then, my stubborn Mistress Oriel, shall we cry truce?"

"Afore God, I doubt anyone can live in peace with you about the place."

"You wrong me. I shall prove my chivalry by promising to go a whole day without teasing you, though it will be hard on me. All I ask in return is that you commend me to your uncle. I admire his learning."

"A whole day?"

He leaned close, causing her to back away in alarm at the tingling of her own skin.

"Yes, *chère*. Think of it. A whole day free of taunts."

"Why would you promise a thing that so goes against your nature?"

"I'm not so light-minded as you seem to think. And besides," he lifted his goblet and stared at the crimson liquid it held. "I've much to learn from your uncle, and little time to do it in. Indeed, I long for privy conversation with so aged and discerning a gentleman."

Chapter
8

*For he who is so tormented by carnal passion
that he cannot embrace anyone in heart-felt love,
but basely lusts after every woman he sees,
is not called a lover but a counterfeiter of love. . . .*

—Andreas Capellanus

He had managed to take himself in hand long
enough to obtain the lady's help in befriending
Thomas Richmond. He'd spent the rest of the evening
distracting himself from his growing preoccupation
with Mistress Oriel's wraithlike person. Leslie Richmond had afforded some entertainment. He had as
much wit as his pretty cousin, and a collection of tales
of exploits in the stews and ordinaries of London.

They compared fencing techniques and gambling
wins, and Leslie had invited him to his rooms in the city
when he was in London.

He'd accepted, and then regretted doing so when
another of those sudden quarrels sprang up between

Leslie and his brothers. He hadn't been listening at first, but when he did, he found Leslie engaged in telling a jest at George's expense.

"And then poor George fell off the poor horse. Landed on his back. God's breath, he looked like a great, fat turnip."

"George isn't fat," Robert said between teeth clamped together.

Livia swore and glared at Robert. "Must you always ruin Leslie's wonderful stories."

By the end of the evening Blade had decided that the Richmond brothers owed their wars more to the blind partiality of Livia than to their own disparate natures. After watching the woman foster the wounding of her own sons' feelings, he'd had sufficient distraction from his own troubles.

Yet throughout the evening he hadn't succeeded in putting Oriel from his thoughts. When they first met he'd believed her a cloth-headed little fairy, but then she'd opened her mouth. Never, since he'd endured his soul-scalding tutelage under Christian de Rivers, had he been so provoked.

Blade walked out of the great chamber behind Lord George with Leslie beside him. Evening prayers had been held, and the family was retiring, everyone except Leslie, who was threatening to go to a tavern in the next valley. They had all mounted the stairs in a procession led by the gentleman usher, who held a candle to light the way. When George heard his brother's plans, he stopped in the middle of the stairs and turned on him.

"If you lose that purse I gave you, I'll not give you more."

Leslie flushed, but didn't answer. Blade gave the younger man a look of sympathy. He had no older brothers to embarrass him in front of a guest, and for this he was grateful. He didn't think he could bear what must be Leslie's lot—a younger son, cast on the mercy and uncertain largess of an older brother who inherited the family fortune, never becoming independent for lack of means. Such dependence fostered deep, gut-roiling bitterness. Considering the provocation, he didn't blame Leslie for hurling an insult at George and stomping out of Richmond Hall altogether.

As Leslie fled, Blade glanced down at Oriel, who was looking after her cousin sadly while Faith and her daughters hissed their disapproval. Their eyes met, and he shook his head. To his surprise, she understood his offered sympathy and gave him a little smile. The more he saw of Faith the more she called to mind cauldrons boiling with frogs and smelling of acid and brimstone.

Soon after Leslie vanished, Blade was conducted to his chambers by an usher. There René awaited him. He, along with Blade's other men, had recovered from the long walk to Richmond Hall in the snow after they were attacked. He stripped and huddled in a dressing gown while he waited for the warming pans to heat his bed.

René was laying his belt in a chest. "The old man fell asleep in his library again, but his man was tidying in his chambers. Then Sir Thomas woke and dined in his rooms. He didn't leave them again, and is now fast asleep. I begin to think I'll never find those rooms deserted."

"Take heart, *mon ami,* for I've a plan to take both Sir Thomas and Mistress Oriel away from the house." Blade wrapped his gown tighter around his body and knelt before the fireplace. "I shall beg for a tour of the chapel. I shall compare it to the finest in France. They go there every day, so they must like it. No doubt the old man will be pleased to give me many long stories about the place."

"*Merci, mon seigneur.*"

Blade went to bed quite proud of his performance that evening. He was beginning to think he'd misjudged himself. No doubt his wound had made him prey to strange fancies about Oriel Richmond when in truth she was little different from any of the women he'd seduced in the past. In the morning his head would be clear, and he would be able to think of her as the tool she really was. A stimulating, arousing tool, but a tool for all that. He drifted off to sleep with images of Oriel's seduction dancing in his head.

He woke while it was still dark. He sprang up in bed, having been startled awake, yet not knowing why. He reached for the dagger beneath his pillow as he heard something metallic clatter down the stairs. A door slammed, and he was on his feet and into his dressing gown as René jumped from his pallet and raced to his side.

"*Tu vas bien?*"

"*Oui.*"

Blade rushed into the gallery with René close behind. As they went, a whining scream came from the landing. He came upon a small group there. Robert was comforting his Aunt Faith, who was snuffling on his shoulder. George held a candle and leaned over the banister to peer down to the ground floor. Blade joined him, and could just make out a pile of clothing in the darkness. Above them another door banged, and Oriel came floating downstairs, a candle held aloft in her hand.

Since George seemed content to gape over the banister, Blade went downstairs. Halfway down, at the first turn, he passed a broken candle and its brass holder. He reached the bundle of clothing. It was a voluminous dressing gown of black velvet lined with fur, and in it was Uncle Thomas. Blade knelt beside the old man and turned him over, but he could already tell from the angle of the neck and the man's stillness that he was dead. He looked up to find George, Robert, and Oriel headed down to him.

Brushing past the men, he took the candle from Oriel, put it aside, and caught her in his arms. "No, *chère*, don't look."

She tried to free herself, but he pulled her close and tilted her head by lifting her chin with his fingers.

"An unhappy chance," he said. "It's your uncle."

"Uncle Thomas?" She shook her head and tried to shove free of him. "This is not possible. No, this can't be so. Not Uncle Thomas."

He heard George swear, but kept his gaze fixed on Oriel. She was searching his face with a bewildered expression. Her eyes grew wide, and she shook her head back and forth again.

"I am sorry, *chère*."

She'd stopped fighting him and now stared at him without seeing him. "Oriel?"

"This can't be," she said.

"Oriel."

She glanced up at him without comprehension.

"It couldn't be Uncle Thomas," she said. "He can't be dead. He's old, but he's not clumsy. He never falls. He's most steady on his feet." She looked up at him as if seeking his agreement. "Surely he but hit his head a mite and will awaken if you call to him."

"I'm sorry, *chère*. I've seen too many dead men not to know that your uncle will never wake."

Without warning Oriel doubled over in his arms and screamed. Her body stiffened as a long wail escaped, carrying with it unending pain. She thrashed about as Blade tried to keep his hold on her. She kicked at him, but he swept her feet out from under her. He lifted her in spite of the blows she delivered to his chest, and carried her back upstairs. At last pain overcame her, and she cried out, overcome by sobs that seemed to rob her of reason.

Over her head Blade snapped at her frightened maid, who waited on the first landing.

"Lead the way to her chamber."

"No!"

Oriel tore at his dressing gown. He clamped his arms about hers, forcing her to be still.

"Listen to me. Your great-uncle is dead, and you must grieve. Let me help you."

She froze, her face wet with tears, then closed her eyes and moaned. The sight of her misery ripped a hole in his heart. Shoving her face down to his shoulder, he ran upstairs in Nell's wake past aunts and cousins too busy shouting at each other to pay heed to Oriel.

In her chamber he lowered her to the bed. She sat there with her arms clasped about her legs, rocking back and forth and shaking her head. He ordered Nell to fetch wine and stayed with Oriel while she went to fetch it. Watching her, he felt helpless and at a loss as to what to do. Nothing could prevent her grief, yet he longed to spare her the pain.

Suddenly her hands twisted in the wild tangles of her hair, and he heard her sob. He flung himself at her without thinking. Gathering her in his arms, he sat with her on his lap, cradling her and rocking back and forth while she wept. He didn't know how long they remained that way, but Nell came with the wine, glanced at them, and put it aside. She went away again and came back dressed, and Oriel still wept.

The maid threw a cover over both of them, for which Blade was grateful. Oriel had her face buried in his neck, and he'd grown cold and cramped from supporting her. Once, when she quieted for a moment, he tried to release her. She clutched at him as if she were a babe in fear of abandonment by its mother, and he gathered her in his arms once more. It was light before she'd exhausted herself with weeping.

He whispered to Nell as Oriel lay in his arms staring at nothing. "Go to my man and have him bring hot wine. He'll know what to put in it."

Nell returned with René, who carried a cup of steaming wine. Blade released his hold on Oriel and took the cup. Oriel shook her head.

"*Chère*, drink this at once. You may not refuse me."

She took a sip when he held the cup to her lips. He

tilted it, and she drained the vessel. He sat with her until her eyes closed, then placed her beneath the covers and stood looking down at her. A teardrop worked its way from beneath her eyelid and trailed down her cheek. Cursing, he sat beside her again and took her hand. In moments the laced wine had done its work, and she slept.

He left Oriel in Nell's care and returned to his own chamber. He washed and dressed, and was belting his dagger in place when he spoke at last.

"I don't believe in such convenient accidents."

"He was an old man, *mon seigneur.*"

"And spry. But in any case, he fell over the banister, which is high. Either he climbed over it and jumped, which seems unlike him, or he was shoved."

"The family thinks he tumbled down from the landing," René pointed out.

"If he had, he would have stopped at the first turn, and mayhap he would have lived. No, he plunged down the well of the stairs like a sack of grain dropped from a loft."

He tugged on the sleeve of his doublet and allowed René to fasten a short cloak over his shoulders. "*Mon ami,* you will go among the servants and ask questions. Did anyone hear or see Thomas Richmond after everyone went to bed? Who was stirring that late? You know to be careful in how you go about it."

"*Oui,* my lord."

Several days passed during which he didn't see Oriel, except briefly at her great-uncle's funeral. She appeared then, pale and silent, only to retreat to her chambers once the old man was laid in the crypt below the chapel. He said nothing of his suspicions to Lord George or anyone else. If someone had killed Thomas Richmond, he had no way of knowing his purpose in doing so. Until he knew the reason behind the old man's death, he preferred to continue as he was.

René found that none of the servants had heard anything that night until the accident. The family had been asleep, except for Leslie, who returned near dawn to find the household disrupted by the tragedy. It was thought that Thomas had either heard a noise or couldn't sleep and had left his chamber for such a reason, only to slip and fall.

Eight days after Thomas's death, in the first week of March, the household routine had been restored except for the black trappings of mourning. Blade noted that Faith and her daughters seemed the least disturbed by the death of the old man. Moreover, Faith could hardly conceal her satisfaction that Thomas's will had provided for considerable increases in her daughters' dowries. In Blade's opinion, Thomas had correctly assessed the girls' chances of obtaining husbands based on their negligible virtues, and, being a practical man, had compensated for this considerable deficiency. He had also left most of his possessions to Oriel, thus enabling the aunts to add to their rich store of resentment.

In truth, no one seemed to miss Thomas Richmond except Oriel. George returned to his routine as lord of the estate, assisted by his mother, the interfering Livia. Robert had responsibilities as a second son, and conducted furtive expeditions in the company of several Catholic neighbors. It took Blade little effort to discover his secret masses and support of an outlawed priest. Leslie too seemed unaffected by the death, for he continued his gaming and carousing.

What changed was Blade's position in the household. Now that her daughters had better dowries, Faith took it into her head to steal him from Oriel for her oldest daughter, Joan. To his chagrin, Blade found himself thrust into the girl's company with little chance to escape, since Oriel rarely left her room.

Another week passed, and by its end, Blade was ready to curse Christian de Rivers for sending him into the bowels of hell. Every minute in the company of Joan and her sister and mother seemed a millennium.

They haunted him so thoroughly he'd had no opportunity to search Thomas Richmond's chambers for any evidence regarding Anne Boleyn's betrothal to Henry Percy.

Finally, he decided to risk searching at night. He endured another evening of boredom during which, despite the onset of Lent, he'd been wheedled into singing for the family. To his surprise, Joan had been able to accompany him on the virginals. If only she had wits to match the talent of her fingers. As it was, he had been forced to undergo the torture of making conversation.

"You play well, Mistress Joan."

"I like playing the virginals. I like music."

"Indeed."

"I play almost every day."

He hid a yawn behind his hand.

"I play the lute as well, but I like playing the virginals better. I like music."

"Really? You like playing the virginals?"

"Yes, I like it."

His sarcasm missed her completely, and by the time the family retired, he was ready to strangle Joan with a lute string. To his dismay, Faith trapped him before he could sneak away and inundated him with a list of Joan's virtues.

"And, of course, she's an heiress now that Uncle Thomas is gone." Faith put a clawlike hand on his arm and leaned close. "Uncle was quite frail, you know. By my faith, I don't know how he lived as long as he did."

Only years of training in courtliness enabled him to escape the woman without insult and retire to his own chamber. He waited until past midnight before he stole out of his chamber through the withdrawing room, leaving René on watch in the passage that led to Thomas's library.

He paused to allow his vision to adjust to the blackness of the passage, then slipped into the library. The door clicked shut behind him.

"Who's there?"

His dagger was in his hand before he realized it was a woman who spoke. Oriel. She was staring at him in alarm from her perch on the window seat. He quickly sheathed his dagger before he caused her further alarm. The room was dark, so he found and lit a candle on one of the tables.

"What do you here at this hour?" he asked.

She sighed and resumed her perusal of the dark court below the window. "I couldn't sleep."

He almost touched her, but they hadn't spoken since he'd left her the day Thomas was killed, and he didn't know if she remembered clinging to him as if he was her only hold on reason.

"You mustn't continue to brood this way. Your uncle wouldn't want you to."

She shivered, and he reached up to draw the curtains that hung over the window to keep out the chill. He was going to order her to bed when she spoke again.

"He was the only one who—" She choked on her words and made a small sound of impatience. Dashing tears from her cheeks, she continued. "After my parents died, he came to fetch me, and he was the only one who cared about me. The others—to the others, I was a nuisance. Aunt Livia and Aunt Faith resented having to look after me. I had no one."

"He was a kind man."

She smiled at him. "I was only twelve when I was orphaned, and somehow I decided that I would have to take care of myself, only I had no idea how I was going to do that. My parents were good to me, even if I only saw them at prayer time and after dinner. I was so frightened. But then he came and took the time to explain to me that I would live with him, and that he would always look after me, and then I wasn't so frightened anymore."

"And now you're alone again."

He hadn't meant to make her cry. He swore at himself when she hid her face in her hands and sobbed. Snatching her from the window seat, he sat with her in his arms and stroked her curls.

"Forgive me, *chère.* Don't cry. Please, you'll make yourself ill."

She cried anyway, and he had to content himself with stroking her hair. After a while the sobs ebbed, and she lifted her head from his shoulder.

"Your wound!"

"Almost healed."

He put his fingers under her chin and looked into her eyes. They were watery pools of darkness made barely visible by the light of the one candle. His lips were almost upon hers when she turned her face away.

"I—I must begin to order Uncle Thomas's things tomorrow."

Blade's gaze was fastened on her profile, but even in his lust, he took advantage of the opportunity she presented to him. "You shouldn't undertake so sorrowful a task alone. I will help if you like."

"You would?" She faced him, her lips trembling. "I am most grateful, my lord. The others, George and Robert and Leslie, haven't the learning to manage the work. My aunts would only throw everything into chests and sell it."

"We can't allow that," he said, his gaze transfixed on her lips. He cleared his throat.

"Are you certain?" she asked. She glanced around the library. "The work will be tedious, for many of the books are in Greek and Latin. Some are in Italian."

"*Chère,* are you suggesting that I haven't the learning to keep up with you?"

"Well, do you?"

"Mock me at your peril, Mistress Oriel."

She smiled, and he paused to look at her inquiringly.

"Did you know," she said, "that you pronounce my name with an accent?"

"Nonsense."

"You do. You say *Ori-elle.*"

"*Mais oui, c'est vrai, demoiselle, Orielle.*"

She smiled again, and suddenly Blade felt as if he'd accomplished a great feat. Then he remembered his purpose.

"*Chère,* I will help you with your sad task beginning upon the morrow. I am much grieved that I won't be able to talk with Sir Thomas now, but perhaps we could speak of him as we work."

"Why?"

"You aren't the only one in this kingdom interested in learning. I would have you know I've a library of my own in France—one much larger than this. Mayhap you will allow me to buy some of Sir Thomas's collection."

"Mayhap."

She stood abruptly, as if only now she'd become aware that they were alone. He got up, and caught her arm as she moved away from him.

"You're afraid again."

She shook her head, but tried to pull free. He smiled as the cloak she'd thrown over her gown fell open. He couldn't resist slipping his arm around her, and felt her warmth through the gown.

"My lord, you are too familiar."

He pulled her close, but she kept struggling in his arms.

"Stop, stop wriggling. You don't know what you're doing."

"I'm trying to free myself."

All at once he remembered his real task. Clamping his teeth together, he grasped her arms and set her away from his body.

"I beg pardon, *chère.* I trespass upon your grief. Sometimes I think I lose every bit of my sense when I touch you."

She was wrapping her cloak about her body. "In faith, my lord, I agree. No doubt your years at the li-

centious French court have made you so, so . . . You
must stop."

"Marry, it isn't a thing one can make up one's mind
to stop. You must trust my knowledge of the matter."

"Since we're not even betrothed, it's a thing you
must somehow accomplish."

"Mayhap we shouldn't speak of it. You're only
arousing my interest further."

He took a step toward her, and she fled. As she
vanished, he tried hard not to chuckle, so precipitous
had been her retreat. Well satisfied that he would be
allowed free access to Thomas Richmond's possessions,
he could take pride in his night's work. He had taken
her mind from her grief, and would continue to do so,
and in the practice, give himself much pleasure as well.

Chapter 9

*Therefore I hold this for certain: that in each one of
us there is some seed of folly which,
once it is stirred, can grow indefinitely.*

—Baldesar Castiglione

Oriel stole a glance at Blade from behind a tall book she'd propped up in front of her face. He was lifting a heavy volume from the top shelf, one Uncle Thomas hadn't touched in years because of its weight. He'd stripped off his cloak and doublet for this dusty work, and through his shirt she could see his arm muscles bunch as he grasped the book. As he turned, she ducked behind her shield.

She rested her hot cheek against the open face of the book and scolded herself. For three days now he'd assisted her in ordering Uncle Thomas's library, and for two of them she'd found herself more interested in Blade than her work. Already unhappy with herself for being unable to accept Thomas's death as God's will, she was even more disgusted with her perversity now that she looked forward to every moment spent in the company of this half-foreign and seductive young man.

Raising her head, she released the book and picked up her quill to record its contents. This was the first day she hadn't wept upon entering the library. No, she didn't cry all the time now. It didn't matter because she cried inside. She cried when she looked at Uncle's printing press model. Her heart ached when she read Greek, knowing she would never read aloud to Thomas again.

She carried her pain with her day and night, and sometimes it seemed as fresh as the night Uncle had died. So new and unabated did it seem that she'd almost decided not to allow Blade to assist her in this sad task. Then she changed her mind. After all, it hardly mattered who bore her company.

She shifted her position in her chair, and a sunbeam cast a patch of gold on her writing hand. She'd been foolish to assume it mattered not who assisted her. It mattered a great deal when her assistant was Blade. The contrast between his youth and strength and Uncle Thomas's age startled her. She hadn't thought how different it would be to sit across from a vibrant man who had but to raise his starlight eyes to her to cast her into turmoil.

Now that she was calm, she'd had time to dwell upon his startling behavior at Uncle's death. She had been drowning, and he had swept her up and protected her from the maelstrom. Never had she expected him to give comfort; still less had she expected to welcome it. He'd held her tightly and stroked her hair that terrible night, and his soft voice and unyielding body had kept her from ultimate despair.

A noise from the bookshelves gave her a start. She stuck her nose over her book. Blade was poking at the back of a half empty bookshelf. Odd how ofttimes he seemed more interested in shelves and chests than books. He made a sound of vexation and stepped down from the stool on which he'd been perched.

"Is something wrong?" she asked.

"No."

He dusted his hands and took up his doublet. When he'd donned it and his short cloak, he stood looking at her, and Oriel hastily directed her gaze to the catalog she was composing. He fetched a stool and sat beside her. She felt a blush rising from her neck and tried to fasten her attention on her writing. She failed when he whispered her name and caused a tremor to crawl through her body.

"Mistress Oriel?"

"Yes."

She dipped the quill in a pot of ink and kept her gaze on the catalog. There was a moment's silence; then he chuckled and plucked the quill from her hand.

"Peace, *chère*. I'm not so dissolute and depraved that I would approach you in your grief. That is, I'll try to remember me of chivalry and courtesy."

"Uncle Thomas has a book about manners."

"What?"

She pretended great concern with the papers in front of her, patting them into an orderly stack. "I've often wondered why manners of other peoples are different."

"Pardon?"

"And have you ever wondered what light is?" She pointed to a patch of light on the table. "I can see it, and it gives warmth, but I can't hold it. Think you firelight is the same as sunlight?"

"Hold!" He put his hands to his forehead and winced. "Marry, I do believe you've given me an ache in my head."

"Haven't you ever wondered such things?"

"I don't know, but I wanted to talk to you, and you're going to make my thoughts vanish if you don't stop."

"Oh." She folded her hands in her lap and looked at him.

"I haven't wanted to speak of this, but it seems I have no choice." He leaned closer, and she leaned away from him as he did so. "But you must understand that what I say is privy between us. Will you give your word not to speak to anyone else about it?"

"That I can't do until you tell me."

He regarded her for a long time without speaking. "I must trust you, it seems, now that your uncle is gone." He seemed to have decided something, for he breathed deeply. "Marry, if he finds out I've confided in you, he'll throw me in the Thames. Oriel, I'm concerned about how your great-uncle died."

"Yes, a terrible accident. I hold on to the banister when I'm on the stairs now."

He shook his head and lowered his voice. "You're a girl of much wit. Think a moment. Your uncle was found in the stairwell, not on a landing or at the foot of the staircase. In order to land there, he would have to topple over the banister. He was old, but hardly that unsteady. He would have to have jumped over or—"

"Or been pushed."

Oriel stared at him, her thoughts following the import of his logic. He was nodding, but she could only gape at him with her mouth hanging open. At last she found her voice.

"But, but that means he meant to die, or someone . . ."

"Killed him."

"Uncle Thomas wouldn't commit so grievous a sin!"

Blade held up his hands. "Peace, *chère*, I agree with you."

"How charitable."

"Now, *chère*, you mustn't lose your temper."

"Don't you speak to me as if I were a child."

He grinned at her, but she only scowled back at him. He suppressed his grin and continued.

"Do you see the reasoning of it?"

She looked away, frowning, and tapped her fingers on the catalog. Finally she nodded. "And you're right. We must keep this news privy until we know more." She looked down, noticed her tapping fingers, and spread them flat on the paper. "Yes, I see the sense of what you say, though the idea seems fantastical to me. Who would want to harm Uncle Thomas? Even my aunts would never kill someone, and they are full of spite and hate."

"There must have been a reason." He put an arm on the table and cocked his head to the side. "There are many reasons to kill someone, but ofttimes murder is done out of passion, or for gain, or to keep a secret."

"Passion?" Oriel shook her head. "I don't think so. I still find it hard to believe. Highwaymen murder people, and so do men who want power. Uncle Thomas wasn't robbed, and he had no power anyone would want."

Blade was looking at her now as if she were an oracle. "And what about secrets? Did your uncle have secrets, perilous secrets?"

"Fie, my lord. Uncle Thomas had lived in the country for many years. He was a scholar, not a purveyor of intrigues."

She jumped when he thrust himself off the stool. "God's blood, think! As infernally clever as you are, you must have noticed something that would give us a hint as to why he might have been killed. Use your wits, girl."

"You'll not address me as if I were a serving maid, sirrah."

He folded his arms across his chest. "You're not as clever as I thought, or you'd realize there may be a killer at Richmond Hall."

"None of my family are killers, and neither are our

servants." Oriel stopped, rose, and turned to face him. A shiver of alarm raced through her body. "But what do we know of you?"

He laughed, took her hand, and kissed it. "God's blood, you've got courage if you face me thinking I'm a murderer. But think further. If I had killed Thomas, would I then arouse suspicions when no one seems to think his death anything but an accident?"

"Oh."

She resumed her seat and tried to think of all he'd said. The idea of someone killing Uncle Thomas was still hard to credit.

"I must have time to reflect."

"You want to ruminate while a murderer runs free?" Blade whirled away from her, his cloak billowing around him. "*Sacré Dieu*, you may have the wit of a man, but you teeter and totter like any other woman when faced with a perplexity. Don't you understand? You could be in danger."

She was on her feet again, her cheeks blazing and her fists clenched. "Teeter and totter? You, a stranger, come to me and talk of murder and danger and suspicion, and then chide me when I take the time to ponder the matter carefully?"

"You aren't taking heed." His voice rose.

She raised hers. "What would you have me do?"

"Think, girl, think."

"Saints, I don't wonder you need me to think for you, since you clearly can't do it for yourself."

His jaw dropped, and for once it was he who turned red.

"God's patience," he said. "I'll not have a virginal, prating, light-headed witch of a girl jibe at me."

"No, sirrah, you'd much rather consort with my cousin Joan and make music for hours and hours."

She wished she could box his ears, for he crowed at her.

"Here's richness," he said. "She's jealous."

"I am not!"

"You are, and I'm most pleased."

"But not pleasing, my lord. You're a haughty jade, over full with self-contentment and too ready to believe the cozenings of dissolute Frenchwomen."

He leered at her, nodded, and began to come toward her. She slipped around her chair so that it formed a bulwark between them.

"Stay away," she said.

"How can I when you taunt and tease me into proving all those French ladies weren't deceiving me?"

She turned and raced to the end of the table, but he kept coming toward her, slowly, with that evil smile still curling on his lips.

"We were speaking of murder, my lord."

"Yes, and now that you have reminded me, I must needs stay close to you, so that I can protect you from danger."

He reached the end of the table as he finished and lunged for her. Oriel cried out, snatched up a large book, and thrust it into his stomach. He grunted and clutched at the book with both hands while she snatched up her cloak and hurried out of the library into the gallery. She risked a look back at him to find he was coming for her. Holding out a warning hand, she forestalled him.

"I'll call George."

He kept coming.

She retreated down the gallery. "I'll call Aunt Livia."

He grinned and stepped into the gallery.

Donning her cloak, she gathered her skirts in her hands. "I'll call Joan."

He halted. "Joan? Joan is a haddock with arms and legs."

"And Jane as well." She headed for the stairs.

"Come back here."

"As I said, my lord, I need time to think."

"If you must needs think, think in my presence."

Oriel shook her head and ran down the stairs before he could reply. She would rather eat slugs than tell him how impossible she was finding it to think clearly when he was in the same room. No doubt he already had guessed.

Fearful that he would chase after her, she left the Hall and went to the chapel. It was past midday, and the sun was shining through the stained glass of the rose window. After saying a few words to the family chaplain, she walked toward the altar and stopped in a pool of azure light cast by a pane of Chartres blue.

Breathing deeply, she tried to calm herself, for Blade had set her body afire and then scattered her wits with his revelations. Try as she would, she couldn't imagine anyone wanting to kill Uncle Thomas. Yet Blade had been right about how strange his accident had been. Thomas had fallen down the gap formed by the twisting angles of the staircase as it rose to the second and third floors. Oriel shook her head, but it felt stuffed with cobwebs.

Dear Uncle Thomas, he'd said when she was troubled she should visit his tomb and read the inscriptions upon it. She decided to take his advice, and went down into the darkness of the crypt. A lone torch shed uneven light in the cold chamber beneath the chapel. She stood in front of Thomas's tomb and regarded the finely carved letters on the face of the stone.

Domine Deus, Agnus Dei, Filius Patris: qui
tollis peccata mundi. . . .

"O Lord God, Lamb of God, Son of the Father, who taketh away the sins of the world," she said.

The words were comforting, but she didn't see why Uncle thought it necessary for her to come down into the crypt and read them when she knew them by heart. After a few minutes of contemplation that gained her nothing, she returned to the chapel. Lighting a candle for Uncle Thomas, she knelt at the altar and prayed for him.

After a while her thoughts strayed back to her bewitching suitor. It had slowly come to her that, in spite of his perverse taunts, Blade had returned to Richmond Hall of his own will. She was certain no threats by his father could have forced him to become her suitor again, and he had no need of her wealth. Therefore . . . therefore, he must truly desire her.

Oriel gasped aloud at this new thought, and a great warmth spread over her body. Images of Blade, his graceful, long-limbed body, came to her. Quick of mind, possessed of a voice that would lure mad beasts, he had come to dominate her thoughts. Never had she imagined that she would attract the interest of so alluring a creature. And yet he must want her, for there was no other reason for him to return after she had sent him away so rudely; no reason for him to remain in the face of her disdain; no reason for him to subject himself to the gloominess of a house of mourning.

He must want her. Mayhap he even loved her. Unused to such ideas, she struggled to believe in her good fortune. She wished Uncle Thomas were here. He'd said Blade loved her, but she hadn't believed him, and now she needed his counsel and assurance that what she suspected was indeed true. Mayhap if she prayed, Uncle Thomas would send her a sign that she was right.

Having only her cousins and suitors as examples, she hadn't realized that a young man could possess both a quick wit and great beauty. Yet Blade could converse with her in any language, match wits with her, and loved learning. If only he weren't so—so tyrannical. If only he didn't roar and rampage like a maddened Viking when she refused to obey him. Ah, well, she couldn't ask God for perfection.

When her knees grew sore from kneeling on the flagstones she rose and left the chapel. Back in the Hall she encountered Livia, who trumpeted at her from the second floor gallery.

"Where have you been? Joan tells me you haven't memorized one line of your part in the masque."

"What masque?"

"I knew it. Come here at once."

Grumbling under her breath, Oriel went upstairs and stood in front of her aunt. Massive of build, Livia was one of those women whom God had given more than a touch of masculinity. She had a man's heavy jaw and an even heavier tread, and the soulless glare of a mercenary.

"I told you yesterday your Aunt Faith has arranged for a masque. I know we're in mourning and it's Lent, but a private and small entertainment may be excused this once if we're to keep the Sieur de Racine at Richmond Hall. You're to play an ugly witch."

"Why should I play the ugly witch?"

"You always play the witch, and you never balked before. It's too late to change now, after your Aunt Faith has taken so much trouble."

"She only wants to give Joan an opportunity to prance and parade in front of the Sieur de Racine."

"Stuff! You don't appear to want him. Why do you object to giving him to your cousin?"

"He's not mine to give, and he doesn't like Joan."

Livia smiled at her. "You're jealous."

This was the second time she'd been accused of jealousy. She scowled at her aunt, who laughed at her and proceeded down the gallery with her heavy tread. Oriel was left with no opportunity to deny the ridiculous charge, which enraged her almost as much as one of Blade's taunts.

Lifting her head high, she turned her back on the retreating Livia and walked to the door of the library. She had to talk to Blade, for she wanted him to speak to George and tell him what he had reasoned regarding Uncle Thomas's death. As she opened the door, she heard a crash and a man cried out. She shoved the door aside and beheld a tangle of arms and legs.

At the foot of a line of shelves to her right lay a toppled stool, and beside it lay Blade. On top of him lay Joan, who was in the act of kissing him. He groaned, and his arms flailed. His hands found Joan's shoulders, and he shoved her back.

"God's blood, my head."

Joan wriggled down his chest, and he yelped. She climbed off him as he snaked his body away from her. Rubbing his wounded shoulder, he cried out again.

"*Sacré Dieu*, don't dig your elbows into a man's groin, you foolish—Oriel."

"So," she said. "You finally took note of me."

"Oriel," Joan said as she got to her feet. "He fell off the stool."

Blade glared at her. "You jumped on me."

"He fell and hit his head," Joan said. "After we kissed."

Oriel lifted her brows and looked at Blade. He was restoring order to his clothing and muttering to himself.

"We didn't kiss. She kissed. I fell on my arse."

"No doubt."

He glanced at her, then at Joan, then at Oriel again, and smirked at her. She whirled about and marched out of the library. He dashed to her side before she could close the door.

"Don't run away again, *chère*. I am most pleased that you're jealous. Remember the rules of courtly love, which say that jealousy and love are one, and that the greater the love, the greater the jealousy."

So furious she couldn't think of a reply, Oriel peered into his smiling face and stomped on his foot. He yelped, clutched his injured foot, and hopped on the other. The sight was most gratifying. Oriel clasped her hands in front of her and watched him.

"You forget another, more appropriate rule, my lord, which is that boys do not love until they arrive at the age of maturity. And you, my lord, have not gotten there yet."

With Blade still hopping and clutching his foot, she left the battleground the victor. It was only when she reached her chamber that she realized she'd forgotten to ask him to speak to George.

The cursed inconstant trifler. No, she was being unfair. Now that she thought of it, Joan had been the one at fault. Still, he could have run from her.

"Fie on it, and fie on him. He deserved to be kicked in the arse, not on the foot."

It was then that she began to worry about how Blade would seek revenge for his injury.

Chapter 10

Treason doth never prosper: what's the reason?
For if it prosper, none dare call it treason.

—Sir John Harington

Having escaped Joan by pleading an ache in his head from his fall, Blade had retreated to his privy chamber. Now he stood clutching one of the tall posters of his bed, pressed his forehead to the wood, and groaned aloud.

"Beshrew all women."

René was brushing one of his velvet cloaks. *"Mon seigneur?"*

"I confided in her, may God protect me. How do I know she won't babble to one of her cousins? I can't believe I decided to confide in her."

"Mistress Oriel?" René held the cloak and blew dust from its folds. "But you said she was the most honest creature you'd ever seen, and the cleverest."

"Yes, but is she discreet?"

"She must be, my lord, for she has yet to succumb to you."

Blade lifted his head and frowned at the man. "Now I'm providing amusement to my servant." He lowered his forehead to the poster again. "I should have waited, but time grows short, and the murderer runs free. Thomas was killed because of what he knew, or what he wouldn't tell. I'm sure of it. If he left any record of it, Oriel is the only one he would have told, and since she now owns his library and the contents of his chambers, I must have her help. Are you sure there was nothing in his chamber?"

"*Oui*, my lord. Did you ask her for her help?"

"I can't ask her yet. Marry, I've only just convinced her of the murder. Besides, what would you have me do? Caper into her chamber and announce that I'm one of the queen's intelligencers and would she please let me dig in her uncle's possessions for that is what spies do? And if I tell her who I really am, I will be risking her life. Almighty God, I have already."

René had stopped brushing the cloak and was looking at him like a priest waiting for a full confession of sins.

"My lord, I've never seen you so worried. Yet the risks are no greater than any we encountered in France."

"I didn't have to worry about Oriel in France."

"Ah." René began to smile.

Blade pounded the bedpost. "Don't leer at me.

"*Oui, mon seigneur.*"

"I told you to stop grinning at me. What's possessed you?"

"Naught, my lord. I but marvel that you spent so many years among the graces of the French court without losing yourself to a woman. You've had your choice of the fairest and most refined noblewomen, yet your heart remained untouched and right well defended."

Blade swore and started out of the chamber. "God

rot your entrails. My heart is still untouched, pristine, damn you. I but lure the girl for my secret purposes."

"As you say, my lord."

"I'm hungry. I'm going to the kitchens, where I can keep company with good, honest folk who are more sensible than you."

He headed below stairs to the kitchen and servants' hall. René trespassed upon their relationship. That's what came of having a servant who had bounced him on his knee as a child—a lack of respect. The man was addled. He hadn't lost himself, especially not to an innocent such as Oriel Richmond. God, he hadn't succumbed to wild curls and dragonfly wits, had he?

Don't. You mustn't. Think of having her near all the time. She might find out. You might destroy her, and certainly she would destroy you.

"Stop!" He heard a bang.

He shook his head, and came out of his reverie to find that he'd stopped at the gallery windows. He'd banged his fist on the window frame, and it ached. Lowering his arm to his side, he resumed his flight to the kitchen. He'd visited there several times already, to the astonishment of the servants. Befriending the ushers, cooks, carvers, baker, and brewer had been no trouble. He sang them a song about upstart gentlemen and told of licentious Frenchwomen.

He arrived out of breath and stalked into the kitchen, a frown still besmirching his face. He was in a room almost as large as the great chamber. Boasting two fireplaces large enough for him to stand in, the kitchen was hung with every possible pot, pan, utensil, basin, and pitcher. He found a great crowd already gathered there, though preparations for tonight's feast hadn't begun. Laundresses, scullery maids, and ushers hovered about the scarred and shining central worktable. From their midst he heard the unmistakable cant of a peddler.

"Snow-white lawn, perfumed gloves, fine wrought shirts, and lace for skirts. What do ye lack? Ivory combs, shining glasses, fit to show pretty faces of lasses."

Several maids cooed as the peddler displayed looking glasses and embroidered gloves. Blade wandered over to the group. The peddler was bundled against the freezing weather in layers of patched wool and torn leather.

So numerous were his garments that he resembled a plump bear. Yet his wrists and neck, which poked out of the bundle of clothing, were slender, even though they were caked with a good bit of dirt. He wore a wool cap so old that the nap had worn away and the fabric shone with age. Beneath it coiled masses of hair damp from the mist outside, and in spite of being layered with dust, it shone a dusky silver, like dried, tawny grass.

What gave Blade pause was a pair of eyes of the deep blue of the gentian flower—eyes that marked the peddler, that set him apart when he looked at everyone as if they were players in a farce. Blade turned away to ferret in a cupboard for dried meat and bread while the peddler regaled his audience with banter.

"Yes, lasses, I've made my way north from London Town where the whole city made merry for Christmas. Why at court, the queen has her own House of Revels with a great wardrobe full of fantastical costumes and disguisings." He bent and dug an elbow into the side of an usher. "And they use thousands of candles, what with all the plays and masques held. Never will you see such gay apparel, such spangles and ribbons and cloth of gold. Why, I saw Her Majesty's Lord of Misrule himself."

Blade had been attending more to his bread and meat than the peddler's chatter. When he heard the word *misrule*, he nearly choked on the hunk of beef in his mouth. He swallowed hard, took a gulp of ale, and stared at the peddler.

Upon closer scrutiny it appeared that the man was far younger than he seemed. There were no lines about his eyes, and they glittered with merriment as he teased a serving girl. He held out a silk lace to her, and Blade noted a long, thin scar that went down the back of his arm. It started at the wrist and disappeared beneath a torn sleeve. That scar couldn't be anything else but the mark of a sword tip.

The peddler hadn't looked at him once, and he soon completed his business and began stuffing goods into his pack. Blade wandered out of the kitchen and up to his chamber again, where he retrieved a cloak and changed into boots. Soon he was in the stables, petting his stallion, while a groom cinched a saddle tight. He rode out the back gate and down the path to the neighboring village. As the road plunged into the oak and hazel forest that covered most of the valley, he could see the peddler trudging through mud and snow.

He kicked his horse into a trot and caught up with the man. The peddler stopped as he approached, and swept him an elaborate bow.

"My lord."

"Stay you a moment, peddler. I've an interest in masking and plays—and misrule."

The peddler smiled at him and pulled off his mittens. His hand waved, and from nothing produced one of the many trinkets he hawked from manor to village. He tossed it in the air, and Blade caught it.

This was no common bauble to catch the eye of a dairy maid. In his palm lay a flat, hollow ring of gold fashioned to resemble a wreath. Within the wreath lay a dragon rampant done in silver and crimson enamel, the heraldic device of Christian de Rivers. Blade closed his hand over the device and looked at the peddler.

"Are you going to sit there gaping at me like a befuddled cowherd?" the peddler asked. He stuck out his arm.

Blade took his hand and drew him up behind him on the stallion. Turning the horse, he rode into the forest until they were out of sight of the road. Once they stopped, the peddler jumped to the ground, and Blade dismounted after him.

"God's truth," said the peddler, "my feet are cold."

The peddler dropped his pack, searched inside, and drew out a pair of leather boots no itinerant should have. Sitting on a log, he drew them on. They fit perfectly. He sighed, stuck his legs out in front of him, and wriggled his feet.

"Are you comfortable?" Blade asked.

"Yes."

"Then give me your message, damn you. I swear I don't know where Christian finds such allies. You'd think you were out for a springtime stroll."

Without warning the peddler's hand flashed to his pack. A dagger jumped into his hand, but Blade leaped at him, his own weapon already aimed at the man's heart. They halted, facing each other, each waiting for the other to move.

The peddler suddenly grinned and lowered his dagger. "He said you were the best, but I had to find out for myself."

"Piss-brained lout, I could have killed you."

"Not before hearing my message."

"Out with it, then."

"Christian's off to Scotland. He said to tell you the Cardinal of Lorraine went to the funeral of the woman named Claude."

Blade sheathed his dagger and said in a whisper, "Claude, poor Claude."

"You must needs make haste, for he said he wasn't the only one going to Scotland."

"Stewart's son."

"Yes. What news shall I bring to him?"

"The old man has been killed, but I may find what we're searching for without him."

The peddler rose from the log and came near. "Killing already? Foul news." He lowered his voice. "When the stakes are kingdoms, many die. Have a care. Mayhap I should remain in the village."

"My thanks, but tell Christian I need no nursemaid."

"A pox take you. It was an offer from my fine and generous heart."

Blade laughed. "You're not one of Christian's vagabond minions from the stews or you'd spout far more lurid curses."

"I'm a familiar of Nora's. She befriended me because I once saved a mongrel pup of hers from drowning. She thinks I'm Parcival reborn."

"That's Nora," Blade said. "Shall I give you a ride to the village?"

The peddler shook his head. "My horse and man aren't far off."

"Then fare you well, peddler."

"I am called Derry by some," the peddler said as he swept a bow and chanted. "Sweep chimney sweep, master, with a hey derry sweep, from the bottom to the top, hey derry sweep."

With a final bow and a laugh, Derry swept up his pack and sauntered off into the trees. Blade watched him go, and noticed his light step and how easily he carried the voluminous and heavy pack. Derry was far younger than his disguising allowed one to see. If Christian trusted him to cavort in so flagrant a manner in the midst of a household infested with at least one traitor, Derry was far more than a simple messenger. Needless as Blade thought it was, his friend had sent someone he trusted to warn him, and mayhap save his life.

That evening Blade conversed in the great chamber with Robert and Leslie as they awaited the performance of a masque by Faith, her daughters, and Oriel. He had almost completed his search of Thomas Richmond's library, and found nothing. He was beginning to think there was nothing to be found, but if this was so, why had Thomas been killed?

"I tell you I can bear this cursed country life no longer," Leslie was saying. "There are no plays, and no bear baitings, nor any good hunting either. Only such as George and Robert could enjoy this place, for they find watching corn grow a tax on their wits. Someday I'm going to build my own house in London."

Robert sneered at his brother. "With whose coin, you arse?"

"Go tup a stable lad."

Robert almost flung himself at Leslie, but Blade thrust an arm in front of him. "Gentlemen, remember where you are."

"Robert." Livia trumpeted at them from her chair by the fire. "Leave dear Leslie alone. God knows why you can't be more like him. Make yourself pleasant company for once."

Flushing from his scalp to his neck, Robert muttered to himself and cast a murderous look at his younger brother. Blade thought he might be forced to come between them again, but two musicians blew a note on their pipes, and everyone turned their attention to the screen set in front of the chamber doors. The musicians stationed beside it struck up a stately tune on viol, pipe, lute, and drum. Faith emerged from behind the screen dressed in a flowing gown and carrying a scroll. She curtsied to the audience, unrolled the scroll, and read.

"Now hear ye, good gentles, one and all, of my tale so dire and doleful. A tale of maidens fair, three in all, and of a terrible witch. The maidens were Beauty, Grace, and Amity; the witch was called Envy."

Blade kept his face expressionless as the three oldest of Faith's daughters appeared as Beauty, Grace, and Amity. Dressed in gossamer robes and floating cloth of silver, they shuffled into the chamber. He supposed they were to have danced, but he could recognize no pacing or steps or gestures.

Joan seemed to have forgotten the dance altogether. She stopped and looked around, and Jane bumped into her. Agnes tripped on the hem of her own gown, then righted herself and followed her sisters to a pile of pillows covered with satin. Plumping themselves down, they struck poses that reminded Blade of sheep settling down for the night.

"The evil witch, Envy, heard of the three beautiful sisters and sought them out to do them harm." Faith turned to the screen behind her. "And sought to do them *harm*."

The screen rattled, and Oriel stomped into view. Blade couldn't stop himself from blinking. She wore a black robe streaked with ashes and black gloves, and held a long black wand. Her hair had been tousled so that it looked as if she'd been in a tempest, and it too was sprinkled with ashes. She wore a black mask with a long, pointed, and hooked nose. She marched into the chamber, sneezed, and tore the mask off her face. Wriggling her nose, she surveyed the audience with a glare.

"I am Envy, mean and evil, jealous and vile. To defeat Beauty, Amity, and Grace is my purpose. I shall not rest, uh, I shall not rest . . . Oh, a plague take it. Where are they?" She sighed and walked over to her cousins to address them in a funereal tone. "Oh what marvelous luck I have found you and no one can save you I shall kill you and reign as Beauty myself take that." She lifted the wand in a desultory manner and poked Joan with it.

Blade clamped a hand over his mouth and disguised a guffaw as a cough. Tears came to his eyes, so great was his effort not to chortle.

Faith was reading again. She paced away from the screen and stopped in front of Blade. Casting a look of unsubtle encouragement at him, she spoke. "Oh, who will save Beauty? Oh who, oh who?"

Blade looked at Robert and then at Leslie. They snickered at him. He glanced about the chamber to find the rest of the family waiting. He stood and bowed to Faith, smiling wickedly.

"I'll save Beauty."

Racing around Faith, he headed for the girls on the mountain of pillows. As he ran, he swerved at the last moment and dived for Oriel. She shrieked as he swirled her up in his arms.

"Fear not, Beauty. I'll save you from vile Envy." Oriel poked him in the ribs with her wand. "Ah-ha! Envy is strong."

He whirled around in a circle, causing Oriel to drop the wand and flail at him and kick her legs. He stopped abruptly, dropped her legs, and threw her over his shoulder. Shoving aside dusty black skirts, he addressed the audience.

"Vile Envy must be imprisoned." He turned to Joan. "Fear not, fair Beauty. I shall take Envy far away and lock her up and guard her so that no peril will threaten you."

Grinning at Joan, he turned and ran behind the screen and out of the great chamber.

"Put me down, sirrah!"

"I never listen to witches." He hurried past amazed ushers and serving men and down to the kitchens. Servants were busy washing dishes and scrubbing floors. He stopped by one kneeling on the floor.

"The cellar?"

The lad blinked at him.

"Don't tell him," Oriel cried.

"The cellar, boy."

The lad pointed to a door, and Blade went through it and found stairs angling steeply down into a black tunnel. He turned back and shouted for a light and a key. The Richmond steward came forward with both, and he ducked down the stairs with Oriel shouting threats in his ear. She jabbed him in the ribs.

"Be still or I might drop you down this hole."

"Put me down!"

He didn't answer. Reaching the foot of the stairs, he encountered another door. It was half open since its stores were providing wine for the company in the great chamber. He went inside, placed the torch in a wall holder, and set Oriel on her feet. She stumbled backwards, out of breath and sputtering. He slipped the key in his belt and shut the door.

"What mean you by this hideous prank?" she asked as she rubbed her stomach and shoved fly-away curls from her face.

He held up his hands to ward her off, chuckling all the while. "Marry, lady, I could see you had no liking for your role, so I decided to rescue you from it. They won't look for us here."

"Everyone will laugh at me." She scowled at him. "You're laughing."

"Yes," Blade said, "I'm laughing. Faith, *chère*, in my life there has been little to give me cheer, and I thank you from my heart for giving me such enchanting merriment."

Her scowl faded, and she took a step toward him. "I make you laugh, but not in mockery?"

"How could I mock such a whimsical little fairy maid?"

"Oh."

He watched as she considered his words. She scuffed her slippers on the flagstones. A puff of ashes billowed up from her skirts and she sneezed. Blade produced a kerchief from his sleeve and handed it to her. She rubbed her nose with it, then began dusting her face and shoulders. "Let me help you."

He took the kerchief from her and dabbed at a sprinkle of ashes on her nose. She went still and caught her breath. He smiled at her, remembering her lugubrious speeches in the masque. His gaze traveled from her smudged brow to the bright rose of her lips, and stayed there. As he looked at her, the blood in his veins turned to molten silver and rushed to his head and groin. How could merriment ruin his designs, banish his intention to coldly seduce? He could feel his will turning to water and trickling away. He felt it vanish, and for once, let it go. There was no other choice but surrender.

He took the ends of the kerchief in his fingers, dropped the silk over her head, and pulled her to him with it. Her lips brushed his, and he opened his mouth. Pulling harder on the kerchief, he sucked on her lips and tongue.

To his surprise, she slipped her hands beneath his cloak and around his waist. She drew him against her body, and as his chest touched hers, he dropped the kerchief. Holding her close, he lowered her to the floor. He cradled her head in one hand, still kissing her, and fitted his body between her legs. Her hands slipped beneath his doublet and worked the flesh at his waist.

Pulling his mouth free of hers, he nipped the flesh of her throat, then tugged at the neck of her gown. His hand slipped inside and closed around her breast. She gasped, then began to wriggle. He lowered his head to her breast, nuzzling the black cloth aside as he searched for her nipple. His hips thrust against hers. She planted her feet flat on the floor and arched her back. At last he realized she was trying to buck him off.

"Don't." He pushed her down to the floor again and arched his own back so that his groin pressed to hers.

"Wait."

He shook his head, too engulfed in the flood of arousal that carried him. His body burned as if he'd been put to the stake. He covered her mouth again, but she pounded his back. He felt the blows vaguely, but it was her cry that stopped him at last. It was a cry of fear muffled by his own lips.

He lifted his head and gazed down at her. "Oriel?"

"Please."

"Have I frightened you?"

She made no reply, but turned her head away and bit

her lip. He closed his eyes and cursed himself and his too-ready body. She mustn't know how near to forcing her he'd come. He didn't want to think of it himself. Pausing to master his body and summon his control, he raised himself so that most of his weight was on his arms. He ducked his head so that their eyes met.

"I beg pardon, *chère*. I forgot all courtesy."

"Will you let me up?"

He got to his knees and pulled her upright, but kept her hands in his. "I didn't mean to frighten you."

"Um, mayhap, if—"

"God's blood, I've frightened you speechless."

"No," she said quickly. "I but meant to say that—" She took in a sharp breath. "Next time I won't be so frightened."

"Ah. Next time. You wouldn't run away if there was a next time?"

She lowered her gaze to the floor and shook her head.

"God is merciful."

She looked up at him in confusion, which made him laugh again.

"Come, *chère*. We must quit the secret cave of Envy the witch before your aunts find us."

"Saints, no doubt they're growling and lashing their tails by now." Oriel picked up his kerchief. "Oh, I had a thing to tell you about Uncle Thomas, but I forgot when I saw you kissing Joan."

"She kissed me!"

"I know. Don't interrupt. I was going to tell you that Uncle Thomas made a great point of instructing me to read his tomb inscription if I was ever troubled. He was most odd about it, so I went down to the crypt again, but I could make nothing of the inscription."

"*Mon Dieu*, why did you not say so? What does the inscription say? Quickly, *chère*."

"It's only a prayer," she said.

"Will you show me?"

"Now?"

Blade took her hand and led her out of the chamber. "After everyone is asleep. I'll come to your rooms." He glanced at her and whispered. "What luck. I'll find you in your bed."

"You won't, sirrah, or if you do, you'll find Nell there as well."

"Faith, I've serviced two wenches before, but I hadn't thought to receive such an offer from my virginal hostess."

Oriel flicked the kerchief in his face. Dust billowed at him and he sneezed, and sneezed again. When he recovered, Oriel was nowhere in sight. He heard her laugh and rushed out of the cellar to see her black skirts disappearing into the kitchen above. He ran up the stairs in her wake.

As he went, he wondered if he dared slip into her bed as he'd promised. He longed to with a violence previously unknown to him. His nights were restless with ungratified desire, and now that he'd touched her skin and lain on top of her, he knew he wouldn't rest until he'd taken her. Would she welcome him in spite of her words? He couldn't be sure, for whatever her learning and wit, Mistress Oriel was as unpredictable as north country weather. And he was beginning to suspect her passions were as violent.

Chapter 11

Art thou fairer than the evening air
Clad in the beauty of a thousand stars.

—Christopher Marlowe

Oriel sat on her bed fully dressed and waited to see if Blade would indeed try to steal into her chamber. The hangings on one side had been thrown back so that she could see the door to the withdrawing chamber. On the floor by the bed and a small brazier lay Nell's cot, with Nell huddled in blankets. She too gazed at the door.

"Ooo, mistress, how can you visit the crypt in the middle of the night? There's bound to be shades walking about."

Shivering, Oriel threw off the cover she'd been using for warmth and replaced it with her heavy cloak. The fur lining enveloped her, and she buried her nose in it.

"I won't be alone."

"You keep well behind his lordship."

The door swung open, slowly, and Oriel clambered off the bed. She had believed Blade's threats and thus had slept a few hours, then rose and dressed so he couldn't catch her abed. Blade's head appeared, then the rest of him, and he scowled at Nell and then Oriel.

"Coward."

Oriel pulled on the hood of her cloak without replying.

"Ooo, mistress, mayhap you should take a knife or something."

"What good would that do against shades?"

Nell oooed again as Oriel preceded Blade out of the chamber.

"You're a distrustful soul," he whispered to her.

"Afore God, I trust you to do what you threatened after what happened in the cellar."

She had reached the stairs when he suddenly took her gloved hand. He bent to look into her eyes. She could see the gleam of his teeth and knew he was smiling.

"Yet you still accompany me privily to a place of darkness and concealment."

Pulling her hand free, Oriel tried to see his expression, but failed. "You said you wished to see Uncle Thomas's tomb. If you intend to try your evil tricks, I will not accompany you."

"But *chère*, you said you wouldn't be frightened the next time."

"I—I was addled by your attempts to cozen me when I said that. I have reflected and remembered my virtue."

She tried to take a step down the stairs, but he caught her arm. She felt his breath on her cheek.

"Liar. You're afraid."

Shrugging off his hand, she continued down the stairs without answering. She didn't hear him follow, but he had, for she heard his whisper just behind her.

"Alas. I've found the exception to Petrarch's rule that rarely do beauty and virtue dwell together."

She stumbled when she heard this, and he caught her. As his arms came around her, she turned and gazed at him. He was frowning at her.

"God's breath, girl, take greater care. You take five years off my life every time you slip."

She nodded. "Beauty?"

He was paying attention to the stairs as they began their trip down again. "Mmm."

"You said beauty."

"Yes. Shhh."

They reached the bottom, and he led the way past a sleeping usher posted at the main entry. She kept silent until they had emerged from the house by a side door. They came to a hedge, and she tugged on his cloak.

"You said beauty."

"Yes. What of it?"

"You think I'm—" She couldn't say the word.

He was looking at her. She could see him in the moonlight, and his face held amazement.

"Never tell me you thought yourself ugly."

"Not precisely ugly. Odd, and plain."

She almost cried out when he cursed, darted at her, and swept her over the hedge. Dropping her on her feet, he snatched her hand and pulled her after him.

"By all the doxies in the London stews, think you I try to seduce monsters? No, I have it. Those cursed aunts of yours have made you believe you're ugly."

"They never said I was ugly, but I've read about great beauties, and I don't look like them."

"Then you've been reading the works of fools."

He put a finger to his lips and slipped inside the chapel, pulling her after him. It was dark except for the altar candles. They waited to make sure the chapel was deserted, and as they waited, Oriel watched Blade.

He thought she was beautiful. That he thought so was to be marveled at, for no one had ever said such a thing to her before. When he had abducted her from the masque, she had thought he was making a jest of her, but she'd been mistaken. Then he'd kissed her and tried to make love to her, and she'd almost succumbed. Until that encounter in the cellar she had found it almost impossible to believe that he could love her.

Now enlightenment burst upon her. This young man who had legions of women tripping over one another to get to him, this man who had pillaged numerous French court ladies, this wild and mysterious interloper, actually fancied her for his mate. Why else would he tell her she was beautiful? If he wished to marry her, he could arrange a contract with George and her aunts with little trouble and even less dealing with her, as long as their relationship was amicable. Yet he hadn't been able to keep his hands from her.

Her life had been lonely for so long, except for Uncle Thomas. Now there was no one to whom she was essential. No one who waited for her to enter rooms, who worried if she was ill, who longed for her presence because it brightened his days. She had longed secretly for such a one, and now he'd come to her wrapped in an alluring package of dark beauty that haunted her days and nights as well. As they waited, she said a quick prayer of thanks to God for this living gift.

Then her gift began to move, and she stopped praying. Blade retrieved a torch from its wall socket, lit it from a candle, and returned to light their way. They crept down the nave to the south transept and gained the stairs to the tunnel that led to the crypt. Nell's warnings about shades and evil spirits came back to her as she followed him down the short tunnel and into the crypt.

Closed in the blackness of the crypt, she said a quick prayer beseeching Uncle Thomas's protection. Blade had stopped at Uncle's tomb and was holding the torch near the inscription on its face. The only sounds in the place were their breathing and the hiss of the flame from the torch. She noticed Blade was caressing the hilt of his sword as he read.

"*Domine Deus* . . . Here lyeth the Right Honorable Sir Thomas Richmond, son of . . . Sometime of the household of His Eminence, Cardinal Wolsey. . . ."

"You see why it's so strange he would tell me to read the inscription if I was in trouble. There's naught in it of great import."

They stood side by side and read the inscription again. The minutes passed as they thought about the words. Finally Blade sighed and turned away. Walking around the tomb, he shoved the torch into a wall holder between two older tombs set in curved archways. As he turned from the wall back to her, he stopped. His hands dropped to his sides and he narrowed his eyes.

"*Chère,* come here."

She joined him while he retrieved the torch. He went to Uncle Thomas's tomb and held the torch next to another inscription carved into the side away from the crypt door. Cut in Roman letters as high as the length of Blade's hand was a phrase in Latin.

Noli Me Tangere

Blade touched the letters with his gloved fingertips. " 'Touch me not.' This is from the Bible. Jesus said it to Mary Magdalene."

"Yes, but it's unlike Uncle Thomas, such a quotation. Why would he warn us away from his tomb? Or mayhap he was afraid of grave robbers."

"Robbers in this crypt?"

"I told you the whole matter was wondrous strange."

"God's blood it's cold." Blade stamped his boots on the stone floor and glared at Uncle Thomas's effigy. "You couldn't have made the puzzle a simple one, put somewhere warm."

"*Noli me tangere*," Oriel said to herself. "*Noli me tangere. Noli me tangere.*"

"Repeating it over and over won't do any good," Blade said.

"I've read that before."

"Of course you have. In the Bible."

She shook her head. Running her gaze over the Latin words again, she cupped her hands over her cold nose and rocked back and forth on her heels.

"*Noli me tangere*," she said.

Blade said nothing, but moved closer to her and never looked away from her face.

"*Noli me*—Sir Thomas Wyatt!"

"What mean you?"

She clutched at his arm and almost danced in her excitement. "In the weeks before he died Uncle Thomas made a great point of having me read the poetry of Sir Thomas Wyatt. He used to say Tom Wyatt knew better how to write verse than to live his life. He had this book of copies of the poems, and he insisted I read all of them."

"Where is this book now?"

"In the library, I think."

He snatched her hand once more and dragged her up to the chapel again. She was out of breath by the time they reached the chapel, but he gave her no chance to protest. Only pausing to douse the torch in sand, he quickly pulled her back to Richmond Hall. By the time they reached the second floor gallery, she was ready to dig in her heels.

"Why are you stopping?" He yanked on her hand.

"Give—*puff*—me—*puff*—time." She gulped in deep breaths.

"Pardon, *chère*."

Instead of waiting, he scooped her up and carried her into the library. Dropping her into Uncle Thomas's old chair, he busied himself making a fire while she regained her breath. He vanished into the adjoining withdrawing chamber and returned with a wine flagon and goblet. He poured some and thrust the goblet at her. She took a sip, then another, and sighed.

"Where is the book?"

"You see that stack beside my table? I put it there after I recorded it on my list. I think."

Blade lit a candle and searched the pile of books resting on a chest beside her worktable. He was forced to remove several stacks before finding the Wyatt poems. He came back to her and placed the book in her hands.

"Which is the poem?"

"I don't remember. All I remember is the phrase *'noli me tangere.'* I will have to search for it."

She began turning pages. Halfway through the book, Blade knelt beside her and watched the pages turn. She pressed another page flat.

"Here! I remember now. Uncle said this one was written about Anne Boleyn. Wyatt was in love with her, you know, but old King Henry got her instead. Uncle said Wyatt nearly died when she tossed him away for the king."

Together they read the sonnet.

> *Whoso list to hunt, I know where is an hind,*
> *But as for me, alas, I may no more;*
> *The vain travail hath wearied me so sore,*
> *I am of them that furthest come behind.*
> *Yet may I by no means my wearied mind*
> *Draw from the deer, but as she fleeth afore*
> *Fainting I follow; I leave off therefore,*
> *Since in a net I seek to hold the wind.*
> *Who list her hunt, I put him out of doubt,*
> *As well as I, may spend his time in vain.*
> *And graven with diamonds in letters plain,*
> *There is written her fair neck round about,*
> *"Noli me tangere, for Caesar's I am,*
> *And wild for to hold, though I seem tame."*

Blade sighed. "What means this hinting with sonnets and circuitous reasoning? Know you why he would put the poem in your way?"

"No, but it's most curious that he would go to all this trouble to give hints only I could understand." Oriel rose and placed the book open on the table. "Mayhap it all means nothing, but signifies our foolish imaginations."

"If that were so, your uncle wouldn't be dead."

She turned back to him in surprise. He had gone back to the fireplace. Having removed his gloves, he was holding his hands near the flames. She went to stand on the opposite side of the fire and removed her gloves as well.

"Mayhap you're right," she said. "But I will have to ponder on this sonnet awhile." She covered her mouth to stop a yawn and blinked slowly as she watched the fire.

"Ponder in secret, *chère,* for we've no way of knowing who might have done in your uncle."

A quiver of alarm shot through her, and she sank to the floor and clutched at the ends of her cloak.

"I'm sorry, but I'd rather have you frightened than dead."

She gazed up at him in mute horror. He knelt in front of her and clasped her arms.

"Someone really killed Uncle Thomas," she said.

"Yes, and it seems your uncle was hiding something of great import. Mayhap he was killed for whatever he was hiding."

"Someone in this house is a murderer," she said. Until now it hadn't occurred to her to be frightened. She bit her lip and wrapped her arms around her waist.

"God rot his entrails, whoever he may be." Blade took her hands in his and fastened his silver gaze upon her face. "No one will harm you. I'll see to it. And no one knows what we're about."

"I've never worried about dying before."

Uttering a curse, Blade pulled her into his arms. He pressed his lips to her hair, and she heard him mutter something.

"Who is Claude?"

"Marry, your ears must have frozen. I said it was cold."

He turned her to face him, drawing her close. She watched him peruse her face. "God, *chère*, I'd rather die than have you hurt."

"Don't say that. I'd rather be hurt than risk you at all."

His eyes widened for a moment. He put his hands on either side of her face, and she saw that he was staring at her mouth. She could see the pulse in a vein at his neck beat faster, and he grew quiet, as a raptor does before diving for its prey. Then he began to lower his mouth to hers. She tried to move away, but he tightened his grip on her. He said something in French, but it was so faintly spoken she couldn't understand him. He was so close she could almost feel the straining of his body.

"I should return to my chamber."

He shook his head. He smiled, but his expression was as intractable as an executioner's. "Too late, *chère*. Much, much too late."

He covered her mouth with his, and she felt his lips suck at hers. As they tugged at her mouth, she began to feel that warmth he'd evoked in her in the cellar. She turned her head to free her lips.

"I—I've never had a suitor before. I mean, not one I wanted to—"

He put his fingers over her lips. "Shhh. Then let me press my suit."

She looked into his eyes and saw fire barely held in check by his concern for her. She craved that fire. She would have it. Pulling him close, she pressed against him.

He surrounded her with his arms and bore her down to the carpet before the fire. The light reflected in his eyes, turning them to molten silver as he lowered his mouth to hers again. She felt his tongue slip into her mouth, and he began to suck with his lips once more. That warmth built in her arms and legs while he kissed her and pressed his body down on hers. Gently he settled between her legs.

His hands slid to the neck of her cloak, and it came open. He spread the garment out beneath her without releasing her mouth. When she put her arms about his shoulders, he loosened his own cloak and used it as a cover. One of his legs came up to rub against her thigh, and her gown inched up her leg. She could hear her own breathing as it grew sharper and more rapid, but when he put his hand on her neck, she forgot to be alarmed.

His hand lay still for a moment on her bare skin, then slowly drifted down her neck to her breast. Through her woolen gown she could feel the heat of his flesh as it rested on her heaving chest. His lips followed the path his hand had first traveled, and she realized that somehow her gown had come loose. It sagged at her shoulders, allowing his lips to nudge it aside as he kissed his way to her breast.

Hardly aware of anything but the feel of his lips, she forgot to breathe when his hand moved from her breast, pulling her gown with it so that her nipple lay bare. When his lips fastened on it, she sucked in her breath and arched her back. Her nipple thrust deep into his mouth, and she nearly cried out, so great was the stab of sensation. Her groin began to ache, and to relieve herself of this ache, she began to move her hips.

Now he was breathing as heavily as she. He shifted his body and took her other nipple in his mouth. Painful pleasure shot through her body, and Oriel began to claw at Blade's back through his doublet. Frustrated, she tore at his clothing and slipped her hands inside to feel his chest and back. As he moved from one breast to another, he rubbed his hand up and down her leg, each time going higher on her thigh. Finally his hand stroked upward to her hot flesh while at the same time he bit lightly at her nipple.

Oriel started and tried to move away from the invading hand, but he moved with her, pressing and murmuring assurances. Soon she calmed, and when he tugged at her nipple, she uttered a groan. He covered her mouth to quiet her, and shifted his weight, lifting his hips away from her.

Oriel tugged at him impatiently, possessed of a mindless urge to have him on top of her. Finally he allowed her to pull him back, and when she did, he shoved her gown up and rested his bare flesh against hers. He swallowed her gasp, then whispered words of reassurance. As he did so, he began to flex his hips and she felt him rubbing against her groin.

That torturing ache built until she thought she would scream. Thrusting her legs wide, she answered the movements of his hips. Suddenly he lifted his body and kissed her at the same time. She felt him press against her, and then cried out. There was a sharp sting, and a great pressing invasion. Oriel writhed beneath him, but he held her trapped beneath him.

"Shh. Be still and I will help you, *chère*."

She opened her eyes and stared into his. Slowly he pushed into her while at the same time he whispered to her. When he stopped, he had put himself into her entirely, and she could feel him quivering inside her. He lay still and took her breast again. With little effort she was aching again, and he began to move.

Slowly at first, and then faster and faster he moved. With each stroke the sensations in her body churned and grew until she could resist no longer and fastened her hands on his buttocks. As he moved, she tried to shove him deeper inside herself, her fingers digging into his flesh. Finally she felt a great explosion, and cried out. He covered her mouth again, and his own cry was smothered as well. He rammed into her harder, then arched his back and gasped. In her madness, she tried to lift her body off the floor and nearly succeeded.

Blade pressed her down with his body as he collapsed. His head fell to her shoulder, and she cradled it. Her flesh still ached, and it burned, but the pain was slight compared to the glorious feeling of union that was its reward. This was right. This was what they both needed. She wanted this creature who beguiled and seduced without meaning to. She wanted him for the rest of her life. She put her hand to his cheek. It was hot. He lifted his head, and she found him staring at her and frowning.

"I am undone."

"I don't understand."

"God's blood, *chère,* I mean I succumbed to mortal lust. I've taken a virgin."

"Is that all?"

"Is that all!" He gaped at her with his mouth open, then began to smile. "I expected laments and tears, you addled fairy witch. It was your hair. It caught the firelight, and seemed to burn a black-red flame."

"But my lord, since you're my suitor, it matters little. Does it not?"

He hadn't heard her. He'd closed his eyes and was pressing his body against hers again. She hugged him close.

"After all," she said as he moved inside her, "we'll exchange betrothal vows soon anyway."

He stopped moving. His eyes flew open, and he started to say something, but a noise in the gallery made them both jump.

"Quick," he said. "Your gown."

He rose and pulled her upright. He was righting his own clothing when George burst into the library. Bundled into a dressing gown and carrying a sword, he stopped just inside the chamber and gaped at them. Oriel turned, her gown hanging open at the neck. George glanced at her and roared.

"By all the devils in hell, Fitzstephen, I'll skewer you to the wall for this!"

Chapter
12

Now unto my lady
Promise to her I make:
From all other only
To her I me betake.

—Henry VIII

Blade put himself between Oriel and Lord George. "I do wish you would forbear from making threats that might get you killed."

George waved his sword at him. Blade glanced at the weapon with little interest.

"By God, Fitzstephen, you'll answer for this. I thank the Almighty that Nell had the good sense to come to me when Oriel was gone from her chamber so long."

"What's amiss?" Robert came in huddled in a dressing gown and cloak. He looked from Blade to Oriel. "Oh."

"I'll challenge you and have your heart on a plate," George said.

He would have smiled if he hadn't been so disgusted with himself for succumbing to his lust. Before he could reply, Oriel darted around him.

"George, you mustn't harm him. He and I, we, oh, fie. He is my suitor."

Blade cursed under his breath and tugged at Oriel's cloak, but she ignored him.

George's sword lowered. "Your suitor. Mean you that you're to exchange vows? Then, why didn't you say so?"

"Wait," Blade said.

George went on as if he hadn't spoken. "Still, there'll be no more of this until the vows are said. The betrothal will take place tomorrow morning. I'll tell the chaplain to arrange for publishing the banns, and the marriage can take place after that."

"Wait."

Raising his sword again, George said, "Is there any reason why the betrothal should not take place? Mayhap you prefer a duel."

Blade opened his mouth, but Oriel turned and caught his arm in both of hers. He glanced down at her and hesitated, for she was gazing up at him as if he were more necessary to her than food. She smiled at him, and he closed his mouth.

"Fie, George," she said. "He's remained in this house of gloom for weeks in order to press his suit. We erred, it's true, in anticipating our marriage, but surely our transgression can be amended upon the morrow."

Lowering his sword again, George glared at Blade. "What say you, my lord? Will it be a betrothal or a duel?"

Blade was still gazing at Oriel's face. She was in love with him. God forgive him, he hadn't taken heed, hadn't realized how innocent she was in spite of her learning and her age. His years among women hardened by licentiousness and court intrigue had made him callous. Oriel had assumed that his seduction was intended to seal their vows, and now he couldn't deny her belief. If he did, he would have to kill her cousin, and his search for Thomas Richmond's secrets would end. There was no choice. He must agree and then delay the marriage.

"Duel," he said. "Why, my lord, how could I fence with my betrothed's own dear cousin and guardian?"

George lowered his sword for the last time and nodded. Robert smiled at them in satisfaction while shivering in his nightclothes. Reaching for Oriel, George tugged her away from Blade.

"No more familiarity," he said. "I shall remain silent about your great sin, mistress, but you will conduct yourself as befits a Richmond lady until your marriage."

"Yes, George."

"To bed," George barked.

Oriel darted away from her cousin and kissed Blade on the cheek. She floated out of the library followed by her bear of a cousin and his brother, leaving Blade to flounder in the shipwreck of his intentions. He covered his face with his hands and uttered every foul oath he had ever learned from Jack Midnight.

He'd gone mad with lust. She'd tricked him with her innocence. Any other girl of her station would have known that a bedding didn't necessarily mean a wedding. Curse her honesty. If she weren't so honest, she wouldn't have expected him to be what he appeared to be. Those aunts were at fault too. If they'd sent her to court she would have learned how to play at love, and then he wouldn't be forced to spurn her once his task at Richmond Hall was completed.

Blade lowered his hands and sighed. There was naught to be done now. He stalked out of the library and went to his own chamber. René was waiting for him.

"You heard?" Blade asked.

"*Oui.*"

"She's in love with me." Blade heard the wonder in his own voice and cleared his throat. He allowed René to take his cloak while he thought.

"God, René, she's in love with me."

"Many have been so. She is but one more."

Blade rounded on his servant. "By hell's torments, I'll have your head on a pike for saying that. She isn't like the others." He began ripping the jeweled buttons off his doublet in an effort to remove it. "She gave her trusting little soul to me, and her love. Don't you see? She didn't just want the pleasure I could give her. She wasn't trying to flaunt me in front of her rivals. She gave herself, and I took her without realizing what I was receiving until it was too late."

Flinging the doublet at his servant, he sat on the bed and tugged at his boots. He got one off and threw it. The boot banged against the opposite wall. He felt no better, and he knew why. The idea of coming so near marriage curdled his entrails. Memories of his parents soured the very word. He'd spent his childhood in torment. Night after night he'd crept from his room to listen to his parents fight. As their voices battled, he would tremble with fear and cry and pray to God to make them stop. But they never did.

Later the fighting turned to war, and his father began beating his mother. It was then that Blade interfered. He would thrust himself in front of his mother, and was beaten as well. He remembered little of those beatings, and tried to forget what he did remember. He survived by not remembering.

If he married and became a husband, he might remember more. And even worse, he might become what his father was. He had within him a rage born of the teachings of his father—a rage he controlled and dared not unleash. There were still nights when he dreamed of killing his father. He couldn't ask any woman to marry someone who longed to kill his own father. Sometimes he woke in a sweat, fearing that his soul was as evil as his dreams.

And if this fear weren't enough, there was his added aversion to marrying at all. He'd been the hope and defense of a clinging, helpless woman at too young an age and for too long to take on another. His mother's death had freed him of that burden, and he could hide his evil dreams. He would give up the freedom if he married, and Oriel was the one person from whom he would be unable to hide his dreams.

Thus when morning came, he took himself to the Richmond chapel with misgiving. In all his intrigues he'd never gone so far as to promise marriage, and never had he been forced to deceive so guileless a maid as Oriel. He stalked down the nave and choir to halt in front of the altar, his features set in an impassive expression as he greeted the Richmond family. All of them were up early for this most precipitant ceremony.

Livia and her sons surrounded him. "It little befits our family honor," she said, "to set about this betrothal in such haste."

"Er, we've been arranging contracts between us," George said. "We didn't want to burden you in your grief for Uncle Thomas."

As he didn't think Livia would grieve if she'd been present at the crucifixion, Blade looked away from the woman and encountered Leslie's speculative stare.

"You do gallop when you're ready, don't you, Fitzstephen?"

"Your cousin has won my heart with her beauty and wit."

"Oriel?" Leslie appeared to consider his cousin's appearance and intelligence for the first time. "Yes, she's clever, if you can get her to leave off those bewildering questions of hers. But beautiful? Think you so?"

"If you don't, you're blind."

Leslie grinned at him. "Perchance it's because I was

raised with her." He nudged Blade with his elbow. "I'm to make myself useful by playing the chaperon for the two of you. I'll be like your favorite hound, always underfoot."

"Then I shall lock you in a kennel."

He was sparring with Leslie when Oriel came into the chapel with Faith and the Richmond daughters. The chapel door opened, admitting a burst of sunlight, and she stood in the entry. With the fiery light behind her, she was lit in gold. Sunlight ignited her dark hair, turning its red highlights into a brilliant crown. For a brief moment Blade forgot his qualms, forgot Thomas Richmond's secrets and the peril of England's queen.

She walked down the aisle, a small figure dwarfed by the columns and high ribbed vaulting, and he noticed that Faith had convinced his stubborn Oriel to don a lady's gown in honor of their betrothal. No wonder she had seemed on fire upon entering. She wore a gown of gold and ivory shot silk trimmed in heavy gold embroidery and pearls. He blinked as the gown and her hair glistened in the sunlight.

He couldn't help smiling at her as she came toward him, for as usual, she had forgotten her lady's graces and was holding her gold and feathered fan as if it were a riding crop. Behind her shuffled the Richmond girls, who slid into the family pew, giggling and whispering. All except Joan, who bore the air of a martyr. As she sat down, he saw her bend and tug at the back of Oriel's skirt. Oriel kept walking, then stopped short and stumbled. He darted forward and caught her arm. The scent of lavender and spice wafted up to him, and he felt a hot spurt of desire that made him set his jaw and curse at himself.

The ceremony was a brief one, an exchange of *de futuro* vows in which each of them said "I will" in response to the chaplain's questions. He was relieved, for if the vows had been *de praesenti*, in which they would have responded "I do," the betrothal would have been much harder to set aside. He thanked the Lord for not making George more farsighted.

He had had the presence of mind to think of a ring even before George had come to him with the offer of a temporary one. He put it on Oriel's finger, marveling at how small her hand appeared when resting in his own. The ring was his own, one handed down in his family for generations from one heir to the next. A thick gold band, it was inscribed with the Fitzstephen heraldic device, a shield upon which was engraved *per pale*, with a falcon addorsed on the right and a great helm on the left. The ring was too large, but Oriel gazed at it in wonder, closing her fingers so that it wouldn't fall off.

He hadn't expected her to provide a ring. Indeed, he hadn't given the matter any thought at all, so when she breathed the words "I will" and took his hand, he simply smiled at her. She smiled back, but then opened his hand and produced a ring that caused Blade to stare like a cowherd at Bartholomew Fair.

Of red gold heavily embossed with scrollwork, it was mounted with a great, square-cut emerald larger than his own thumbnail. The piece was old and more valuable than anything he'd seen Oriel wear. He knew she was an heiress, but now it occurred to him to wonder at her indifference to the riches she so clearly possessed. She had given him a ring that would purchase a small castle.

He allowed her to slide the jewel onto his finger, and suddenly, the betrothal was complete. He took a deep breath, then kissed her. Her lips opened under his mouth, and he slipped his arms around her, pressing her to his body. A harrumph from Faith brought him to his senses. When he lifted his head, Oriel looked up at him, and he forgot the restive aunts in the fire in her eyes.

Livia trumpeted at them. Recovering themselves, they knelt before the altar for the service that was to follow. As the chaplain droned on, Oriel surreptitiously groped for his hand and clasped it. His lips quirked but he maintained his composure when she tickled his palm with the tips of her fingers. At the end of the ceremony, Blade took Oriel's hand and placed it on his arm. They led a procession out of the chapel and into Richmond Hall, where a midday feast had been provided.

His misgivings about his situation returned and he found he had little appetite. Since it was Lent—mid-March—there was fish and more fish. He contented himself with helping Oriel to salmon. She declined the oysters and fried cod, and he observed with fascination the way her nose crinkled at any suggestion of eel. Finally he persuaded her to eat some candied strawberries.

In deference to the season, there was no dancing. By the afternoon he was freed from the attentions of the aunts and cousins. Oriel had retired earlier to change, having lost patience with her farthingale and the scratchy embroidery on her gown. He was pacing in his withdrawing chamber, imagining how Oriel would take his inevitable request to be released from their vows when he heard a muffled sob coming from the library. He crossed the passage between the two chambers and found Oriel collapsed in Thomas Richmond's chair, raining tears on the carved arm. He knelt before her, wondering if she had sensed his unwillingness at the betrothal.

"*Chère?*"

The sobs stopped. She lifted her head. Her lashes were wet, as were her cheeks, and she covered her nose with a kerchief.

"*Chère*, what ails you?"

"Oh, naught."

Blade took her hands, and she turned her face away from him.

"Tell me, for I won't let you stir from this spot until I know what has caused you grief."

She caught her bottom lip between her teeth, then met his gaze. "I quarreled with Aunt Faith."

"Not a difficult thing to accomplish."

She almost smiled at him.

"She is furious at me for—for . . ."

"Last night."

"Yes, but not because I've lost my virtue. She said I, I opened my legs for you so that you'd be forced to marry me instead of Joan. She made what we did sound so ugly. And then she said the Bible condemns harlots like me. It says more bitter than death is a woman whose heart is snares and nets. Then she quoted Proverbs: 'Her end is bitter as wormwood, sharp as a two-edged sword.' "

"Your aunt has the soul of a pig. How could you listen to her?" He put his hand to her cheek. "Listen to me instead, *chère:* 'Behold, thou art fair, my love; behold, thou art fair; thou hast doves' eyes.' "

He was rewarded with a brilliant smile. She took his hand from her cheek and clasped it in both of hers.

" 'As the apple tree among the trees of the wood,' " she said softly, " 'so is my beloved among the sons. I sat down under his shadow with great delight, and his fruit was sweet to my taste.' "

Rarely had a woman made him blush. What was happening to him? Blade lowered his eyes and studied their joined hands.

"Blade," Oriel said.

"Yes."

"I'm afraid I called her a jealous old termagant."

He laughed, forgetting his discomfort, and gave her a kiss on the cheek. "I rejoice to hear it."

"Blade."

"I haven't gone away."

Now she was staring at their hands. "I . . ." She cleared her throat and started again. "I did forget all virtue, but—but I couldn't seem to help it. I wanted you so. I never thought to find someone who would capture my esteem and my—my longing at the same time."

Never in all his dealings with women had one so astonished him. As she looked at him, he saw both love and desire, mingled in a heady brew he'd never before longed to taste. It was almost as if he was being offered the Holy Grail. He had no words of response, but to his relief, she seemed to expect none and changed the direction of her thoughts as if she assumed he returned her feelings.

"I came in here to think, you know, not to fight with snarling aunts." She leaned over the arm of the chair and produced the book of Sir Thomas Wyatt's poems. "I was trying to think of why Uncle would go to such trouble to direct me to this sonnet."

Grateful to be distracted from uncomfortable thoughts, he nodded. Now was the time to guide her thinking in the right direction. "Thomas Wyatt" he said, "was in love with Her Majesty's mother long ago. He was in love with Anne Boleyn."

"Yes, you can see it in his poetry. Did you know Uncle was great friends with a man Anne Boleyn almost married? His name was Henry Percy, and he was the heir to the Earl of Northumberland, but Cardinal Wolsey broke their betrothal. Uncle said Henry Percy never recovered from losing Anne Boleyn." Oriel looked up from the book to regard him solemnly. "She must have been a creature of great fascination."

"*Chère,* a thought just came to me. These hints of your uncle's, they all have to do with Anne Boleyn."

She nodded slowly. "They do."

Silence fell as he allowed her a few moments to think. Watching her piquant face absorbed him. He studied her wide brow dusted with fine curls, her adamant little chin.

"You know, now that I think upon the matter, Uncle Thomas was greatly absorbed in that old story about Her Majesty's mother—so much so that he purchased a painting."

"What painting?"

"That one." Oriel turned to point to a portrait on the wall behind her.

He rose, offering his hand to her. Together they went to stand before the painting. The portrait showed a woman in a black gown trimmed with gold and pearls. She wore an old-fashioned French hood also trimmed with pearls, and a long strand of pearls wound around her delicate neck. At its center was suspended a gold pendant in the shape of the letter *B*. From the pendant hung three large, teardrop pearls.

The woman herself appeared far less beautiful than he would have imagined her to be considering that for her, old King Henry had defied the Church and dragged his kingdom to the brink of war. Her face was long, as was her nose, and she had a small, bow-shaped mouth. Its diminutive size gave her a pinched, self-satisfied look. But her black, almond-shaped eyes stared back at him in mocking amusement, as if she knew what he was thinking and saw the incongruity of her situation. Now he knew where the queen got her dark, flashing eyes and not a little of her wit.

He was studying Anne Boleyn's long neck, which had been severed when Henry VIII decided she wasn't going to give him sons, when suddenly Oriel gasped and stuck her face close to the picture. She seemed to be inspecting a portion of the dark background behind Anne Boleyn.

"Look," she said.

He bent and stared at the patch of paint at the tip of her finger. Barely discernible was a faint design done in a paint that blended into the background.

"It's a leaf," he said.

"Yes, a leaf that is just floating there. The background is plain. There are no trees or bushes. Why is a leaf hidden in the background of the queen's painting?"

"Mayhap it's a device of the artist."

Oriel shook her head until her curls flew in his face. "It wasn't there when Uncle hung the portrait. I know because we inspected the painting thoroughly."

"Wondrous strange. Think you it's another of your uncle's hints?"

"Perhaps. But why a leaf?"

Blade studied the faint design. "It's an oak leaf."

"Uncle Thomas loved oaks. He used to say he'd spent the happiest hours of his youth in the north country dales, lush with oak and hazel."

Blade threw up his hands. "Another fine hint from your uncle. No doubt he meant us to search an entire dale."

"I think not," Oriel said.

"We haven't time for such machinations. I'm losing patience with your uncle, *chère*."

She smiled and patted his arm. "He did love puzzles."

"Ha!" Leslie burst into the library and stopped before them, beaming with merriment. "George grew worried because you both left the table. I'm here as I promised, Fitzstephen, your faithful hound."

"Damnable oaf, you're as welcome as a cutpurse in the merchants' guildhall."

Leslie bowed, laughing at him. "I know it well, and therefore I suggest that we go riding. The exercise will distract you from thoughts of further seducing my fair cousin."

"Leslie!" Oriel batted him on the shoulder.

"Don't chastise me, coz. You're the one with the great appetite for grey-eyed wastrels."

"Close your mouth, Richmond," Blade said, "and lead the way to the stables before I box your ears for insulting my lady."

They followed Leslie out of the library. As they walked down the gallery, Oriel snapped her fingers.

"Oak leaves! Uncle used oak leaves to mark his place in books."

"Then there must be quite a number of oak leaves in the library."

"Yes. Let's go back."

Blade shook his head and pulled her along with him. "We can't. Leslie would come with us. We must find another opportunity to sneak away."

"You know," Oriel said. "There's one place more than any other where there are oak leaves aplenty in the library."

"Where?"

"In Uncle's journal. The binding is covered with embossed oak leaves. Oh!" Oriel clutched his arm as they walked. "Do you think Uncle was killed because of something in his journal?"

"Mayhap, *chère,* and if he was, and we find it, we will be in danger as well."

Chapter 13

Love, which absolves no beloved one from loving,
seized me so strongly with his charm that,
as thou seest, it does not leave me yet.

—Dante Alighieri

To be in love and in danger at the same time made her shiver with fear and excitement, or mayhap it was the cold. She was riding beside Blade in the forested dale surrounding Richmond Hall. She might as well have been riding on a cloud, for in spite of Blade's warnings of danger, her happiness wafted her along as though she was flying.

She'd lost her senses and allowed him to make love to her, and it was the most fortunate thing she'd ever done. Even now she could imagine the pressure of his hands on her body. She still tingled from this new passion that banished all others. She loved him.

Stealing a glance at Blade, she watched his legs flex as he rode, saw the ripple of thigh muscles. Her gaze wandered to his lips. She thought of all the places they'd been, and she blushed. Best turn her thoughts to less arousing matters since Leslie rode behind them.

Where had she put Uncle Thomas's journal? Shortly before his death she'd come across it while piling books out of the way. She remembered being surprised that it was among the works on mathematics, history, and other texts to be cataloged, for Uncle always kept it in his room. Before she remembered to ask him about it, Uncle Thomas was dead. It was still there, somewhere, among the hundreds of books still to be looked at.

Uncle must have believed someone wanted the journal, someone evil, or he wouldn't have hidden it by placing it in the library. She shied away from the idea that someone in the household might have killed him, though she knew it was a possibility. She turned her thoughts instead to Anne Boleyn, dead for so many years. What about her could be so important? Anne Boleyn was only of note because she was Her Majesty's mother. King Henry had gone to great lengths to make their liaison official so that Elizabeth would be born legitimate. He'd been furious that she was a girl, legitimate or not. Legitimate.

"Legitimate!"

"What did you say, chère?"

Blade was regarding her inquiringly. She looked over her shoulder at Leslie, and he grinned at her. She shooed him away with her hand, and he slowed his horse so that the distance between them widened. She nudged her horse closer to Blade's stallion.

"I have an idea—something that Uncle Thomas may have known and written in his journal." She stopped and glanced back to make sure Leslie was too far away to hear. "Perhaps he knew something about Her Majesty's birth. Something that might cause her legitimacy to be questioned. Perilous knowledge to have. If so, no wonder he never spoke of it."

"Think you so?" Blade frowned and appeared to

consider her suggestion. "God's blood, we'd better find that journal soon, for who knows what evil purpose the murderer intends for it."

"The murderer," she said. "Surely he must be one of the servants. I can't believe anyone in the family would kill Uncle Thomas. Why, families don't do that to each other."

He leaned down to pat the neck of his stallion before he answered. "You'd stand amazed at what people of the same family can do to each other. Think of what old King Henry did to his wives, and to his daughter Mary. Your cousin Robert is a Catholic, *chère*, and one who thinks the Queen of Scots is the rightful queen of England. Mayhap he's decided to help her gain the throne by destroying the legitimate claim of our good Queen Bess."

She didn't answer at once. At first she was angry with him for impugning Robert, but then logic demanded that she acknowledge the truth. Robert made no secret of his opinions, which was the chief reason George and Aunt Livia disliked him so. Afore God, she wasn't used to intrigue and machinations, and found it difficult to think in the twisty, deceitful ways necessary to divine the secrets of this mystery. Blade, however, seemed at ease with plots and danger.

Something about this last thought gave her pause. Blade Fitzstephen seemed to take to intrigue and mystery as if he were born to it. And now that she thought about it, he had spent all those years at the French court. He'd told her he'd even met the Queen of Scots when she was married to the French King Francis II. He'd been there when her husband died and she had to go back to Scotland, the queen of only one country instead of two. He had said he stayed in France because of his French possessions, and because he and his father didn't bide well together. She knew little of his father, except that he must have a cruel nature to have made so dire an enemy of Blade.

"*Chère*, we must find the journal quickly."

"What? Oh, yes, we must, but Leslie won't leave us alone, so I will search later by myself."

"You will not. What have I been telling you about the peril of searching for something for which your uncle was killed?"

She cast an irritated glance at him. "I must search. I know what the journal looks like and I also know the library better."

"Then we must search while Leslie is with us."

"But you said we must be secret."

Blade assumed an air of innocence. "True. Therefore Leslie will sleep while we search."

"What mean you?"

"Have you ever heard of the root called All Heal?"

She nodded, then gasped, "Saints, you mean tó put some in his drink?"

"We'll send for ale when we return to the Hall."

"This root—it won't harm him, will it?"

"Marry, think you I would poison him?"

"Of course not."

She looked back at Leslie and found that her cousin had stopped and was talking to a peddler bearing a large pack and wearing layer upon layer of tattered and patched clothing. As she watched, their voices raised, though she couldn't make out what they said. Suddenly Leslie's booted foot shot out and jammed into the peddler's chest.

"Blade, look!"

As they turned their horses, Leslie jumped from his mount and landed on the prostrate peddler. Blade's stallion leaped past her, and she watched as he galloped back down the path to the men, who were rolling on the snow-packed ground. Without waiting for the horse to halt, Blade dropped from the saddle, raced to the fighters, and shouldered his way between the two.

"Out of my way!" Leslie backed up and drew his

sword. "I'm going to teach this bastard a lesson in manners. He'll learn not to mock his betters."

"Sodding caitiff, it was you started it, calling me a bloody whoreson lout."

"God's breath," Leslie said. "I've never met a common wretch with such a desire to die."

Leslie tried to lunge past Blade, who rammed his shoulder into the younger man's chest. Leslie bounced back and cursed. The peddler meanwhile was shouldering his pack. He tramped through the snow past Oriel. As he went by he grinned at her, placed a wooden box in her hands, and winked. She stared at him as he left, but Leslie's curses distracted her. Blade had her cousin in a bear grip.

"Release me!"

"Master yourself, you fool. Would you shed blood in front of Oriel?"

Leslie stopped struggling, and Blade dropped his arms.

"I forgot myself," Leslie said. "But the foul jade wouldn't show me his papers. I'm sure he hasn't got permission to sell his wares. No doubt he's a thief."

"Someday," Oriel said, "someday your temper will land you in a fine mess, Leslie Richmond." She glanced around. "The peddler's gone."

Blade whistled to his horse and held out his hand to the stallion as he came trotting up. "In any case, I'll have no quarreling and bloodshed in Oriel's presence. And now that you've trounced him, we'll not see him again."

Oriel looked down at the box in her hands. "He gave me this."

Both men came to stand beside her horse as she opened the box.

"Comfits," she said.

"Comfits," Blade repeated. "Comfits. No doubt he meant them as atonement for his misbehavior."

Oriel picked up a piece of candied fruit, a date, and popped it in her mouth.

Later, after they had returned home, Oriel waved a serving man out of the withdrawing room next to the library and grasped a flagon of ale by its handle. The silver vessel knocked one of the goblets on the tray that was on the side table.

"Let me help you, *chère*."

Blade came to stand beside her while Leslie picked up an ivory lute he'd found resting in a chair and sank to the pillows beside it. Oriel's hands were shaking. She was glad when Blade took the flagon from her and poured the ale. She couldn't stop herself from sneaking a glance at Leslie. He wasn't watching. He plucked at the strings of the lute.

She returned her attention to Blade and watched, fascinated, as he touched the heavy signet ring on his right hand. The bezel slid aside to reveal a compartment filled with fine, dark powder.

"Know you a tune?" he asked calmly as he tipped the ring and emptied its contents into a goblet of ale.

Swallowing hard, Oriel watched the powder dissolve instantly.

"I prefer," Leslie said, "to listen to you, Fitzstephen, rather than embarrass myself by singing before one so gifted."

Blade swirled the ale in the goblet and handed it to Oriel. She took it, and their eyes met. He was no more disturbed than if he were a priest serving communal wine. He'd done this before, she realized abruptly, perchance many times.

"Who are you?" she whispered, suddenly frightened.

He looked from her to the goblet and back again. "Why, I'm Blade. Serve the ale, *chère*."

She didn't move. He stared at her for a moment, then took the goblet and sipped from it.

"Now," he said. "Serve the ale."

She took another goblet for herself, went to Leslie, and handed him the one with the powder in it. Leslie thrust the lute into Blade's hands and pleaded for a song. As that unequaled voice surrounded them with magic, Oriel considered her discovery.

In her obsession with this beautiful creature, she had failed to discern his complexity. In faith, she knew little about him, though she had his body committed to memory. He moved from France to England easily. He frequented the company of great lords and ladies. His clever mind perceived mysteries where others did not, and he drugged people's ale. For the first time she realized how much he hadn't confided in her. She knew nothing of his beliefs, his aspirations, his feelings, his principles. Curse her inexperience. Dear God, she'd been so enamored she'd promised herself to a stranger, all because his touch aroused her to mindless passion and his voice charmed her as if he possessed the magic of a sorcerer.

Blade's song ended, and the silence brought her back to the present. She looked at him, but he was studying Leslie as if he were examining a bull at market. Leslie had lain back on his pillows. His head had dropped to the side, and he snored. Blade rose, set the lute aside, and offered his hand to her. He pulled her erect and guided her out of the withdrawing chamber into the library. He shut the door to the passage between the two chambers.

"Well, *chère*, where shall we begin looking for the journal?"

"I'm not looking for anything until you explain."

He lifted his brows, but said nothing.

"What are you that you are so experienced at poisoning people's wine? How do I know I can trust you?"

"Marry, you trusted me last night."

"Don't try to distract me."

He lifted her hand to his lips and pressed a kiss to it.

"I yield," he said with a mocking smile. "If you would know the truth, I must tell it. Mayhap you've heard how violent a man my father is. To be honest, when I was a child, he was more than violent, he was a monster."

He dropped her hand, folded his arms over his chest, and stared at the floor. "I seldom speak of it, but he used to beat me unmercifully when I angered him. Once I knocked over a bowl of soup and ruined a Turkey carpet. He backhanded me so hard I sailed over the table. Then he took his riding crop to me. I couldn't leave my bed for most of a month." There was such bitterness in Blade's eyes that Oriel put out a hand to touch his arm.

"To this day I dream of those attacks, and of avenging myself on him. I dream of beating him as he beat me, only I don't stop until he's dead and can no longer hurt me. Sometimes I wake up sweating and—" He stopped and looked down at her hand on his arm. "*Chère*, I know about the powder because I use it myself when nightmares rob me of sleep and peace."

She couldn't help the tears that rolled down her cheeks. Flinging herself into his arms, she hugged him hard.

Laughing softly, he held her at arm's length. "It was long ago, *chère*, and he can't hurt me now. Don't cry. It was long ago."

"I can't help it," she said. "I keep seeing you as a little boy, so sweet and beautiful, and the thought of that man hurting you, well, it makes me want to kill him."

She wiped her cheeks and smiled at him, then gasped. "The journal! We must hurry."

They searched among the piles of books for over a quarter of an hour before Blade found the journal beneath a treatise on geometry. Fortunately, her family seldom came to the library, for none of them cared for learning as had Uncle Thomas.

Thus when Blade opened the journal, they were able to examine it in peace. Most of the journal concerned Uncle Thomas's private musings and memories, but near the end he began to write of his experiences as a page in the household of Cardinal Wolsey.

"Here," Oriel said, pointing to the top of a page. She began to read. "When I was a youth my family placed me in the household of Cardinal Wolsey, the king's chief councilor and friend. While there I became friends with Henry Percy, who became enamored of one of the queen's maids, Mistress Anne Boleyn. We ofttimes accompanied the cardinal when he took counsel with the king, and thus Percy had many opportunities to woo the girl. They even swore *de futuro* vows of betrothal to which I was a witness. But the cardinal heard of it, and chastised Percy most woefully, saying that his station was too high, and the alliance unsanctioned by Percy's father and the king. Percy, being a weak sort, succumbed to the pressure of the cardinal and his father, and broke with Anne Boleyn, who was banished to the country for several years. Later, of course, she caught the king's eye, and was wed to him."

The narrative ended here, and beneath it Thomas had drawn his device, an oak leaf, within a rectangular frame. Oriel turned the last page in the journal, but it was blank on the reverse side.

"There is no more," she said.

"*De futuro* vows," Blade said. "Such vows may be set aside, and they were." He took the book from her and examined the passage. "It is well. Naught can be made of this for evil purposes, for now that we have it, no one can alter its meaning to suit their designs. Shall I guard this?"

"Yes. I've no doubt you're used to keeping things secret."

He didn't answer.

"So," she said as she watched him slip the book inside his doublet. "That was your fear? That someone

might use Uncle Thomas's journal to destroy the claim
of our queen to the throne?"

"A frightening thought, is it not?"

"There would be war, civil war," she said. She was
sitting in Uncle Thomas's chair again, and rested her
chin on her hand. "Were I Uncle Thomas, I would have
destroyed the journal."

"Perchance he meant to, but was killed before he
could do so."

She rose from the chair and went to the withdrawing
room door. She opened it and listened to Leslie's snoring.

"What shall we do with the journal?" she asked.

Blade was busy clearing books to make a path to the
gallery door. "I must take it to London."

"Why? I think we should burn it."

Kneeling on the floor by the paneled wall, Blade
glanced up at her. "There is someone who will want to
see it."

"Who?"

"The queen."

Oriel shut the door quickly and put her back to it.
"You're going to take it to Her Majesty? You're mad.
You'll never gain an audience."

"I have friends who will help." Blade hefted a stack
of books and shoved them against the wall.

"Listen to me, Blade. It's too dangerous for you to
keep the journal. We must destroy it.

He shook his head. "You must trust me in this,
chère. Her Majesty will want to see the journal for herself."

"How do you know?"

"Because if I were king, I would want the same
thing. It's a dangerous thing to wear a crown. Think of
the three queens King Henry got rid of. Think of the
unbounded ambition of the Queen of Scots."

"When will you leave?"

"Soon. But I must prepare your cousin George for

my leave-taking, or he will challenge me to a duel again."

"Not if I come with you."

"You can't!" Blade lowered his voice. "Think you your family will allow you to travel with me? God's blood, who taught you modesty and behavior?"

She lifted her chin and scowled at him. "Are you questioning my virtue?" She heard a chuckle that ignited a rage she didn't know she could feel.

"Marry, *chère*, you have none now."

Oriel felt as if her head would explode from fury. She made a fist and rammed it into Blade's stomach. He doubled over and gasped, and she stomped on his foot. He yelped, and she darted away from him as he made a grab for her. She raced to a table and picked up a heavy book, turned, and dropped it on Blade's head as he rushed at her. He swore and staggered backwards while she ran around him and made for the door. She was almost there when he caught her from behind and lifted her off her feet. She kicked and scratched at his hands, but couldn't free herself.

Blade turned her, fastened his arms around her, and dragged her back to the table. He shoved her against it, trapping her between it and his body. He buried a hand in her hair and made her look at him.

"I beg pardon," he said, and she stopped fighting him.

"You do?"

"I, to whom you gave the gift of your self, who took that gift and gloried in it, have no right to question your honor." He smiled at her, and his eyes glittered. "I was but teasing, *chère*. You are the most estimable and worthy of women."

"You make me sound like a fat old widow."

He tightened his grip on her hair and rubbed his body against hers. "Neither fat nor old, *chère*, and most entirely savory."

He lowered his mouth to hers, and she felt his lips

begin to suck. In little more than a moment she was lost in the feel of those warm lips. He bent over her, and she sank back on the table. His hands slid to her thighs, nudged them apart. As she wrapped her arms around his chest, he began to press his hips back and forth. She was running her fingers through his dark, soft hair when she heard a voice.

"Well, coz, I chose the right moment to wake."

Blade groaned and lifted his body from hers. She rose, blushing hotly, and jumped off the table.

"Leslie," she said, "you're as welcome as the pox."

"Alas, such is the price of duty."

She glared at him. "I shall go to my chamber. I must bathe after all the riding we did."

"Allow me to bear you company," Blade said. As Leslie began to sputter, he raised his hand. "Only to the door, Richmond, only to the door."

In the entryway Blade kissed her hand. As he bent over it, he whispered, "I'll come to your chamber to-night."

She smiled, kissed his cheek, and whispered back, "You can't. Nell sleeps there, but I know a place where we won't be disturbed."

Offering her cheek to him, she went on. "Come to the old hunting lodge at midnight. One of the servants will tell you where it is."

Blade drew back from kissing her cheek, grinned at her, and spoke aloud. "Fare you well, *chère*. It seems we must resign ourselves to waiting."

Chapter 14

Surely there is nothing more wretched than a man,
of all the things which breathe and move upon the earth.

—*Homer*

His body was aflame, unsatisfied in a way he'd never experienced. His skin felt as raw as if a hive of bees had stung him, and he admitted to himself that no other woman had ever driven him to this pass. He'd behaved like a randy youth in a brothel. He couldn't allow it. Blade pounded his fist into the door of the library.

"Damn, damn, damn."

When they first met he had thought her even-tempered and malleable, but he'd been fooled by her air of distraction brought on by her intellectual curiosity. Now he knew better. Still, he hadn't expected her to turn into a spitting viper. He also hadn't expected her temper to ignite his and then hurl him into a maelstrom of desire that vanquished his resolution not to touch her again. The more he saw her, the more he wanted her. Blade looked at his reddened knuckles. They throbbed, and he cursed himself again.

At least he was rid of Leslie now that Oriel had gone to her chamber. The man knew when to give his victims respite from his company. Blade quit the library, shaking his throbbing hand, and returned to the withdrawing chamber. There lay the small comfit box given to Oriel by Derry. He had secreted it beneath a cushion.

"Sodding doxy's brat," he muttered to himself as he carried the box to his chamber and examined it. "Handing messages to Oriel."

Oriel and Leslie had finished the candied fruits, and the box was empty. Blade turned it over, knocked on the wood, then pushed on the bottom. A panel slid back to reveal a small scrap of paper. Blade shut the panel and put the box on the table beside his bed. He lifted his head and listened, but could hear no one. He returned to the paper and studied the images upon it. Beautifully drawn, they were of a red bird and a falcon.

Each detail of feather and beak was carefully traced, but the picture was odd, for the red bird was attacking the falcon. In fact, the red bird had its claws around the falcon's neck, its beak embedded in the heart of the falcon. The feathers of the red bird were painted a vivid shade, between scarlet and crimson, which is called cardinal. The falcon was his own heraldic device.

Blade crumpled the paper in his fist and tossed it into the flames of the fireplace. Leaning on the chimneypiece, he stared into the fire. The Cardinal of Lorraine knew about him, possibly from Claude. As he was contemplating how long he could survive with Charles de Guise hunting for him, René returned with a pile of his master's clothing in his arms. Blade hardly glanced at him.

René knelt in front of a chest and began transferring hose and shirts to it. Blade spoke softly to his man in French.

"We're in trouble. The Cardinal of Lorraine has discovered who I am."

René paused in the act of lifting a shirt. "Then we are fortunate to have left France when we did."

"The cardinal's reach is long." Blade sighed as he looked over at René. "No doubt he searches for us at this moment. Marry, it's fortunate we've found what we were looking for."

René dropped a shirt and let out a breath. "At last, *mon seigneur*. Then we leave."

"I leave soon, but you will remain."

"But my lord, the cardinal."

"There's the matter of the killer of Thomas Richmond," Blade said. "There's a murderer in this house, and I can't leave Oriel unprotected. You will guard her until I can return to find the culprit and break this cursed betrothal."

"My place is at your side."

"You will do as I command," Blade said. When René continued to frown at him, he went to the man and put a hand on his shoulder. "I have hurt her enough by misleading her into this betrothal. I won't have her harmed, and you're the only one I trust to keep her safe."

"*Oui, mon seigneur.*"

Blade turned back to the fire and braced his arm on the mantel. The emerald on his left hand caught the flames and gleamed, reminding him of his folly.

"God's blood," he murmured and closed his eyes.

"My lord?"

At first he didn't answer, but then he opened his eyes and stared at the emerald. "God, René, I hate myself, but how could I have known what would happen?" He closed his fist over the emerald. "I vowed long ago never to endanger any woman by marrying."

"It was your father, not you, who—"

"I'll hear no more, damn you. Now that I have what I came for, I will begin to remove myself from her affections. Tonight I'm to meet her at the old lodge. I'll begin then."

"Meet her?" René's frown deepened. "But my lord, the old lodge is almost a league's distance from Richmond Hall. How will Mistress Oriel go there?"

"A league?" Blade left the fire to join René by the chest. "A league. By the rood. She meant to travel a league to this lodge by night? *Sacré Dieu*, I thought she had more sense." As he realized the danger in which she would place herself, his fury at Oriel grew.

"Pardon, my lord, but Mistress Oriel's sense seems to be directed more toward Greek and Latin than the business of everyday living."

Blade's voice rose. "God's sacred body!"

He charged toward the door. "I'll take a whip to her. I'll, I'll—" He stopped. "She's with her maid. Curse her, I'll have to wait until tonight when we dine."

He kicked the door, turned, and swept back into the chamber. How many other foolish things had she done before he had come? What would she do once he'd gone? God's blood, he would give her a scolding that would soon teach her sense.

That night, after everyone had dined in the great chamber, chivalry prevented him from refusing Aunt Livia's demands for a song or two. He was tuning his lute while seated on a stool near the fire with Oriel on a cushion beside him. They hadn't spoken much, for she seemed absorbed in glaring at Leslie for some reason of which he was ignorant.

Most of the family were ranged in a half circle on cushions and chairs. They were chattering among themselves while he tuned the lute. Twisting a peg, he plucked at one of the strings. With everyone talking at once, he was about to chastise Oriel for her foolish plans to go to the hunting lodge when Leslie sauntered over to them.

He yawned, then gave them a lazy smile. "God's

foot I'm drowsy this night. It's unlike me to fall asleep in company as I did this afternoon. I must beg your pardon again, Fitzstephen."

"There's no need." He twisted another peg. Oriel said nothing and continued to glare at her cousin.

"Most unlike me," Leslie said.

He was suspicious. Blade gave Leslie a wide-eyed glance. Leslie waited with an air of expectation, but Oriel interrupted them.

"Leslie Richmond, you're a foul toad."

They both stared at her.

"Not two hours ago I caught you with Nell—again—this time in Uncle Thomas's chamber. You had your arms around her, and if I hadn't come upon you, I know what would have happened. Why is it that men demand chastity of women and then try to debauch them? Why is it that chaste women are hounded until they yield and then blamed when they succumb? Why is it that men are praised for their debauchery, but women who behave the same way are considered depraved?"

Blade stared at Leslie. Leslie returned his gaze, his mouth working. He finally got out a reply.

"Men are different."

"Men are unfair, as you are," Oriel snapped. "And now Nell's gone into hiding for fear of my wrath, and it's all your fault."

"I'll not remain here and listen to your silly complaints." Leslie stalked away to join his brothers.

Striking a chord on his lute to gain Oriel's attention, Blade scowled at her. "Where do you find these strange notions?"

"They're not strange."

He held up a hand to forestall another argument and spoke to her under the cover of the sound of his tuning.

"Never mind. I would speak with you about this journey to the lodge. I've heard the hunting lodge is over a league's distance away. By God, you try my temper. I'll not have you putting yourself in such danger."

"I've been to the lodge many, many times," Oriel whispered back fiercely.

"At night?"

"Well, mayhap not at night."

Blade placed the flat of his hand against the lute strings and spoke louder. "You're not to set foot out of this hall. I forbid it."

She scrambled upright, and to his surprise, poked him in the doublet with her finger. "Don't you order me about, Blade Fitzstephen. I'm not one of your pliable French harlots."

"Marry, I hope not, for a harlot might brave the roads at night. You, mistress, will not."

"I will do as I please." She lifted her chin and glared at him. "Faith, I like not this tyrannical manner of yours. I'll not be spoken to as if I were a slave."

"You're my betrothed lady. You owe me obedience and submission."

"I have a mind with which to think, my lord."

"According to the Bible, wives should be obedient to their husbands. I will be your lord, and you must obey me."

Furious, Oriel managed to kick him on the ankle surreptitiously.

"The Bible also says that maids should be chaste, but I haven't noticed you worrying about that particular admonition."

Faith tapped her fan on the arm of her chair. "Oriel, stop chattering and allow Blade to finish his work. We're all waiting."

As Blade returned to his tuning, Faith continued.

"By the rood, Oriel, we must put you to work quickly at learning the rightful tasks of a wife. You've spent far too much time in useless learning, and now you're ill fit to marry anyone, much less a lord with holdings in England and France. What was the name of your chateau, Blade?"

"Mirefleur."

"Ah, such a beautiful name. It's a pity Oriel won't be able to manage it as she should. Now, Joan would know what was needful, for I've taught her well."

Oriel tossed her head. "I can order a steward about just as well as Joan."

"And how will you know what orders to give?" Faith asked. "How will you know if he's performed his duties correctly or if he's cheating you?"

"I have studied mathematics."

"But you don't know the price of pepper," Faith said, "and you have no knowledge of the salting of meat or how to dry fruit or how to distill herbs and flowers for medicines. Why, I don't even think you know when pigs should be slaughtered."

"Oh."

Blade heard that small, desolate reply and glanced up from his lute. Oriel's cheeks were flushed, and she was staring at her hands, which were clasped in her lap.

"I'm sure Oriel can learn what she needs to know," he said. "As for me, I found myself enchanted by the jewel-like qualities of her mind and person. All the rest fades when compared to that."

Oriel looked up at him, eyes wide and startled. She bit her lip. "Aunt Faith speaks the truth. She tried to instruct me, but I would forget what she taught me as soon as I returned to my studies in Latin or French."

"Il n'importe, chère."

"But it is important," she said. "Mayhap I should study householding a bit."

"As you wish. At least it will keep you at home instead of wandering where you shouldn't."

He drowned her irate reply with a chord from his lute and began to sing. He entertained the family with a few songs, but found it hard to enjoy the music himself. He longed to resume his quarrel with Oriel, for now he had no idea what other foolhardy risks she was in the habit of taking. She defied him simply because he had ordered her to do something, whether the order was reasonable or not. A plague take her, he wouldn't suffer her churlish, willful disobedience. She needed curbing.

He glanced down at her, his ire fermenting as he remembered her defiance. She was watching his hands as they plied the lute, her gaze moving with each stroke. Blade smiled nastily and began a new song. As he sang, Faith began to frown, while Livia and Leslie chortled and clapped in time with the music.

> *When he and I got under sheet,*
> *I let him have his way complete,*
> *and now my girdle will not meet.*
> *Dear God, what shall I say of it?*
> *Ah dear God, I am forsaken*
> *Now my maidenhead is taken!*

When he finished, everyone except Faith and Oriel clapped and laughed. He rose and bowed to the group, then turned to offer his hand to Oriel. She was staring at nothing, her face drained of color. He had expected fury.

He bent low and took her hand. *"Chère?"*

She allowed him to help her rise, then went with him when he retrieved their goblets and guided her to a side table where flagons had been set out. She was silent while he poured. When he shoved a goblet into her hand, she wet her lips and whispered "I might be with child."

He choked on his wine.

"God save me, *chère,* I hope not," he said, after he had recovered. "I would spare you that heavy burden awhile. After all, we know so little of each other. Um, plenty of time for children later."

"I warrant you're right. Still, I'm glad we're to be

married soon. George says we should be married in four weeks' time."

"He does, does he?"

"You don't agree?" she asked.

"Oh, marry, I do. Four weeks. Yes, four weeks. Now, about the lodge. Perchance we shouldn't meet alone anymore. After all, we're betrothed and—"

"Don't you want to be with me?"

"Yes, too much. So much that I'm in constant pain from the wanting, but honor demands that we be circumspect."

"Damn honor." Oriel grinned at him. "Let us hence tonight to the lodge where I may assuage your pain."

"God's blood, I told you you're not to venture out of the hall at night."

"But—"

Blade glanced around to see if anyone was looking, then grabbed her arm and squeezed it. Fixing her with his most commanding stare, he said, "Oriel Richmond, if you try to stir from this hall at night, I'll strip you of your clothes and lock you in your room."

"You will not."

"*Sacré Dieu*, after what has passed between us, do you doubt it?"

"Foul toad."

She jerked her arm free and tried to leave him, but he snatched her arm back.

"Release me," she said. "I like not your arrogance, my lord. Mayhap I no longer wish to meet you at the lodge or anywhere else."

Knowing he'd won, he couldn't resist a taunt. "Don't spurn me, *chère*. You only tempt me to show you who's master."

She rounded on him, and he lost his smile when he saw her face.

"God's holy patience. Is this what I may expect? A man who seeks to master me as he does a wild horse? Indeed, I thank you for showing me your true nature before we married. Now I shall have to consider whether I want to be married at all. Afore God I do believe I'd rather remain a spinster than subject myself to your governance."

"Now, Oriel—"

"Good e'en to you, sirrah."

Chapter 15

Full of wiles, full of guile, at all times, in all ways,
Are the children of Men.

—*Aristophanes*

Oriel stalked into her bedchamber, her mind in a tempest. Beshrew the man, he was as autocratic and inflexible as her aunts. If only he hadn't addressed her as if she were his serf. He could have asked her not to travel at night by herself because he feared for her safety without playing the slave master.

She stopped in the middle of her chamber and found the new girl from the village, Meg, in attendance. "Nell still plays the mole?"

Meg bobbed a curtsy. "Yes, mistress."

Sighing, Oriel turned around so that Meg could remove the pins that held some of her wayward hair out of her face.

"She hasn't hidden this long since she was caught in

the stables with Lord Montague's heir. Ah well. Tomorrow I'll go to the village and search her out."

She relapsed into silent fuming. Why did men assume that women possessed no logic simply because they were constructed differently? Fie, she was quickly discovering that even an enticingly handsome man could be intolerable if he played the feudal master. She'd spent half her life prey to the hissing and bared fangs of two aunts. Now that she had a little freedom, she wasn't going to subject herself to the rule of a domineering overlord.

But if she were with child, then there would be no choice. She helped Meg pull a smock over her head and scrambled under the bed covers. Blade had too much power over her, for he'd made her forget her honor. She must resolve to govern her passions. Yet how could she when, even while he was at his commanding worst, the sight of him evoked an urge to slip her hands beneath his clothing and knead the muscles of his chest? It was a perplexity.

She wished Uncle Thomas were here, so she could confide in him and ask his advice. Instead, he was gone, leaving only a trail of hints and puzzles behind. Oak leaves. Uncle had been quite clever in hiding his secrets, for of all the family, only she had had the wits to follow the trail he'd left. Leslie could have done it, as well, had he the interest.

Uncle Thomas must have been concerned about the threat to Her Majesty from the great northern families. The Earl of Westmoreland and the Duke of Norfolk were Catholic. Most of the north was Catholic, yet loyal to Queen Elizabeth. No doubt Uncle Thomas had anticipated some attempt to depose Her Majesty on the grounds of illegitimacy, and had tried to do his part to prevent it.

She remembered Uncle Thomas telling her he admired Elizabeth. That was why he'd left his journal record. Elderly as he was, he'd taken the trouble to do his duty to the queen. Oriel called up the image of the shaky script in which the journal's last pages had been written. The writing had been legible, however, even at the end, where Uncle had placed the drawing of his oak leaf device. Under it had been one of Uncle's favorite sayings, *fronti nulla fides*—no reliance can be placed on appearance.

Oriel snuggled under the covers while Meg drew the hangings about the bed. Uncle Thomas had been the only person she could talk to until Blade. Blade, whose mind was as quick as his body was beautiful, and whose manner was as gentle as his nature was domineering. She drifted off to sleep with the resolution to confront her despot of a betrothed upon the morrow.

She had been dreaming of Blade's hands and long legs when oak leaves invaded her fancy. They began to fall upon her as she opened her body to Blade, and soon they were covered with them. Blade ignored them and continued to kiss her as he lay upon her, but one of the leaves landed on her nose, and she sneezed.

Oriel's eyes flew open. She sat up in bed and rubbed her nose. She was still enclosed in the draped four-poster, and she could hear Meg snoring on the thick pallet at the foot of the bed. Something had awakened her. She listened, but no other sound came to her ears except Meg's snorts. She remained sitting and thinking of her dream of lovemaking and oak leaves.

Oak leaves! The device at the end of the journal. God's holy apostles, Uncle Thomas had been clever again. She fished for her heavy dressing gown, wrapped herself in it, and found her slippers. Pushing aside the hangings, she slipped from the bed. Meg was still snoring when she left her chamber and went down to the second floor.

She flitted along the dark gallery, then stopped in a puddle of moonlight shining in from the tall windows that overlooked the courtyard. She listened, but there was only the sound of the night wind blowing against the windowpanes. She tiptoed over to the library door and went through it. Once inside, she went through the library, the passage, and the withdrawing chamber to the door to Blade's chamber. As she pushed it open, it creaked a bit, but not loudly.

The chamber was as dark as the library. The window was closed, as were the hangings on the bed. Clutching her gown against the cold, she went to the bed, grasped the edge of a hanging, and shoved it aside. Something grabbed her wrist and pulled. She cried out as she sailed off her feet and landed on the bed. A great weight landed on top of her, and something pricked the skin above her heart.

"Oriel?"

"Ouch!" She peered into the black shadow that lay upon her and spoke in that familiar, magical voice.

Another shadow loomed behind Blade. *"Mon seigneur?"*

"It's nothing, René. You may go."

The shadow vanished.

"You're hurting me," she said, and the pricking at her breast stopped.

"Sacré Dieu, woman, I almost killed you."

He was still lying on top of her, and she felt his hands running over her chest.

"That was a dagger I held to your heart, you witless little blight. What do you here?"

She was much warmer now that he was covering her. She nuzzled into his shoulder and found it bare. Curious, she searched his body with her hands. The rest of him was bare as well. She heard him suck in his breath as she rubbed his thighs.

"God's blood, stop that!"

He tore himself away and scrambled under the covers. He yanked her close by the wrist and snarled at her.

"What do you here? When we parted you were snapping at me like a deranged trout. Ouch!"

"Did I hit your nose?"

"Yes."

"Good. Keep a mannerly tongue in your head."

"Oriel, you're becoming a shrew."

"I am not. You're becoming a tyrant, and a rude one at that. Now listen to me. I've discovered something about Uncle Thomas's journal."

"Is that why you crept into my bed?"

"Yes."

"Oh."

He sounded disappointed, which made no sense to her, for her discovery was significant. "Uncle Thomas left another puzzle."

She described the oak leaf device and the saying at the end of the journal. "You remember it?"

"Yes, but writers often end their texts with such flourishes."

"Not Uncle Thomas, and besides, that oak leaf—I've seen it before."

"It's all over the library."

"But not placed in a rectangle, as in the journal."

"And?"

"And I know where we will find such an oak leaf. In the old lodge."

She heard a groan.

"Will this chasing about after puzzles never end?"

"I think this will be the last one," she said. "There are no more libraries or lodges or rooms decorated with oak leaves."

"I pray God you're right." Blade squeezed her hand. "Very well, my jewel, we will go to the old lodge upon the morrow. You go for your morning ride, and I shall slip away later to meet you. Marry, this last puzzle worries me. What could be of such import that your uncle wouldn't include it in his hidden journal?"

"I don't know, but Blade, whatever it is, mayhap he was killed on account of it instead of the journal."

She was drawn into his arms and squeezed until she couldn't breathe. "*Chère*, I fear for your safety. God's blood, I don't think I could bear it if you were harmed."

Snuggling close, she put her face against his neck. "So, this is why you play the tyrant. Fear has turned you into a master of slaves."

"I was being reasonable."

"A reasonable man explains himself instead of dictating as if he were Caesar." Shivering, yet anxious to argue the point, she began to climb beneath the covers.

"What are you doing?"

"I'm cold. If we're to continue our discussion, I need cover." She snuggled down into the pillows and scooted close to him.

He shoved his body away from her and rose on his elbows. "Get out."

"What's wrong?"

"I told you. It isn't meet that we should conceive a child until we're married."

"But Uncle Thomas told me that happens all the time, and besides, what about your other ladies? The ones in France and other places? You didn't worry about children then."

She heard him groan, but it was too dark to see his expression.

"God, I'm well repaid for my callousness."

"What mean you?"

She reached out and felt for his arm, but encountered his hip. She ran her hand down his thigh, and he grabbed it.

"*Sacré Dieu*, those other women knew how to—most of them were married, and the rest knew how—God defend me, I've never had such a conversation with a maid before."

Oriel was less and less interested in the ladies of Blade's past. His warmth called to her, and the low vibrancy of his voice made her skin tingle. She slid closer to him, knowing he couldn't retreat since his back was to the hangings already.

"*Chère*, don't. Go back to your room."

"Why?"

"I told you."

She put her free hand on his bare shoulder. "Then why did you make love to me in the first place?"

"Because I went right mad, and have suffered from lunacy ever since. Christ, don't touch me, I beg of you. I think I would prefer the rack to this torment. Oriel, I am trying to preserve your honor, and getting no help from you."

She had freed her hand from his grasp and was pressing her body close to his again. "Fie, I don't want honor. I want you."

She removed her gown, tossed it at him, and heard him wrestling with the cloth.

"What are you doing? Put this back on!"

"If you want me to go to my chamber, you must carry me there."

"I won't touch you."

Oriel slithered next to him, so that their bodies touched. His hands skimmed over her bare back.

"That," he said through clenched teeth, "was a mistake. Don't do this. I want you to leave me alone."

"Are you sure?"

Oriel was finding her mastery quite pleasing. To be the hunter had many advantages. Catching Blade unaware, she fastened her mouth on his neck. He jumped, caught her face in his hands, and shook it once.

"Damn you, can't you see I'm trying to protect you?"

Mayhap she had offended him with her forwardness. She bit her lip and whispered, "Have I disgusted you?"

"What?"

"I know I'm not as pretty as all those women who— all those women. Mayhap I'm one of those insatiable women the Church is always complaining about."

"You are not."

"But I must be, because when I touch you, even if I

don't touch you, I tingle in the oddest places, and now that I'm on top of you, my chest is heaving as if I'd run up a mountain. There must be something wrong with me that I'm so unchaste."

She heard a long, low groan, and without warning she was tossed off him and crushed under his weight. He put his lips to her ear.

"There is nothing wrong with you. You're passionate, and therefore a delight." He ran his lips across her cheek. "You drive me near to madness with your passion." His mouth slid over her skin, down her neck to her breast. "Oriel, tell me to stop. Please, tell me to stop."

Too awed by his words to speak any of her own, she answered him by moving so that her breast pressed against his lips. His lips fastened upon it. Her reward was that special tingling she'd grown to crave. As he tugged at her breast, his hands smoothed their way up her thighs. They pressed her legs apart, then drifted upward to caress her.

Made bold by her pleasure, Oriel imitated the movements of his hands. She traced the line of his thighs. Though she could feel her face grow hot, she grasped him. Blade threw back his head, inhaled sharply, and moved against her hand. At the same time he stroked her, driving her to the brink of her own madness. She gave a short gasp, sank her nails into his back, and bit his neck.

"Damn you," he said, and thrust into her.

She stopped breathing for a moment. He began to move with practiced ease, and she responded with her own hips. Together they climbed each pinnacle of sensation until she cried out, lifted her hips off the bed, and shuddered with her climax. He rammed into her, and they fell back to the bed as he took his own pleasure. Then they both sank into the covers, arms and legs tangled together and limp.

For a while she lay there panting, enjoying the feel

of his body on hers and him inside her. Her world had turned golden and blessed because of him. She kissed his hot cheek and he stirred, propping himself on his forearms to kiss her forehead. She touched his lips with the tip of her finger.

" 'For when I look on you a moment, then can I speak no more, but my tongue falls silent, and at once a delicate flame courses beneath my skin, and with my eyes I see nothing, and my ears hum, and a cold sweat bathes me, and a trembling seizes me all over. . . .' "

There was silence for a moment, then his head sank down and he rested his forehead against hers. "Oh, *chère,* I think I've lost the battle."

In a chateau on the Loire, floating in mist and encased in frost, lay a stair in a tower. At the top of that winding stair lay a polished mahogany door, and behind the door a room of Persian carpets, silken tapestries, and sweet incense. Before the arched and faceted window was set a carved table graced with a silver quill holder and ink pot, a golden drinking cup inlaid with amethysts and pearls, and the Cardinal of Lorraine, its owner.

His soft golden hair was combed and crowned by a black cap, and he wore riding dress instead of his cassock. In demeanor he looked and was almost a prince. Son and brother of a duke, he wielded the power of a prince with as ruthless a will as his opponent, the Queen Mother, Catherine de Medici.

At the moment he was engaged in exercising that power. He held a much-folded letter in his hand and read it by the light of a candelabra on the table. A man in traveling clothes waited, hat in hand, while the cardinal read and slapped his riding crop against his boot. Whimsical dark eyes lifted to glance at the messenger.

"So, Alain," the cardinal said. "The old man is dead, and his secrets remain hidden."

"Oui, mon cardinal."

"And my English intelligencer only now has been warned of the Sieur de Racine."

"*Oui, mon cardinal.*"

"I like it not, this delay." The cardinal touched the letter to the candle flame and held it while it burned. "Nor will I suffer being confounded by a young Anglo-French minstrel who seems to have cavorted freely about the court and played havoc with all our stratagems for years."

The cardinal turned and went to the window, where he looked out at the roofs of the chateau and the mist that curled and twisted on the ground below. His long, manicured fingers tapped a diamond-shaped pane.

"I think, Alain, that we must capture ourselves a nightingale, a nightingale too dangerous to be allowed to fly free and untamed." He turned to face the messenger. Examining the ebony handle of his riding crop, he continued. "You will return to my English confederate and communicate my wishes. I charge you with the governance of this matter, for the English lack the subtlety and refinement so necessary for successful treason."

Resembling a cadaver more than a man, Alain smiled. The grimace disfigured his already macabre appearance, giving his face the expression of a tortured soul in hell.

"And the Sieur de Racine, Your Eminence?"

"Ah, the Sieur de Racine."

The cardinal turned back to the window and unlatched it. He pushed it open with the tip of his riding crop and leaned against the casement as he gazed at the white-shrouded stonework below.

"An enticing problem. One needful of careful consideration as to the solution." The moments went by while the cardinal slapped the palm of his hand with the crop.

"Frenchmen," the cardinal said at last, "belong in France, Alain. Do you not agree?"

"Oui, mon cardinal."

"Even those whose blood has been tainted by the barbarian blood of the English."

"Oui, Your Eminence."

"Then you have your charge. I will expect your return anon, with the proof I require, Alain. With the proof I require."

Alain departed, and the cardinal lifted the heavy drinking cup to his lips. The discovery of the Sieur de Racine had rankled. He wasn't used to being bested. He prided himself on knowing everything of importance, on his guile and perception. This boy had outwitted him. He would pay for it, and in doing so, learn what it was to cross the path of the Cardinal of Lorraine.

Chapter
16

Nothing is secret, that shall not be made manifest.

—*Luke 8:17*

Oriel leaned over her mare's neck and slapped the reins against her withers. Plunging through the forest at a canter, she skirted trees and ducked overhanging branches until she broke free of the vegetation. Kicking her mount to a gallop, she hurtled across a meadow toward the old hunting lodge. It lay at the edge of the forest in the narrow meadow between the eastern hills and the trees. A small place, its red brick crawled with ivy, and its latticed and mullioned windows sparkled in the sunlight.

She galloped up to the entryway, reined in, and sent pebbles flying as the mare dug her hooves into the ground. Out of breath, she was dismounting as Blade came out to meet her. He caught her and lifted her to the ground. Taking the mare's reins, he walked with her around the back of the house while she took in great gulps of air.

Blade chuckled as he looked at her. "Why such haste? I would have waited."

"N—Nell." She wiped her forehead with her sleeve. "It's Nell. She fell in the well behind the house in the kitchen yard. She's dead, and all this time I thought she was hiding."

They had reached the stables where Blade's stallion was. He didn't reply as he removed the mare's saddle and began wiping the horse down.

"Poor Nell. She was a good woman."

Blade threw a blanket over the mare, put her in a stall, and shut the door. "Children fall down wells, *chère*, not grown women."

"Not so. Old Goody Alice fell in this very well not three years ago."

"An old woman." Blade took her arm and guided her back to the lodge. "I had just finished with my horse when you came. Are you sure no one will disturb us?"

"Yes. George and the others sometimes use the lodge for hunting, but they're to go to Norfolk for a boar hunt soon, so they won't come here. Mostly we use it for a retreat when Richmond Hall is sweetened in the spring."

They entered the lodge from the rear and passed through the kitchen and scullery. She led Blade to the front, to a room off the hall. Walking to the center of the chamber, she lifted both hands to indicate the oak paneling that lined all four walls.

"I told you. Oak leaves. And look."

She pointed to the lintel of the door. Upon it, flanked by two oak leaf devices set in rectangular frames, was inscribed the Latin saying they'd seen in Uncle Thomas's journal.

" '*Fronti nulla fides*'—no reliance can be placed on appearance. You see, Uncle Thomas used to live here when he was much younger, and this was his study. He took most of his books and papers away though."

Blade looked at the inscription, then paced to the windows that took up most of one wall. They formed part of the front face of the lodge. He looked out, sweeping the meadow with his gaze.

"Is aught wrong?" she asked.

"I like not this second death so near the first. You're sure no one knows where you are?"

"Yes. I stole away while everyone was still at table. The head groomsman wanted to send a man with me, but I had a fit of temper and frightened him." Blade was looking at her with a sadness she'd never seen in him.

"*Chère,* there is danger. Don't you see it?"

"Of course I see, but we must continue our search."

"You're not thinking. Someone close to you has been killed, and I fear for you. I'm leaving my man René with you while I'm gone to London."

Blade was still gazing out the window. She waited for him to continue, but he didn't. He pulled off his gloves and slapped them against his thigh. "Very well. Now that we've found these oak leaves of great import, what shall we do?"

"I suppose we must search."

She went to a group of chests that had been shoved into a corner and began opening them. Blade joined her, but the search only yielded old tradesmen's bills and accounts of expenditures from the time of Uncle Thomas's residence at the lodge. Sitting back on her heels, she dusted her hands while Blade closed the last chest and glanced about the room.

"Not a cupboard or a wardrobe," he said.

He went to the chimneypiece and ran his fingers along the foliate carving. She watched him, still crouched beside the chests, and tried to ignore the tiny sliver of suspicion that jabbed at her. Blade Fitzstephen seemed to know a great deal about searching someone else's possessions. She rubbed her chin and followed his movements as he left the fireplace and started tapping the oak leaf panels. Pausing, he looked over his shoulder at her.

"Get off your delicious bottom and help me."

"How haps it that—"

"Not now, *chère.*"

She sighed and joined him in examining the wall panels. She progressed with no results until she came to a long table set against the wall opposite the windows. Oriel grasped one end and shoved, pushing it away from the wall. Here, as elsewhere, the paneling was divided into rectangular insets bordered with carved oak leaves, and the floor was covered with plain tiles. She was tapping panels when one of the floor tiles caught her eye. Unlike the rest, it had a decoration in one of the corners, an iris. Her fingers paused in mid tap. An iris.

"Blade."

She beckoned to him, and he joined her. Pointing with the toe of her boot, she indicated the floor tile. The iris design was faintly etched.

"An iris," he said, meeting her gaze, "Meaning . . ."

"A message," she finished for him.

"Was this always here?"

"I know not."

"I don't think so," he said. "There is no dirt in the etching at all."

Blade stooped and pressed the tile, but nothing happened. He produced a dagger and stuck the tip in between the tile and its neighbor.

"Hold a moment," she said. She stepped on the tile with the toe of her boot and heard a click. Above, one of the wall panels swung open.

He stood and smiled at her. "I do so love your keen wit, Oriel Richmond."

She flushed at the praise and pushed the panel open. Within was a compartment the size of the panel, and there lay a single roll of parchment. Blade took it, and she closed the panel. The floor tile clicked back into place. She followed Blade to the window. He was holding the parchment to the light and examining the seal with its dangling ribbons.

"An ecclesiastical seal," he said.

"Should we wait?"

"Marry, *chère*, there's too much danger to wait."

He broke the seal and unrolled the paper. They read the text together. Her gaze traveled to the bottom of the page and took in the signature of Uncle Thomas, and of Henry Percy, Earl of Northumberland. It was Henry Percy's deathbed confession. In a fine Italianate script were set out the last words of the earl, in which he confessed that in the year 1523, he and Mistress Anne Boleyn had consummated their betrothal vows. He begged forgiveness from the Almighty and commended his soul to Christ. Three witnesses signed the document —Percy's chaplain, his steward, and Uncle Thomas. All of the men were dead.

"*Christ.*" Blade released the bottom of the parchment and it curled up.

Oriel found that her hands were cold, even in her gloves. She removed the gloves, and saw that her hands were shaking.

"No wonder Uncle Thomas hid it so well," she said.

"But how could he have kept this, knowing the danger?" Blade asked. "Why didn't he destroy it?"

"You must understand Uncle Thomas. He would never destroy anything so important to his friend, and as a scholar he would have valued the truth as well. Knowing him, I believe he kept the confession for the sake of history."

Blade rolled the parchment into a tight cylinder. Turning to her, he said, "Nevertheless, we must destroy this at once."

As he spoke, the chamber door crashed open.

"Don't do that if you value my cousin's life."

Leslie walked into the room followed by several

armed men. One held a bow with an arrow aimed at Oriel. Leslie came toward her, reached out and grabbed her arm. Blade moved, but the bowman pulled back on the arrow, and he subsided. Leslie hauled her to his side.

"What are you doing?" she asked.

"He's betraying his queen," Blade said.

Oriel looked up at Leslie. "You?"

"Yes, me. You see, coz, I'm tired of being treated like a beggar by my own brothers. Tired of being the useless extra brother, the one no one trusts with money, the one who gets nothing because he was born last. The reward for my service will be a barony, or perchance an earldom. And I will have made a queen." Leslie drew his dagger and pointed it at Oriel's stomach. "The paper, Fitzstephen."

Oriel felt as if she were in a dream. She could hardly credit what she was seeing. Blade held out the parchment, and one of the men took it. The man brought it to Leslie and held it open while his master glanced at it. Leslie smiled, then turned back to Blade.

"Take him."

"Leslie, stop this," Oriel said.

Two of the men approached, but Blade's hand went to his sword, and they stopped.

"Come, Fitzstephen. You have no choice." Leslie put the dagger to Oriel's throat.

"Leslie, you can't do this." She tried to twist in his arms, but he grabbed her hair and yanked her back so that her neck was exposed.

"I'm sorry, coz, but my need is great, and you're interfering."

Fighting tears of pain, Oriel went still as she felt the point of the dagger nick her skin.

"Don't," Blade said.

He held his arms away from his body. One of the men snatched his sword and dagger. Two more grabbed him and bound his hands behind his back. Once Blade was tied, Leslie released Oriel. She went to Blade and rounded on her cousin.

"Greedy traitorous whoreson."

Leslie clicked his tongue against the roof of his mouth. "Now coz, if you had been deprived as I, you would have done the same. Mayhap if Grandfather had left me a fortune as he did you, I wouldn't have had to kill Uncle Thomas."

Nausea clogged her throat. She looked to Blade, who met her gaze with that expression of sadness she had seen before.

"You guessed?" she asked.

"Yes, chère. After you said Nell drowned in the well. I think she found your dear cousin in Uncle Thomas's chambers, searching for the journal."

Leslie shrugged. "She threatened to tell you what I was doing if I didn't reward her. I was luring her with promises of a tumble in the stables when you interrupted us. But enough of this chatter."

"You killed Uncle Thomas!"

Oriel flung herself at Leslie, clawing at his eyes and kicking. Blade tried to go to her, but he was caught and held by two of the men. She heard him shouting, but so great was her rage that she continued to claw and kick at Leslie until another man dragged her off him. Leslie shoved her away and put the back of his hand to a long red slash on his cheek. Her captor held her by both arms so that she couldn't move.

"God's arse, coz, you're a tempest. No wonder Fitzstephen is as addled as a randy coxswain in a London brothel."

Oriel spat at him, but he dodged and laughed at her, tucking the confession into his doublet. "I do regret having to toss old Tom over the stair rail, but he wouldn't comply with my request that he tell me the truth about Anne Boleyn. He admitted he'd set down in writing what he knew, but he wouldn't hand over his journal. I tried one last time to convince him. I feigned a trip to drink and carouse and then returned after everyone was abed. The old fool wouldn't give me what I needed, and finally threatened to tell the family of my endeavors." Leslie threw out his hands and sighed. "What was I to do?"

"Kill an old man, naturally," said Blade.

"How astute of you to agree," Leslie said. He turned to one of his men. "Samuel, take them into the hills to Jack Midnight. Tell him to finish his work this time."

"I should have guessed," Blade said, and began to curse fluently.

"Leslie!" Trapped by the man who held her, Oriel was too furious and too heartsick to do more than shout.

Leslie turned to her. She saw regret flicker across his face and then vanish. "I wouldn't have had to embark upon these adventures if it hadn't been for you, coz. But you got the riches I should have had—Grandfather's and Uncle Thomas's. Do you know how I felt seeing all that wealth go to a mere woman?"

"I thought you were fond of me," she said. "I never meant you harm, and I would have shared if you had asked. Don't you care at all?"

Leslie came to her and patted her cheek. "Sorry, coz, but not enough to die a traitor's death for you. If it's of comfort, I'll name my first girl child after you."

Blade called out to him as he left. "Richmond."

Leslie turned and glanced at Blade.

"The queen would pay you far more for that document than will the Cardinal of Lorraine."

"So," Leslie said. "You know about His Eminence."

"She would pay you in gold, and mayhap reward you with an earldom."

Leslie laughed and bowed to Blade. "A good try, Fitzstephen, but I'm sure our queen would be far more likely to clap me in the Tower and lop my head off than reward me. God give you good rest." He waved at them merrily and vanished.

She shouted after him. "Leslie, you come back here."

Her answer was the slam of a door at the back of the lodge. The man holding her squeezed her in his arms, and she cried out. Blade tried to jump at him, but his captors held him fast.

"Here," Samuel growled. "None of that."

Blade jerked at the leather cords that bound his wrists. "If you harm her, I'll cut your heart out and feed it to the pigs."

One of his captors kicked him, and his leg folded. "Let's kill them now. Less trouble."

"You addlepated sod, he wanted them taken to Midnight so's they wouldn't be found on his land. They're supposed to be attacked by highwaymen."

"Wait," she said. "I'll pay you more than my cousin is. I have caskets full of jewels."

She couldn't understand why they all laughed.

"Don't bother," Blade said as he got to his feet again. "If they're Jack Midnight's men, no bribe will touch them."

"And how do you know so much about Midnight?" Samuel asked.

"Marry, sirrah, because when I was a youth I served him."

Samuel scoffed, and the other three men guffawed and began hauling Blade and Oriel out of the lodge.

"Served Jack Midnight," said Samuel as Blade was hauled past him. "That's a jolly tale, that is."

"Mayhap you've heard of me. I am called Blade."

The laughter stopped abruptly, and Oriel looked from one dirty face to the other. An uneasiness stole over their features, and Samuel appeared to examine Blade minutely.

"You're lying, you," Samuel said.

"I only thought to tell you so you won't kill us in the hills before we reach Midnight. He'd be—annoyed."

"Hold him," Samuel said, and Blade's captors tightened their grip on him.

Samuel ran his hands over Blade's body. He touched the sleeve of his doublet and stopped. Tearing at it, he withdrew a slim dagger. He found a knife strapped to the small of Blade's back, and one in each of his boots.

Oriel joined the others in staring at him. He smiled and shrugged.

"You would have searched me before you put me on a horse."

"Yes," Samuel said.

The complaining thief, who held Oriel, spoke up again. "Now can we kill them? You saw what he's like."

"Sod you, Johnny. If he's this Blade, Jack Midnight would roast us alive if we didn't bring him back. Get on with you."

Johnny released Oriel, only to grab her by the arm and drag her out of the lodge. She looked over her shoulder at Blade, who was being hauled out behind her. He'd said he'd once been a thief, but he'd never told her about it. The ruffian called Johnny yanked at her arm, and she stumbled, bumping into her own mare. She was plunked onto the horse while Blade was shoved onto his. He'd been blindfolded, and his hands retied in front of him so he could remain upright. Samuel took the reins of his horse, while Johnny controlled hers.

She wasn't bound or blindfolded. It seemed the highwaymen had a low opinion of her ability to thwart their designs. The two remaining thieves flanked Blade, confirming her suspicions. Samuel kicked his horse and set off, leading Blade. She and Johnny followed at the rear.

As they galloped toward the hills to the east, Oriel grabbed her horse's mane. Low clouds had rolled in while they were inside the lodge. They hugged the tops of the steep hills, heavy and blue-grey with rain. At the horizon they darkened almost to purple and obscured another line of hills. It was all she could do at first to keep herself on the mare, so fast did they ride. They climbed a spiny hillock and scrambled down the other side, skirting the lake and surrounding mires that lay below. Once Blade nearly toppled from his horse when the stallion stumbled on the rocky ground, but he was quick to clutch at his mount with his arms and legs.

She still wore her cloak, and she was grateful for it, for as the sun vanished beneath the clouds, wind whipped up and cut at her cheeks. Its bite woke her from the fog of confusion into which she'd sunk after Leslie had abandoned them. She must do something. Blade couldn't, and she realized he was trusting to his old affiliation with Midnight to save them. She wouldn't. It was beyond her imagining that she could trust the benevolence of a highwayman, especially one who consorted with Leslie.

Therefore she must try to escape, thus offering Blade a chance to elude his captors. She was a good rider. After all, what difference did it make if she died now or later, at the hands of Jack Midnight?

Assuring herself that Johnny was busy marking the way up a nearly vertical slope, she shifted in her saddle, bringing her leg more securely against her sidesaddle. Most probably she was going to break her neck.

She watched Johnny. Her mare had been climbing reluctantly behind. Suddenly the horse tossed her head as Johnny yanked too hard on the reins. Oriel lurched forward, grasped the leather straps in both hands, and yanked hard. As she pulled, Johnny's arm jerked, and he fell backward. His feet shot up and out of the stirrups, and he toppled to the ground with a yelp.

Oriel gathered the reins and tugged her mare's head to one side. The horse spun around. Before Samuel and the others could gather their wits, she had kicked her horse and started back down the hill at a run. She heard shouts, but didn't dare look back.

Clinging to her mare, she watched the jolting ground in front of her. The field below rose up, and she and her horse landed on it with a jar. Once on level ground, she risked a look behind her in time to see Blade's leg shoot out and jab Samuel in the stomach. Johnny and another of the thieves scrambled down the hill toward her.

She kicked her horse and was soon galloping down the dale, swiping at the mare's flanks with her reins. A gully loomed ahead. She felt the mare gather her strength. Forelegs lifted as haunches sprang, and together they sailed over the obstacle. She rounded the base of another hill, and came up against the steep side of a line of hills.

Behind her she could hear the rumble of hooves. With no choice, she began to climb the hill. If she could reach the razorlike top, she might be able to scramble down the other side ahead of her pursuers. Again she clung to her mare, but this time, the horse stumbled and balked. She wasted precious moments calming the horse, and by the time she reached the summit, Johnny was close behind.

She heard him cursing, and turned to see him reach out for her. She sliced at his face with her reins. He screamed, covering his eyes. She was over the hilltop as the second man passed Johnny. She careened down the slope, heedless of the dark and glassy mountain lake at its base.

A hand clamped onto her arm. She bent and fastened her teeth on it. The man yelped and shook her off, only to grab her reins. The mare swerved, then whinnied and reared, and Oriel sailed backward into the air.

She slammed into the ground on her back, and her head banged against a tuft of grass. The air rushed out of her body. Stunned, she lay helpless as Johnny galloped up and sprang down from his horse.

"Bleeding highborn bitch."

Head swimming, barely able to hear, she felt

Johnny's hands fasten on the neck of her gown. He began to shake her like a wet puppy, and her head wobbled. Without warning the world filled with loud indistinguishable noises. When Johnny dropped her she collapsed, closing her eyes to block the sight of spinning ground and blurred figures.

Moments later she heard the singing of steel sliding against steel. A man screamed. She tried to lift herself up on her elbows, but she only succeeded in raising her head. Two legs straddled her.

Her blurred glance took in soft leather boots and long, muscled legs encased in black hose. A sword whirled and made an arc in the air. She heard a chime as sword clashed with sword. Someone grunted. The legs flexed, and the body above her bent forward and shoved at another man. There was a thud. She watched a bloody sword withdraw from the body of the man, then drop to the ground. The legs straddling her vanished.

She tried to turn over and get to her feet, but the effort was beyond her. Suddenly, strong arms surrounded her. She felt her body being lifted gently. She was propped against a muscled thigh.

"*Chère?*"

"Oh, good." She licked her lips and opened her eyes to peer into dark grey eyes. "I feared you might be Johnny."

"Are you well? Can you move your arms and legs?"

"Did you kill them?"

"Answer me, damn your interfering little self."

She wriggled her feet and moved her arms. "Everything seems to be attached." She groaned and sat up with his help. "My head."

"You're fortunate not to have broken your neck."

She was swept up into the air and hugged to Blade's chest. She squealed in protest, having had enough of sailing through the air. He lowered her feet to the ground, but kept her in his arms. She clutched at his doublet and tried to meld herself to his body. Wrapping his arms tighter around her, he lowered his mouth to hers. He seemed determined to devour her, sucking and probing with his tongue until she mumbled against his lips. When he lifted his mouth, she gasped for air.

At last she opened her eyes, and met his gaze. She caught her breath, and a tremor of apprehension went through her. She had never seen him more furious. He looked at her as if she were a stranger. His eyes held the chill of a sword thrust into snow. He released her and let his gaze travel the length of her body.

"By God, mistress, instead of kissing, you deserve a good whipping. You take too much upon yourself. You should have trusted to my judgment and waited for me to give you deliverance. Did you not understand that I know Jack Midnight?"

This was her reward for saving them. Oriel's fear burned away in the flames of her anger.

"You, sirrah, may trust murdering highwaymen, but I do not." She planted her fists on her hips. "I have no time to assuage your bruised pride, or have you forgotten that every moment sends Leslie farther and farther away."

She almost smiled when he cursed and stalked to his waiting stallion. Now she must fix her determination on preventing him from leaving her behind when he chased after Leslie. No doubt he would object to her accompanying him, but after all, Leslie was dangerous, and she wasn't going to let him go alone. He'd killed four men just now, but that didn't mean he wouldn't need her later.

Chapter
17

Hell hath no limits, nor is circumscribed
In one self place, but where we are is hell,
And where hell is, there must we ever be.

—*Christopher Marlowe*

Blade stalked up and down in front of the fire-place in Uncle Thomas's study at the old lodge. He stopped as he passed Oriel, who was sitting in a chair, rolling her shoulders and wincing.

"You're not coming," he said.

"I am."

Muttering, he busied himself retying the strap to his scabbard. "I just killed four men. Don't you understand that? I'll not expose you to greater peril. It's well after noon, and I'll be riding at night. I'm losing light by arguing with you, and if I'm wrong and he's not gone to London, my losing him will be your fault."

"He's gone to London. Leslie always goes to London, and you said he would most likely take the confession to the French ambassador."

He lost patience. Bending over her, he grasped her by the shoulders and growled at her. "God's blood, woman. You're not coming. You're going back to Richmond Hall where you'll be safe."

"I will not, and if you try to leave me behind, remember that I know all the byways and short paths. I'll catch up."

She glared at him, and her chin went up. Even as he felt his anger grow, he couldn't help admiring her courage. He released her and walked to the windows to look out at the forest in the distance. She knew little of the world beyond her books and Richmond Hall, but she was prepared to risk her life in a misguided attempt to protect him. He couldn't let her. He had never known such fear as when he'd seen her break from her captor and hurtle down that steep hillside. His fear had bestowed upon him the swiftness of a merlin, and he'd dispatched Samuel with his own blade.

After skewering the second man, he'd raced after Oriel. He'd had to kill the third man to get to the man called Johnny in time to stop him from ramming his fist into Oriel's face, a blow that could have killed her. When he thought of her death, his body went cold. No matter the cost, he would prevent her from casting herself into further danger. It was time for the truth.

He would tell her the truth, and she would hate him, but she would be safe.

He put his forehead to a cold pane and raised his voice. "*Chère*, I've a thing to tell you."

"Make haste, for we must go to the Hall for fresh horses for our journey."

The bitterness of his laughter was apparent even to himself. "You're not going, *chère*, and to assure myself that you won't, I'm going to tell you the truth." He turned, but kept well away from her, for she was looking at him with those wide, innocent eyes the color of new spring leaves. "Do you remember the proverb that says the bread of deceit is sweet to a man, but afterward his mouth is filled with gravel?"

"Say you that you've deceived me?"

He nodded and summoned all his skill at pretense to disguise his pain. He drew his gloves from his belt, slapped them against his palm, and allowed a mocking smile to grace his lips.

"Forgive me, *chère,* but I came to Richmond Hall this second time for a secret purpose. You see, you were right to suspect me when you found me drugging your cousin. I came in the service of the queen, to search out your uncle's secret knowledge about Her Majesty's legitimacy."

"You came in the service of the queen." She said it as if learning a lesson from a tutor and then stared at him.

"I was best suited for the task, as I could justify my presence by courting you. I beg pardon, *chère,* but it is my calling, you might say."

She rose, then sat down again and twisted her hands in her lap. "Mean you that you never . . . You're an intelligencer, a spy. You pretended to—to woo me so that you might find Uncle's journal and expose Leslie."

When she lapsed into silence, he found that he couldn't go on. Perchance what he'd said would be enough. She sat in that chair looking small and broken, and he closed his eyes to stop himself from going to her.

"I don't believe you."

She rose and came toward him. She looked up into his eyes.

"The way you touched me, the words you spoke to me . . . That can't be a lie."

"Marry, a man says many things to the woman he wants. Your innocence has deceived you." He held up a hand when she would have spoken. "Don't, *chère.* You don't know me."

Her lips trembled and she clasped her hands in front of her body. "You must say it. You must say you don't love me. That all your words and the proof of your body, all these were lies. Perhaps then I might believe you."

"*Sacré Dieu,*" Blade said, raking a hand through his hair. "Very well. Even if I loved you I wouldn't marry you, for I will never marry at all. You see, *chère,* my past lives within me, and with it a rage so boundless that it would destroy the woman I love. My father is a monster, and I am his son. His blood taints mine. It flows through my body, and with it flows a ravening desire to destroy, to hurt, to kill. My only salvation is to avoid being with my father, and never, never to take a wife. I've done many a deceitful and foul thing, but that I will not do."

"Even if you loved me."

He laughed bitterly.

"Do you know how many young and foolish girls have yielded to me? Please, I do not wish to shame you with the telling of it."

At last she released him from that wide-eyed stare. Turning her back on him, she said, "It is good of you to spare me. I release you from your vows. No doubt you're well versed in wriggling free of such encumbrances. I do not wish to see you again in this life, Sieur de Racine."

He felt the blood drain from his face. Walking to the door, he spoke without looking at her.

"We will return to the Hall at once."

"Get out, my lord. I know well enough where I belong, and it isn't with you."

"Very well. I will send an escort for your safety."

In all his life he'd never done a more difficult thing than walk out of the lodge and get on his horse. Forcing his thoughts away from Oriel, he rode back to the Hall and stormed into his chamber, shouting for René.

"Send grooms to the hunting lodge to escort Mistress Oriel home," he said as he grabbed a saddlebag from a chest. "Leslie Richmond is the traitor, and he's fled."

"Then I may come with you since he's quit the Hall?" René asked.

Blade paused as he stuffed clothing into the saddlebag. "After what has passed between us, I doubt she'd have you about her. We'll leave two men here with her anyway. After you've spoken to the grooms, tell the men and get me a fresh horse."

George burst into the chamber while he was fastening the saddlebag.

"Where have you been, Fitzstephen, and where is my cousin?"

"Oriel will be home soon. She's been riding."

"And where are you going?"

Blade threw the saddlebag over his shoulder and a cloak over his arm. "To London. There's no time for chatter, Richmond. Oriel will explain."

Outside, Blade found René and his men waiting. His roan had been unsaddled and René was leading him. Blade jumped onto a long-legged gelding and set off with René close behind. He took the road to London, raking the snow-soaked ground for traces of Leslie.

He'd been riding south for less than half an hour when a rider came toward him around a bend in the road. They both slowed to a trot and stopped several yards apart. René and the others stopped behind him. Blade inspected the stranger, noting the golden hair, heavy, mink-lined cloak, and Thoroughbred mount. It was the eyes that led him to guess the identity of the rider, for they were the color of gentians touched with frost.

"Derry."

The golden head inclined. "Blade."

"I've no time to ask why you're still about. Have you seen Leslie Richmond?"

"Who?"

"That foul-tempered viper who tried to kick your

face in. He murdered Thomas Richmond and tried to kill Oriel and me."

"So, it's Leslie Richmond. Yes, I saw him galloping south not two hours ago."

Blade nudged his mount closer to Derry and grasped his arm. "We're well met, my friend. Since you so desire to guard someone, go you to Richmond Hall on some pretext. Guard Oriel for me. She won't accept protection from me, but she knows about her cousin, and about me, and insists upon meddling in this business. Keep her safe."

Releasing Derry, he kicked his horse. Derry reined in his own mount as Blade and his men galloped past.

"Wait!"

"No time," Blade called as he raced down the road. "Take care of Oriel Richmond."

Derry shouted after him, "It will be my delight."

Blade rode across England as if the hound of hell nipped at his heels. He left one man behind due to a fall from his horse, and lost another to the chill from night air. By the time he rode into London, he could barely keep himself in the saddle. He went straight to the tavern on the south bank of the river called the Bald Pelican.

Leaving René and his men to tend to the horses and themselves at a stable nearby, he went into the tavern, which was known to every cutpurse and bawd in London. Close and dark, brimming with vagabonds and harlots, the Bald Pelican was owned by Marvelous Mag, and at one time Christian de Rivers had owned Mag. Blade shoved his way through gamblers and foolish young sots on his way to the stairs at the back of the tavern. He might just make it to his usual room before weariness caused him to drop to the ale-slick floor.

As he mounted the stairs, Marvelous Mag herself came out on the landing, her blond hair tousled, her bare breasts swaying. Blinking up at her, Blade smiled and brushed the hood of his cloak from his head. Mag's painted face lit with amusement. She put her hands on her hips and leered at him, which brought out the lines at the corners of her eyes and mouth.

"Come home at last to Mag, lovely?"

Blade dragged himself up to the top step and kissed Mag's hand.

"Ooooo," she said, "aren't we gallant this night. Come, lovely, I'll reward you for your gallantry."

Blade shook his head, but Mag grabbed his hand. She dragged him down the landing, turned a corner, and thrust him into a chamber. He was flat on a bed before he could open his mouth. Mag's lips fastened on his mouth. He pushed her back.

"Please, Mag, I've traveled from the north country with little rest and no sleep."

Mag took his hand and patted it. "You're that worn, you are. And pale, too. You need rest, lovely."

"First, I've a chore for you."

"You're not up to it."

"Mag!" He hadn't meant to snap, but his weariness wrought havoc with his temper. "I'm looking for a man. A young man not two and twenty. Auburn hair, tall, fond of gambling, swilling, and carousing. Fair of face and fond of murdering. His name is Leslie Richmond."

"Never heard of him, lovely, but if you want him, I'll give him to you."

"My thanks, Mag. Set every bawd and cutpurse in your pay to hunting for him, and I'll give you a purse of gold."

"And a more pleasureful reward, as well, if you want him quick."

"I'll do whatever you want, only find him for me, Mag. I can't tell you how important it is."

"You don't have to, lovely. He must be near to God in importance if you almost kill yourself chasing him."

"Find him, Mag."

He felt her hands pressing him back down on the

bed. His boots were being pulled off, and he couldn't seem to keep his eyes open.

"Rest now, lovely. Mag will find your quarry for you. Rest you well and safe."

He woke from a black death of sleep a day later to find Mag at his side gently shaking him. Another girl as bare-breasted as her mistress stood behind her with a tray of food. He smiled at Mag, then bolted upright.

"Have you found him?"

"Easy, my lovely. Not yet, but soon."

Blade looked down at himself and found that she'd removed his clothes. He shoved the covers back.

"I must search for him."

Mag pushed him back down on the bed and threw the sheets over him. "Rot. If you don't eat, you won't make it down the stairs. René said you refused to eat all the way south. I'm not having that. I want you fit and ready to reward me for giving you this Richmond fellow."

"I'm not hungry."

Mag plumped herself down on the bed and took the tray from the girl, who left them alone. Mag placed the tray on his lap, and Blade sighed. She tore a piece of bread and stuck it in his mouth.

"Chew," she said.

He chewed. As soon as he swallowed, she shoved a cup of ale to his lips. Mutton and cheese followed, alternating with ale and bread. Finally he turned his head away, and she put the cup down on the tray. Popping a candied apple slice in his mouth, she surveyed him from head to foot.

"Now, are you going to tell me who she is?"

He choked on a piece of apple. Clearing his throat, he took a sip of ale.

"Who?" he asked.

"Listen, my pretty stallion with eyes like a thundercloud, you may not have Christian de Rivers's evil tongue, but you abjure food as he did when he ran afoul of Mistress Nora. I've seen you twist women into knots with a smile. I've seen you beguile and lure and enchant as if the devil gave you dominion over everyone in skirts. I know what you are, and why you spend so much time in France. And I've also seen you ply sword and dagger so swiftly I couldn't mark their paths. I've never seen you so sick of heart as to refuse nourishment."

"Your tongue clatters like a windblown shutter, woman."

"Then I'm wrong?"

"Yes."

"Prove it," Mag said, and took the tray from him.

She set it on the floor, then bent over him. Bracing her arms on either side of his body, she lowered her head to kiss him. He remained still, allowing her to do as she wished, for as her lips moved on his, he felt a surge of unhappiness, and a desolation so great it threatened to pitch him into a black and endless abyss.

When Mag ended the kiss she pulled away to peer into his eyes.

"Who is she, lovely, that her loss has brought you such sorrow?"

"Leave off, Mag," he replied harshly.

"Ah well, you're young, and if I were this girl, I wouldn't allow you to gad about London on your own for long. So, you want to know where this Richmond man is?"

"You know!" Blade grabbed her and shook her until her head bounced.

"Stop, you damned harlot's cub."

"Where is he?" Blade released her, leaped out of bed, and began donning his clothes.

"In a town house on the north bank near the Strand. One of them French conies owns it, but he's not there. He's an auburn-haired swaggerer, right?"

"Yes."

"Well, he sent for five expensive bawds from Goody

Jen's house last night and rode them all. Paid in good coin, too. That kind of patron gets talked about."

Mag picked up the cup of ale and took a drink. "No need to hurry, my lovely. Your cony is waiting for someone, sure as straw burns. He's burrowed into that deserted house and he peers out the windows on the hour. He's got two men with him on guard, and they chase away tradesmen and cutpurses alike."

Blade was relieved to hear it. It seemed he was in time. Stuffing his shirt into his hose and pulling on his boots, he said, "There's no reason to tarry either. Have someone show me where Leslie Richmond is. At once."

Chapter 18

The joy of love is too short,
and the sorrow thereof, and what
cometh thereof, dureth over long.

—*Sir Thomas Malory*

The sun was touching the tops of the leafless trees by the time Oriel emerged from the forest and pulled her mare up so that she could stare at the gates to Richmond Hall. She had sent on ahead the men Blade had provided as escort. She felt as empty as a beggar's cup in a famine. Even her shame had faded, the shame that had assaulted her after her first anguish. Now she mused with blessed numbness at her guilelessness and credulity. What a marvel she must have appeared, priding herself upon Blade Fitzstephen's wooing.

How witless of her to have expected a man of such beguiling charm to have given his heart to her. Her, with her dried pea eyes, frazzled locks, and head stuffed with useless learning. She nudged her horse into motion again and thanked God for the numbness that had come over her after an afternoon of near-hysterical weeping in the deserted lodge.

She must take care to conceal what had passed this day. Should her aunts discover her rejection, they would chastise her endlessly for her failure. She didn't need a pack of aunts nipping at her heels.

Upon her arrival at Richmond Hall she discovered that a visitor had made an appearance and she was expected in the great chamber. George met her in the gallery.

"Where have you been?" he asked. "I've had men searching for you for hours."

"I went riding and got lost."

"Lost? You? Mother is furious, and we've a guest." George puffed up, roosterlike, and forgot her bad manners. "The son of Viscount Moorefield has arrived with an invitation from the queen for me to come to court and consult with Her Majesty's ministers on border affairs."

George began herding her toward the great chamber. "Try to behave with courtesy and maidenliness, Oriel. Lord Derry is a friend of your betrothed, and has the favor of the queen."

She was propelled into the chamber, where she curtsied before someone who, to her disinterested eye, appeared to be a tall mountain of leather, gold braid, and flaxen hair. Around her rose the baying and howling of aunts and cousins, to which she paid little heed. After a few minutes, she excused herself and fled the great chamber. Wearily she set foot on the bottom stair of the flight that would take her to her own chamber when a sudden thought came to her.

As devious and unprincipled as Leslie had proved, it would be well to search his rooms. There was no imagining what other foul designs and plots he'd hatched. How many others were in danger because of him? Mis-

erable as she was, she couldn't neglect her duty, which
was to stop him from hurting anyone else. After all, that
beautiful fiend Blade wouldn't have had time or the opportunity to search for tokens of Leslie's disloyalty before he raced off after his quarry.

Having something to do pushed her agony away
somewhat, so she directed her steps to the opposite
wing of the house, where Leslie and his brothers
dwelled. Leslie's chamber was a small one, and as usual
festooned with discarded possessions and clothing. His
prized possession lay to the left of the entry, a giant
four-poster bed. The posters were thick, carved columns, each ending in a tall, rectangular base. The hangings were of midnight blue brocade. He'd won them at
the throw of a pair of dice in London. Another win at
gambling had brought him the tapestries that hung on
the walls.

As she looked around the room, her sorrow at Leslie's betrayal returned fullfold. Her love for him had
been destroyed by his murder of Uncle Thomas, his
deceit, and by his casual forfeiture of her own life, yet
some tiny measure of feeling for him remained, foolish
as it was. Blade was going to hunt him down, and now
she realized that she wanted to be there when Leslie was
captured, for Uncle Thomas's sake.

She would search Leslie's room, and if she found
anything, she would take it with her to London.
Though he'd done murder, she would stand by him, for
in the end, he would die condemned as a traitor. And
that was another reason for finding him, because traitors' deaths were hellish. They were hanged, then cut
down while they lived, and their entrails cut out before
their eyes and burned. Her thoughts veered away from
more details.

Oriel stepped into the room and over a pile of discarded doublets and cloaks. Leslie had packed and left
hurriedly. This sudden departure would have been no

surprise to the family. They were accustomed to Leslie's cavorting from Richmond Hall to London and back.

Slowly she turned in a circle in the middle of the room and tried to imagine where Leslie might secret any treasonous documents. At least she'd learned a few useful skills from Blade. Wincing at the thought of him, she went to the fireplace and pushed on the decorative molding of the chimneypiece with no results. She opened the chest at the foot of the bed, but it held only a spare sword and other weapons. A cabinet was stuffed with ruffs, hose, codpieces, kerchiefs, and the like. She peered into caskets and even tested the floorboards. She was stomping on the last of them when a stranger entered the room. She paused, her foot raised in the air, and stared at him.

"Who are you?"

"By my faith, Mistress Oriel, you slay my heart."

"Oh, you're the guest."

The young man bowed. "At last you remember."

"Your name?"

He covered his heart with his hands and sighed. "Alas, she does not remember, though it was but a short time ago. I am Derry."

"Hmm." She stomped on the last floorboard and scowled at it.

"A dance, mistress?"

"No doubt you've lost your way, my lord. I'll call a servant."

He was at her side swiftly. "Don't call anyone, mistress, for I've come at the request of your lord to protect you."

"My lord? My lord? I have no lord."

"Blade Fitzstephen."

"I have no lord. Go away." She went to the wall opposite the bed and began rapping her knuckles on the wood paneling.

He followed her, matching his steps with hers and

knocking on the wood above her head. "Does this noise drive away evil spirits?"

"Go away."

He bent and whispered in her ear. "I know about your cousin. Blade sent me to help you."

"God's patience!" She sidled away from Derry, glaring at him. "I'll have naught to do with him or any of his friends." She clamped her mouth shut when she realized she was shouting.

He stopped tapping on the panels and stared at her. "Ah. So the notorious Blade has made an enemy of a woman, for once. You find me amazed, but please, mistress, rail not at me, for I know your lord only slightly."

"I told you he's no lord of mine."

"Forgive me. We'll not speak of him at all, if you desire, but I have come to do what you appear to be doing now—to search among the possessions of Leslie Richmond for anything that will help us foil this vile plot against our queen."

"And how do I know you're trustworthy?"

He cast a reproving glance at her. "Mistress Oriel, the queen has given me her favor. She has even given me one of the royal manors as a reward for certain services I've performed for her. I've no desire to see the Queen of Scots take the place of a sovereign so generous and wise enough to appreciate my remarkable self."

In spite of her own sorrow, she had to smile. He spoke jeeringly of himself, and with great affection of the queen. She offered her hand, and he kissed it.

"I've searched everywhere and can find nothing," she said.

"The chimneypiece, the walls behind the tapestries, the cushions?"

As he went through his list, she nodded at each item.

"Under and on top of the bed and in the bolster and mattress?"

"Yes."

"The posters?"

"What mean you?" she asked.

He went to the foot of the bed. The base of the massive posts that supported the hangings was carved and thicker than her torso. He knelt and banged on it. Unsatisfied, he moved to the opposite post and knocked on it. A hollow rapping sound resulted.

After much pushing and tapping on the carving of the post, he finally hit a raised portion of the relief that pushed inward with a click, and a small door jarred open. Inside lay a wooden casket. Derry brought it out and held it while she threw back the lid.

Inside lay a pile of buttons. Frowning, they each picked up one. Buttons were commonly transferred from one costume to another, which was why everyone kept boxes and caskets of them.

"Why put his buttons in a place of such concealment?" she asked.

Derry shook his head. He sank to his knees and emptied the contents of the box on the floor. Oriel knelt beside him and helped sort the buttons. There were some of silk, others of velvet, and still others of pearl and gold. There were a few aglets and gold clasps for doublets and cloaks, and five ornate gold buttons larger than all the rest. They were so large they were almost brooches. Of red gold, their bases were octagonal and supported intricately filigreed gold tops in the form of curling serpents.

She picked up one of these. It was heavy and the top seemed to be loose. Twisting the top, she found that it slid back to reveal a hollow. Derry dropped the pearl he'd been inspecting as a tightly rolled piece of paper fell from the button.

They stared at it in silence as she picked it up and unrolled it. At the top was a drawing of a griffin. There was writing on the paper, but it was gibberish.

"I know Latin, Greek, French, and Italian, and this is none of them," she said.

"It's a cipher, mistress."

She glanced up at him to find he was staring at her with eyes of brilliant gentian blue. "Can you read it?" she asked.

He shook his head. "Such work needs an artist in the craft."

He began to open the other octagonal buttons. Each held a roll of paper similar to the first.

"Each bears a drawing at the top," Oriel said. "These are mythical creatures used in armorial bearings. Look, a unicorn, and a griffin, but what may this be?"

She pointed to a black, leopardlike creature.

"That is an ounce, according to heraldry," Derry said, "and this is the wyvern—a two-legged, winged dragon—and this merman blowing a shell trumpet is called a triton."

"A unicorn, a griffin, an ounce, a wyvern, and a triton," she said. "Think you these symbolize the persons for whom the messages are intended?"

"You would make a good intelligencer, mistress. The difficulty lies in the identity of each. The meaning behind the symbol will not be one easily surmised by anyone."

Oriel began rolling up the papers and restoring them to their compartments in the gold buttons. "I must take these when I go to London."

"God's breath, mistress, you can't go."

"Why not?"

"I will take the ciphers to London."

Spilling the buttons back into their container, she said, "And me as well."

"I cannot. You're a lady, and I can't endanger you."

"Then I'll go myself."

"No, mistress, I shall tell your Aunt Livia to keep you here."

She clutched the box in her lap and gave him an unsmiling stare. "Then I shall tell my cousin George everything, and you'll have the entire family at your heels, including my dragon aunts."

"I think I need a physic," Derry said on a groan.

"Content you, my lord. All I wish to do is seek out my cousin. No doubt by the time we reach the city he'll be captured. I would plead with the queen for leniency so that he is put to death mercifully. What ails you, my lord?"

Derry had helped her rise and had lowered his bright gaze to the floor. He sighed and looked at her.

"Lady, I fear you don't know Fitzstephen's reputation. If your cousin resists, he's not likely to live through a minute's swordplay with him. That's why he's called Blade."

"Then I will bring the body home." She headed out of the room, but hesitated as she passed Derry. "I have a duty to my family, such as they are, and to Uncle Thomas, who gave his life protecting his secrets."

A little over a week later Oriel was in London. With Derry's help, she had stolen away from Richmond Hall before dawn the morning after Leslie had tried to kill her and she had learned the truth about Blade. On the journey, to her relief, she discovered she wasn't with child. To carry one without Blade at her side was something she could not imagine.

Once in London, she insisted that they ride immediately to Blade's town house near the Strand, taking an escort of Derry's liveried men with them. The thought of seeing Blade again made Oriel's stomach curdle, but she'd be damned if she would allow him to think her so destroyed by his charms that she couldn't face him.

Blade wasn't at home. The steward, intimidated by Derry's aristocratic bearing and his claim of an invitation from Blade, allowed them inside. The man reported that his master was indeed in the city, but he knew not where. Blade had sent for clothing through his man René, but hadn't appeared himself. Establishing Oriel in a guest chamber, Derry sent messages by several of his own men and retired to bathe and change his clothing.

She was downstairs in a small dining chamber, picking at an assortment of dried fish and breads and staring at the button box, when Derry joined her.

"I've sent men to William Cecil's house and to several ordinaries and taverns," he said. "We should find him quickly."

She shoved her plate away, left the table, and dropped into a chair where she wouldn't smell the fish. Rubbing her fingers over the smooth wood of the box in her hands, she pursed her lips.

"He hurt you badly," Derry said.

"What folly."

"God's breath, Oriel, you're turning into a shade. You're shrinking before my eyes, and your hands are shaking."

She looked at her hands, then hid them under her skirt.

"Come," he said. "We've grown to be friends. You even remember my name now. I beseech you to allow me to give comfort."

"There's nothing you can say that will comfort me. He cozened me, and I was a lackwitted arse, and I hate him, and I wish I could wipe his memory from my mind. If I thought it would help, I'd blind myself so that I wouldn't have to see him again. But then, I would also have to make myself deaf, for even now I still hear his voice, his sparkling, brilliant voice. Oh, God. Look what you've done." She dashed a tear from her cheek and squeezed her eyes shut to stop others from falling.

They were quiet for a while. She stared at her box, while he rested his hip on the dining table and poked holes in a fish with an eating knife.

"I don't understand," he said.

"What?"

"This man who cares so little for you that he spurns you callously . . . this same man sent me to protect you from harm. He risked his life to save you when he could have done nothing. He knew Jack Midnight wouldn't harm him, yet he fought those thieves to save you."

"Out of duty, no doubt."

"All I know is that the last time I saw him, he looked at me with the same torment in his eyes that I see in yours, and I cannot believe that anguish was on account of Leslie Richmond."

"You make no sense," she said. "You're trying to say that he—he loves me. Why then, my lord, would he hurt me so grievously?"

Derry stuck his knife in the roasted fish. "I know not. I know only that he was in hell. If you care to, you could discover for yourself why he would cast you aside when it so obviously cost him his very soul."

"What is this talk of souls?"

Oriel jumped, and the button box fell to the floor. Derry turned and smiled at Blade.

"Well met, Fitzstephen. We've brought you a present."

She bent to retrieve the box, thus giving herself a few moments to recover from the way her heart froze in her breast at his sudden appearance. He walked into the chamber, his eyes a flat metal grey.

"Give me a reason not to kill you for bringing her near to danger," Blade said to Derry.

"She threatened to bring her whole family down on us, including those aunts."

He turned to her, and she took refuge in her chair again.

"Why?" he asked.

She worked her mouth, but no sound came out. Instead, she shoved the box at him. He opened it and inspected the buttons, then lifted a questioning gaze to her. She took one of the buttons and opened it to reveal the cipher. In silence he picked up the roll of paper and examined it.

"Another puzzle of your uncle's?"

"They're Leslie's," she said.

"I have a clerk who can decipher these."

He replaced the paper and held the button out to her.

She plucked it from his hand, taking care not to touch him. "I—I wish to be there when Leslie is taken."

"That is not possible," he said.

Derry shrugged. "I told you."

Unsmiling, she went on. "He's my cousin."

"He's a murdering traitor," Blade said, "and I'll not have you near him."

He turned his back on her to address Derry, and she felt her face redden.

"The bastard is hiding in his town house. He's—"

"Leslie doesn't have a town house," she said.

He didn't look at her.

"He's in a town house nearby," he said. "He's been there for days, and hasn't stirred except to go to a tavern and gamble. He's waiting for someone, and it's not the French ambassador, or he would have seen him by now. I'm waiting to see who he gives Percy's deathbed confession to, and then I'll take him."

Derry rubbed his chin and asked, "There's danger in waiting."

"Richmond's a tool," Blade said. "I must find out who the wielder of that tool is. And now you will take Mistress Oriel to the house of her cousin George."

She was tired of being ignored. Scowling she marched around Blade to stand beside Derry.

"I'll not be sent away like a troublesome child. I've had a hand in solving this mystery, I'll see it through to its conclusion."

"You will not," Blade said.

"I will."

"Will not."

Derry's chuckle interrupted this exchange. "By my faith, I've never seen two such quarrelsome lovers."

Gasping, she rounded on him. "We're not lovers."

Derry lifted both brows and glanced from her to

Blade. She noticed that Blade had said nothing and looked at him as well. What little color he'd had in his face drained from it.

Oriel took a step toward him and reached out to touch his arm. "Blade?"

He glanced down at her hand and then met her gaze with one that held the iciness of a sword encased in snow. "*Dieu*, seldom have I met so unrelenting and importunate a mistress. Will you make me repeat my wish to be quit of our dealings together in the presence of Lord Derry?"

She removed her hand. Her eyes stung with unshed tears, and she closed them. She felt him leave her and heard a barely whispered curse. Something in that one word caused her eyes to fly open. He was leaving the room, walking away from her with that careless yet graceful walk.

"Why, you foul, dissembling, imperious liar," she said.

Chapter
19

*Love and War are the same thing,
and stratagems and policy are as
allowable in the one as in the other.*

—*Miguel de Cervantes*

He would hang Derry by his toes for bringing her to London. He stopped in midstride as Oriel spoke.

"Vile dissembler," she said as she rounded the dining table. "You lied."

"Marry, lady, I'm a spy. Lies are my currency."

She fixed him with a challenging stare. He looked down at her, frowning. Her defiance invited a contest for mastery, a contest in which he had no intention of indulging.

"You said you didn't love me," she went on, "that your wooing was but a pretense, a disguising by which you gained residence at the Hall."

"I did."

"Very well," she said as she paused and folded her arms over her chest. "Say it again."

"I know not what you mean."

"Repeat your avowal that you but cozened me and don't love me."

"It is as you say."

"Repeat the words, my lord."

He opened his mouth, and nothing issued forth. A coldness invaded his arms and legs as he watched her eyes grow larger and her whole face soften. If he couldn't summon his wits, she would undo him simply by looking at him.

"I—I came to Richmond Hall to—to—*Sacré Dieu. C'est impossible.*"

Fortunately the door opened at that moment and René entered.

"*Mon seigneur*, a party of French arrived, but Richmond has gone to a tavern. Quickly, my lord."

"Thank God," he said and turned to Derry. "Come. You may explain yourself as we ride. René, guard my lady."

"I'll come with you," she said.

"You will not."

"I will."

"You will not."

Derry chuckled. "I tried to refuse to bring her to London, and she's here, Fitzstephen. Mayhap you should surrender with grace."

"I don't surrender to fey little witches who have no more sense than to desire to place themselves in the middle of a fight."

"He's my cousin. And besides, did I not save you from those thieves who were going to kill us?"

"You did not. You risked your life when you should have waited for me to save you. I knew what I was doing, but you nearly got yourself killed, and I had to slice my way through a pack of highwaymen to prevent it."

"You're just angry because I was the one who saved us."

He thought his head would burst from the futility of the argument. "God's blood, you'll do as you're commanded, for once."

Vaulting toward her, he bent and shoved his shoulder into her stomach and lifted her. She gasped as she lost her breath, and then started kicking.

"Blade Fitzstephen, release me!"

"When I return."

He went out of the dining chamber and climbed the stairs. Derry had covered his ears when Oriel began to shout, and René stood aside, impassive. He was halfway up the staircase when something clawed his buttocks. He yelped, but managed to keep his grip on Oriel's legs.

He entered his chamber and dumped her on the bed. She bounced and scrambled off. Realizing his mistake, he raced her to the doorway, bounded through it, and shut her in as she caught up with him. He heard her pound on the door and shout at him. Taking a key from the pouch on his belt, he locked the door. René joined him, and he handed the key to him.

"Don't release her."

"*Oui, mon seigneur.*"

He raised his voice. "Forgive me, *chère,* but I can't have you so near danger." He listened, then turned to René. "What did she say?"

"I fear, my lord, that I cannot repeat it."

Blade heaved a sigh. "I'd rather face Jack Midnight than her. Don't leave her until I return."

It was a short ride to the house occupied by Leslie Richmond. He and Derry left their horses in the care of a servant in the next street and made their way to the corner of the road on which Leslie's house lay. Vendors hawked their wares up and down the street. Carts of hay and produce fought their way down the narrow, cobbled street and liveried servants jostled each other and gave way to gentlemen when they passed.

Blade led the way down the street and paused to look at the wares of a vendor selling perfumed pomanders. The man was a tall stick figure who had great trouble not tripping over his own feet. Blade picked up a silver pomander ball and studied it.

"Well, Inigo, has he returned from the tavern?"

"Just now," said Inigo.

Blade sniffed the pomander, discarded it, and picked up another. "How many went in?"

"Only two. Frenchmen I've never seen before. They're in his chamber."

Derry picked up a pair of scented gloves and waved them under his nose. "One is the wielder of the tool?"

"Yes," Blade said. "Or a messenger. Whatever the case, we must catch the lot of them now. Inigo, you come with me. The others will watch the house."

A high stone wall surrounded Leslie Richmond's abode. Blade climbed on top of it with a boost from Inigo and Derry. He helped the others to join him, then jumped into the branches of a tree near the wall and climbed down into a deserted garden. Slinking into the house, he led the others in search of Leslie Richmond. Neither he nor his guests were on the ground floor. Indeed, there was no one there except two guards.

Since arriving in London, Leslie had kept only the two guards and no servants in the house. The first guard was stationed at the foot of the stairs in the entryway. Inigo produced a cudgel, tiptoed up behind the man, and smacked him on the head. Blade and Derry caught him as he fell, and they dragged him back to the kitchen. The second guard stood outside at the front door. Inigo and Derry flattened themselves on either side of it while Blade scratched at the wooden panels. He jumped back as the guard opened the door.

"*Bon jour,*" he said as the man stuck his head inside.

Inigo plied his cudgel once more, and Derry caught the falling body.

"*Bon nuit,*" Blade murmured and closed the door as

his companions carried the guard to the back of the house.

Once the man had been disposed of, they crept back to the entryway.

Drawing his sword, Blade whispered to Derry, "Richmond's chamber is the third to the right of the landing."

Taking the stairs quickly but quietly, he approached the room. The darkness and silence of the house oppressed him, but the quiet allowed him to hear the muffled voices of the chamber's occupants. He put his ear to the closed door, then tested the handle of the lock. It moved easily. He nodded to Derry, and gently opened the door a crack. There was no pause in the conversation within. He stood back, glanced at Derry and Inigo, and rammed his boot at the door.

The portal crashed open. He and the others leaped into the room, swords at the ready. Within, three men turned from the table where they had been studying a document by the fading light of the afternoon sun. Their hands went to their swords, but Blade palmed his own dagger and hurled it at one of the Frenchmen before any of them could draw. The Frenchman cried out and fell to his knees. Leslie moved, and Blade jumped at him, touching his sword point to the man's throat.

"You'll be dead before you draw."

Leslie and his companion raised their hands away from their swords. Blade jerked his head to the side, and they moved away from the table. While Inigo and Derry held the two at sword point, Blade strode over to the table and glanced down at the paper. To his relief, it was the confession.

"Fitzstephen," Leslie said. "How discourteous of you to have survived. And I suppose my dear coz lives, as well?"

"If she weren't alive, you would be dead."

"I shall complain to Jack Midnight. He's failed me again."

"Not Midnight," Blade said. "Samuel. But I haven't come for your conversation. Inigo, light that candle. I've a paper to burn."

"Stay!" Leslie reached for his sword, but Derry prodded him and he stilled. "Fitzstephen, you could claim riches beyond imagining for that piece of paper. I have an ally—"

"Marry, sirrah, you've a master. The Cardinal of Lorraine doesn't make allies of minnows such as you."

"How do you know who—" Leslie whistled. "I bow to your skill, Fitzstephen. I never suspected you of being more than an interfering fool. It seems I'm in more trouble than I thought."

"Consorting with foreign spies is madness and treason," Blade replied. "Trouble hardly describes your plight. I marvel that you would gamble so recklessly with your life."

Leslie slowly lowered his hands and shrugged. "You wouldn't understand, being firstborn. An accident of birth cast me in the role of beggar. How would you like to wait upon the whim and charity of brothers whose wits wouldn't fill a comfit box? Year after year coddling their fancies, cringing under their censure, condemned to rot in that mold-ridden heap in the north country."

"Fear not," Blade said, "I've arranged for you to rot in a mold-ridden cell in the Tower until your execution. Inigo, if I mistake me not, has brought manacles."

As Inigo approached the two prisoners, there came a shout from below and the explosion of fighting. Everyone looked through the open door at once, but Leslie recovered first and kicked at Derry's sword hand. The weapon flew out of Derry's hand and slid across the floor. Blade dashed for Leslie, but was too late to prevent him from drawing his sword.

Swinging his manacles like metal whips, Inigo attacked the Frenchman, Derry dived for his sword as Blade thrust at Leslie. There were more shouts from the first floor. Evidently more Frenchmen had arrived and

Blade's men had tried to prevent them from coming upon him unaware. He parried a thrust from Leslie, but was distracted by a cry from Inigo.

The manacles had twisted around the Frenchman's sword and the man had taken the opportunity to dash Inigo against a wall. As Inigo sank to the floor, Derry rushed at the Frenchman, who quickly freed his weapon, swinging around to meet this new attack.

Leslie had taken advantage of this diversion to leap for the table and the confession upon it. Blade plucked a dagger from the sleeve of his doublet and hurled it. The weapon sank into Leslie's hand as he reached for the paper. He cried out, pulled the dagger from his hand, and, snarling, raised his sword and rushed toward Blade.

Blade grasped his weapon in both hands and bent his knees. Leslie charged at him, putting the full force of his momentum behind the attack. Blade raised his sword, and their weapons clashed, sending off sparks. As he rammed into Blade, Leslie brought his knee up and tried to jam it into Blade's stomach. Blade leaped aside, turned, and parried a second thrust from Leslie's sword.

Derry swept by him on a charge at his own opponent. Blade now stood between Leslie and the confession on the table. Knocking Leslie's weapon aside, he backed toward the table with Leslie matching every step. Without taking his eyes from his opponent, Blade picked up the confession. Stepping to the side, he approached the candle. Using one hand, he rolled up the paper.

"You'll have to take your gaze from me to put it to the flame," Leslie said. "It will cost you your life, and I'll get the cursed paper anyway."

Blade moved so that he could see the flame in the corner of his eye while holding Leslie at bay with his sword. In one corner of the room Derry still battled the Frenchman. Blade lifted the roll; it wavered near the flame. The paper flared, and in that instant Leslie pounced. The two weapons clashed, and Leslie's sword slithered down Blade's until their hilts locked. Leslie grabbed for the confession with his free hand, but Blade threw the burning paper out of his reach.

Leslie cried out in dismay as he saw the confession consumed by flames, then looked back at Blade. "You bastard."

Breaking free of Blade's sword hilt, he jumped backward. Rage burning from his eyes, he took his sword in both hands.

Holding Leslie at bay with his sword, Blade retrieved a dagger from his boot without taking his gaze from his opponent. "You don't want to continue this fight, Richmond. I've earned my name, believe me."

"I want to bathe in your blood," Leslie said. He raised his sword high and charged.

Blade held his ground, crossed the hilts of his sword and dagger, and thrust them at Leslie's sword as it soared down at him. The impact filled the chamber with the ringing of metal against metal. Roaring his frustration, Leslie pulled free and sent his weapon slicing at Blade's neck. Blade whirled and met the blow with a backhanded parry. As he turned, he brought the dagger underneath his sword arm.

Intent on his own charge, Leslie impaled himself on the dagger. As the weapon sank deep into his chest, he sank to his knees. Leslie gaped at Blade in surprise, then slowly closed his eyes and fell to the floor.

As Leslie died, Blade heard a scream from the Frenchman. Derry had sunk his weapon into his enemy, but as he pulled his sword free, a club sailed through the doorway and smashed into his head. Dropping his sword, he collapsed.

Blade scrambled to his feet, sword raised, but as he did so, five swordsmen rushed into the room and surrounded him. He lowered his sword and glanced at the confession. Only a few ashes remained. He had succeeded, in part.

As he stood in the middle of a circle of steel, a sixth

man entered the room, his sword still in its sheath. Cloaked and clad in black velvet, he was tall and skeletal, giving the appearance of a body that had been placed in a crypt nigh onto three days. He walked without making a sound, and the circle of men around Blade parted for him. He stood surveying the fallen men, glanced at the burned paper and then at Blade.

"*Salut, mon seigneur.*"

"Who are you?"

"Your sword," the man said.

Blade glanced around the circle of men, then dropped his weapon. One of them kicked it away.

His captor bowed to him. "I am Alain Le Brun, and you are the Sieur de Racine."

"What you came for has been destroyed, Le Brun."

"*Non, mon seigneur,* only part of it has been destroyed."

Dread filled him, and he glanced about the room for signs of other documents.

Le Brun made a noise that sounded like a devil laughing. "It is you, Fitzstephen. I came for you. You see, there is someone who wishes to speak with you, someone whom you have annoyed. And when he hears that you've interfered with his plans in such a devastating manner, well, shall I say that minstrels will compose laments about your untimely death."

As he listened, Blade felt a tremor of apprehension crawl up his spine. Then he stopped breathing, for behind Le Brun, in the doorway, a small white hand crept out to grasp the hilt of Derry's sword. He could have sworn he felt his hair turning white. He hastened to keep Le Brun's attention. If he survived, he was going to lock Oriel in a high tower for at least a year.

"By now the watch has been summoned. You'll leave this house as a prisoner, Le Brun."

"Bind him," Le Brun said.

Two men grabbed him, but he dared not resist, for the little hand had grasped the sword and was raising it unsteadily. His hands were bound in front of him with leather straps. As the last knot was tied, Oriel jumped into the room and bashed one of the swordsmen with the flat of the sword blade.

The man plummeted to the floor, and Blade jammed his elbow in the chest of another. Kicking a third in the ribs, he snatched the man's sword. Lifting it, he swung around to meet Le Brun, who stood with the tip of his sword touching Oriel's breast. She glared at him, her own sword wobbling in her hands.

"Look what you've done," Blade snapped at her as he dropped his weapon.

She transferred her glare to him. "Someone had to try to save you."

"Where is René?"

"Putting out the fire in your chamber. He thinks I've fainted on the landing."

"God's blood!"

"Silence, s'il vous plaît." Le Brun motioned to his men, who imprisoned Blade between them while another grabbed Oriel. "And now, *mon seigneur,* if you wish to preserve the life of this foolish demoiselle, you will obey me."

"How do I know you won't hurt her?"

"You don't know anything except this: I will most certainly hurt her if you do not do as I say."

Le Brun produced a bottle from beneath his cloak. No larger than a perfume vessel, it was of dark green Venetian glass. He withdrew a cork from it, then handed it to one of his men. Blade watched as the man came toward him. The arms holding him tightened, and his head was pulled back by his hair. He struggled, but Le Brun's voice came to him as the man holding the bottle loomed over him.

"Drink, my boy, drink, or watch her die."

He couldn't help fighting them as the bottle was pressed to his lips. Someone pinched his nose, and his mouth opened. Bitter liquid flooded his throat. He choked, swallowed, and choked again. Finally he tore his head free and sputtered obscenities at Le Brun.

"Poison is a coward's device."

"What foolishness." Le Brun's skull-like face swam before him and his voice seemed to come echoing from a long tunnel. "Don't struggle so. You will but sleep."

Blade felt his legs turn to water, and he was caught and supported by the men holding his arms. A cold hand touched his face, and Le Brun looked closely into his eyes.

"Calm yourself. Fighting the potion only makes the experience unpleasant."

"Oriel."

He heard her scream, and began to thrash at his captors.

Le Brun shook his head. "Unfortunately, it is necessary to kill both your lady and your friend with the golden hair."

From a great distance he heard the shout of the watch. He smiled as he heard Le Brun curse.

"Leave them. There's no time."

Somehow he was sailing through the air, upended so that he floated with his head pointed at the floor. A door slammed. He heard Oriel shouting and pounding on it. He watched as stairs rippled by. The world skimmed to a halt as he was propped upright before a door below the staircase. It opened, and he was dragged into a dark cavern, then carried down into a hole. A torch flared, but all he could see were billowing flames. He closed his eyes against the brightness.

He was hauled upright and forced against a rock wall. He struggled uselessly until someone placed hands on either side of his head to still him. He swore and blinked, trying to clear his vision. Le Brun's face swam before him, and he felt another bottle press at his lips. He tried to turn away, but he was trapped. The burning liquid rushed into his mouth. A hand rubbed his throat, and he swallowed.

He heard the bottle smash on rock. A great black cloud enveloped him, and he began to smother in it. No longer able to move his body, he held to that thread of consciousness remaining. But with the swiftness of a merlin, it flew from him and at last, with a flicker of wrath at his own helplessness, he let it go.

Chapter
20

Some stealthy demon in dead of night
With grisly horror and fiendish hate
Is spreading unheard-of havoc and death.

—Beowulf

Oriel threw herself at the door, clawing at it, but that terrible Frenchman had shoved something against it when he had fled. Frantic, she whirled around and ran to the windows, which faced the street. No one left the house, but she could see five members of the watch running down the street toward the house.

Behind her, Derry groaned. Oriel ran to him. He was lying facedown, and she helped him turn over. As she did so, another groan issued from the heap of bodies tangled in chains and manacles nearby. She helped Derry lift his head, but he moaned and sank into her lap. She shook him, her voice growing louder with each word.

"Derry, wake up. Derry, they've taken him and we have to go after them. Derry!"

As she called to him, she caught sight of Leslie's body spread out in a pool of blood. For a moment she felt a stab of pain. Once Leslie had been good to her. Once they had been friends. Or had they? Had he ever cared about anyone other than himself? He'd tried to kill her, and Blade. For trying to hurt Blade, she would have killed him herself.

A movement from Derry distracted her from the body. He tried to rise, but fell back again, gasping a name.

"Inigo."

The man called Inigo levered himself to a sitting position and clutched his bleeding nose. The shouting and pounding began again downstairs.

Propping Derry up, Oriel shook his shoulder. "Derry, please, they've taken Blade."

"They didn't kill him?"

"They made him drink some potion and he collapsed. They were going to kill me, but they heard the watch and dragged Blade away with them."

Derry sat up and touched the back of his head. Oriel tore a piece of her petticoat and dabbed at the bloodied wound there.

"Jesu Maria," he said, "why did they take him? Who were they?"

"I know not. Their leader was a horrible man who looked like a cadaver."

Derry lifted his head and stared at her. "A tall man with a head like a skull and grayish skin?"

"Yes."

"Le Brun. God's blood, it was Le Brun."

Derry rose to his knees, and Oriel helped him get to his feet. He went to Inigo, who was still nursing his nose.

"You're of no use," he said.

Oriel was back at the door, trying to shove it open. "Make haste, Derry. We must follow Blade."

"Wait," Derry said. "Let me think. Le Brun is the cardinal's man."

"The Cardinal of Lorraine?"

"Yes, and it seems the cardinal wants Blade."

"Then Le Brun will take ship for France."

Derry nodded, then winced. "If we can't prevent him."

Something scraped against the door, and it was thrown open. A man with a pike stuck his head into the chamber cautiously. His gaze fell on Derry.

"Lord Derry, isn't it?" He came into the room. "My lord, there's a heap of bodies downstairs. Frenchmen mostly." His tone suggested that since they were foreigners he needn't trouble himself.

Derry stumbled as he brushed past the man. Oriel caught hold of his arm and helped him downstairs, over several dead men littering the steps. In the entryway lay more bodies. Derry called to the sergeant of the watch.

"Did you see anyone quit the house?"

"No, my lord."

Derry drew the sergeant away from Oriel and spoke to him quietly. When he was finished, the man saluted Derry and went upstairs. Derry returned to her.

"If Le Brun is going to France, we but need to find the right ship," she said.

"Not 'we,' " Derry said.

Oriel wanted to smack him on the head. "The last time you went without me you lost Blade. I'm going."

"There is too much danger. I'll not allow it."

She lifted her skirts and stepped over a dead Frenchman still clutching a sword. "Argument is futile, and you waste time. I'm going to the docks. Will you accompany me, or shall we conduct a double search?"

Almost a fortnight later Oriel rode through a French forest with René, Derry, and five of his men. They had failed to find Le Brun and Blade at the docks, and so had sailed to Calais. Derry had arranged for a tale to be put out that Leslie had been killed in a quarrel over a dice game with foreigners. He'd sent word to Richmond Hall as well, but none of these arrangements mattered to Oriel.

Each moment that passed tightened the knot of fear in her chest. She imagined Blade being tortured or killed, and she could hardly govern her desire to rush out and search every inch of French soil until she found him. Instead, she waited while Derry and his men skulked from one unsavory tavern to another until they traced Le Brun's path.

After days of inquiry, Derry paid a purse full of coins for the news that Le Brun was headed for his manor near the royal chateau of Amboise, on the Loire. The Cardinal of Lorraine was in residence at Amboise. Now she fixed her will on remaining in the saddle as they picked their way through the forest. They had avoided the main roads, resting seldom, and had been riding for so long that she'd lost track of the days. Her bones ached and her eyes burned, and she still wanted to rush to the manor house and tear it to the ground in search of Blade.

Her fury at his deception had receded. He had lied to her. As deceitful as he was beautiful, that's what he was, but no more. They had both discovered something in his house in London. Blade no longer had the art or the will to deceive her. Even in her fear, a quiver of excitement ran through her. He loved her, and she wasn't going to allow some rabid cardinal to have him now that she knew it.

They were stopping. Derry turned his horse back and joined her.

"The manor is still over a league away, but we dare go no farther until dark. We'll find a place of conceal-ment and make camp."

By late afternoon they had burrowed deep into the

tree cover of the forest and camped around the base of
an oak so large that its trunk resembled a gnarled keep.
Though it was almost Easter, winter had been stubborn,
and France was still wrapped in its chill. Derry made
her promise to try to sleep while he left to inspect the
manor house, and left René behind to see that she did.
She closed her eyes for an hour or so. She didn't sleep,
but she didn't try to follow Derry. She knew when to
trust to the expertise of another.

In any case, she would be hampered by having to
thwart René. Since Blade had been taken, his French
servant had appointed himself her guardian and had become her shadow. She was sure he hadn't forgiven her
for tricking him into releasing her from her prison in
Blade's house. Now he watched her, catlike, vowing
that Blade would carve him for stew meat if she were
harmed. So she waited.

When Derry returned, her guts twisted as she beheld
his expression. She ran to his side as he handed the reins
of his horse to one of his men.

"What news?" she asked.

She dogged his steps as he walked to the giant oak.
René lurked nearby.

"I mislike what I've seen," he said, "and like even
less what I found out. I spoke to one of the maids from
a village at the edge of the forest. It lies a league or so
from the manor, but they know Le Brun well. I do so
love wheedling news from dairy maids."

"Stop babbling and tell me," she said.

"Le Brun arrived two days past and brought with
him a young nobleman who was quite ill."

"Blade."

Derry sank down to a blanket spread beneath the
oak and rested with his back against the trunk. "The
manor was shut up for the winter. Now Le Brun has
returned suddenly with this unknown young man. Most
likely Blade is kept in a tower room, for that would be
the most secure. Le Brun has sent for no servants, and

his men warn away any villagers who seek to sell goods at the manor."

"It is as you guessed, then," she said. "Le Brun holds Blade for some fell purpose. They must be feeding him that potion to keep him quiet, or . . ." She twisted the hem of her gown in her fingers. "Or they have so hurt him that he is indeed sick unto death."

"Don't think upon it," Derry said. "Le Brun has some reason for keeping Blade rather than killing him."

Oriel got to her knees in front of Derry. "Yes, and while you've been lurking about taverns, I have been pondering. If, as you say, Blade has destroyed the plans of the Cardinal of Lorraine, mayhap the cardinal wants revenge."

"My reasoning has taken the same course," Derry said.

"But I had another thought today. If I were the cardinal, and I had discovered one of the English queen's chief spies, I would want to know what he'd been about."

"Which means. . . ."

"Which means we'd best pluck Blade from that nest of shrikes before the Cardinal of Lorraine puts Blade to the rack to prize his secrets from him."

The room had turned gold with the fading of sunlight. Blade kept his eyes half-closed and watched Alain Le Brun storm into his prison chamber and over to the bed. The old woman they'd hired to nurse him rose and shoved her stool out of the way.

"How does he?" Le Brun asked. "Well?"

"The same," the old woman said. "He's as weak as a dying babe, and I want no part of the blame if he dies."

Le Brun shoved the woman aside and leaned over the bed. He grasped Blade by the shoulders and shook him.

"Fitzstephen, open your eyes, damn you."

He shook Blade again, then slapped him. Blade's head snapped back under the blow, and he went limp.

"He won't get well if you beat him," the old woman said without much interest.

Le Brun released Blade, who fell back to the mattress.

"This illness," Le Brun said, "it must be a ruse."

The old woman shrugged. "If he'd puked all over my boots like he did yours, I wouldn't put a wager on it."

"That was two days ago."

"I've held his head over a chamber pot every day since then." The old woman shook her head. "A pity. He's a fine one, he is."

She picked up the aforementioned chamber pot and waddled out of the room. As she went, she complained that she needed food if she was to nurse her patient through the whole night. Le Brun turned back to Blade and grabbed his face, bending close.

"You listen to me. Well or ill, you're to kneel before the cardinal tonight. Do you hear me? Fitzstephen!"

Blade's lashes fluttered, then lowered again.

Uttering a growl of impatience, Le Brun released his prisoner again and stomped out. A lock clicked, and Blade was alone. He slowly raised one eyelid, then both. He darted glances about the room and listened for footsteps. Hearing none, he threw back the covers and sprang out of bed with a grim smile. He enjoyed baiting Le Brun.

They had stripped him before depositing him in bed. Goose bumps rose on his skin and he shivered. He flexed muscles stiff from lying in bed all day and stole over to the latticed windows. He remembered little of how he had gotten to this place. What he did remember was being awake, and then being awake again, and sick near to death from that foul potion they kept feeding him.

During that nightmare time of helplessness and pain,

he'd wanted Oriel. Several times, when he could hardly lift his head or the blackness threatened, he cursed at his own foolhardiness. He should have admitted the truth to her once she guessed it at his town house. Now he might never again have the chance. Too late he understood how essential she was to him, and now it was most unlikely he would ever be able to tell her.

"Blade Fitzstephen, you're a crack-brained lackwit."

He forced his thoughts back to gaining his freedom. He was in France, so he must have been on a ship, but he only remembered waking in a place of vile smells and loud music and voices, with Le Brun bending over him. More of the potion had been forced down his throat. The next time he woke, he was tied to a horse and even sicker than before. He remembered retching with the motion of the animal.

As time passed, Le Brun seemed to realize the stupidity of feeding him too much potion, and had refrained. Once the poisonings lessened, his wits gradually roused from their stupor. When they did, he decided to disguise his recovery in hopes of allaying his captors' watchfulness long enough to escape. He'd succeeded in part, for Le Brun now left only the old woman to nurse and guard him.

It was the puking on his boots that convinced Le Brun of Blade's weakness. That trick had been born of desperation. He'd leaned over the bed, putting his face near the chamber pot, and taken a deep breath. The scent had produced the result he'd wanted.

His time had run out, however. The cardinal was coming tonight. Therefore he must escape or die. The old woman was stuffing her ample self with food, and from experience he knew he had almost an hour to himself. He flattened his body beside the windows and peered down at the rooftops below the tower. He was in a manor house surrounded by a forest. Not far off he could see a river and an arched stone bridge spanning it. The rooftops below him were leaded, steep, and

broken by dormer windows. If he could lower himself
the thirty feet to the next roof, he might be able to cling
to the nearest dormer and then jump to the ground—or
break both legs. He was looking down at the ground
below the dormer when one of Le Brun's men came out
of the manor and crossed the drive in front. Blade
whipped his head back and flattened himself against the
wall once more, praying that the man hadn't seen him.
He waited, listening intently, but no alarm was
sounded.

Sliding along the curved wall of the tower, he
dropped to the floor and scrambled to the chest at the
foot of the bed. His nurse had stuffed his clothes in the
chest after they'd been cleaned. He would dress, make a
rope from the bed sheets, and climb down the side of
the building. It was almost dark, and time to leave the
rough care of Alain Le Brun.

His hand was on the torn cambric shirt that lay top-
most in the chest when he heard horses outside. He
closed the chest and stole back to the windows. In the
fading light he saw three men dismounting. One was
taller than the rest and slim. He brushed the hood of his
cloak back to reveal red-gold hair topped by a priest's
cap. The cardinal.

Cursing, Blade returned quickly to the bed. He
summoned thoughts of nausea, dog carcasses, and refuse
heaps. He closed his eyes. Boots pounded on the bare
floor outside. The lock clicked again, and the boots
drew near. He heard the rustle of a heavy cloak, and
breathing, but nothing else.

Without warning a hand touched him. It took all his
control not to start or shrink from that touch. He felt a
warm palm lay against his cheek. It lifted, and the covers
were pulled down to his hips, then replaced. Still the
silence continued.

Suddenly his head exploded with the force of an
openhanded slap. His head snapped to the side, and he
moaned weakly. He was shaken and slapped again. This

time his eyes flew open, and he met the dark, amused gaze of the Cardinal of Lorraine.

"Ah, *mon fils,* you but needed encouragement to join us."

Blade said nothing and blinked slowly at the cardinal, then closed his eyes again.

"Come, my dear boy, don't force a man of God to strike you again."

He opened his eyes, slowly, as if doing so took all his strength.

"*Bon,*" the cardinal said. "The English nightingale is with us. Ah, you're startled. I do remember you, *mon seigneur,* though I didn't at first. I remember the lovely Claude gave a masque last year, and at this masque— this quite dreary masque—you sang. Your voice suffused the night with the brightness of the sun."

The cardinal motioned to Le Brun, who stood behind him, and Le Brun brought a chair. Seating himself and arranging the folds of his cloak, he placed his hands on the arms of the chair and regarded Blade as though inspecting a novice.

"You have caused me great inconvenience, boy. I like it not, nor being made to appear the fool. You may thank God that I admire your cunning, or you'd be worm's meat by now. You're a marvel, you know. You speak French as well as I. You'll speak a lot of it, and to me, in the coming days."

Blade whispered, taking care to slur his words slightly. "I'll tell you nothing."

He hated lying here, helpless, while the man toyed with him as if he were some amusing lapdog. The cardinal's soft laughter alarmed him as Le Brun's brutality could not.

"Make no vows, for I warrant you, I have yet to fail when I set myself to turn a man to my purpose. But perchance I am hasty. Would you like to submit now and save yourself much travail? Tell me how you knew about the old man Sir Thomas Richmond, and the names of your fellow intelligencers."

Blade stared at his captor and said nothing. The cardinal sighed.

"Infortuné, mon fils," he said. He made a steeple of his fingers and gazed at Blade over them. "You see, I have a suspicion that the secrets in that pretty head are worth far more than those of that damnable Thomas Richmond. Tell me, Nicholas Fitzstephen, Sieur de Racine, what know you of the affairs of Her Majesty, the Queen of England?"

"Naught."

Charles de Guise gave him an amused, even affectionate smile. He lowered his hands and began to stroke the miniver that lined his cloak. "I have an apothecary named Cosimo. Italians are so versed in the lore of herbs and potions. Cosimo studied for a while under Nostradamus. He amazes me with his philters, infusions, and decoctions, and he has created for me a most useful tincture. I believe he combined lavender, rue, and mandrake root, and other such herbs."

The cardinal leaned on the bed. "Mayhap you know the lore of the mandrake. It grows under the gallows of murderers and it is death to dig up the root. If one tries, it utters shrieks and groans so terrifying that none may hear them and live. Thus one must use dogs to dig it up."

"I shall take care not to dig for it at all," Blade murmured.

"It is a funeral herb, an herb of magic and of visions —one of great potency."

As he spoke, the cardinal drew a gold chain from beneath his leather jerkin. Suspended from it was a vial of transparent crystal filled with a black liquid. He held the chain over Blade's head, and the vial began to spin. Blade watched it, but the whirling of the crystal caught the light of the candles by the bed. His vision blurred, and he turned his head aside.

"I have given this tincture to certain condemned heretics," the cardinal said. "Unfortunately I was too generous with it at first, and several of them died before they could be burned for their crimes. I've mastered the art of administering it though. It seems that Cosimo's tincture reduces a man to a willing slave within hours."

"I don't believe you." Blade tensed as the cardinal lowered the vial and caught it in one hand.

"It matters not." The cardinal glanced at the vial. "Enough chatter. You have a choice, my boy. You may walk down to your horse with Le Brun's help, or I can give you a taste of Cosimo's tincture now. I would prefer to wait a day or two until you are stronger, but if you force me, I will begin your schooling now."

"Where are you taking me?"

"Why, to the royal chateau. I vow it's really as much fortress as chateau, which is fortunate, for I've a mind to keep you in the dungeons of Amboise, my dear Anglo-French spy. For there, no one will hear you scream."

Blade's fingers twitched as he sought to prevent himself from leaping upon the cardinal. He understood how the man had gained so much power, for he worked subtly and slowly, teasing apart the fabric of his victim's defenses until the quarry found himself exposed.

"Come, your answer," the cardinal said. "I would advise obedience, for in the end you will be transformed into a meek and biddable slave. Comply, and I will deal with you gently."

Blade watched his enemy rise and loom over him. The cardinal took his hand, and he allowed the man to help him rise. He glanced about the chamber to find himself outnumbered by Le Brun and five guards. Even he couldn't fight seven men. It was best to feign submission and hope for a chance to escape along the road to Amboise. If he was fortunate, they wouldn't bother to tie his feet to the stirrups when he was mounted.

He was dressed and propelled down the winding tower stair and out to the court where the horses

waited. A guard bound his hands in front of him. The
cardinal snapped an order, and someone threw a heavy
cloak over him. Its folds were wrapped about his body.
He hung between two guards while a third steadied his
mount. They shoved him into the saddle, where he took
care to slump a bit.

The cardinal rode over and surveyed his captive.
"Watch him closely. If he falters, throw him over the
saddle and tie him down. I don't want him falling and
breaking his neck."

He'd succeeded. They thought him too ill to do anything but acquiesce to their commands. A guard took
the reins of his horse. At the cardinal's signal the party
set off. Blade huddled in his saddle and took in a deep
breath of icy night air.

Excitement set fire to his body. He was outnumbered and unarmed, but at least he was out of his prison.
The next hour would see him free or it would see him
dead. Either way, he would rob the Cardinal of Lorraine of the chance to threaten the life of his queen.

Chapter
21

Nobly to live, or else nobly to die,
Befits proud birth.

—Sophocles

At the edge of the forest near the manor of Alain Le Brun, Oriel put her hand on Derry's shoulder and stood on tiptoe to gaze at the house. In the darkness eight figures strode about by torchlight and readied horses.

She hissed into his ear. "God's toes, what are they doing?"

"They're leaving." Derry uttered two words she'd never heard before. "Christian will have my head for this. He sent me to help Blade, and I've given him to the cardinal."

"Who is Christian?" She jerked Derry around to face her. "Did you say the cardinal? He's there?" She shoved him aside and peered around a tree at the house again.

"Are you certain?" she asked.

"Yes. Jesu Maria, they're leaving, with Blade."

She nodded, then clutched at his arm. "They're taking the road to Amboise. We must free him before they reach the chateau, or we'll never get him at all."

"We must go before them," Derry said as they rejoined the men and horses. "What we need is a place in the road where the trees lie close. Make haste."

She followed Derry in a perilous dash through the forest, dodging saplings and low-hanging branches. Behind her she heard swearing as one of the men caught a branch in the face. The full moon was high by the time Derry called a halt. He dismounted and drew his dagger. She took his reins and those of René and the other men and wrapped them around her fist.

"Remember," Derry said. "You vowed you would let me do the fighting."

"I promise to guard the horses. If I knew how to use a sword, I would fight, but I don't."

Derry snorted. "And the last time you tried, you nearly got killed."

"You needn't belabor the matter. I don't wish to put myself in your way and risk endangering Blade."

"Good."

At a signal from Derry, his men took up their positions. Derry shinnied up a tree trunk and climbed out on a thick branch that hung over the road. Imitating Derry, René chose a tree on the opposite side of the road. Three men nocked arrows in their bows and hid behind trees on either side of the path. The fourth settled in another tree and loaded a crossbow. Oriel fixed her attention on quieting the horses. She led them some distance away, but couldn't go too far, for the mounts must be nearby for a quick escape. From her station she could barely make out the road, and she couldn't see Derry or his men at all. Her task was to ride in with the horses once the fight was won.

She sat still, her arm aching from holding fast to the bundle of reins. Tree branches creaked in the breeze, and dead leaves skipped along the forest floor. She heard an owl, then realized it was Derry. They were coming.

At first she could only hear hoofbeats and the sound of clinking bits and bridles. Then she glimpsed the line of horsemen. Her skin crawled as she watched them pass beneath Derry's branch. Why didn't he attack? Then she saw a slumping figure riding between two upright ones. Blade. Derry whistled again, and Blade straightened in the saddle, his head raised toward Derry's perch.

The three passed beneath Derry's branch, and he dropped on top of the guard nearest him with a howl. He raised his dagger and plunged it into the man's chest. As he did so, Blade's leg shot out, and he kicked the second guard. The man grunted, but didn't fall. He drew his sword, and lashed out at Blade, but before he could strike, an arrow hit him in the back. He fell to the ground. Other arrows hissed through the trees, and a man screamed.

A clamor rose as the Frenchmen drew their weapons and dismounted under the hail of arrows. Two of Derry's bowmen fell under their swords. The third ran out of arrows and ducked behind a tree to draw his sword. A French guard riding just ahead of Blade turned his horse. Drawing his sword, he headed for Derry and Blade, but René hurled himself on the man from above, and the two vanished behind horses and fighting men.

Derry was trying to cut Blade's bonds when a guard kicked his horse and charged toward them, sword drawn. Another man rode close behind. Oriel shouted, but the noise of the fight drowned her warning. For a moment she fumbled with the knot of reins, then cast it aside and kicked her horse into motion. The mare leaped forward, and she charged through the trees toward Blade in a race with the Frenchman.

Derry's dagger cut the last of Blade's bonds. She sprang into the road and screamed at him.

"Blade, behind you!"

He turned. A sword sliced through the air. Blade ducked, hauling his mount around. Derry shouted something and threw him his sword. Blade caught it just as the guard thrust at him. He parried the thrust, feinted left, then brought his sword down in a slicing blow across the man's shoulder that knocked him to the ground. Without pause Blade brought his weapon up to meet the attack of a second man.

It was the cardinal. He parried, and their swords locked. The cardinal glanced over his shoulder at Oriel and Derry, then smiled at Blade.

"Is this English luck?"

"English guile, more like," Blade said.

The cardinal laughed and raised his voice, summoning his men. Three were left, including Le Brun, and they all charged at Blade. Derry cried out, and Blade immediately broke from the cardinal, sliding his weapon up so quickly that his opponent had no time to respond. The tip of the sword danced, then dipped and sliced at the cardinal's cheek. The man gasped, cursed, then turned his horse and galloped back toward the manor.

The three Frenchmen followed their master, passing Oriel and Derry who were running to Blade. They reached him as the last man drew abreast of them, his sword raised. Blade shouted a warning at Oriel. She hauled her mare aside, but the animal was too slow. The sword arced down at her, but before it could strike home, something else hit her, hurling her out of the saddle and to the ground.

Landing face down with a thump, she felt a great weight crush the air from her body. It lifted, and she sucked in gulps of air.

"God's blood. Mother of heaven. Christ and the apostles."

Strong hands turned her over. Blade's face hovered over hers.

"Are you hurt? What do you here? Have you no wits at all? Where is Derry? I'll skewer him to a tree, so help me."

Oriel took a last deep breath, then grabbed his shoulders. "Thank the Almighty. They haven't hurt you too much or you wouldn't have the strength to harp at me for saving your life."

"God's patience. Woman, I should take a whip to you."

Wrapping his arms around her, he covered her mouth with his and squeezed the air from her lungs at the same time. Her ribs ached, but she devoured his lips in return, then caught his face in her hands and peered at him.

"Are you truly well?"

"Yes, *chère*, and you?"

René appeared from behind horses and bodies. He whispered something in French, and Blade whirled around to face him. Hauling him into his grasp, the Frenchman rasped out questions so quickly Blade had no chance to respond. Finally, without waiting for answers, René pulled his master into a crushing hug.

Derry pulled them apart. "Enough cosseting. He's well, but not like to be for long if we don't quit this place. Now mount your horses, before the cardinal decides to reclaim his prisoner."

They set off with René guiding them, leaving Derry to gather his men and follow. They rode through the night, only stopping at dawn when they reached a town large enough for them to hide in. There Derry caught up with them. Two of his men had survived the attack, and these he sent to an inn separately. They would make their way back to England by a different route. Oriel, Blade, and Derry took refuge in a modest tavern.

While Derry kept watch a while before retiring, Blade escorted Oriel to a room on the second floor. He ushered her into the chamber, shut the door, barred it, and leaned against it. He'd been quiet during their strenuous ride, but none of them had had the time to talk. He'd spoken briefly with Derry, but had said nothing to her.

Now he regarded her as she dropped her bundle of possessions on the floor and sank onto the bed. She gave him an eager smile, but it faded when he did not respond.

He drew a dagger from his boot and examined the blade, testing its weight in his hand as he surveyed her from head to foot. She began to grow anxious as he spun the weapon by its tip on one finger, staring at her all the while.

As suddenly as it had appeared, the dagger vanished, and still he stared at her. Finally she could bear the silence no longer.

"I was afraid they would hurt you."

Nothing.

"Do you think they will follow?"

Nothing.

She frowned at him. "I know Plutarch says it is wise to be silent when the occasion requires, but this occasion requires speech, my lord."

No answer.

As the silence wore on, it abruptly occurred to her that they were alone. How odd that the thought disturbed her. She hadn't seen him in so long, and now he was different, so silent and almost threatening.

Mayhap it was because she'd seen him kill, quickly and without hesitation—seen him ply his sword as if it were wind. When he'd killed Jack Midnight's men, she hadn't been in a position to see him do it. Now she wasn't sure of him. How could one alluring body contain the unequaled skills of a courtesan and of a killer?

At last he did something. He shoved away from the

door and began to walk toward her. She scrambled to the opposite side of the bed and off it to the floor. He paused as she retreated, then swung around the bed, still walking slowly. Too late she noticed she'd put herself in a corner. Anxious, she retreated with each of his steps until she ran up against the wall beside a cabinet. He leaned close, his hand resting beside her head. She tried to duck his arm, but he caught her wrist and pressed it to the wall.

"What are you doing?"

He flattened her against the wall with his body, and she tried to wriggle away from him. He pinned her other wrist against the wall and bent so that his lips were close to hers.

"Don't," she said.

"Hush, *chère*. This is an occasion for silence."

His lips closed over hers, and she felt their warmth invade her flesh. His chest pressed against her breasts, and his tongue flitted about inside her mouth before he began to suck. He put his hand to the side of her breast and held it there while he kissed her, then his other hand came to rest on her other breast.

Still pinioned between his body and the wall, she felt his hips press against hers. A knee nudged between hers, and her legs were spread. Immediately he began a steady flexing of his hips so that they rode against hers.

Slowly, with each kiss, each small stroke of his hands, every sensual movement of his hips, her body began to simmer. His hands lifted her skirts, then stroked their way up her thighs, and the simmer turned to a boil. He had made her so sensitive that when he touched her, she started. He lifted his mouth from hers, but only a little, and their lips still touched. At long last he whispered while he continued to touch her.

"Oh, *chère*, I thought I would never see you again. I thought I would be killed without being able to say farewell."

She tried to respond, but his lips devoured hers. As

he kissed her, he lifted her and placed her on the bed. Shoving her legs apart, he settled between them.

She felt her gown rip at the neck, and he covered a breast with one hand. His palm brushed against her nipple, and she sucked in her breath. He was right. This was an occasion for silence.

She woke many hours later to find Blade resting on his side and staring at her. He plucked a stray curl from the bridge of her nose and tossed it over her shoulder.

"I am afraid for you, *chère*. I've tried to cast you from my heart and I've failed."

"I don't understand. Why are you afraid?"

He turned away. Lying on his back, he stared up at the ceiling. "Why do you think I'm so good at killing?"

"I know not."

"Because within my soul there lies a great hellish rage. A rage I have learned to govern by keeping myself alone, allowing no one too near. When I was younger I turned my rage against others. I couldn't seem to stop myself. Once I even hurt a lady—an innocent, sweet lady named Nora."

"Did you kill her?"

He shook his head. "But I have killed men. Men who deserved death. I use my rage. I send it through my body to my sword, and it kills." He turned to look at her, his eyes dark in the shuttered room. "I am afraid of my own rage, afraid that it will strike you, as it has others. It's in my blood—a curse inherited from my father."

Oriel sat up and leaned over him, but he wouldn't look at her. "You have said this before. But never in all our time together have you ever hurt me. I've never seen you raise your hand to a woman."

"When a man and a woman live together, they can grow to hate each other. I've seen it. And hate turns to violence. I couldn't endure it if that happened to us."

She sat back, her eyes wide with hurt, and gathered a

sheet to her breast. "You still want to be released from our betrothal, because of this fear that you're as great a monster as your father."

Propping himself up on one arm, Blade drew close, so close that she could see his face. She saw pain, yet he was almost smiling.

"No, I don't wish to be released, for I have discovered a far greater fear, the fear of never seeing you again. No torture by the cardinal could have surpassed the pain of losing you." Blade sat up and put his hand against her cheek. "I have told you what I am. Now that I have, you must decide whether you want me. *Chère*, will you be my wife?"

She threw herself into his arms, and he sank back down on the bed beneath her weight. She kissed him hard, then released his lips so that she could gaze at him, taking in the glitter of amusement that had crept into his eyes.

"I will," she said.

"And I see I must marry you to keep you safe from harm. As your lord I will forbid you to take any more risks with your life."

She pounded him on the chest. "Fie. It's your fault I had to gad about the countryside and risk my life. If you would but keep still and refrain from intrigue, I wouldn't find it necessary to embark upon perilous adventures."

"We're still in danger," he said as he rose from the bed.

Sunlight filtered through the shutters, casting intriguing beams upon his thighs and buttocks. Oriel cocked her head to the side and watched as he washed in a basin and drew on his clothing.

He picked up a boot and yanked the sheets from her body. "Come, *chère*, it's well past noon, and we must be on our way. I've sent René among the townspeople to see if anyone has been searching for us. The cardinal may have sent men to find us."

"I'll hurry," she said. "But think of it. I'll be able to watch you take your clothes off every day."

He stopped in the middle of pulling on a boot and looked at her. She grinned at him, and his gaze washed over her body, lingering on her breasts. Then he shook his head.

"Stop that, you wanton baggage. I'll find Derry and see to the horses while you dress."

He left, and Oriel set about washing and dressing. She was attempting to restrain her wild hair with pins and a ribbon when she heard someone outside the door. She tied the ribbon and hastily stuffed her old gown in the pack she'd brought to hold her belongings. As she bent over the pack, the door opened. She was tying the leather laces of the pack.

"Don't scold. I'm almost ready."

"I should have killed you in London."

She cried out and whirled around. "Le Brun."

"Oui, demoiselle."

With his sword drawn, Le Brun advanced on her, towering over her like an ensorceled corpse. She stepped to the side, drawing in her breath to scream.

He lifted his sword. "If you warn him, I'll stick you now and wait for him to come searching for you."

At once she knew he intended to do what he'd described no matter what she did. She was about to launch herself at him in a desperate attempt to escape when a great din began in the tavern below—a man's shout, the clatter of pans being thrown, the thud of furniture upended. Then she heard Blade yelling for her. Le Brun smiled.

His sword thrust at her without warning. She screamed and dodged. As he recovered, she bounded away from him to the bed, grabbed her pack, and threw it at his sword. The ties wrapped around the blade.

Oriel took advantage of the few moments it took for Le Brun to free his weapon by jumping up on the bed and picking up a candlestick from a nearby table. As Le

Brun tossed the pack aside, she hurled the candle and pewter holder at him. It struck him on the temple, and he yelped as blood gushed from the wound.

Staggering slightly, he wiped the blood with his sleeve, and swore at her. Having run out of weapons, she scooped up a pillow. When he stepped toward her, she bashed him in the face with it and screamed Blade's name. She swung the pillow again, but Le Brun skewered it with his sword and tossed it aside. She glanced frantically around, but found nothing else to use as a weapon.

"Stand still, *demoiselle*, and your suffering will be slight. Make me chase you, and I'll slit your gut and leave you to die slowly and in torment."

Oriel said nothing. She fixed her entire attention on the tip of his sword. Standing on the bed with legs apart, she waited. The sword tip darted at her, and she jumped aside with a bounce. He drew back, cursing, and thrust again. She dodged again, but lost her footing on the mattress and fell to her knees. Le Brun recovered, lifted his sword again, and grinned at her.

"Well fought, *demoiselle*. And now I would suggest making your confession quickly, for I've your lover to kill before I can return to the cardinal with your dead bodies for his entertainment."

Crouched on hands and knees, she readied herself for his attack, knowing she would never be able to avoid the sword in this position. She watched him raise his sword over his head. The weapon paused at the highest point of his reach, then soared down upon her. She sprang forward, sending her body lunging toward him into the air. As she sailed off the bed, the sword arced down at her, and she realized her gamble had failed.

Chapter
22

Anger is a weed; hate is a tree.

—*St. Augustine*

Blade had been on his way to the stables with Derry when Le Brun and his men had attacked. They had charged out of the kitchen just as he'd put his hand on the back door of the tavern. He turned, drawing his sword and dagger, and gutted one man as he charged Derry. Past a mob of six men he saw Le Brun head for the stairs. He and Derry had fought their way through the pack of guards, hurling stools and tables as they went. One guard fell as a stool hit his head, another beneath Derry's sword. He shouted a warning, hoping Oriel would hear him. As he mounted the stairs, he turned and parried the thrust of one of the guards. Kicking out, he knocked the man backward and thrust, driving his sword into the man's shoulder. Leaving Derry to fight off the two remaining men and bar the stairs at the same time, he took the steps three at a time.

When he heard Oriel's voice screaming his name, he hurled himself up to the landing and ran to his room, vowing to slice the throat of the tavern keeper for selling the news of their residence to Le Brun. He kicked the door open. Oriel was on the bed. Just as she dived at Le Brun, Blade launched himself and rammed into him, knocking him off balance and sending his sword arcing down to impale the floorboards.

Blade thrust himself away from Le Brun and leaped on the bed. Le Brun pulled his sword from the floor and whirled to meet Blade's challenge. Oriel scrambled from the bed to the farthest wall.

Now that he was between Le Brun and Oriel, Blade smiled.

"*Bienvenue*, Le Brun. I see you've come to be killed. Come hither and I shall oblige you."

Blade twitched his hand; his sword flashed. Le Brun cried out and clapped a hand to his chin. Blood trickled from a fresh cut.

Blade tossed his dagger up and caught it by the blade. "I have no regrets at killing you, may God forgive me, for you've touched my lady, and for that you die." He cocked his arm, and the hilt of the dagger bent back over his shoulder.

Le Brun held up a warding hand. "Wait, Fitzstephen."

"Don't trust him," Oriel said behind him.

"God's blood, *chère*, what makes you think I would?" He eyed Le Brun. "Speak quickly, I beseech you, for I've more important things to do today than kill vermin."

As Le Brun reached inside his doublet, Blade's fingers tightened on his dagger. Le Brun slowly withdrew a sealed letter from a hidden pocket. He held it out to Blade, who lifted his brows.

"I'm not a fool," he said. "Put it on the floor and kick it toward Oriel."

Le Brun complied. Oriel snatched up the letter and retreated to stand behind him.

She opened the letter. "Madness."

"What?"

"It's a safe conduct. From the cardinal."

"*Oui,*" said Le Brun. "My instructions were to kill you, and failing that, to offer you safe conduct if you will leave at once."

"You make no sense," Blade said.

Le Brun reached inside his doublet again. "Mayhap this second letter will explain."

He pulled his hand free. Blade shouted at Oriel as he saw the edge of a knife. They both ducked, and the knife stabbed into the wall behind them. Blade landed sideways on the bed. Le Brun thrust at him as he fell, but Blade brought his sword up, and the two weapons clanged together. Le Brun hurled himself on top of Blade, trapping his dagger hand. The dagger, which Blade still held by the blade, dropped from his hand.

Their swords were still locked. Le Brun rammed his knee into Blade's gut, and Blade gasped, his arms going limp from the blow. Le Brun lifted his sword, but as he raised it, something hit him in the back. He fell onto Blade, who grunted under the weight of Le Brun and Oriel.

Le Brun reared up, furious. As he did so, Blade's hand found the dagger that had fallen on the bed in their struggles. Le Brun screamed as Oriel clawed his face and he struck her with the hilt of his sword. She collapsed and slid to the floor.

Blade rammed the dagger into Le Brun's heart. As the man fell forward, Blade scrambled over him to Oriel's side. Blood was streaming down her cheek from a cut on her forehead. He picked her up, kicked Le Brun off the bed, and lay her upon it. As he tore her petticoat into rags and dabbed at the cut, Derry rushed in.

"How does she?" he asked.

Blade wiped blood from her forehead. "He hit her, but she will be well. The others?"

"I killed one," Derry said. "The other fled. We must do the same."

Blade pointed to the letter on the floor behind the bed. Derry picked it up.

"A safe conduct from my loving host," Blade said. "What make you of that?"

"I know not, except that our dear cardinal is as twisted and devious as our friend Christian, which makes me give thanks that Christian serves Her Majesty."

"Keep the safe conduct," Blade said. "And give thought to why the cardinal would offer it. I think Le Brun disobeyed orders. I think he was told to give us that safe conduct, and he decided to rid his master of a nuisance instead."

Oriel's moan caught his attention. Derry stuffed the letter in his jerkin and brought a basin of water. Blade dipped a rag in it and pressed it to the cut on her head. Her eyes opened slowly, and she gazed up at him. He let out the breath he'd been holding when she smiled at him.

"You can see me?"

"Yes, and a pretty sight it is."

Derry snorted. "I'll ready the horses."

When he was gone, Blade kissed her gently. "*Chère*, Le Brun is dead, and we must go, if you're able."

"I can ride." She tried to rise, but sank back. "Oh, my head feels as if it's been beaten like an egg."

"I'll give you something for the pain."

"Not one of your powders."

"A few herbs, my love."

She nodded, then groaned. He wound a bandage around her head and tied it, then went downstairs to frighten the tavern keeper in revenge for his ill-dealing and to obtain his herbs. She might not want to drink his concoction, but for once she had no choice. She would drink it and sleep while they rode, and with her safe in his arms, he wouldn't have to worry that she would gallop into danger and get herself killed before he could marry her.

The journey to Calais and across the channel was much easier than he'd expected. They spent Easter crossing to England. No one chased them, and the crossing was smooth, except for Oriel's fury at his taking charge of her. He never allowed her out of his sight, and she resented his attentions, telling him she had no more need of a nursemaid than he. Finally he admitted the truth, that he could hardly bear to let her out of his sight for fear of losing her again. To his consternation, this admission of weakness gained him more compliance and sweet kisses than all his peremptory orders ever did. Women were fey, unpredictable creatures.

During the voyage he'd decided that the cardinal had sent the safe conduct for a good reason. It wouldn't do for two English lords to run about the countryside stirring up attention with their claims of persecution at his hands. They might attract the attention of the cardinal's rivals or even the Queen Mother. The idea that Charles de Guise was concerned with keeping him out of the way was an interesting one worth much contemplation.

The channel crossing was uneventful, and their ship docked in London at midday. René went ahead to arrange for horses for Blade and Oriel while Derry took his leave of them. He was due to join Christian de Rivers in Scotland. Before leaving he would take news of Blade's success to the queen's chief minister, William Cecil. Blade joined him on deck to say farewell as they watched the crew securing the ship.

"I'll attend to the button ciphers," Blade said, "and send word when we find those to whom they are addressed."

Derry nodded. "And what of Robert Richmond?"

"I'm not sure, but Oriel says he's not the kind of man to back his faith with action, especially not action that would cause him to lose his head."

"And you believe her?"

"I've learned to trust Oriel's judgment, and her wits. She led me to Thomas Richmond's journal and to the deathbed confession."

"And now she's leading you to marriage." Derry slapped Blade on the shoulder with his gloves. "Take care, Fitzstephen, or you'll end up the slave."

"Love isn't slavery."

"Mayhap not with Oriel, but there is but one Oriel, my friend."

"And I'm not sharing her."

Derry grinned at him, and he grinned back.

"Fare you well, Lord Derry. And be wary in Scotland. I don't wish to hear of you ending up slit from neck to groin on some barren mountain."

"I go to the court of the Queen of Scots, who cultivates poets and musicians and French food. God's blood, I wish her noblemen were as civilized as she, but I fear you're right. The Scots nobles are rabid and untamed wolves. I will take heed. Fare you well, Blade, and your lovely Oriel."

He watched Derry vanish into the crowd on the docks and felt a small hand on his arm. Oriel joined him, slipping her hand into the crook of his arm.

"He's gone?"

"Yes, chère."

"He kissed me farewell and—"

"Kissed you!"

She smiled at him. "A most brotherly kiss."

"Brotherly my arse."

"Blade."

He fumed and swore. "Someone should teach him—"

"Blade, look." Oriel pointed to a group below on the docks.

Closing his eyes, he pinched the bridge of his nose. "Is it the whole of your family?"

"Not Joan and her sisters, but the aunts have come breathing fire and pawing the ground. Saints, there's George. He must have had men watching the docks. And there's René with your horse."

He lifted his head and turned to her. "Ah well, *chère*, this battle won't be as terrible as those we've just survived."

"Your ordeal has made you simple if you believe so."

"Then come, we'd best charge and rout them before they gather their legions."

Taking her hand and placing it on his arm, he guided her down the ramp to the dock. He nodded at René, who saluted him but remained a good distance from the others. As they stepped down, Aunt Faith saw them, raised an arm to point, and screeched. He winced, for the noise was like the scraping of metal against metal. George, Robert, and Livia rushed at them, and they were surrounded.

"By the rood, Fitzstephen, I'll hang you by your privy parts from my highest turret."

"A good morrow to you, George."

George lunged at him. He dropped Oriel's hand, touched his sleeve, and flicked the point of his dagger at George's nose. Robert grabbed his brother and pulled him back while Livia shouldered both her sons aside with little effort.

"Oriel Richmond, you've disgraced the family," she bellowed. "After all I've suffered with dear Leslie's death, now you cavort abroad just to shame me."

Faith joined her and whined. "The whole kingdom will know of your harlotry."

"We'll never be able to go to court again."

"My daughters will grow old in spinsterhood."

"My sons will never get worthy brides."

"I shall die of dishonor and shame."

Blade saw Oriel cover her ears and flush. "Silence!" He was gratified that he could roar louder than Aunt Livia. The woman's mouth popped open, then snapped closed when he rounded on her and stared.

"A great misfortune befell me. An old enemy from France attacked, and Oriel was caught up in the fray. We'll amend the mishap at once by—"

"God's sacred arse, Nicholas, what have you done?"

Blade turned to see his father shouldering his way through dockhands and sailors. His father . . . The world seemed to fade from his perception, which fixed upon the dark-haired man looming in front of him.

He stared at that working mouth and remembered a time when he'd been so small that he had had to look up into that gaping maw. His ears filled with humiliating taunts from the past, with his mother's screams, with his own. And in that moment his father's face seemed to alter, and it seemed to Blade that he was looking at his own face in years hence.

"*No*," Blade said under his breath, his hand closing around the handle of his dagger. He wanted nothing more than to sink the dagger deep into his father's gut.

Then Oriel touched his arm. He looked down at the small, vulnerable hand on his sleeve and jerked away from it.

A chill settled over his body and spirit. Oriel touched his hand, but he could not bring himself to meet her gaze. He did not want to be like his father. But the moment he'd encountered the man, he'd nearly killed him. He would be a danger to Oriel as long as she was married to him. What madness had led him to take that risk?

His father was bellowing. "Cursed brat, you'll marry this girl at once or I'll beat some honor into your skull with my fist."

"Please," Blade said softly, "do try. I've longed for a chance to ram my boot into your face."

"You're a caitiff puling wastrel, and you'll marry at once."

"I think not, dear Father. For one sight of your loving face has convinced me that I will never marry. Good morrow to you all," he said and shoved past George, leaving behind a white-faced Oriel.

Sending René to collect his possessions, Blade rode to the Bald Pelican. He would attend to the button ciphers. Finding five traitors would keep him busy and catching them without getting killed himself would require all his attention, leaving little time in which to feel pain, or to feel at all. But first he had a letter to write.

After a short ride that skirted the riverbank, he found the Bald Pelican. He slipped inside quietly, but as he did so, the patrons of the tavern fell silent. Gamblers, harlots, and pot boys stared at him. A wanton named Nan whispered, and his name hissed around the room. Mag emerged from the kitchen into the unaccustomed silence. Wiping her hands on her apron, she grinned at him.

"Ah, it's my lovely, come home at last."

Everyone resumed his own activities when she pursed her lips and sent a kiss floating toward him. She came to him as he headed for the stairs and trapped his arm, crushing it to her bare breasts.

"You vanished like one of them pixies, lovely."

"You never complained before."

"You never sent Inigo back with two black eyes and a broken nose. Why do you think these sods mooned at you? Word is you've run afoul of Jack Midnight again. He's been looking for you."

"If he's fortunate, he won't find me."

"It's the talk of the streets. Every cutpurse and bawd in the city knows he's on to you. He says you ruined a bargain he'd struck. He's prowling around like a baited bear complaining you've destroyed his plans for his old age."

"No doubt."

Blade freed his arm and mounted the stairs. She caught up with him on the landing.

"Jack Midnight's a bad man to cross, lovely."

He paused at the door to his chamber. "Mag, Jack Midnight's a sodding angel compared to the man who made me his guest these past few days. And now, if you will send for a barrel of ale, I would like to drink until I can't see or stand."

Chapter 23

Benign, courteous, and meek,
With wordes well devised,
In you, who list to seek,
Be virtues well comprised.

—John Skelton

"God's wounds, this is all your doing!"

Oriel's voice boomed throughout the hall of her cousin George's house on the banks of the Thames River. She paced back and forth before Lord Fitzstephen, her cousins and aunts, her skirts whipping about her legs. She poked a finger at Livia.

"We were to be married this very day."

"I'll find him," Blade's father said.

Oriel rounded on him. She advanced upon Lord Fitzstephen, pinioning him with her gaze. "If you don't quit this city at once, I'll pay a cutpurse to slit your throat. I'll pay a hundred cutpurses, and I can pay the price to have the work done quickly."

"You little harlot, you need a whipping." Lord Fitz-stephen raised a fist.

George barked at him and would have stepped between the man and Oriel, but she shoved him aside. Planting her feet apart, she doubled her fists and put them on her hips.

"Lift a hand to me, and I'll tear it from your arm with my teeth. I know about you. You're a beater of women and children. You may thank God I was raised a Christian, or I'd have cut off your privy organ for what you've done to my Blade."

Her relatives gaped at her, mouths working silently. She jabbed a finger into Fitzstephen's chest. By now the man was so swollen with repressed fury his head looked like a ripe apple.

"Get you gone, sirrah, or I'll have my cousins toss you out in the streets so hard you'll land among the sops and dead dogs of Houndsditch."

Lord Fitzstephen sputtered and gave an impotent roar. He eyed George and Robert, whose hands had touched their swords, then stomped out of the hall.

"O—ri-el!" bellowed Aunt Livia.

Faith wailed. "The disgrace. I shall be mortified."

She ignored them and turned on George and Robert. Buffeting George on the shoulder, she snapped at him.

"Cease your mewling. You're going to find my betrothed or I'll hire those cutpurses to slit your throats instead, and remember, I've five caskets full of baubles to spend on the task. Off with you."

George shoved Robert out of the hall before him.

Livia gawked at her son's retreating back, then threw back her head and howled. "Geeooorge!" George vanished, and she scowled at Oriel. "You shameful little trollop."

Oriel raised her fist until it floated in front of Livia's nose. "It has been my dearest wish to poke you in the nose these eight long years."

Livia's eyes rounded and swelled to the size of pomegranates. "You dare not."

"You've cost me my love. I would dare far more." Oriel drew back her fist.

Livia squawked, turned, and fled. Oriel spun about and marched on Faith, who picked up her skirts and scampered after Livia. Slowly, she lowered her fist, but both hands remained clenched. She closed her eyes and saw again Blade's storm cloud eyes looking at her, but not seeing her for the cloying mist of pain that surrounded him. Those eyes, they had shown her a glimpse of hell, of a self-hatred she'd never dreamed existed.

He believed himself a danger to her, and would destroy himself rather than imperil her with his presence. She had watched him transform once faced with the specter of his own father. He'd closed up, marshaling his unyielding will, and she had been left alone.

She wouldn't allow him to abandon her again. She would hunt him down and crack that armor of resolve before he took himself off in search of some new intrigue. She would hunt him down and make him face her, and quickly, for the longer they were apart, the stronger his rage and fear would grow until they would engulf his love for her, and burn it to ashes.

George and Robert searched for three days before they found the man she knew only as Inigo. Shoving him into her presence in the hall, they grinned at her like two hounds presenting their master with a pheasant. He peered at her over the thick bandage that covered his nose. He sported two black eyes and still spoke as though someone had stuffed wool up his nose.

"You are Inigo."

"Yes, lady, and you're the one what tried to save, er," he glanced at George and bobbed his head. "Yes, lady."

"You will take me to Blade at once. He's not at his house, and you no doubt frequent the same foul haunts."

"I can't do that, lady."

"Inigo, I've been abducted, stabbed at, hied me clear across the channel and back, slept in leaves and dirt, and all to lose my lord once I got home again." She drew a dagger she'd stuffed in her girdle and tapped it on Inigo's bandage. "If you don't tell me where he is, I'll show you that my lord isn't the only one worthy of the name Blade."

Inigo put his hands over his nose. "God save me, you're just like him."

"No, for he would give you a moment to think. I am going to slit your nose." She moved the dagger.

"Wait, lady!" Inigo shrank away from her. "You won't like where he's gone. It's not a place for you."

"I'll slit each nostril."

"He's at the Bald Pelican."

"Show me."

"He'll do more than slit my nose if he finds out I've told you."

Oriel picked up her cloak from a chair. "Then you have a choice. I can slit it now, or you may put off the ordeal a while. George, you and Robert will escort me."

"I'm not challenging him," Robert said as he followed her.

George grunted unhappily. "Nor am I."

"You won't have to. I will."

The hour was near sunset, but they found the Bald Pelican before dark. It lay in a road congested with the traffic of pack animals, porters, apprentices, and merchants, squeezed between two old timbered buildings whose use couldn't have been any more savory than the tavern's. Inigo led her inside, and she was blinded for a moment by the darkness.

None of the windows had been opened in this century, and the stink of tallow candles nearly made her gag. She had worn an old cloak and pulled the hood close to her face, but their arrival gave the inhabitants pause, for George and Robert wore clothing seldom seen in the Bald Pelican except when stolen. She surveyed the patrons, and her jaw fell as she encountered a bare-breasted woman being fondled by a tattered gallant.

George rumbled under his breath. "Leslie would have loved this place."

She was tempted to speak upon the subject of Leslie and his habits, but restrained herself. No good would come of such an indulgence, and George would be hurt.

Inigo tugged at her cloak. "Come, lady. Don't linger here."

He took her upstairs, but paused on the landing when a plump blond woman turned a corner and confronted them. She looked at Inigo, then at Oriel and her escort, then at Inigo again.

"You're daft if you think you can bring a strange bawd into my house, Inigo Culpepper."

"Mag," Inigo said, "this is no bawd."

Oriel threw her hood back. "She knows that."

Mag sauntered over to her, taking care that her breasts jiggled. "Yes, I know it right well. He doesn't want company, especially not yours."

"You know who I am."

"I know. He's described that wild hair and those puke green eyes so many times I nearly screamed. Course, he does that, does Blade, makes a woman scream."

Oriel unclasped her cloak and handed it to Robert. She smoothed her hands over blue and silver brocade and studied Mag. "Indeed."

Mag strolled to the banister and leaned on it. She leered at George, who squirmed and muttered to himself.

"In—deed," Mag said. "So you might as well take yourself off. He doesn't want to see you. He won't see any woman but me."

"George, show Mag the color of your coin."

George produced a pouch fat with money, but Mag

tossed her head. "His door's locked, and I got the key, which I ain't giving to you."

"Then, since you've no fear of my getting into his chamber, you may entertain my cousins."

George tossed the pouch in the air and caught it. Mag heard the clink of the coins and smiled at him.

"There's been five girls tried to get into his room; the likes of you won't do it." Mag took George and Robert each by the arm. "Come on, gentlemen. Let Mag show you what a fat purse like that can buy."

"She doesn't like you," Inigo said as he led the way to Blade's chamber.

"It's only fair, since I detest her."

He stopped at a closed door in the middle of a dark corridor. She immediately pounded on it with her fist.

"Go away, Mag."

"Blade Fitzstephen, you show your cowardly face at once."

There was a pause, then a stream of fluent gutter language followed. Inigo shivered and started to tiptoe back down the corridor. Oriel caught him by the neck of his jerkin while pounding on the door again.

A familiar, musical voice answered. "Go away."

"I will not."

"Stay there all night then."

She kicked the door, but there was no response. Giving the portal a scowl, she pulled Inigo down and whispered something to him. He gaped at her.

"He'll kill me."

"Die now, or later."

He groaned, but cupped his hands around his mouth and shouted in a rasping voice. "Here's a pretty maid, my lads, ha!"

Oriel screamed and cried out Blade's name. The latch on the door rattled, and Inigo sprinted for the stairs.

Blade burst through the door calling for her, and as

he ran by, she darted into the chamber. He veered around to stare at her, then hurried back inside.

"You tricked me."

"A small device when measured against your beguilements, but I haven't had as much practice."

She looked around the chamber, which was littered with his clothing and the remains of meals, and at least twelve casks and flagons.

"You will leave," he said.

She faced him and shook her head. He blinked at her slowly, and she realized that he was drunk, though his hands and walk were steady. Hair tousled, face shadowed with several days' beard, he nevertheless presented a delectable sight, all glowering male fury and tense muscles. Distracted by the sensuality he seemed to emanate without intent, she floated over to him and caught his hands. He shook her off with a curse and retreated behind a table littered with scraps of bread and cheese. Undaunted, she kicked the door shut and turned the key.

"There is always the window," he said.

"And leave me alone in this place unprotected?"

"René will escort you home."

Oriel approached the table, planted her hands on it, and stared into his silver-grey eyes. "Who would have thought the infamous Blade a coward."

"Me? I," he said carefully, "am not a coward."

"You're afraid to love me."

He looked away. "That is another matter."

"Blade," she said in a low, breathy voice.

He glanced at her, wary.

"God's toes," she said. "You'll fight traitors and French demons for the queen, but shrink at the challenge of fighting for yourself and for me."

"I am fighting for you, for what's best for you."

"Have you ever hit a woman?"

He shook his head.

"Ever killed one?"

He shook his head again.

"Do you know why?"

"My father—"

"Ah-ha. Your father." Oriel grasped the table and shoved it aside. "I ran your father out of the city the day you left me on the docks." She took a step toward Blade, who took a step back.

"You?"

"Yes." She walked toward him, and he backed away. "He wanted to beat me, but I told him I'd put a price on his head if he so much as disturbed one of my curls."

"You don't know me," Blade said. "All you see is, is this body. Inside there's a fiend, a mindless ravening monster."

"If there were such a fearsome creature, it would have gained mastery of you long ago."

Oriel placed herself before him, her body almost touching his. She flattened her hands on his chest, ran them down his torso to his thighs, then stroked up the inside of his legs to his groin.

"Here," she said. "Here is the only ravening beast I've seen, and it is indeed most ungovernable."

Blade grabbed her wrists and pulled her hands away. His eyes glittered. "If I wanted servicing, I'd pay one of the other doxies under this roof."

Oriel gasped, her face draining of color, her eyes filling with tears.

From the tavern below came René's voice. As René rushed into the chamber, followed by a man in Fitz-stephen livery, Blade shoved Oriel away. The man bowed to Blade and handed him a letter. Blade broke the seal. After a quick glance, he folded the letter again and handed it to the messenger.

"René, find Inigo so that he may escort Mistress Oriel home. We leave at once."

"You're not leaving without me."

He fixed her with a wintry stare. "He's dead. My father is dead, and I must go home to Castle La Roche.

He's dead, and when I die, our cursed lineage ends as well. Not even you, Oriel, will change my mind."

When he was gone she looked at René, who regarded her sadly.

"I am afraid, my lady. A blackness of spirit has overtaken him, and he cares not what perils he undertakes. For one such as he, such negligence could cost him his life."

René and the messenger left, and she was alone. A blackness of spirit, René had said, a sword-bright soul eaten with the acid of cruelty, the cruelty of a monstrous father.

She wasn't giving up, which meant that she would have to follow Blade to La Roche. Now that his vicious father was dead, she must convince her tormented betrothed that his fears were but the stuff of nightmares left over from a time long gone. However, no matter how strong her resolve, she couldn't lay siege to Blade if he was sequestered in that great pile of stone—not without an army. Therefore, she would need aid from within. René!

Rushing out of the chamber, she stopped on the landing and surveyed the tavern below. Potboys and maids were busy clearing up a wreckage caused by the battle between two patrons over a dice game. Several groups of men played backgammon and diced. From two of the upstairs rooms nearest the landing George and Robert emerged, tucking bits of clothing back into place. They joined her, but she waved them away when her attention fastened on a slender, tall figure below.

Blade stood at the front door, and Mag with him. She was talking, and he bent down to hear her, frowning. She chuckled and smiled at him, but he only stared at her. She put her arms around his neck, snuggled up to him, and took his mouth in a long, leisurely kiss. Oriel clamped her hands on the banister to keep from screaming at the two.

Finally Mag released Blade, whose frown hadn't

lessened for all her efforts. He said something to her, and she laughed and glanced up at Oriel. Blade followed the direction of her gaze and met Oriel's scowl. For an infinite moment he continued to stare at her, unsmiling, then turned and left without a word to Mag.

Once he was gone, Oriel was able to think clearly. There was one task that needed doing at once. Catching Mag's eye, she marched down the stairs. The woman ambled across the tavern to meet her.

"Mag, if you ever touch him again, I'll cut your lips off."

Mag hooted and looked her up and down. "You? I could have a few of my friends at you right now. Break your neck and toss you in a ditch."

"And then Blade would kill you."

The sneer on Mag's face disappeared.

"I see you understand. No other woman has ever been able to make such a promise, or expected it to be kept."

Mag shoved her. "Get out of my house, you bleeding witch's spawn."

"Where is René?"

"He's in the kitchen with that messenger, but you're not going in there."

"If you want me to leave I am."

Mag snorted and flounced past her to mount the stairs with injured dignity. George came up to her.

"Please, Oriel. We should leave."

"A moment longer, George."

With him close behind, she went to the kitchen. The place was crowded with cooks, scullions, and turnspits all bustling about. At a table in a corner sat René and the messenger, who was gulping down hot stew. René saw her, lifted a brow, and rose. Bowing, he murmured a greeting in French. She responded in the same language before launching into her request. She had already decided that George would be happier not having full knowledge of her plans. As she spoke, René's eyes brightened. When she finished, he bowed to her in salute.

"*Oui, demoiselle.* On the battlements, one hour past midnight."

"*Merci*, René. Until then."

With her arrangements settled, she left the kitchen. George followed, catching her arm.

"What is this talk of battlements and midnight. What have you done? I'll not play your fool any longer, Oriel. It's plain you've failed. The time has come for me to—"

"Oh hush, George. Blade's father has died."

"But he just left the city."

"He died on the way home. Died of fury, it seems. A groom annoyed him, and he whipped him, but as he was flaying the poor man he turned purple and died. God is just, it seems. Where is Robert?" She waved at her cousin, who was ogling a bawd.

"Nevertheless," George said, "I will defend your honor."

"No need, I thank you." She put her hand on George's arm. "I told you I would settle with Blade myself, and I have. I'm going to Castle La Roche, to be married."

"Good." George beamed at her as he led her from the tavern with Robert in their wake.

Silently Oriel prayed to God for forgiveness for her untruths. After all, she must journey north to La Roche, for which she would need George's escort. And by the time poor George discovered her ruse, it would be too late to turn back.

Chapter 24

*For as well as I have loved thee,
mine heart will not serve me to see thee,
for through thee and me is the flower
of kings and knights destroyed.*

—Sir Thomas Malory

The trees bore leaves of new green. May and spring had come at last to the north of England. Blade touched the knobbed branch of an apple tree. It bounced under his finger, then swayed in the breeze. He lifted his face to the sun, eyes closed. No matter how many springs came and went, he would always feel encased in a winter frost.

He glanced back at the inner ward of Castle La Roche. The old, square keep rose high behind the inner battlements, its pennants signaling that he was in residence. The spires of the chapel could be seen just above the merlons. He had buried his father in the crypt below it this morning—and felt nothing.

For most of his life he'd longed for this day, and now the reality seemed far less satisfying. Only this morning had he understood that he hadn't wanted his father to die. He'd wanted him to magically transform into a loving, gentle sire, a man like Christian de Rivers's father. He had longed for such a father, and he would never have one. This need had left a flaw in his construction, as if masons had built a wall and left a gap that weakened the whole structure.

He walked between the rows of apple trees in the castle orchard and tried to throw off this mantle of gloom that had beset him since first confronting his father on the London docks. Useless. Oriel's loss haunted him. He would never spend days with her reading Ovid and Thomas Wyatt, never laugh at her attempts to remember names, touch her hair.

Cursing, he muttered aloud. "But at least she's safe —safe from me."

He would give away all his father's possessions. They reminded him of nothing but pain. His steward would protest. His distant relatives would protest more, for he had yet to inform them of Lord Fitzstephen's death. No matter. They could do nothing but complain, for he was lord of Castle La Roche.

He left the orchard and walked across the inner ward, passing stables and the mews. The castle was built in two concentric circles of battlemented walls, each thicker than he was tall. He'd spent his childhood here in the new house beside the keep.

The former owners had built the fortress at the behest of Henry II to guard the border between England and Scotland, only to have it confiscated when they did more raiding than guarding. It had passed from family to family until Edward III handed it to Blade's ancestor, in whose family it had remained for more than two hundred years. Now it was his turn to guard the border for his queen. Because of the tumult caused in the last few months by the Queen of Scots, his task would be a perilous one.

Yet his greatest fear wasn't the threat of the Queen of Scots. It was that his own sovereign, upon hearing that he'd succeeded to his father's title, would insist upon his marriage to produce an heir. Elizabeth was a great one for insisting her lords do their duty, though she herself had yet to marry. He'd never be able to stomach looking at some inbred, pale and mincing maid when he only wanted Oriel.

He walked through the gate house of the inner ward and into the outer bailey. His head groom was training a new stallion in the art of keeping his rider alive in battle. Most of the gentlemen and boys of his household had gathered to observe. He left them behind, acknowledged the salutes of guards at the outer gate, and walked across the drawbridge over the moat, then down the steep slope of the hill upon which Castle La Roche was built.

He must try to prevent every thought from veering off course and leading to Oriel. After arriving from France he'd sent a letter to the Cardinal of Lorraine. He'd kept it a secret from Oriel, for he hadn't wanted her to worry. He knew better than to expect the cardinal to give up hunting him simply because he'd crossed the channel.

That letter had contained a solution to this threat, one the cardinal wouldn't like at all. He waited for a response. Meanwhile, he'd set a clerk to work on the button ciphers. The man was closeted in the Black Tower in the castle at this very moment, studying the papers.

"Mon seigneur!"

He turned to see René hurrying after him.

"Mon seigneur, you must not leave without escort."

"Go away. There is no need at the moment."

"But my lord—"

"I forbid it," he said, his voice rising. He threw his

cloak over one shoulder and patted the hilt of his sword. "I've protection enough, and my need for solitude is too great. Leave me."

Without waiting for a reply, he turned and resumed his walk down the rocky hillside to the forested dale below. Here the trees grew thick. Their branches, fluttering with light green leaves, formed a dais overhead. Most wore a coat of lichen that contrasted with the blacks and greys of hazel and oak trunks. He could feel the evidence of spring in the warmth of the sun on his face.

He walked some way into the forest until the keep pennants were barely visible through the trees. His father and grandfather and great-grandfather had reserved the forests surrounding La Roche for game, and the nearest village was some leagues away in another valley. He picked up a dead branch and started breaking it into tiny pieces, which he discarded as he walked. When he moved, shadows cast by the branches above him crawled along his body.

His stride slowed as an unexpected memory tore at him. In his imagination he saw Oriel, tongue peeking out of the corner of her mouth, bent over her catalog of Thomas Richmond's books, her hair glinting in sunlight. She glanced up at him, and that enthralled expression came over her eyes. He'd seen women appraise him before, but never had he been so sure that the appraisal included his true self as well as his person.

The branch in his hand snapped, and he shook his head. There was another snap, and he whirled around, his cloak swinging, his sword already halfway out of its sheath. A man stepped from behind a thick tree trunk— a young man. Richly dressed in black patterned silk, gold chains, and an ornate rapier, he spread his arms wide to signal his peaceful intent. He smiled at Blade and propped one shoulder against the tree.

Blade looked from him to the surrounding forest and kept his sword trained on the stranger, who waited patiently for him to finish his survey. Finally he returned his gaze to the stranger. He was smooth of face, with silken black hair and the smile of an angel confronted with a cherub. His cheeks bore a maiden's rosy hue, yet he wore his sword with the ease of a mercenary.

"Sieur de Racine," the young man said. "His Eminence is most displeased with you."

Blade pointed his sword at the stranger's heart. "And I with him. What do you want?"

The young man bowed gracefully. "I am Jean-Paul."

"You bring an answer to my letter to the cardinal."

"I am the answer."

Blade lifted his brow and waited. Jean-Paul crossed his legs at the ankles and cocked his head to the side.

"I must say you don't look the troublesome interloper, nor do you seem capable of eluding His Eminence."

"What do you want?"

Jean-Paul gave an impatient sigh and straightened. Leaving the tree, he approached Blade, who kept his sword pointed at the stranger. Jean-Paul stopped two sword lengths from him.

"You're half French, I am told. Surely you appreciate the refinements of courtesy, even between enemies."

"I'm also half English, and therefore have no trust in Frenchmen. Speak or draw your sword."

Jean-Paul sighed again, then made the sign of the cross before Blade in benediction. "Peace, my son."

"God's blood, he's sent a priest." Blade lowered his sword a few inches. "A worldly priest, as befits Charles de Guise."

A lazy smile rippled over Jean-Paul's lips. "I was raised in a monastery until the cardinal found me. He took me into his household, where I received a much more—thorough education. But, as you say, I must speak. His Eminence is most displeased at your letter."

"Good," Blade said. "Then he appreciated that the

Queen Mother of France would also be displeased if she were to learn of his dealings with English Catholics and his attempt to put his niece on the throne of England. You forget, Father, I've lived in France. The kingdom is torn apart by the struggle between Protestant and Catholic, and the Valois king and his mother are caught in the middle. They balance between the Catholic de Guises and the Protestant house of Orléans. The Queen Mother would be more than displeased to learn of the cardinal's plots."

"His Eminence is thinking of confiscating your French estates."

"She might be so alarmed as to accuse the cardinal of treason."

"He is also most concerned about your health."

"The house of Orléans would dance a jig upon learning of his dealings with the English, and would no doubt send their armies to aid the Queen Mother in arresting His Eminence."

"And the health of Mistress Oriel Richmond."

Blade smiled at Jean-Paul. "No doubt the king of France would arrange an auto-da-fé with the cardinal as the chief entertainment. Has a cardinal ever been drawn and quartered?"

"*Bien touché*, Fitzstephen. Well hit." Jean-Paul laughed and rested the palm of his hand on the top of his sword hilt. "He told me you wouldn't respond to threats. His Eminence offers a truce. Your silence for his tolerance. You may live in peace, even keep your lands."

"How generous, considering I've already told him that should harm befall me for any reason, there are five secret letters concerning his doings which will be posted to various interested persons."

"His Eminence is always solicitous of the health of his friends."

"*Merde.*"

Jean-Paul laughed, then his hand twitched, and five men emerged from the forest to surround them. "I had to be sure, *mon seigneur*. As you see, I am a careful man."

"You're a strutting, overconfident boy."

Blade whistled. Behind the Frenchmen appeared a company of his men, headed by René. Jean-Paul chuckled and signaled to his men to be still.

"Well played, Fitzstephen." He met Blade's gaze coolly. "Have I your word upon our contract?"

"You have it. As long as the cardinal keeps his fingers out of English pies, his guilt will not be published on the church steps of France."

"Then I will take leave of you."

Jean-Paul glanced around at Blade's men. Blade nodded to René, and the Englishmen fell back to allow the Frenchmen to leave. Jean-Paul bowed to him, and returned the courtesy.

"My men will escort you to London, priest, and see you safely aboard a ship."

"Your care for my safety is generous, but unnecessary."

"God's blood, sirrah, I consider your departure from England of great portent to me and to my queen. Fare you well."

He watched Jean-Paul stride off surrounded by his men, who in turn were surrounded by his. René joined him, sheathing his sword.

"You followed me despite my command."

"Of course, my lord."

"No doubt you will castigate me for my carelessness from now until Judgment Day."

"God forbid, my lord."

"You'd better send word to Inigo. He should double the number of men watching Mistress Oriel. I won't rest well until I'm sure the cardinal means to honor our bargain."

He began walking back toward the castle with René at his side. He wasn't surprised that the man cast censorious looks at him and finally spoke.

"Before, you wouldn't have been taken by surprise —before you left Mistress Oriel. Since you parted from her you're like a pup that's lost its dame."

Blade halted and faced René. "Keep your place, man, or I'll send you back to France."

"Brooding," René continued undaunted, "and roaming about the castle like a besotted lover in a play."

Hurling himself away from his tormentor, Blade marched up the steep slope toward the castle. "I'll not listen to this mawkish prattling. I told you. I've no desire to saddle myself with any woman. Women need protecting, and they can do nothing for themselves. They must be guided and advised, and they're helpless. I despise being burdened forever with a whining, frail, dependent maid."

"Are we speaking of Mistress Oriel Richmond?"

He glared at the skeptical tone René used and stomped across the drawbridge. Clearing the gate house, he turned on René, hissing at him.

"*Sacré Dieu,* you know why I must not have her. You know why. Saints give me peace, and you as well."

René stuck his thumbs in his belt. "Will you keep men about her for the rest of her life? What will you do when she marries?"

"Marries?" Blade gaped at his servant as if he'd spoken Arabic. "Marries?"

"Marries," René repeated firmly. "Her cousin won't allow her to remain a maid, especially now that, well, especially now that she's—especially now. He will find a complaisant husband for her, one who will be glad to overlook certain points of honor for her dowry."

"He won't if he wants to live," Blade said. "And don't leer at me."

He swore and flung himself away from René and his mirthful visage, only to encounter his steward hurrying toward him.

"My lord, you have a guest."

"God's bones, not another Frenchman."

"Lord Braithwaite, my lord." The steward nearly danced with excitement. "Of the queen's household."

Suppressing a groan, he headed for the inner ward and the great hall. No doubt the queen had heard of his father's death and sent Braithwaite with her condolences. He must summon his courtly manners, though his temper had been sorely tried. He entered the hall, a chamber built to hold several hundred retainers, and greeted Lord Braithwaite.

An older man with a head shaped like a quince, Braithwaite bowed stiffly to him and presented a letter to him from the queen. In it she expressed her sympathy upon the loss of his father, and her good wishes to him upon his succession to the barony.

Braithwaite snapped his fingers at a servant. The man came forward with a long, gilded box set on a velvet pillow.

"Her Majesty sends this token of her good will and thanks Lord Fitzstephen for his service to her, and those good offices she is sure he will perform in the future."

Braithwaite took the box and held it out to Blade. Opening the lid, he revealed a quillon dagger. It was a ceremonial one of gold, and its hilt was set with emeralds and diamonds symbolizing the queen's colors of green and white. Just below the hilt, engraved on the blade, were the queen's initials, ER—Elizabeth Regina. Blade picked up the weapon, unable to speak.

"Her Majesty sent this letter and instructed me to tell you that henceforth she names you her Dagger."

He took the proffered letter and heard himself making courtly replies, ones which seemed to please Braithwaite. He offered the man wine and food, but he only desired to be conducted to his chamber, saying that his journey had been a long one. Relieved, Blade escorted his guest to his quarters and left him there.

He locked the dagger in a heavy chest in his own chamber, and knelt beside it with the key in his hand.

Finally alone, he broke the royal seal of the letter and read.

> *Right trusty and well-beloved Dagger,*
>
> *We have received news from our Derry of your vigilant care for our estate. Know you right well that such goodly service and bravery lodge within our heart, and that we do not forget faithful subjects. This token of our thanks cannot fill up the half of our debt to you. Have a care, my lord, for your health. We have heard of a great plague spreading from France, and would see you come to no harm.*
>
> *Your loving sovereign,*
> *Elizabeth R*

He folded the letter, reopened the chest, and placed the letter inside the gilded box with the dagger. He rose and deposited himself in the carved oak chair by the window seat and glanced around his chamber. The favor of the queen was priceless.

Men spent their lives cultivating the affection and gratitude of their sovereign, for that was the path to riches and power. He had gained that favor. How he wished he could rejoice in it. Yet somehow, the praise of Her Majesty struck no chord of pleasure within him. The idea was frightening.

Was this a portent? Would he spend the rest of his life comparing happy events to the dizzy tumult caused by one of Oriel's smiles? He would go right mad.

Wyatt had understood. He'd been forced to give up his love. Blade rubbed his eyes with thumb and forefinger. He should go to the Black Tower and take counsel with his clerk about the button ciphers, but his head throbbed and he kept hearing one of Wyatt's songs in his head. He rose and knelt on the window seat, gazing down at the servants, guards, and peasants in the courtyard.

He shoved the window open and breathed in air smelling of horses and hay, and murmured to himself, " 'Now must I learn to live at rest/ And wean me of my will/ For I repent where I was pressed/ My fancy to fulfill.' "

Chapter
25

*I have seen the wicked in great power, and
spreading himself like a green bay tree.*

—*Psalms 37:35*

George took over a week to ready himself for
their journey to Castle La Roche, which was
fortunate, for Oriel was busy making her own arrangements. She hired five new and unique servants and sent
them on ahead to wait for her in a village near the castle.
Once she was ready to leave London, her greatest fear
was that Livia or Faith would come along. To her relief,
neither wished to accompany her. After their last con-
frontation, they had retreated from the battlefield in defeat and wished for no further skirmishes.

Thus she set out with George and Robert as her
escorts. Along the way, Oriel listened with tolerance to
George's complaining, and decided that, in spite of having a trumpet with legs for a mother, he'd taken after his
Aunt Faith. For the better part of their journey north

he'd whined like a bagpipe. At this moment he was quite noisy, for his midday meal had settled and he had grown accustomed to the saddle once more. It was her misfortune that he'd chosen to ride beside her instead of Robert. Their men had slowed their pace so that she and George rode well ahead. No one cared to listen to him if he could avoid it.

"You'd think Fitzstephen would have provided an escort," George said. "I can't stay away from Richmond Hall forever, and I'm in mourning for Leslie."

She hadn't noticed any tears on his cheeks, or Robert's. Leslie had been Livia's favorite. She had expended her small store of love on him, and they had known it.

"And how haps it," George continued, "that your betrothed frequents the company of such rogues as this Inigo? How haps it that we found him all comfortable and cosseted in that stew with that blond doxy? And how haps it that he and Leslie were attacked by thieving gamblers in some strange house, and how haps it that all of you ended up in France? I don't believe your tale of abduction. Who would abduct Fitzstephen?"

"I told you. A noblewoman of the court who was enamored of him sent ruffians to bring him back to France."

"A scurrilous falsehood."

"George, you've seen for yourself what happens when he but walks into a chamber where there are women. Remember Joan and Jane?"

"Then he should stop."

"Stop walking into chambers?"

George cast an irritated glance at her. "Stop beguiling women."

"It happens whether by his design or not. George, must we discuss these grey-haired old troubles over and over? Content you that I'm to be married and will quit Richmond Hall."

George reined in his horse and looked at her. "I will miss you."

She nearly slipped off her saddle.

"In truth?"

"Yes. You're the only one who ever routed Mother and Aunt Faith. One of my chiefest amusements was listening to her bawl your name when you hid from her. Robert and I would place wagers upon whether her head would burst open like a dropped melon with the force of her fury. I cheated by directing her to places I knew you hadn't gone."

She patted his arm. "You're a good man, George."

"But not a brave one, I fear."

They continued riding, for Castle La Roche was still some distance away, and George was anxious to reach it before sunset. Poor George, he would be disappointed, for she had no intention of entering the castle before nightfall.

Indeed, she planned to camp at least a league away upon the excuse of illness or a fever of the brain caused by anticipation of her wedding. Then, when everyone was asleep, she would go to La Roche alone. René would be waiting on the battlements to let her inside, and she would lay siege to Lord Fitzstephen in a way he'd never imagined, despite all his experience at the licentious French court.

They had topped a hill and were riding on a track down the slope that led to another forested dale. The closer they got to La Roche, the thicker the woods became. The trees boasted leaves of a bright pale green that spoke of their newness. She surveyed them as they fluttered overhead, narrowing her eyes against the brightness of the sun. They continued amicably for some time until George informed her that they were now on the road to La Roche.

It wound and twisted through a dense forest made dark by the long shadows cast by the setting sun. George complained of a sore backside. Overhead she spotted a merlin hurtling after some unfortunate prey. She was just about to fluster, dither, and flutter herself into a pretended maidenly fit when something inhuman began to howl.

She turned to see men dropping from trees and springing from bushes. Without warning a smelly ruffian plummeted from above her head to land behind her on her horse. The animal reared, and she fought to stay atop it while her attacker rolled off the animal's back.

Behind her a line of thieves separated her and George from the rest of their party. As she flayed about her with her riding crop, George attempted to draw his sword, but was felled by a rock hurled by a thief who couldn't have been more than sixteen. She screamed at George, but he was oblivious. The young thief dragged George's horse away.

Her crop whacked the head of one of her attackers, and she glimpsed Robert as he shrieked and bolted from the fray. Those of his men left upright galloped after him.

"Robert, you worm, come back!"

Suddenly a man with silver and black hair appeared on a horse at her side. He snatched her from the saddle. She twisted in his arms and swatted him with her crop. He cried out as the weapon slapped the top of his head, and she heard several thieves laugh. He wrenched the crop from her and began to shake her so hard she was sure her head would pop off her neck. When he stopped, she was sick to her stomach and so dizzy she couldn't see him. She could hear, though.

"Well done, my happy sots. Willie! I told you no killing. Leave the cony, or we'll have the whole county after us, and I'm tired of being chased about the countryside."

Oriel groaned as the man flipped her on her stomach and launched his horse into a gallop. Her head hit his knee, and she yelped. Suffering from this last blow, jounced by the gait of the horse, she had no hint of their direction. She was about to retch all over her captor's boots when the horse slowed and then halted. She was dumped off the horse and landed on all fours. Sick and frightened, she kept reminding herself of the leader's injunction against killing.

The boots of her captor appeared beneath her nose, and she looked up. He was grinning down at her in the twilight. Grabbing the back of her gown, he jerked her upright and to her feet. Holding her arm as she swayed, he chuckled and addressed her at last.

"Mistress Oriel Richmond," he said. "Such a scrawny little hen to fetch so high a price." He bowed, still leering at her. "Jack Midnight, mistress, your host for this night."

"Midnight." Oriel glanced around for a way out, but his men had surrounded them, though most were busy examining their spoils. "Midnight. I think I've heard that name. God's toes, Jack Midnight! You're the one who attacked Blade Fitzstephen."

"Yes, mistress, several times."

He held out his hand, but she only stared at it until he took her arm and began to stroll toward a fallen tree.

"Sit you down," he said. "My plans are going well, and if they succeed entirely, you will be in Castle La Roche before midnight."

Somewhat calmed by his placid demeanor, she sat on the log. "What plan?"

"Ah," he said. "A bit of fun, mistress. Revenge and spoils, all at the same time."

One of the thieves brought a water bag, and he offered it to Oriel. While she drank, he continued.

"You see, your betrothed has cost me much of the loot I was planning to collect for my old age. I was in the city watching him, but he bolted. Now you've put yourself in my way, and I am grateful."

"Loot for your old age? Sooner or later you'll be hanged. You won't have an old age."

"I will on the Continent." Midnight drank from the water bag, then grinned at her. "Your betrothed will provide the funds."

"He'll kill you."

"Nah. He and I are old friends, though I confess we're also old enemies. Blade's a clever boy, he is. He'll see the sense of paying for you, and then I'm gone. My messenger is already on his way. Now you needn't be frightened. I rarely kill women."

Oriel found his protestations of little comfort. "What of George?"

"Who?"

"The man who was riding beside me."

"He'll wake in a few hours. Willie gave him a nasty rap on the noggin, but he'll be fine. Your other men, now, they showed us their backsides right quick."

"I know. They've more to fear from Blade than do you."

Midnight studied her face. "You're a bold little runagate, for all your highborn manners."

"I've had to be, I've lived with two entire aunts and a gaggle of cousins."

"You've got no family?"

"My parents died."

Midnight faced her and straddled the log. "I could have had a daughter like you. Put off my land, I was, by a bleeding, piss-spewing nobleman."

"But why?"

"Noblemen don't need reasons to treat honest men like pig's swill. Once I would have taken pleasure in running your George through, but time changes a man."

"And why are you confessing to me?" Oriel asked.

He smiled at her and took another swig from the water bag. "Quick of wit, you are, for a gentry mort. Well, mistress, in the past year or so I've grown tired. I used to live on hate—fed on it like mother's milk. But lately it's as if the old rancor is like a shirt so old it's only clinging to me by a thread or two. Mayhap I wore it so long because it was familiar."

"So you will withdraw from active thievery and spend your days in comfort, living off your plunder."

"Yes, you're clever." He gave her an admiring look, which faded into a frown. "My wife and her babe starved, you know, like many of us when the lords began to enclose lands. But after all these years, I can hardly remember their faces."

Oriel watched his face. It bore the lines of hardship, rage, and grief, but his eyes reflected some measure of peace. Perhaps his own wrath had worn him out.

"Time to go, mistress." Midnight stood and pulled her to her feet.

"Where are we going?"

"To a place where I'll be safe when my sweet Blade comes charging out of his castle in search of you. He's been told the time and place, you see. And how much you will cost as well."

Darkness had closed in by the time they reached the place of assignation. To her it seemed unremarkable, a mere clearing in the thickest part of the woods. Midnight ordered a fire built in the middle of the clearing, but he and his men avoided it once it blazed high. Guiding Oriel to a place beside a tree that looked as tall as a keep, he snapped his fingers, and all but one of his ruffians vanished. They accomplished the feat so quickly she couldn't see where they went. The remaining man looked like a tree with legs, so tall was he.

"Mistress Oriel," said Jack Midnight, "meet Long Willie. It's time, Willie."

Long Willie swooped down on her from behind. Wrapping his arms around her, he lifted her in the air. Oriel screamed, but her cry was muffled when Willie clamped a hand over her mouth. She kicked Willie's shin, but he responded by squeezing the air out of her body, and she subsided.

Midnight stood back, hands on his hips, and examined her. "Now, is that any way for a gentry mort to behave?"

"Mmmfff."

"Now, you mind your manners. Your pretty betrothed should be here soon. He's been told to come to the fire with the ransom. He'll be furious, but he's got no choice but to comply, considering the things I said I'd do if he disobeyed. Willie, take Mistress Oriel for a ride."

She was tossed over Willie's shoulder, and she began pounding his back. Without warning they rose in the air, and she realized he was climbing the tree. The ground receded quickly, yet still Willie climbed. She stopped pounding him and clutched at his belt. Squeezing her eyes shut, she prayed for wings.

When they stopped, she opened her eyes again, and was immediately sorry. Willie had climbed almost to the top of the tree. She never knew she was afraid of heights. Hanging upside down, the branches beneath her seemed mere threads that would break under her weight if she fell. Mayhap the sight of Jack Midnight far below, dwarfed by the height of the tree, worsened her fear.

Willie shifted her, then set her on a branch next to the trunk. Once free, she clutched the trunk with both arms. Willie drew a knife and held it to her stomach.

"Now you be quiet, mistress."

She looked down at the knife, but caught sight of the ground, hugged the tree, and shut her eyes again. Silence fell as they waited for Blade to appear. She heard the logs on the fire hiss and pop. An owl hooted in the distance, and to Oriel it seemed she'd been in the tree for the better part of a year. Every time she braved a peep down at Jack Midnight, she grew short of breath and buried her face in the crook of her arm. She was never going to leave the tree. She would grow old in this tree.

Willie stirred, and she braved a look. A cloaked and hooded figure walked into the light of the fire. Jack Midnight called out Blade's name, and she heard the singing of metal as a sword was drawn from its sheath. She forgot her fear as the sword appeared at Midnight's back, its point digging into his doublet.

"Midnight," Blade said as he stepped from the shadows, "you're a curse on mankind."

Midnight turned to face Blade. "Recovered from your little cut, have you, my treasure?"

"My thanks, René," Blade said to the figure by the fire. He looked at Midnight. "I've had my fill of cheats and cozeners of late. What do you want?"

"Why, to return Mistress Oriel to her lord."

"Oh, her."

"Don't you want her?" Midnight sounded surprised.

"I suppose I do. She's unruly and quite mutinous to my rule, and she continually puts herself in danger when she should be in some withdrawing chamber sewing, but she is wealthy."

Oriel hugged her tree and glared at Blade. Willie was sniggering.

"Where have you put her?" Blade asked with little interest.

"She's nearby. Where is my loot?"

"It's nearby."

Midnight laughed and looked up. "Willie?"

Willie shook Oriel by the arm, and she screamed. At the sound of her voice, Blade's attention wavered, and Midnight sprang aside, drawing his sword. Blade attacked at once, driving his weapon down at Midnight.

The thief parried and countered with an upward-slicing cut. Blade hopped backward and slashed down with his own sword. Thieves emerged from their hiding places, but they contented themselves with cheering their leader on. By the fire, René remained motionless, separated from his master by a crowd of ruffians.

Forgetting her fears, Oriel peered down at the two opponents. They danced across the forest floor, scattering thieves in their wake. Firelight glinted on sword blades, and she saw Midnight lunge at Blade.

Blade turned sideways and smashed his weapon down on Midnight's. The thief pulled his sword free, and without pause, lunged again. Blade swirled his weapon around that of his opponent. His sword circled Midnight's in a dizzying maneuver that flicked the thief's weapon out of his hand. He darted forward and touched his sword point to the base of Midnight's throat.

An abrupt quiet fell over the thieves. Several turned to René, but he was gone. Blade smiled at Midnight, who was out of breath.

"Tell your man to bring her down," Blade said.

"I think not, my treasure. I want my gold, and I don't believe you'll kill me."

"You know me, but not well," Blade said. "I'll cut off your nose."

"And my men will cut off your pretty head."

At this, Oriel decided to tip the balance of this impasse. She was sitting on a branch level with Willie's shoulders. She stuck her foot out and jabbed him in the stomach.

Willie cried out and flew backward, arms flailing. He disappeared, falling through cracking branches to land on a thick limb far below. After her kick, Oriel had clutched the tree trunk again and hidden her face. Another long silence ensued.

"Oriel?"

"Mistress?"

She peeped over her arm to see Blade and Jack Midnight goggling at her. Blade still held his enemy at sword point. She closed her eyes again.

"This is your doing, Midnight."

"How was I to know she'd kick Willie out of the tree?"

"If she falls she'll be killed, damn you."

Willie groaned, and Jack Midnight raised his voice.

"I want my gold."

"I want my lady."

Keeping her eyes shut, Oriel called down to Blade. "He only wants something for his old age. He wants to give up thievery."

"You be quiet," Jack Midnight yelled.

"You?" Blade said. "You've been aiding traitors, not gathering funds for your retirement."

"I know nothing of treason."

"You deny serving Leslie Richmond?"

"Richmond and I were partners, Blade, my sweeting. Being a penniless younger son gave him a powerful dislike for lords, not unlike my own. He sent me word when travelers were to pass, and I robbed them. We shared the booty."

"Never mind your thievery," Oriel shouted. "Get me down."

Midnight swept his arm up, indicating Oriel. "Your fair lady wants rescuing."

"I'm no more of a fool than the last time we met," Blade said. "Oriel, climb down."

"If I could, do you think I would be hugging this cursed tree?"

Midnight leaned toward Blade and spoke in a low, caressing voice. "A fair puzzle, my gem. If you lower your guard to help her, you lower your guard to me. If you make her climb down alone, she's like to fall." Midnight laughed softly. "Like to fall and die at your feet. What is your choice, my love?"

Chapter
26

Come live with me, and be my love,
And we will some new pleasures prove
Of golden sands, and crystal brooks,
With silken lines, and silver hooks.

—John Donne

Blade looked into the mocking eyes of his old enemy and cocked his head to the side. "Do you know how near you are to death?"

"And you?" Midnight asked.

"If you had harmed her, I would have hanged, drawn, and quartered you and every one of your men."

Midnight's smile slipped a little. "Is this my dear apprentice speaking?"

"It is." He nudged Midnight with the tip of his sword. "I still may impale your head on a pike and stick it on top of my keep if she's hurt getting out of that tree. René, take my sword."

René now reappeared from his hiding place behind

Jack Midnight, and skirted the line of thieves. He took
the weapon from Blade, holding Jack Midnight at bay.
Having relinquished the sword, Blade removed his belt
and scabbard, and tossed them on the ground. He went
to the tree and gazed up at Oriel. He could barely make
her out in the darkness, and only because the moon and
firelight aided him. He began to climb.

She was sitting in the bend of a limb close to the
trunk in the uppermost branches, with her arms
wrapped around it. He stood on an opposite branch.

"Oriel, come to me."

"I'm not letting go of this tree."

"Nonsense, come here." He touched her arm, but
she shrank from him, her eyes squeezed shut.

Gripping her wrist, he pulled, trying to free her
from her perch. She cried out, and he dropped her wrist.
She was too frightened for him to reason with her.
Foiled, he chewed his lower lip for a moment, then
crossed to the limb on which she was perched. Sitting
beside her, he snuggled close and spoke to her calmly.

"Now, *chère*, I've come to take you down. You'll be
safe with me."

"We'll both fall."

"I never fall. I've climbed trees much higher than
this."

He reached around and tore her arm from the trunk.
She cried out again, but he put her arm around his
shoulder. As he expected, once she felt his body, she
threw herself in his arms and buried her face in the
crook of his neck. Her arms squeezed so tightly he had
to fight for breath.

"Put your legs around me, *chère*."

She complied, and he chastised himself for the licentious thoughts that suddenly came to him. Whispering
encouragement, he began the long climb back to the
ground.

"One last jump, *chère*, and we're on the ground."
He winced as her arms constricted even tighter, then

hopped from the lowest branch to the forest floor. Planting his feet apart, he said to her, "We're there. You can open your eyes and let go. Please, *chère*, you're going to suffocate me. Start with your legs."

He unwrapped one of her legs from his waist and guided her foot to the ground. She opened her eyes and lifted her head from his neck then, and stood. Slowly she relaxed her grip on his neck. He held her hands, and they stared at each other.

"I was in the tree," she said.

"I know."

"It was high."

He grinned at her. "You're beginning to sound like Joan."

"Fear has made me simple." She took a deep, quavering breath, then glanced at Jack Midnight. "What are we going to do?"

"You are unharmed?" he asked.

"Yes."

"Then I'll forbear killing him." He pulled her close and addressed Midnight. "I've had enough of your interfering in my doings. I suggest you take yourself off and give up thievery before I really have to kill you. And take my advice. Don't hire yourself out to traitors."

Midnight laughed at him. "How was I to know Richmond was a traitor? I was only trying to earn a penny or two in honest labor."

"Honest!"

Holding up a hand, Midnight forestalled his comments. "As I told your lady, I am retiring from the life of a highwayman. I don't suppose you brought my gold at all, did you, my gem?"

"You know me."

"As I feared." Midnight clicked his tongue against the roof of his mouth. "I was looking forward to giving up thievery, but now it seems I must work longer than I intended."

"Not here."

"Why not? I hear there's a rich young lord at the castle now."

"Midnight, if you—"

"Here," Oriel said.

Blade went speechless as she bent down, lifted her skirts, and pulled a tiny pouch from where it was tied to one of her garters. She dug inside the pouch and retrieved a brooch. Set with garnets and pearls, it was made in the form of the letter R. She held it out to Jack Midnight.

"What are you doing?" he asked, snatching the jewel from her.

"I'm saving you a great deal of bother and most likely a few lives as well." She snatched the brooch back and handed it to Jack Midnight. "There, now you go away, and don't come back. If you do, I won't interfere with what Blade will surely do to you."

Midnight glanced from the brooch to her, then at Blade. Blade scowled at him, which seemed to give him great pleasure. Midnight laughed and patted his cheek. Blade jerked his face out of reach.

"Get you gone, Midnight, before I regain my senses and make you eat that brooch."

"And I love you, my treasure." Midnight signaled to his men, who faded into the darkness. "Fare you well, my gem. I entrust you to the keeping of this lady. She tests and taunts you even more unmercifully than I did, which will give me great comfort. Do tell our friend Christian of my great sorrow at not being able to bid him farewell."

He watched Midnight follow his men into the darkness. Staring at the place where he vanished, Blade wondered if the highwayman would keep his word. Oriel tugged at his hand.

"What of George and Robert?"

"I sent men to find them. They should be at the castle by now."

He looked down at her, noting the tousled curls that always made her look like a wanton fairy. She was weary. He could see faint purple smudges under her eyes. He stopped himself from picking her up. Instead, he looked over her head at René, who handed him his sword. Releasing her hand, he took it and found his belt. Fastening his scabbard in place, he sheathed his sword while René brought their horses. René mounted, and before Oriel could protest, he swept her up in his arms and handed her to the man.

"Blade?"

"I will lead the way. I left a party of men not far off."

Mounting, he guided his horse away from her, not daring to glance her way.

"Blade Fitzstephen, you come back here."

"I will give you shelter for tonight. Then you and your cousins must leave."

He expected a challenge from her. When he got none, he risked a glance over his shoulder and saw her whispering with René. The sight of those two deliberating caused him much unease. What did they have to say to each other? No matter. He'd decided what was best, and he would continue to act upon that decision. Oriel Richmond would come to understand that his will ruled, and not hers.

After finding his men, he led the party back to La Roche, where he managed to evade Oriel by having her conducted to her cousins, who descended upon her with agitation and relief. He retreated to his own chambers, leaving the settling of his guests to René and his steward. As he'd told her, both George and Robert had been found, along with their men, and were waiting for Oriel.

He went to bed determined not to think of how her body had felt wrapped around his as he climbed out of that tree. He didn't, but he dreamed of her body wrapped around his as they made love. He got little sleep.

Dawn found him sitting up in bed trying to think of a way to avoid bidding Oriel farewell this morning. He would order René to make some excuse for him and ride to one of his manors in the next valley. Throwing on his riding clothes, he descended to the hall, intent on grabbing bread and meat from the kitchen to take with him.

He ran down the winding stairs only to halt at the bottom, for his way was blocked by five of the biggest men he'd ever seen. Evidently the Almighty had decided not to spare himself when he made them, for each seemed to have received the height and bulk of three men. They all gazed at him with oxlike placidity.

"Who are you, and what do you in my hall?"

Two of them moved, and Oriel stepped between them.

"Good morrow, my lord. They're mine."

"Oriel, what have you done?"

She turned to point at the first man. "This is Hal. Next to him is—is—now, don't tell me. I memorized your names. This is, um, Edmund, then Bevis and James, and the last is Martin, um, Martin Holydean. They're brothers." She clasped her hands in front of her and beamed at him. "I hired them and told them to meet me here. They're my new guards, my very own."

He eyed them. They seemed rooted to their posts. He stepped aside, and one moved in front of him. He scowled at Oriel.

"What mean you by this, you devilish little badger?"

She latched onto his arm and pulled him with her to a window seat well away from the giant Holydeans. She sat down and grinned at him. Puzzled, he leaned on the wall next to her.

"These Holydeans, they will protect you on your way home?"

She arranged a fold of her skirt, studying it for a moment before glancing up at him archly. "No, Blade, they're my answer to your fears."

"You make no sense."

"You said you were afraid you would hurt me." She indicated the five men who were staring at them from their post at the stairs. "This is my answer. You can't."

He stared at her. She looked back at him and smiled.

"It's right mad you are," he said at last.

She clasped her hands in her lap. "Hit me."

"I will not!"

"But you said you would."

"In anger, no other way. And you must think me addlepated if you think these Holydeans make any difference. God's blood. If we married, I would own them as well as you, and send them away."

"And then?"

"And then," he stopped and pondered. "And then some day I might . . ."

"Hit me?"

He couldn't say the words, so he nodded. She startled him by jumping to her feet with a curse.

"Very well, suppose you did this thing which is so against your nature. Suppose you hit me. Then, Blade Fitzstephen, I can promise you this. You would hit me only once."

"How so? I could hurt you badly."

"Then, sirrah, you had better not sleep."

Never had a woman threatened him. He had never heard of a woman threatening any man in such a manner. Mayhap it was her learning that had made her so bold. Hot spikes of temper jabbed at him.

"You insolent wench, you hired these ruffians to threaten me."

She rose and planted herself in front of him, smiling as if she'd been invited to court. "I have indeed."

Furious, he shouted at her. "I won't be cozened by a

fey changeling of a girl. God's blood. I rule here, not you, and I'll not be threatened."

"But I love you." Her eyes rounded with bewilderment and she tried to touch his arm.

He yanked it out of her reach. "I don't care. Do you hear me? I don't care." His anger was so great he didn't pause when tears began to roll down her cheeks. "I've important matters that need my attention. I expect you to be gone when I return. If you are not, I'll throw you out of the castle myself."

He hurled himself out of the hall and across the ward. He didn't stop until he reached the stables. Shouting at the grooms, he nurtured his wrath until his horse was saddled. She'd dragged his fears into the open, and somehow, the exposure had curdled his entrails. No woman was going to strip him naked like that. He urged his horse into motion as if a hoard of demons were after him instead of one tearful young woman.

Oriel watched Blade race out of the hall, her vision blurred by tears. He hadn't understood her at all, and now he hated her. She ran after him, pausing in the doorway to watch him hurtle across the bailey, dodging men at arms and servants. Then she frowned. He was angry with her. The only reason he could be angry with her was because he loved her. He ran from her because he couldn't run from himself.

With that thought, she sprang out of the hall after him. He'd gained the outer ward and disappeared by the time she emerged from the bailey, and she lost time searching for him in the barracks, the smithy, and the mews. She came out of the mews in time to see him mount his horse. Launching herself after him, she raced for the gate house.

He hadn't seen her. His horse was trotting slowly, gathering speed for a canter, when she drew alongside. She saw the gate house ahead. If he gained it before her, she would be left behind. Desperate, she burst ahead of

Blade and dashed in front of him. As she did, the horse sped up, and she felt a great weight thrown against her shoulder. She cried out at the massive jolt, and flew backward. Hitting the ground, she fell on her back, and her head bounced off the packed earth of the outer ward.

The blow flung all perception from her body except pain. She tried to lift her head, but it fell back. It seemed as if she were fading, like light at sunset. She heard Blade calling her from a great distance. He must have ridden to the next valley, and was shouting at her from there.

Her next awareness came slowly. Her head throbbed and had swollen to thrice its accustomed size. Her bones seemed to be sore, and she couldn't open her eyes. She tried to move a hand, and found it still attached to her arm. Moaning, she put one of them to her head. It was smaller than she'd guessed. Something was weighing her other hand down. She ventured to lift an eyelid, and saw Blade's dark head resting on her hand. She was lying on the bed in the chamber she'd slept in last night.

"Mmmm."

His head shot up, and she could see terror recede from his eyes.

"Oriel?" He squeezed her hand, and she protested. He kissed it. "*Chère*, can you hear me?"

"Mmmm." She moved her head and winced.

"Don't," he said. "I've sent for an apothecary. *Sacré Dieu*, why did you run in front of my horse?" He put her hand against his cheek and stared into her half-opened eyes. "God's blood, I thought you were dead. I forbid you ever to take such a risk again. *Chère*, you can't keep endangering yourself so. I won't allow it."

She wet her lips and whispered so that he was forced to lean close. "Your fault."

"What?"

"You ran away. Coward."

She tried to sit up, and he helped her, supporting her in his arms. Leaning her aching head on his shoulder, she gasped as a sharp pain stabbed at her temple. The strength seemed to leak from her body, and she fell heavily against him. He cursed and gently returned her to the pillows, keeping his arms around her. When she opened her eyes again, he was looking down at her in helpless fury.

"Oriel Richmond, the moment you're out of my sight, you try to get yourself killed. I vow I'll not live a month if you don't cease this madness."

"I only wanted to show you—"

He put a finger against her lips. "I know. God's blood, in the last hour you've taught me a lesson, though not the one you intended. When my horse hit you, and you flew into the air and hit the ground like an egg thrown by a catapult, I thought the fear would kill me. I was trying not to hurt you and did so anyway."

"I wasn't finished." She rubbed her temple and gazed up at him, hoping the pain wouldn't increase before she could tell him what she needed to tell him. "I could go away, if you hurt me. I have my jewels and my inheritance. I will keep them." She clutched his hand. "Don't you see? I have a power of my own, a will of my own, ungoverned by you, and thus I can prevent your treating me unfairly. Though I will make you a wager that you'll never do these terrible things you fear."

"Hush, *chère.*" Blade lowered his head, then faced her again. "You must let me speak now." He took a deep breath and continued. "I have been thinking, since I nearly killed you just now, and realized that if I don't keep you with me, I won't be able to protect you from yourself. Now, don't get angry. It isn't good for you in your state. By my troth, *chère,* I don't think I can live knowing you'll continue to cast yourself into peril this way. If I could be sure you wouldn't stir from your uncle's library, I might be content. I don't suppose you would care to promise not to get yourself into trouble?"

She shook her head and waited without breathing. He looked at her without smiling for long moments, meeting her gaze and searching it as if pondering a great mystery. Then, slowly, his lips curled, his eyes brightened to shining silver, and he gave a sigh of relief.

"Thank God," he said.

"I don't understand."

"I think, *chère*, that the only way I can be certain of your safety is to keep you near me, and the only way to do that is to make you my own. Will you allow me to become your lord?"

Irritated, she poked him with her elbow. "God's toes, why think you I've engaged in all these machinations?"

He spoke to her softly. "Now, *chère*, if I'm to be your husband, you must give me deference."

"My head hurts."

Laughing, he kissed her lightly and rose. "I'll see if they've found the apothecary."

He left, but returned with the apothecary, who gave her herb tea and ordered her to rest. The tea soothed the ache in her head, and she fell asleep with Blade holding her hand. She woke to find the setting sun casting golden light through the windows of her chamber. Her head no longer ached, but she was alone.

Had she dreamed that he'd returned to her? Had he run away instead? After all, she'd hit her head. Mayhap she'd imagined that he'd come to her in a delirium. Dread sent her heart crawling up her throat, and she sat up. Her head twinged, but she ignored the discomfort and tottered across the room to the door.

As she went, her fear grew. He'd abandoned her, and she would be alone again, without his strength and wit and magical presence. She reached the door knowing that if he'd left her, he might as well have trampled her beneath the hooves of his stallion. She flung the door open, and a group of men standing in the room beyond turned as one to look at her. One of them broke from the group and rushed to her.

"*Chère,* you mustn't race about like this."

He caught her shoulders, and she twisted her fingers in his leather jerkin. He smiled at her, oblivious to her disquiet, and calmly picked her up. Carrying her back to the bed, he deposited her there as if she were a delicate crystal.

George and Robert came to the door and gave her their good wishes, but a look from Blade sent them away, and the door shut. He locked it and returned to her.

"You must rest, *chère.*"

She touched his cheek. "Sing for me then."

He took her hands in his and complied, but instead of making her drowsy, his voice resounded throughout her body. She watched his lips, reveling in their movement, and let her gaze melt down the length of his torso to his thigh. He stopped singing.

"*Chère,* you mustn't do that."

"What?"

"Look at me. *Sacré Dieu,* one would think you learned that in the bedchambers of Amboise."

He stirred restlessly. She noticed the way his body strained toward hers and smiled. He swallowed and gripped the covers with both fists.

"Don't, Oriel."

She rose and slipped her hand inside his jerkin and shirt to knead his bare shoulder. " 'Vanquished by desire for a youth through the work of soft Aphrodite.' "

"You're not well," he said as he pulled her hand from his shoulder.

She wrapped her arms around his neck and sank back into the covers. Her weight pulled him down on top of her, and he braced himself by pressing against the mattress. She countered by pulling herself up to meet him. Before their lips touched, he spoke.

"Are you sure? I don't want to hurt you."

"I know that full well. Now kiss me and still that beautiful voice, my love."

He began to lower himself on top of her. "As you command, *chère*. In this it will always be as you command."

About The Author

SUZANNE ROBINSON has a doctoral degree in anthropology with a specialty in ancient Middle Eastern archaeology. After spending years doing fieldwork in both the U.S. and the Middle East, Suzanne has now turned her attention to the creation of the fascinating fictional characters in her unforgettable historical romances.

Suzanne lives in San Antonio with her husband and her two English springer spaniels. She divides her time between writing and teaching.

Suzanne Robinson

loves to hear from readers. You can write her at
the following address:

P.O. Box 700321
San Antonio, TX 78270-0321

Coming next from
Suzanne Robinson
in the summer of 1993 . . .

Lady
Valiant

A richly romantic new historical romance set
during the spellbinding Elizabethan era, *Lady
Valiant* is the passionate love story of Rob Savage
—highwayman, nobleman, and master spy—and
the fiery young beauty he kidnaps.

Here's a tantalizing glimpse . . .

Thea Hunt refused to ride in the coach. Heavy, cumbersome, and slow, it jounced her so that she nearly vomited after a few minutes inside it. She preferred riding at the head of her party, just behind the outriders, in spite of Nan Hobby's objections. Hobby rode in the coach and shouted at her charge whenever she felt Thea was riding too fast.

"Miiiiiistress!"

Thea groaned and turned her mare. There was no use trying to ignore Hobby. It only made her shout louder. As the outriders entered the next valley, Thea pulled alongside the coach. The vehicle jolted over a log, causing Hobby to disappear in a flurry of skirts and petticoats.

"Aaaaow," groaned Hobby. "Mistress, my bones, my bones."

"You could ride."

"That horrible mare you gave me can't be trusted."

"Not when you shriek at her and scare her into bolting."

"Aaaaow."

Thea pointed down the track that led into the oak-and hazel-wooded valley. "We'll be following this road. No more spiny hills for a while."

She glanced up at the hills on either side of the valley. Steeply pitched like tent tops they posed a hazard to the wagons, loaded with chests and furniture, and to the coach. Yet she was glad to see them, for the presence meant northern England. Soon they would reach the border and Scotland. She heard the call of a lapwing in the distance and spotted a merlin overhead. The countryside seemed deserted except for their small party.

She'd insisted on taking as few servants and men-at-arms as necessary in order to travel quickly. She and Hobby were the only women and the men-at-arms numbered only seven including her steward. Still, the baggage and Hobby slowed them down, and she had need of haste.

The Queen of Scots was to marry that fool Darnley. When Grandmother told her the news, at first she hadn't believed it. Clever, beautiful, and softhearted, Her Majesty deserved better than that selfish toad. Thea had pondered long upon Grandmother's suggestion that she go to Scotland. Grandmother said Mary Stuart would listen to no criticism of Darnley, but that she might listen to Thea. After all, they had both shared quarters and tutors with the French royal children.

Thea had been honored with Mary's friendship, for both found themselves foreigners among a clutch of French children. Later, when Thea had need of much more than friendship, Mary had given her aid, had seen to it that Thea was allowed to go home.

Slapping her riding crop on her leg, Thea muttered to herself. "Don't think of it. That time is over. You'll go to Scotland for a time and then return to the country where no one can hurt you."

Nudging her mare, she resumed her place near the front of the line of horses and wagons. Only a cause of great moment could have forced her to leave her seclusion. She'd made her own life far away from any young noblemen. Some called her a hermit. Some accused her of false pride. None suspected the mortal wound she nursed in secret—a wound so grievous and humiliating it had sent her flying from the French court determined to quit the society of the highborn forever.

Her steward interrupted her thoughts. "Mistress, it's close to midday. Shall I look for a place to stop?"

She nodded and the man trotted ahead. Hunger had crept up on her unnoticed, and she tugged at the collar of her riding gown. Her finger caught the edge of one of the gold buttons that ran down the garment, and she felt a sting. Grimacing, she looked at her forefinger. Blood beaded up in a small cut on the side. She sucked the wound and vowed to demand that Hobby remove the buttons. They'd been a gift from Grandmother, but one of them had a sharp edge that needed filing.

It was a good excuse to replace them with the old, plainer buttons she preferred. These were too ornate for her taste. She always felt she should be wearing brocade or velvet with them, and a riding hat, which she detested. Only this morning Hobby had tried to convince her to wear one of those silly jeweled and feathered contrivances on her head. Refusing, she'd stuffed her thick black hair into a net that kept the straight locks out of her way.

She examined her finger. It had stopped bleeding. Pulling her gloves from her belt, she drew them on and searched the path ahead for signs of the steward's return. As she looked past the first outrider, something dropped on the man from the overhanging branches like an enormous fruit with appendages. The second outrider dropped under the weight of another missile and at the same time she heard shouts and grunts from the men behind her.

"Aaaaow! Murder, murder!"

A giant attacked the coach, lumbering over to it and thrusting his arms inside. A scrawny man in a patched cloak toppled into her path as she turned her horse toward the coach. He sprang erect and pointed at her.

"Here, Robin!"

She looked in the direction of the man's gaze and saw a black stallion wheel, his great bulk easily controlled by a golden-haired man who seemed a part of the animal. The stallion and his rider jumped into motion, hooves tearing the earth, the man's long body aligning itself over the horse's neck. Stilled by fright, she watched him control the animal with a strength that seemed to rival that of the stallion.

The brief stillness vanished as she understood that the man who was more stallion than human was coming for her. Fear lanced through her. She kicked her mare hard and sprang away, racing down the path through the trees. Riding sidesaddle, she had a precarious perch, but she tapped her mare with the crop, knowing that the risk of capture by a highwayman outweighed the risk of a fall. Her heart pounding with the hoofbeats of her mare, she fled.

The path twisted to the right and she nearly lost her seat as she rounded the turn. Righting herself, she felt the mare stretch her legs out and saw that the way had straightened. She leaned over her horse, not daring to look behind and lose her balance. Thus she only heard the thunder of hooves and felt the spray of dirt as the stallion caught up. The animal's black head appeared, and she kicked her mare in desperation.

A gloved hand appeared, then a golden head. An arm snaked out and encircled her waist. Thea sailed out of the saddle and landed in front of the highwayman. Terror gave her strength. She wriggled and pounded the imprisoning arm.

"None of that, beastly papist gentry mort."

Understanding little of this, caring not at all, Thea wriggled harder and managed to twist so that she could bite the highwayman's arm. She was rewarded with a howl. Twisting again, she bit the hand that snatched at her hair and thrust herself out of the saddle as the stallion was slowing to a trot.

She landed on her side, rolled, and scrambled to her feet. Ahead she could see her mare walking down the trail in search of grass. Sprinting for the animal, she felt her hair come loose from its net and sail out behind her. Only a few yards and she might escape on the mare.

Too late she heard the stallion. She glanced over her shoulder to see a scowling face. She gave a little yelp as a long, lean body sailed at her. She turned to leap out of range, but the highwayman landed on her. The force of his weight jolted the air from her lungs and she fell. The ground jumped at her face. Her head banged against something. There was a moment of sharp pain and the feeling of smothering before she lost her senses altogether.

Her next thought wasn't quite a thought, for in truth there was room in her mind for little more than feeling. Her head ached. She was queasy and she couldn't summon the strength to open her eyes. She could feel her face because someone had laid a palm against her cheek. She could feel her hand, because someone was holding it.

"Wake you, my prize. I've no winding sheet to wrap you in if you die."

The words were harsh. It was the voice of thievery and rampage, the voice of a masterless man, a highwayman. Her eyes flew open at the thought and met the sun. No, not the sun, bright light filtered through a mane of long, roughly cut tresses. She shifted her gaze to the man's face and saw his lips curve into a smile of combined satisfaction and derision. She could only lie on the ground and blink at him, waiting.

He leaned toward her and she shrank away. Glaring at her, he held her so that she couldn't retreat. He came close, and she was about to scream when he touched the neck of her gown. The feel of his gloved hand on her throat took her voice from her. She began to shake. An evil smile appeared upon his lips, then she felt a tightening of her collar and a rip. She found her voice and screamed as he tore the top button from her gown. Flailing at him weakly, she drew breath to scream again, but he clamped a hand over her mouth.

"Do you want me to stuff my gloves into your mouth?"

She stared at him, trapped by his grip and the malice in his dark blue eyes.

"Do you?"

She shook her head.

"Then keep quiet."

He removed his hand and she squeezed her eyes shut, expecting him to resume his attack. When nothing happened, she peeped at him from beneath her lashes. He was regarding her with a contemptuous look, but soon transferred his gaze to the button in his palm. He pressed it between his fingers, frowned at it, then shoved it into a pouch at his belt.

"I'll have the rest of them later," he said.

Reaching for her, he stopped when she shrank from him. He hesitated, then grinned at her.

"Sit you up by yourself then."

Still waiting for him to pounce on her, she moved her arms, but when she tried to shove herself erect, she found them useless. He snorted. Gathering her in his arms, he raised her to a sitting position. She winced at the pain in her head. His hand came up to cradle her cheek and she moaned.

"If you puke on me I'll tie you face down on your horse for the ride home."

Fear gave way to anger. In spite of her pain, she shoved at his chest. To her chagrin, what she thought were mortal blows turned out to be taps.

"Aaaow! Look what you've done to my lady."

"Get you gone, you old cow. She's well and will remain so, for now. Stubb, put the maid on a horse and let's fly. No sense waiting here for company any longer."

Thea opened her eyes. The highwayman was issuing orders to his ruffians. From her position she could see the day's growth of beard on his chin and the tense cords of muscle in his neck.

"My—my men."

"Will have a long walk," he snapped.

"Leave us," she whispered, trying to sit up. "You have your booty."

The highwayman moved abruptly to kneel in front of her. Taking her by the shoulders, he pulled her so that they faced each other eye to eye.

"But Mistress Hunt, you are the booty. All the rest is fortune's addition."

"But—"

He ignored her. Standing quickly, he picked her up. Made dizzy by the sudden change, she allowed her head to drop to his shoulder. She could smell the leather of his jerkin and feel the soft cambric of his shirt. An outlaw who wore cambric shirts.

She was transferred to the arms of another ruffian, a wiry man no taller than she with a crooked nose and a belligerent expression. Her captor mounted the black stallion again and reached down.

"Give her to me."

Lifted in front of the highwayman, she was settled in his lap a great distance from the ground. The stallion danced sideways and his master put a steadying hand on the animal's neck. The stallion calmed at once.

"Now, Mistress Hunt, shall I tie your hands, or will you behave? I got no patience for foolish gentry morts who don't know better than to try outrunning horses."

Anger got the better of her. "You may be sure the next time I leave I'll take your horse."

"God's blood, woman. You take him, and I'll give you the whipping you've asked for."

His hand touched a whip tied to his saddle and she believed him. She screamed and began to struggle.

"Cease your nattering, woman."

He fastened his hand over her mouth again. His free arm wrapped around her waist. Squeezing her against his hard body, he stifled her cries. When she went limp from lack of air, he released her.

"Any more yowling and I'll gag you."

Grabbing her by the shoulders, he drew her close so that she was forced to look into his eyes. Transfixed by their scornful beauty, she remained silent.

"What say you?" he asked. "Shall I finish what I began and take all your buttons?"

Hardly able to draw breath, she hadn't the strength to move her lips.

"Answer, woman. Will you ride quietly, or fight beneath me on the ground again."

"R—ride."

Chuckling he turned her around so that her back was to his chest and called to his men. The outlaw called Stubb rode up leading a horse carrying Hobby, and Thea twisted her head around to see if her maid fared well.

"Look here, Rob Savage," Stubb said. "If you want to scrap with the gentry mort all day, I'm going on. No telling when someone else is going to come along, and I'm not keen on another fight this day."

"Give me a strap then."

A strap. He was going to beat her. Thea gasped and rammed her elbow into Rob's stomach. She writhed and twisted, trying to escape the first blow from the lash. Rob finally trapped her by fastening his arms about her and holding her arms to her body.

"Quick, Stubb, tie her hands with the strap."

Subsiding, Thea bit her lower lip. Her struggles had been for naught. Rob's arm left her, but he shook her by the shoulders.

"Now be quiet or I'll tie you to a pack horse."

"Aaaow! Savage, Robin Savage, the highwayman. God preserve us. We're lost, lost. Oh, mistress, it's Robin Savage. He's killed hundreds of innocent souls. He kills babes and ravages their mothers and steals food from children and burns churches and dismembers clergymen and—"

Thea felt her body grow cold and heavy at the same time. She turned and glanced up at the man who held her. He was frowning at the hysterical Hobby. Suddenly he looked down at her. One of his brows lifted and he smiled slowly.

"A body's got to have a calling."

"You—you've done these things?"

"Now how's a man to remember every little trespass and sin, especially a man as busy as me?"

He grinned at her, lifted a hand to his men, and kicked the stallion. Her head was thrown back against his chest. He steadied her with an arm around her waist, but she squirmed away from him. He ignored her efforts and pulled her close as the horse sprang into a gallop. She grasped his arm with her bound hands, trying to pry it loose to no avail. It was as much use for a snail to attempt to move a boulder.

The stallion leaped over a fallen sapling and she clutched at Savage's arm. Riding a small mare was a far less alarming experience than trying to keep her seat on this black giant. She would have to wait for a chance to escape, but escape she must.

This man was a villain with a price on his head. She remembered hearing of him now. He and his band roamed the highways of England doing murder and thievery at will. Savage would appear, relieve an honest nobleman or merchant of his wealth and vanish. No sheriff or constable could find him.

As they rode, Thea mastered her fears enough to begin to think. This man wanted more than just riches and rape. If he'd only wanted these things, he could have finished his attack when he'd begun it. And it wasn't as if she were tempting to men, a beauty worth keeping. She'd found that out long ago in France. And this Savage knew her name. The mystery calmed her somewhat. Again she twisted, daring a glance at him.

"Why have you abducted me?"

He gaped at her for a moment before returning his gaze to the road ahead. "For the same reason I take any woman. For using."

He slowed the stallion and turned off the road. Plunging into the forest, they left behind the men assigned to bring the coach and wagons. Several thieves went ahead, while Stubb and the rest followed their master. Thea summoned her courage to break the silence once more.

"Why else?"

"What?"

"It can't be the only reason, to, to . . ."

"Why not?"

"You know my name. You were looking for me, not for just anyone."

"Is that so?"

"Are you going to hold me for ransom? There are far richer prizes than me."

"Ransom. Now there's a right marvelous idea. Holding a woman for ransom's a pleasureful occupation."

As he leered down at her, fear returned. Her body shook. She swallowed and spoke faintly.

"No."

There was a sharp gasp of exasperation from Savage. "Don't you be telling me what I want."

"But you can't."

His gaze ran over her face and hair. The sight appeared to anger him, for he cursed and snarled at her.

"Don't you be telling me what I can do. God's

blood, woman, I could throw you down and mount you right here."

She caught her lower lip between her teeth, frozen into her own horror by his threats. He snarled at her again and turned her away from him, holding her shoulders so that she couldn't face him. Though he used only the strength of his hands, it was enough to control her, which frightened her even more.

"I could do it," he said. "I might if you don't keep quiet. Mayhap being mounted a few times would shut you up."

Thea remained silent, not daring to anger him further. She had no experience of villains. This one had hurt her. He might hurt her worse. She must take him at his word, despite her suspicion that he'd planned to hold her for ransom. She must escape. She must escape with Hobby and find her men.

They rode for several hours through fells and dales, always heading south, deeper into England. She pondered hard upon how to escape as they traveled. Freeing herself from Savage was impossible. He was too strong and wary of her after her first attempt. She might request a stop to relieve herself, but the foul man might insist upon watching her. No, she would have to wait until they stopped for the night and hope he didn't tie her down.

Her gorge rose at the thought of what he might do once they stopped. She tried to stop her body from trembling, but failed. Her own helplessness frightened her and she struggled not to let tears fall. If she didn't escape, she would fight. It seemed to be her way, to keep fighting no matter how useless the struggle.

As dusk fell they crossed a meadow and climbed a rounded hill. At the top she had a view of the countryside. Before her stretched a great forest, its trees so thick she could see nothing but an ocean of leaves.

Savage led his men down the hillside and into the

forest. As they entered, the sun faded into a twilight caused by the canopy of leaves above them. Savage rode on until the twilight had almost vanished. Halting in a clearing by a noisy stream, he lifted Thea down.

She'd been on the horse so long and the hours of fear had wearied her so much that her legs buckled under her. Savage caught her, his hands coming up under her arms, and she stumbled against him. Clutching her, he swore. She looked up at him to find him glaring at her again. She caught her breath, certain he would leap upon her.

His arms tightened about her, but he didn't throw her to the ground. Instead, he stared at her. Too confused at the moment to be afraid, she stared back. Long moments passed while they gazed at each other, studying, wary, untrusting.

When he too seemed caught in a web of reverie her fears gradually eased. Eyes of gentian blue met hers and she felt a stab of pain. To her surprise, looking at him had caused the pain. Until that moment she hadn't realized a man's mere appearance could delight to the point of pain.

It was her first long look at him free of terror. Not in all her years in the fabulous court of France had she seen such a man. Even his shoulders were muscled. They were wide in contrast to his hips and he was taller than any Frenchman. He topped any of his thievish minions and yet seemed unaware of the effect of his appearance. Despite his angelic coloring, however, he had the disposition of an adder. He was scowling at her, as if something had caught him unprepared and thus annoyed him. Wariness and fear rushed to the fore again.

"Golden eyes and jet black hair. Why did you have to be so—God's blood, woman." He thrust her away from him. "Never you mind. You were right anyway, little papist. I'm after ransom."

Bewildered, she remained where she was while he stalked away from her. He turned swiftly to point at her.

"Don't you think of running. If I have to chase you and wrestle with you again, you'll pay in any way I find amusing." He marched off to shout ill-tempered orders at his men.

Hobby trotted up to her and began untying the leather strap that bound her hands. Thea stared at Robin Savage, frightened once more and eyeing his leather-clad figure. How could she have forgotten his cruelty and appetite simply because he had a lush, well-formed body and eyes that could kindle wet leaves? She watched him disappear into the trees at the edge of the clearing, and at last she was released from the bondage of his presence.

"He's mad," she said.

"Mad, of course he's mad," Hobby said. "He's a thief and a murderer and a ravager."

"How could God create such a man, so—so pleasing to the eye and so evil of spirit?"

"Take no fantasy about that one, mistress. He's a foul villain who'd as soon slit your throat as spit on you."

"I know." Thea bent and whispered to Hobby. "Can you run fast and long? We must fly this night. Who knows what will happen to us once he's done settling his men."

"I can run."

"Good. I'll watch for my chance and you do as well." She looked around at the men caring for horses and making a fire. Stubb watched them as he unloaded saddlebags. "For now, I must find privacy."

Hobby pointed to a place at the edge of the clearing where bushes grew thick. They walked toward it unhindered. Hobby stopped at the edge of the clearing to guard Thea's retreat. Thea plunged into the trees looking for the thickest bushes. Thrusting a low-hanging branch aside, she rounded an oak tree. A tall form blocked her way. Before she could react, she was thrust against the tree, and a man's body pressed against hers.

Robin Savage held her fast, swearing at her. She cast a frightened glance at him, but he wasn't looking at her. He was absorbed in studying her lips. His anger had faded and his expression took on a somnolent turbulence. He leaned close and whispered in her ear, sending chills down her spine.

"Running away in spite of my warnings, little papist."

Thea felt a leg shove between her thighs. His chest pressed against her breasts, causing her to pant. He stared into her eyes and murmured.

"Naughty wench. Now I'll have to punish you."